# CATCH
## AND KILL

# EDEN FRANCIS COMPTON
### WITH MELISSA B. ROBINSON

Level 4 Press, Inc.

This book is printed on acid-free paper.

Published by:
Level 4 Press, Inc.
14702 Haven Way
Jamul, CA 91935
www.level4press.com

Library of Congress Control Number: 2019943903

ISBN: 9781646300587

Printed in the United States of America

For Harper, Dylan & Darcy. Who always believe in me.

# PROLOGUE

Kristy Wong powered her way across the asphalt of the studio lot in new knock-off Jimmy Choos, which were killing her, a tablet in one hand, her cell phone in the other. Goddamn it, Scarlett was never late.

The movie had wrapped that afternoon. Champagne flutes lined the table, platters of sushi were chilling, waiters were readying trays of steak tartare bites, shrimp satay, and edamame dumplings. But no Scarlett. Charles had made clear he wanted to toast the completion of the film, which he'd announced in the press would continue DreamWeaver's reputation as a place that made great movies, meaning money *and* art. Yet he couldn't toast without his star, and Kristy could tell he was getting impatient—and no one wanted an impatient Charles. He was bad enough when he got what he wanted.

Kristy knew she was lucky to have landed her job at the studio. But as glamorous as it seemed from the outside, it was work. Hard work. And sometimes demoralizing work. That was a detail she never mentioned to her parents back in Michigan. Once she'd started at the studio, she soon learned what everyone in Hollywood knew—working for Charles Weaver wasn't easy and definitely not fun, but much was forgiven because he had built the largest of the mini-majors from nothing. And he'd done it through constant hustle, a genius for understanding how to produce and package the right movie at the right time, and a vise-like grip over his company.

As she made her way across the lot, Kristy felt confident in her new turquoise silk blouse, unbuttoned to the point of being sexy but still professional—the unspoken DreamWeaver dress code for female employees—and her slim white skirt. She wanted to look good at the wrap party, her first.

Skittering up the few short steps to Scarlett's trailer, she knocked on the closed door. "Scarlett?"

Super-loud music blared from inside, which wasn't typical of Scarlett.

"Scarlett, hey! Can you hear me?! It's Kristy. Charles and everyone are waiting for you." She waited for a response but wasn't sure she would be able to hear anything over the music. She could barely hear her own voice. "Are you ready? C'mon, the party's starting."

Nothing. She knocked one more time, paused a brief moment, then opened the door and leaned in. "Scarlett?"

A vase of red poppies on a table caught her eye first, before her gaze fell to the body on the floor. Scarlett's wavy dark hair and makeup were still as they'd been for her final scene of the shoot earlier, but now sticky blood pooled behind her head, a gun near her hand.

Kristy gasped.

Then screamed.

# 1

A shriek pierced the air as a small girl in a pink-and-blue winter jacket landed with a thud on the playground dirt. The child gazed up, startled, at the stormy red face of the boy who had pushed her. She stared at him for a split second before her sense of injustice could no longer be contained and she broke into a loud wail.

"Mooommm, he pushed meeeeee!"

The angry boy's mother stalked over and half-heartedly tried to intervene. "Now, Billy, what is going on with you? Say you're sorry."

"She wouldn't race me," he said, pouting.

"Well, maybe she didn't want to run," his mom replied. "She doesn't have to run if she doesn't want to. Now say you're sorry."

But her words were lost in the din of howling as the girl's mother rushed over to hush her daughter's sobs. "Now, honey, it's okay, shhhhh, it's okay." She smoothed her dress gently then embraced her.

"But he pushed me!" the little girl cried, looking at the bloody scrape on her elbow.

"He didn't mean for you to get hurt, he only wanted to play," her mother assured her.

"I'm so sorry," the boy's mom said. "Billy, apologize."

Billy grumbled a "sorry" as his mother led him away, past Angie, who had watched the drama unfold as oil congealed on her slice of cheese pizza. Unable to muster much enthusiasm for the rest of her lunch, she tossed it in a nearby trash can. Then she crossed the street and headed back to the old narrow office building, half-hidden between two skyscrapers.

As she fished for the office key in her purse, the scent of stale cigarette smoke wafted into the building's dingy hallway.

"Hey, Angie. The weather's changing, you know. It's not quite cold enough for my warm winter coat, but . . . Did you get through the Kuppersmith yet?" Rita Ray plunged her key into the old mortise lock and then jiggled it. It seemed to stick every single time they unlocked the door. "The manuscript I gave you two days ago? Are you almost through it? I mean, the guy can write. Sometimes. Whenever he decides it's time to come back down to planet Earth. Jesus, some of the stuff he comes up with. Wrap that one up as soon as you can. I want to figure out if there's a pitch there pronto. If it needs revising, that's gonna be a fight. I sure as hell hope it's good . . ."

Angie liked her boss. Along with the sorry begonia on Angie's desk, Rita, a legend in New York literary circles, provided all the color the office needed. She'd once confided to Angie that she'd made a fair amount of money over her long career and inherited her family's Greenwich Village apartment, so she was able to keep working as an independent agent in her tiny office in Chelsea, scouring manuscripts with a sharp eye for spotting rare talent. Many of Rita's old contacts in the publishing industry were gone, retired or dead, but her name alone was still enough to get her calls put through at big and small houses alike. She still had it despite her steadfast refusal to "rebrand" or revamp her outfit into a sterile glass-and-chrome structure with a gleaming plaque outside the door announcing The Ray Agency. She'd told Angie, "No, thanks!"

It had been almost ten years since Angie had come home with a newly minted BA in French and English and had stared at her phone for a full fifteen minutes before she got up the nerve to call The Ray

Agency. Lacking a better plan, she was acting on the advice of her professor who had advised the college literary magazine. Dr. Barker had suggested a master's in literary studies or, if she didn't want to go straight into graduate school, a job in publishing where she could spend time reading and analyzing writing, something that would play to her talents and temperament.

"Ray Agency."

"I'm looking for work in the literary field," Angie had managed to get out. "I . . . I just graduated . . . I have a BA in French and English."

"Well, I've got sixty manuscripts on my desk," Rita had responded through what sounded like puffs of a cigarette. "Someone quit four months ago. Moved to Oregon with her girlfriend to work on some organic wildlife preserve or reserve or whatever. What do you know about books?"

There was some requisite hand-holding of writers, but even so, it wasn't a job for extroverts, and that was fine for Angie. Rita mostly left her alone except to drop manuscripts on her desk, confab about pitches, and ask at least once a day if she had seen her reading glasses that were, invariably, perched on top of her messy pile of hair dyed an unnatural shade of red.

Rita opened the office door and they squeezed past the battered coffee table, lumpy armchair, and struggling fern. Rita strode down the narrow hallway to her office after Angie promised to prioritize Kuppersmith.

Angie headed for her own office, intent on finishing the Kuppersmith manuscript that afternoon. The room's muted-green walls that recalled the avocado kitchen appliances of the seventies. The pot of semi-alive begonias on her desk provided a much-needed pop of color, but the plant never really thrived. Angie was never sure how much to water it, so it continually hovered between states of bloom and decrepitude. Whenever it tipped too much toward death, she'd add water and move it to a different spot until it recovered. Then she'd put it back on her desk, and the cycle repeated itself.

She put her bag down, took out the Kuppersmith, and sat down, but couldn't start in. She was feeling out of sorts. The bratty boy in the park stuck with her.

Angie identified with the little girl. At five, she too would have been startled, frozen by the boy's bullying. But Scarlett would have put him in his place without hesitation.

Scarlett.

Her older sister had always been a protector. Of the weak, the frightened, the hesitant. Of Angie. Angie didn't know what she'd have done growing up without her guidance, her insight, her shielding.

When Scarlett moved to Los Angeles after college, Angie had felt like a foundation card had been removed. She flailed, more than she had before, and she had always been flailing. She didn't remember a time when she had felt comfortable, when she had felt competent, when she had felt . . . safe.

Even as a child, sandwiched in the back between Scarlett and their younger brother, Scott, she couldn't stop fearing that they would be in an accident, that she would be thrust through the windshield, despite the security of her seatbelt.

The immediacy of her fears was an odd contrast to her siblings and peers. They found joy in so much: television, video games, sports, friends, music. Angie found them to be mild distractions, but they weren't the balm they appeared to be to others. Boys didn't gravitate toward her, makeup and fashion eluded her, even school, at which she excelled, didn't give her any sense of completeness. She went through the motions with her friends, but in the end, she felt more separate than ever. She knew it was her, she was the problem, but that knowledge didn't help give insight into what was wrong.

In time, she graduated college, got the job with Rita. She was okay. Okay enough. Her life worked.

Until the news of Scarlett's suicide. Then, it wasn't just a foundation card that shook Angie's core. The whole house of cards she'd carefully maintained came crashing down.

"Hey, you want some tea?"

Angie gave a start, so caught up in her thoughts. She turned in her chair to find Rita coming through the doorway. She dropped two more manuscripts on Angie's desk. "I'm gonna nuke myself a cup of chamomile. I had Greek for lunch, which usually agrees with me, but I think they put too much oil in the orzo today."

Angie preferred being alone, but she'd learned over the years to deal with people when necessary. Rita, though her boss, didn't make her nervous. For one, Angie was used to her. For two, Rita was predictable. She never changed, so Angie didn't have the stress of always being on edge during a conversation, wondering what to say next or how to escape.

"Thanks, Rita. I'm fine."

"Okay, honey."

Rita had told Angie she was profoundly saddened when she'd heard about Scarlett's death. She hadn't said much, except to tell Angie to take as much time off as she needed and that she would have a job whenever she returned. Angie had stayed home for two days and then went back to work. Being home on her own was much worse than being at work.

"Listen, let me know if things get to be too much for you," Rita had told her on her first day back. "If you want to talk or just open a window and yell, you just tell me. I mean, it's not as if people in New York are gonna be shocked by a woman yelling from a window."

But Angie never yelled. She'd never been one to yell, or even complain. She disliked attention, squirming at holidays when relatives would inevitably ask how school was, what was her favorite subject, what did she want to do when she got older. How was she supposed to know? She would murmur a few short answers and, as soon as her parents were occupied playing host, retreat to her room until someone dragged her out for dinner, so she didn't appear impolite. As a kid, when she couldn't cope on her own, there'd been Scarlett. Like when Angie had suddenly come down with a horrific case of tonsillitis in the fifth grade and woke up in the middle of the night with a throat so sore she couldn't get back to sleep.

"Scar, are you awake?" Angie, her voice a rough whisper, cracked Scarlett's bedroom door open.

"Hmmmm . . ." Scarlett murmured, turning over in her bed. "Are you okay?"

Angie started to cry. "My throat hurts so bad, I don't know what to do. I'm scared."

"Awwww, Ange. Come here." She scooted over, pulled down the covers, and patted the space next to her. Angie crawled in. "Hang on a minute." Scarlett got up and Angie could hear the water go on in the kitchen sink then the refrigerator door open and close. When Scarlett came back, she had two Tylenol capsules and a glass of water. "Okay, now take these."

"I don't want to. It'll hurt."

"It'll hurt just for a second, then it'll help you feel better. C'mon."

Angie placed the pills in her mouth and grimaced as she washed them down her inflamed throat.

"Plus," Scarlett added, "I got you something that will really help." And with a "Ta-da!" flourish she produced a cherry popsicle from behind her back. "Have some of this. It'll soothe your throat a little." She propped her little sister up so she could suck on the ice pop. "You don't have to finish it. When you're done, just put the rest in the glass."

Angie nodded.

"Now I gotta sleep." Scarlett gave her a kiss on the forehead and slipped back under the covers. "Goodnight, boogie-boo. Tomorrow things will be better."

Angie nodded, then turned thoughtful. "Scarlett? Do I have to go back to my room after I eat the popsicle?"

Scarlett lifted her head from the pillow. "Of course not, boogie-boo. Stay right here with me."

As she got older, Angie continued looking up to her kind,

effervescent older sister. Scarlett took life as it came, greeting it like a sunrise that would never turn into a sunset. She had an innate optimism that things would turn out fine in the end. Angie would look at her and wonder if her natural gifts of beauty and athleticism—she played soccer in school and competed in a summer swimming league—gave her the self-assurance and easygoing attitude that she herself lacked. Angie was the stronger student, but she dismissed that as a result of simply studying more. She buried herself in books when her sister wasn't dragging her out to a basketball game or bonfire. Still, she was never more than a tag-along. Scarlett's friends, though nice, treated her as more of a mascot than an actual person. It wasn't her crowd. Then again, she didn't have a crowd.

At SUNY New Paltz, a college far enough away that she could feel like she'd left home but close enough to return for a weekend if she wanted, Angie did the usual things: got a fake ID, drank too much beer with the girls in her freshman hall and threw up—that was never repeated—and had sex for the first time. The latter was with a chemistry major from New Hampshire named Robby with a head full of dark curls. Robby earned money over the summer giving kids tennis lessons and was sweet and funny. But the romance fizzled after a few months, leaving Angie, to her surprise, not devastated. She mostly wondered why everyone made such a big deal out of college.

Things picked up junior year when she joined the literary magazine and spent many an afternoon and weekend laying out pages, reading short stories, assigning reviews, and writing her own criticism. That was more her pace: being alone to soak in other people's words and reflect on them. A month of study in France awakened her senses and, for the first time, it occurred to Angie that a person could reinvent oneself. Wandering the streets, she thought of herself as "Angelique," literary wanderer, Francophile, lover of coq au vin and walking through the Bois de Boulogne. She stayed with a family, dove into street photography, learned to cook cassoulet, and read Baudelaire. But somehow, she still felt the impostor. No matter what she did, and no matter how much she liked something, be it a boy, a book, or a great pair of boots, nothing sustained her for long. Various things promised to lift her out of the semi-fog she seemed to perpetually exist in, but inevitably she would drift back to her solitary ways, falling into her ruts and routines, wondering if that was all there was.

No one ever mentioned depression, though Angie did start to question what she had always assumed was a normal, reserved, solitary nature when Dr. Barker posed a simple question as they worked on the layout for a special edition of the magazine comparing modern and classical poems.

"What do you guys do for fun?" he asked the group huddled around a desktop where they argued over fonts, design, and poem order. Georgie and Vina were competitive swimmers. Chris ran track. Edmund did photography. Andre was in an a cappella group. A few students with part-time jobs didn't have time for much else.

"What about you, Angie?" Dr. Barker asked.

"Um, well . . . this is fun," she offered, unsure what else to say.

"But what *else* do you do?" Barker pressed. "Look, it's not for me to tell you guys how to live. But you're what? Nineteen? Twenty? If you don't stretch yourself now, work up a sweat, scream from the rooftops, drink too much, fuck too much, do it all too much—"

There was a little awkward laughter from the group.

"—before you know it, you'll be hanging out with some pretentious assholes in grad school, you TA for a few years, get your degree, start teaching, and, if you're me, marry one of your doctoral students. Then you have a couple of kids and BAM!—no more free nights to recite poetry until dawn on the steps of the library . . . Carpe diem, guys. Trust me."

Angie did trust Dr. Barker. He wasn't sleazy, and he treated his students as peers, with respect, as he prompted them toward more critical thinking with every session. Still, nothing changed until the fall of her senior year, when Dr. Barker had asked her, "What's next?" as they hunted for illustrations to accompany point-counterpoint essays on the merits of free verse.

Angie gaped at him. "What?"

"After graduation. Is there a job you're pursuing, or grad school, or motorcycle racing?"

Angie kept staring, blankly.

"I'm kidding—about the motorcycle," Dr. Barker said. "You don't strike me as the biker type."

Angie had to smile at the thought of her riding around Long Island with a posse of leather-clad compatriots on a ginormous Harley. Even funnier was the thought of her mother watching her ride by the house. Perfectly coiffed Ellen Norris with her Ralph Lauren slacks and sweaters. And her father? Not even worth contemplating.

The truth was Dr. Barker's casual inquiry had slammed Angie into reality. She hadn't a clue and no idea how to get one. It occurred to her that she'd been drifting for a long time, and that that would no longer do. College was coming to an end in a few short months.

"I guess I'll move back home, get a job," she mused. "I'm not sure, actually. I haven't given it much thought, though I suppose I should. I'm just not really sure, you know." She hesitated and finally spluttered, "I don't really know what I want."

"Angie, let me tell you something. It's a hundred percent okay to not know. In fact, I'm sort of suspicious of students who think they have the world figured out at twenty-one. But here's the thing—you're a smart girl, and you have good literary insights. I've worked with thousands of students, some more promising than others. The difference between students who go places and those who don't isn't promise. It's a willingness to take a risk, to do something, to screw up, to hate a job, to do something else, but always, always be moving. Move forward, move in another direction, it's even okay to retreat sometimes, but do something. Read, write, create art, listen to music, work, quit, fail, or 'fail better,' as Beckett said. But don't not do things because you're afraid. That's the real killer. Remember our friend William Ward," he added, pointing to her open laptop.

Angie read the poem on her computer screen.

> To live is to risk dying,
> To hope is to risk despair,
> To try is to risk failure.
> But risks must be taken because the greatest hazard in
> life is to risk nothing.

Two days later, Angie awoke at 2:00 a.m. with her heart pounding so hard she had trouble catching her breath. She was dying. That had to be it. She would die and leave her family to grieve her. But twenty-year-old women didn't have heart attacks. Maybe she was having a nervous breakdown? What was a nervous breakdown, anyway? It was something that afflicted middle-aged women in old movies whose husbands left them. Whatever it was, maybe that was it, maybe she was too skittish to handle life so she was falling apart and EMTs would come and cart her off to a psychiatric hospital where she would be overly medicated and left drooling in a wheelchair. The thought only made her more anxious but she couldn't just lie in bed, struggling to breathe, so she did the only thing she could think of. She went into the bathroom, turned on the shower, took off her clothes, and sat directly under the torrent of water, hoping it would save her from insanity and death.

A few minutes later there was a tentative knock at the door. She couldn't gather herself enough to respond. Finally, Suzanne poked her head in. "Everything okay?"

As the water cascaded over her, Angie repeated between choked sobs, "I don't know what's wrong. I don't know. I can't . . . I can't . . ."

"It's okay. Here, here . . ." Her roommate looked alarmed as she turned off the water and helped Angie out of the tub. She wrapped her in a towel, sat her down on the toilet seat, kneeled in front of her, and took her hands. "Listen. You've got to breathe. Angie, look at me."

Angie cried quietly, her eyes wide with panic.

"We're going to breathe now, in through your nose, out through your mouth. Ready? Breathe in, two, three, four, and now out, two, three, four. Good, that was good. You can do this. Now again. This will help. Ready? In, two, three, four. And out, two, three, four . . ."

Angie closed her eyes. She could feel water running in rivulets down her back from her drenched hair. The voice telling her to breathe seemed far away, like a distant echo. Her heart was racing. *Please don't let me die, please don't let me die*, she pleaded to whatever universal force or deity might be out there, willing to save her.

Suzanne still held her hands. "Just breathe. Come on, breathe steadily. It will calm you and help you focus. Come on, Angie, you can do this."

Gradually, the breathing, the repetition of counting, and Suzanne's steady presence brought calm back into Angie's body. She started to feel less lightheaded. The terror, the panic subsided. The better her body felt, the less scared she became. Maybe it was just some weird chemical glitch. Maybe she wouldn't die after all.

"Better?" Suzanne asked as they headed back to bed.

"Yeah. I'm not crazy, I swear I'm not."

"I know. I know," she assured Angie.

It had taken a couple of days and a few rounds with a campus psychiatrist and some therapists specializing in young adult behaviors and disorders before Angie had a diagnosis: generalized anxiety disorder and underlying clinical depression. The latter made it hard for her to get excited about much in life or muster enough energy to do more than get through each day. The former, the doctor thought, had spiked into a panic attack because her time at school was coming to an end, forcing her subconsciously to confront the looming question of what to do next.

\*\*\*

At the end of her work day, Angie felt no panic, just weariness, as she trudged up two flights to her one-bedroom apartment in Astoria.

"Why, hello, Brontë," she greeted the gray tabby who rushed toward her as she came through the door. She bent down to pet the cat, who immediately rolled onto her back with a deeply contented purr.

Angie's evening routine didn't tend to vary. She would change into yoga pants and a sweatshirt or shorts and a T-shirt, depending on the season, feed Brontë, pour herself a glass of seltzer over ice with a slice of lemon, and sit on the couch with her microwave dinner—that night's was chicken tikka masala—while Brontë settled on her lap. She would read a manuscript for Rita or a book or watch a movie. Sometimes she had an evening event, like a book signing. She knew and liked some of the writers Rita represented. Part of her job was meeting with them about changes to their manuscripts and pitches to publishers. Still, those nights were tiring for her, and she preferred to go home and sink into her solitude.

A couple of hours later, Angie picked up Brontë, the cat meowing in protest, and plopped her on the couch so she could stand. "I know, I'm sorry. I need some water." She checked her phone—1:40 a.m. She must have dozed off during her British mystery. She had a headache and wandered over to the kitchen, where she kept her ibuprofen. But as she rooted around in a drawer, her hand slammed up against a sharp edge. "Shit!" She pulled out the offending object: a small, framed photo of her, Scarlett, and Scott, on Scarlett's high school graduation day. She'd forgotten she'd stashed it there. It had gotten too hard, seeing it every day.

She clutched the picture with both hands and leaned against the kitchen counter. It had been windy that day, and Scarlett held the mortarboard on her head with one hand while she casually draped her other arm around Scott, then a goofy twelve-year-old with tousled hair, as shy fifteen-year-old Angie leaned into her other side. She wished she could remember what they'd talked about before the picture was taken. Were they laughing about how their hair was flying in every direction possible? Had their father told a dad joke? No, maybe the wind had blown their mother's skirt above her knees. Scandalous! Was that it? The details of their childhood years were fading. That made her feel a bit panicky. What if her memories of Scarlett faded, too?

Angie started to pace, treading the well-worn path from the kitchen to the living-room window fronting the busy street below. *How could it be?* She paced more quickly, back and forth, looking at the picture, arriving at the kitchen, turning around, striding to the window, turning again, crossing back. Seeing the three of them in that frame. *How could it be?* They'd been a normal, middle-class family on Long Island, with a vibrant, beautiful older sister, a rambunctious, nerdy kid brother, and a quiet girl in the middle who liked to read. It was your basic happy suburban set-up.

Smart parents. Good kids. It wasn't supposed to turn out the way it had. Her breath quickened, and she could feel her heart rate start to pick up.

*Why, Scar?* Now everything was gone, shattered. *I can't put the pieces back. No one can ever put the pieces back.*

Angie's hands shook. She went back to the couch and sat with her head between her knees. "God, please stop. Please stop." Her heart was pounding, and she knew she should practice the rhythmic breathing she'd done for years, but all she could manage to do was sit and rock. "Please, God, please let it stop, please, I don't want to feel this, please help, please help me . . ."

No matter how many times they happened, the attacks had the potential to shock and terrify. She tried to lift her head and open her eyes but that made her queasy, so she closed them again and tried to soothe herself: "You won't die, you didn't die before, you won't die now, this always passes. It'll be okay, it'll be okay . . ."

When she finally felt a modicum of equilibrium, she grabbed her phone and called her brother. Her anxiety spiked when he didn't pick up until the fourth ring. She didn't even give him time to say hello:

"Scott? Scotty, oh, my God, it's happening again. My skin feels like it's burning. What if I really die this time? What about Mom and Dad? What about Brontë!" Her words came out in bursts between gasping breaths. "Scotty, I can't die. Mom and Dad already lost Scarlett, please don't let me die."

"You're not dying—"

"Jesus, I feel like I'm going to throw up. I'm so sick of this, I can't stand it, it's like I want to rip my skin off my body." Her voice was growing louder and more agitated. She hated feeling like she was losing her mind and was terrified at the prospect of actually getting seriously ill. *Could the panic attacks damage my heart?* She pushed the thought aside.

"Scotty, listen, if I die, please take Brontë. Promise me." She looked over at the cat sprawled on her desk. The thought of her alone and frightened was more than she could bear. "Please. Otherwise, they'll take her to the pound and kill her."

"Angie, you are not dying," he assured her. "You are not going to die. We know what this is. This is panic. Plain and simple. We've been through this before."

"Brontë. Promise."

"Yes, yes, I promise, no one will take Brontë. But you are not dying. Now, I want you to listen to me and go and close your eyes and breathe, slowly. Repeat to yourself, 'I'm okay. This will pass. I'm safe. This will pass.'"

"I can't, Scott, I can't, I can't . . ." Angie couldn't think. She was trembling and scared of her thundering heart even though she knew she wasn't having a heart attack. Her limbs were hot and itchy; she couldn't stop clawing at her skin.

"What are you doing, are you sitting or standing?" Scott asked. "Go sit down. C'mon, you can do this."

Angie trudged over to the sofa and sat. Closing her eyes, she hugged herself, her hands moving up and down her forearms to calm her raging skin. "I'm okay. This is just a panic attack. This will pass. It's passed before. I'm okay."

Angie hated bothering her brother so late when they would see each other in eight hours anyway. She envied Scott. He was a chemical engineer with a steady, friendly manner. He had been rocked by Scarlett's death, too, but not as much as Angie, it seemed.

"That's it. Breathe in, two, three, four. Out, two, three, four. Slowly."

They stayed on the phone for several minutes, silent except for Angie's rhythmic breaths.

Finally, Scott asked, "How do you feel now? Is it better? How is your skin?"

"I . . . I don't know . . . Yeah, better, better." Her heartbeat had slowed.

"Where's the lavender? Do you have the lavender oil? You need to keep that handy."

"Yeah, okay." Angie kept Scott on the phone as she went into the kitchen and took a small vial of essence of lavender from the cupboard. She opened it and breathed deeply. Then she opened the tap and poured a glass of cool water.

"Ange, are you gonna be okay now? You feel better?"

"Yeah, it's passing." Her skin felt cooler and her breathing more relaxed. "I got some water."

"Sounds like the worst is over." Usually, once Angie started to drink water, it meant the attack was ebbing. Scott knew that, too. "Call me back if you need to. Otherwise, I'll see you at ten and we'll go out to Mom and Dad's. Okay, kiddo?" Even though Angie was older, she knew he still seemed to see her as his younger sister in need of protection.

"Thanks, Scotty," Angie whispered. "Scotty . . . ?"

"Yeah?"

"How could we not have known? If we knew Scarlett was hurting like that, we could have done something, gotten her help."

"Ange, we've been through this. Scarlett never let on that she was at all depressed. She seemed to be on top of the world, so how were we to know? This wasn't our fault. You can't stop something you don't know about."

"Yeah, okay. Love you, Scotty. Thanks for putting up with me."

"Hey, c'mon, we're family. I love you too. We'll see you in the morning. We'll bring muffins, your favorites, the carrot cake ones with the golden raisins, okay?"

Angie allowed herself a small smile. Suddenly, she was very, very tired. "Muffins sound good."

"Night, kiddo."

"Night."

Angie disconnected, more grateful than ever for her brother. In the shadow of Scarlett's absence, his presence meant more than it had before. And it had always meant a lot.

She would ask her doctor about adjusting her meds. Her depression had been fairly well controlled for years, ever since she got her diagnosis in college. After some trial and error, a regimen of nightly medications, along with therapy, had made her life manageable. She could live on what Rita paid her. On weekends, she read new books, watched movies, napped, went running, hung out with Brontë. Her panic attacks almost vanished.

Until last year, when the call came very early one morning.

It had been Angie's father, his voice so low and raspy she could hardly understand him. "Something's happened," he said. "You need to come home. Come now."

"What's wrong?" She struggled not to panic.

"I'll explain when you get here. Don't check the news, don't check your phone."

It was so ominous, Angie dialed her brother immediately. "Scott, what's happening?"

With just a few words, he had sent her ordered world spinning into a vortex of grief and confusion.

"The LAPD phoned Dad. Scarlett's gone. She killed herself."

# 2

The next morning, Angie opened her living room curtains to reveal a cold, clear February day. When her brother rang her buzzer at 10:10, she grabbed her coat and emerged from her building in boots, jeans, and a baggy oatmeal sweater. Scott, his wife, Sarah, and their two kids, five-year-old Michelle and three-year-old Brendan, were waiting in their SUV, ready to head out to Naw-naw and Pop-pop's on Long Island.

"Hey, guys," Angie said as she climbed in the front. Sarah was in the back between the kids who were strapped into their car seats. "Thanks for getting me."

"Good to see you," Sarah said.

"Thanks, Sarah." Angie knew her sister-in-law was making an effort in spite of the late-night call to Scott.

"We have muffwins, Aunt Angie," Michelle chirped. "Do you want a muffwin?"

Angie pivoted to smile at her niece, who clutched a bakery bag in one hand and a stuffed llama in the other. "Why, yes, Michelle, I would love a muffin." She turned to the little dark-haired boy on the other side of his mother. He held fistfuls of Star Wars Lego figures. "Hi, Brendan."

"Hi." He was focused on his toys.

"How are you?" Sarah asked. She was a nurse practitioner, very practical and adept at juggling patients with the parenting of young children.

"I'm well." Angie didn't feel like talking or explaining herself. And what was there to say, anyway?

Thirty-five minutes later, they pulled up in front of the manicured garden that framed the Norrises' colonial in Farmingdale. Angie's father, Gerry, was an English professor who taught at Fordham University. Her mother, Ellen, was a museum curator, a forensic anthropologist by training, who'd taken a leave after Scarlett died. She'd recently told Angie that, although she missed work, she wasn't sure she would ever return—she still didn't feel up to facing people. She volunteered once a week at a women's shelter. Other than that, she spent hours in her garden, culling daisies and tending to climbing clematis vines, losing herself in dirt and seeds, flowers and greenery.

Gerry Norris was methodical. His immaculate library was alphabetized, and he read several newspapers each day, plus *The Atlantic* and *The New Yorker*, and skimmed online news sites and political forums. He was possessed of a withering eye and could be wryly funny. He lacked patience for sloppy thinkers and messy emotions and when he drank too much at dinner parties or family gatherings, he grew belligerent. Ellen usually had to intercede before an ugly argument ensued.

The front door opened and Angie's mom stepped onto the portico, smiling broadly in welcome. To Angie, Ellen never seemed truly happy after losing Scarlett, but she very clearly put on a brave face for others. A teen beauty queen and high school cheerleader—Angie and her siblings were all familiar with the photos from Ellen's youth, and the stories about her and her father's early days. They met when she was studying for her master's and he was working toward his doctorate in rhetoric and writing. They married and bought the house in Farmingdale shortly after Angie was born.

"Hello, hello, my darlings!" Her mother beamed at the children as they scurried up the walk with cries of "Naw-naw! Naw-naw!" She started to tear up as she embraced them. There was always so much emotion just under the surface, as if any of them could tip into grief at any moment.

"Hey, Mom." Scott put an arm around her. "You look beautiful, as always."

Ellen wore green linen trousers, a white blouse, and patterned V-neck sweater, her champagne-colored hair arranged in a chignon. A thick gold chain lay against her collarbone. She was ever chic, even though the past year had etched lines in her face.

"Hi, dear." Ellen kissed her son on the cheek. "Hello, Sarah! And, Angie, sweetheart, look at you, that sweater's darling. Come in, come in."

By then, Gerry had appeared in the doorway. "Well, well, look what's blown in! Come here, you rascals!" he called to his grandchildren. "You get bigger all the time, do you know that?" He crouched and gave them each a tickle that prompted squeals of laughter.

Sarah led the two children toward the backyard as Angie, Scott, and their parents went inside. Angie sat at the kitchen table while her mother arranged the pastries on a plate. The antique butcher block on wheels Mom had found a few years before at a specialty shop sat in the middle of the airy room. Through wide, clear glass panes they could see Sarah playing with the kids. The backyard, which included Ellen's garden and a swing set (the same one Scott, Angie, and Scarlett used to play on), was expansive, the grass still covered in a white frost from the night before.

"So, how are things?" Gerry asked.

"Oh, you know, fine," Angie dodged. She loved her father, but he could still make her nervous, even as a grown woman.

"How's work?" he pressed. "Has Rita found the next literary wunderkind? Honestly, I don't know why she insists on keeping her own shop. She could have sold to one of the big houses years ago, made a small fortune."

"Well, maybe she likes being her own boss," Scott offered.

"Not everyone likes being told what to do, Gerry." Ellen's voice had a brittle quality.

"Oh, for the love of God. She could have made her life a dozen times easier, but never mind. Scott, what's new in the engineering world?"

Scott and Gerry grabbed their coats and drifted out the sliding doors into the backyard, leaving Angie and her mom alone in the kitchen.

"So, really, how's life these days?" Ellen asked.

Angie looked into her mother's clear, green eyes and thought she would always be beautiful but would never seem young again. Ellen had become much more prone to distraction. One minute, she would be mixing tuna salad for lunch, and the next she would be staring into space, her knife poised over a stalk of celery, lost in thought.

"Things are well," Angie replied after a moment. "Well enough. I'm reading a decent manuscript by an established writer. It's a fantasy-adventure-romance and it's pretty engaging."

"Well, that sounds promising. Are you sleeping? And eating?"

"I had . . . Last night was . . . I had a few bad moments." She didn't want to go into detail. Her mother was much easier to talk to than her dad, who had an answer for everything. He didn't understand how others lived in the gray spaces between absolutes and, even worse, made decisions different from what he thought they should. "But it passed."

"Good," her mother said. "Did I tell you, the Tuckers are selling their place and moving to Scottsdale? Their son is out there, and one daughter is in California, so they'll be closer to their grandchildren. I don't know, it sounds awfully . . . barren or something. Not sure I'd like it."

Angie had caught sight of the FOR SALE sign when they'd pulled up. She and her siblings had grown up across the street from Chris, Charlotte, and Amanda Tucker. They'd walked to school together, shared birthday celebrations, and confided first crushes. They'd drifted apart in high school, when the Norris siblings went to the local public high school while the Tuckers went to Our Lady of Divine Salvation.

The Tuckers had sent flowers when Scarlett died, and Ellen mentioned how kind Mrs. Tucker had been, knocking on Ellen's door a couple of times a week to see if she wanted company.

The days of hanging around with the Tucker kids seemed like eons ago. *So much time gone by. So much is different.*

They fell silent and Angie joined her mother in slicing kiwis and oranges for a fruit platter. Once they had filled the plate, Angie carried it to the table where she set it down. "Mom . . . Have you heard from the Academy Awards?"

Ellen finished washing her hands and reached for a dish towel. "Yes, we got a call when they announced the nominations. I'm so proud of all that she was able to accomplish."

They both fell silent. The first anniversary of Scarlett's suicide was coming up in a month—March 20.

"What's that?" Gerry asked.

They both turned with a start. They hadn't heard him and Scott come back in. Ellen cleared her throat. "Angie was just mentioning the Oscars, Gerry, and—"

"Angie, why would you bring that up and upset your mother?"

"I'm not upset, Gerry, for heaven's sake. Scarlett is nominated for Best Actress. It's hardly a secret."

"There's no need to talk about any of that," Gerry snapped. "As if we would all head out to Los Angeles. We don't want anything to do with the movie industry, or Hollywood, or their fake award nonsense. For the love of God, that place killed your sister."

"Dad," Scott started, "don't blame Angie just for—"

"I'm not blaming Angie, I'm blaming Hollywood. This is still my house, and I'll decide what we do and don't bring into it, and we are not bringing in Hollywood, or those goddamn awards, or any of that film industry crap here. None of it comes in here."

"Gerry, Angie was just—"

"Ellen, you know how I feel about this!" her husband shot back.

"Enough." He looked at each of them, swallowed hard, turned, and strode out.

Angie's throat was tight, but she wasn't going to cry. "I'm sorry, Mom, I should have known better."

Ellen put her hands on her daughter's shoulders and leaned in, pressing the side of her face against Angie's. "There is no need to apologize, dear." She pulled back and looked her square in the eye. "You did nothing wrong. He's just . . . He can't face it."

With that, she let go of Angie's' shoulder, grabbed a jacket, and drifted out to the yard to join her daughter-in-law and grandchildren. Angie squeezed Scott's hand and then went down the hall to the stairs that led to the second floor. Looking up, she felt a stream of childhood memories rush toward her.

She pushed past them, through them, until she stood at a pale-yellow bedroom at the end of the upstairs hall. She hesitated, girding herself, then gingerly crossed the threshold.

Scarlett's many high school awards still stood in place on top of a white bureau, heavy under the weight of her accomplishments. Her brass bed gleamed, dolls still piled high in a corner rocking chair. Ellen said she was saving them for Michelle who had yet to express much interest.

The walls held a framed photo of Scarlett on the opening night of her first major movie. Angie opened the sliding door of the double closet. Much had been given away since Scarlett moved out, but there were still a few sweaters hanging there, an old denim jacket, a cowboy hat Scarlett wore one Halloween when she was Annie Oakley, a pair of ice skates in a corner. Angie reached into the far recess and felt the stiff tulle of the blue gown Scarlett had worn to her prom. They'd all laughed when her date, handsome Doug Jenkins, asked if her fairy godmother had conjured up the dress.

Angie closed her eyes, allowing the memories to wash over her, inhaling deeply.

*In, two, three four. Out, two, three, four.*

A knock at the door roused her and she opened her eyes to find Scott poking his head in from the hall. "Sorry," he said. "Didn't realize you were . . . having a moment?"

"I was just . . . Nothing. What's up?"

Scott stepped inside. "We need to talk about Dad."

"About what a dick he is to Mom?"

"He's suffering too. He just doesn't show it much."

"Uh, I think he is showing it."

Angie lay down on Scarlett's bed, and Scott lay next to her. They stared up at the ceiling in silence for a few moments, ruminating in their separate thoughts.

Finally, Angie turned to her brother. "How did we get here?"

"The Long Island Expressway?" he joked, and she couldn't help but laugh. "I think about her, too, you know. A lot." He suddenly sounded sad. "And I don't know what happened in California. She seemed happy. She was certainly successful. I wondered sometimes why she never talked much about her personal life, who she was dating, that kind of thing, but I figured she was just busy making movies. It's gotta be a lot of pressure. I had no idea she was depressed, or whatever."

"Did anyone call you about the Oscars?" Angie asked.

"Yeah. And I thought about going, but I've got a conference that week, in Taipei of all places. And Sarah's got a few shifts at the hospital, so we're going to bring the kids here to Mom and Dad's for a few days. It's already complicated without me trying to get to LA in the middle of it. And, like, what are they going to do, anyway? Introduce me to Ryan Reynolds? I mean, I wouldn't know what to do. I'd like to go for Scar, in a way, but it's not like it's going to change anything."

It was hard to know how much attention Scarlett's career and tragic death would get at the ceremony. She'd be included in the traditional tribute to film notables who'd died over the past year, of course. And the Academy had reached out, which Angie supposed was something.

Attitudes were changing, but dying of a horrible disease was seen as somehow noble, while killing yourself out of misery and desperation from your mental illness wasn't. Angie could never understand it.

"I sort of feel like someone should go," she said. "I mean, if none of us shows up, isn't that, you know . . . like we don't care?"

"Well, Dad sure as hell ain't going. Mom probably wouldn't go without him, considering she'd never hear the end of it. We've been through my schedule. That leaves . . ." He turned to her and pointed both index fingers.

"Yeah. I know, I know. But what if I have a panic attack? It's so unpredictable. I can't fall apart when E! TV starts asking me about Scar and who designed my dress."

"Actually, that alone would be worth it. Just picture it, some size-two fashionista wearing fourteen pounds of eyeliner shoves a microphone under your nose, flashes her blinding smile, and says, 'Miss Norris, thank you so much for being here. Now, do tell us, who designed the dress you're wearing tonight.' And you could look at her and say, 'Um . . . T.J. Maxx?'"

"Cut it out!" They both laughed, Angie playfully shoving Scott, and then she thought a moment. "I'd like to do it, for Scarlett, but, God, all those people watching . . ."

"Yeah, I know. You don't have to go. No one *has* to go." He got up and straightened his pants. "I'm gonna go find Sarah and the kids. You coming?"

"Yeah, I'll be along." Angie was picturing herself on the red carpet, totally panicked, cameras flashing and celebrities slinking by in hundred-thousand-dollar gowns. *No one wants to look at me.* The thought dredged up the memory of the time she was about to pop into Rita's office to deliver a manuscript but stopped just outside the door when she heard her boss on the phone.

"She'll be there tonight, at the launch, instead of me. Irv, she's fantastic!" Rita had enthused. "She's been with me years, and, man, oh, man, did I hit the lottery with her."

Angie had realized she must be talking about her, and her cheeks grew hot.

Rita paused, clearly listening to whomever she was speaking with. "She's cute, slender but not skinny. Bobbed hair, dark blond. Intense gray eyes. And, oh, boy, has she got style. But, understated, you know? Flair. She's got flair."

Angie had stepped into the doorway with a sheepish smile. "Hi. Just dropping off this manuscript." She set it on Rita's desk.

"Hi, doll. Just singing your praises to Irv Winkelman. You remember him."

"Uh. . ."

"She says hi, Irv."

The conversation had stuck with Angie, who had never once considered she had style. And she'd always been self-conscious about her thinness. She kind of liked the idea of slender instead of skinny. Still, the thought of being scrutinized at the Oscars twisted her stomach.

She shook off the feeling of terror and left Scarlett's room.

She found everyone in the living room. Her mother sidled up to her. "So, my dear. Anyone interesting in your life these days?"

"No, Mom. I'm not really up to meeting anyone just now. It's not been the best year. Obviously." It came out sharper than she intended.

Ellen sighed. "My friend Jean has this very smart son. He's a writer and lives in Brooklyn, and we just thought, wouldn't it be nice if you two could get together and just have a coffee? I mean, it couldn't hurt, honey."

"Mom, I'm really not interested in having coffee with some guy I've never met."

"Sweetie, people have been going on blind dates for years. I just think it might make you feel better."

"Feel better?"

"Honey, we've all been through a lot. Too much. I just think you might be happier if you had someone in your life. I wouldn't worry about you being sad all the time . . ."

Angie understood. Her mother had only so much bandwidth for worry and anxiety. And if Angie was happier, it was one less thing for her to stress about. "I don't mean to sound so . . . ungrateful. I'll meet . . . Who is it?"

"Matthew. He's Jean's son. Jean Mandelbach. From the museum."

"You can give Matthew, Jean-from-the-museum's son, my number. He can call me. Who knows, maybe he'll turn out to be a literary genius and Rita can make millions off him."

"Honey, I'm not trying to force you into anything, I just think it might add something to your life, that's all."

"It's fine. I get it." She tried to speak more gently. "I do."

Scott sauntered up behind them. "Has Mom got you all sorted out to meet the love of your life, Ange?"

Angie could tell he'd been listening. Why couldn't he have swooped in sooner to save her from their mother's matchmaking?

"Yes, Matthew Mandelbach is going to be the love of my life, for sure. I can't wait to have coffee with him and plan our wedding."

"Oh, now, don't be silly," Ellen admonished. "I meant nothing of the sort. I only mentioned it—"

"No, Mom, honestly, it's fine." Angie caught her brother's eye. "I'm happy to meet Matthew, really."

"And I'm sure Matthew is going to love meeting you," Scott said. "He'll probably turn out to be some nerd desperate to get in your pants—"

"Jesus, Scott!" Angie chastised. But they both burst out laughing.

"Oh, my goodness, now I'm really sorry I mentioned it." Ellen was flustered, her cheeks pink, but she smiled just the same.

When they got ready to leave later that day, Angie went to the closet to get her jacket and stopped short. Posters of Scarlett's movies hung in the front hallway. Every Christmas, she'd had one framed for their parents as a fun memento of her success, something they could show off to their friends. But now . . .

Angie went slowly, one by one.

*Even Steven*, an early film that had gotten Scarlett some recognition, was a black comedy about a group of college girls who come up with creative ways to get back at their exes.

Then she had made the thriller, *Danger Zone,* a murder whodunit, and *Every Time I Kiss You,* in which she was cast as a lonely young wife in the 1960s. She realizes she's a lesbian and precipitates a scandal by embarking on a damaging affair with one of her kid's teachers. The film had marked Scarlett's emergence as a serious actor, and better scripts soon came her way. Then she starred in a well-received series for three seasons to rave reviews.

But her biggest coup ended up being her last. Angie remembered the big announcement, some two and a half years ago, that DreamWeaver Studios had signed Scarlett Norris to star as Chloe in their upcoming drama, *Catapult,* about a heroin-addicted prostitute who inadvertently saves a congresswoman's life and gets pushed into a high-powered political career. Scarlett had been so excited about landing the role and told her family all about DreamWeaver. Though not the biggest studio in town, she had said, it was among the hottest, thanks to the virtually unerring eye of founder Charles Weaver for making films that were as excellent as they were popular.

*Catapult* was no different. The film opened in November to critical acclaim, eight months after Scarlett was found dead on the set the final day of shooting. It was a tragic detail that only served to magnify its allure. Theaters were packed.

In spite of herself and the pain of her grief, Angie followed the movie's ever-growing success. DreamWeaver orchestrated a no-holds-barred publicity campaign: the director gave interviews everywhere from Hollywood to Cannes. Cast members appeared on talk shows. Enormous ads featuring images of Scarlett popped up in *Variety, The Hollywood Reporter*, the *LA Times, The New York Times*, and more. No one was surprised when the movie garnered numerous Oscar nominations, including Best Picture and a posthumous Best Actress nod for Scarlett.

*What went wrong, Scar? What?*

"Ange, you coming?" Scott called from the front door.

She snapped to and turned from the tunnel of memories. "Yeah. I'll be right there."

Angie's dread mounted as the days ticked by, the anniversary of Scarlett's death looming. Over the next week, Angie focused on work to keep her mind busy and her body calm. She got through three more manuscripts and wrote up some pitch ideas, successfully keeping her panic attacks at bay. By the time Friday night rolled around and she found herself fiddling with a plate of seafood pasta while Matthew Mandelbach made a fervent effort at conversation, she was utterly drained. But she hadn't wanted to cancel on the son of her mother's friend, who had called the day he got her number.

*How do clams breathe anyway?* Angie wondered as she considered the bivalves in the yellow dish. *Do they even have a central nervous system?* She remembered how she and her siblings would dig for clams on family outings near East Hampton every fall. She could picture Scarlett, laughing in her bright green bathing suit at low tide, holding out her shovel to Angie, urging her to get in on the action. Angie smiled at the memory. That was how it always went. She would hang back while Scarlett was out front, trying to bring her along. *God, without Scar, I probably never would have done much of anything.*

"Do you know what I mean?"

She looked up.

Matthew appeared animated. "I mean, it's crazy how many different types of operating systems they had to go through before they found one that wouldn't crash if you had a smaller hard drive."

"Oh, yeah, crazy, right."

"Gosh, I'm boring you." Matthew was cute and a writer, just like Ellen had said. He wrote technical manuals for setting up home computer networks.

"No, it's not that, Matthew. I'm just a little wiped out. You know—Friday night after a long week. I'm sorry I'm not very good company."

"No way, I really like your company. Let's finish up here and get the check."

As they walked a few blocks in search of a taxi, Matthew took Angie's hand. It was pleasant, if not exhilarating, and she didn't pull away. As they rode, she took a leap of faith. "Would you like to come in for tea?"

Maybe her mother was right, that she had to give dating more of a chance.

Over steaming mugs of mint tea, they talked about publishing. Angie told him about Rita and her work.

"Wow, that sounds so interesting," he enthused, seemingly earnestly. "Working with real writers and all."

"I mostly enjoy the reading, but some of the writers are cool."

When they had endured a comfortable silence, she cleared the mugs to the kitchen sink. When she turned back, Matthew was standing there. He took both of her hands and, gently, leaned in and put his lips to hers. She kissed him back, at first hesitantly, but then with more intensity. Then she led him to the bedroom. *Why not?* she thought. *This is what people do. Go out. Have sex. Get to know one another.*

In Angie's small bedroom, Matthew began unbuttoning her blouse. They kissed, pressed up against one. Slipping his hand under her bra, he unhooked it, and then unbuttoned his shirt. She wriggled out of her slim black pants as Matthew unbuttoned his jeans. Angie didn't have any particular sense of desire, but she didn't particularly mind, either. It was almost as if she were having an out-of-body experience, watching herself as she and Matthew ran their hands over one another's bodies before falling onto the bed, naked, until Matthew got on top of her. Afterward, as they lay there, she stared at the ceiling as Matthew, one arm slung across the top of her pillow, twirled a strand of her hair.

"What are you thinking?" he asked.

"I should probably get some rest. It's late and I have work to do this weekend. For Rita—my boss. I'm behind on a book." She knew she was being distant. She didn't want to hurt him. He was sweet and obviously interested in her, but she just couldn't face awkward morning small talk.

"Oh, okay, then, um, should I go?"

"Do you mind?"

"Yeah, no problem."

So Matthew Mandelbach got dressed and left. Angie felt bad, knowing he was disappointed. As for the sex, it was much like the last time she'd slept with someone, over a year ago, when, after a reading, she'd gone home with a big-shot agent. The sex wasn't great—she didn't have an orgasm—but the guy was interested. Angie felt detached. *Does twice make a pattern?* She was still thinking about that when the intercom buzzed. It was nearly 1:00 a.m.

"Who is it?" she queried into the speaker when she'd approached the door.

"It's me, Matthew. I have a package for you. Someone just dropped it off."

Confused, Angie buzzed him back in. What would someone be dropping off in the middle of the night? She waited until there was a gentle knock, and she opened the door to find Matthew standing there with a manila envelope with her name in typeface.

"I was waiting downstairs for my Lyft," Matthew explained, "and this guy on a motorcycle pulls up. I guess he's a messenger, but I didn't think they worked this late. Anyway, he asks me if I can receive a delivery. I look down and it's addressed to you, so I said sure. I figured I should come up and give it to you. I mean, it's so late. So, maybe it's important?"

"Oh, yeah, thanks." She took the envelope from him. A pause. Matthew still stood there. "Is your Lyft close?" she asked. She just couldn't deal with anyone else at the moment, not even nice tech writer Matthew.

"Yeah, I'd better get back down there. Take care. I'll call you." He gave a sweet grin then headed back to the stairs to the street.

Angie sat on her couch and studied the envelope. Too thin to be a manuscript. She had a strange feeling as she opened it and pulled out a single sheet of lined paper.

*Your sister was the bravest woman I knew*
*Make this right*
*Scarlett deserved better*
*CD-1447789 1st Precinct*

# 3

The day after her lackluster date with Matthew, she slept in, finally venturing out for a soy latte and a few newspapers and magazines. Back home, she tried to read but her eyes kept wandering over to her desk, where she'd placed the mysterious envelope. She went running, but the message kept playing in her head. On Sunday, she picked up groceries, made carrot soup, and started a new manuscript. But the message would not be vanquished.

She tried to rationalize it away. Surely it was the work of a crazed fan. Scarlett died in Los Angeles. Why would there be a police report in Manhattan? Scarlett was a beautiful actress who became a star after her death, and the world was probably full of Scarlett-obsessed lunatics.

"Make this right." What could that mean? She took her own life. A studio assistant found her dead on the floor of her trailer her final day on *Catapult*. Scarlett's prints were on the gun. The coroner said she had fired the shot herself, based on the bullet's trajectory and how she fell.

*What is there to make right?*

Angie tossed it over and over in her head. It was exhausting. She went to bed early that night but couldn't sleep, despite the fatigue. She grabbed her phone. "Scotty?"

"Ange, it's nearly midnight. What's going on? You okay?"

"Scotty, this weird thing happened. Somebody sent me a message about Scar."

"What do you mean?"

"Someone dropped off an envelope at my apartment building and inside is a sheet of paper with a message about Scarlett. And there was a number." She paused. She didn't want to sound delusional or obsessive, like someone who'd watched one too many episodes of *Law & Order*.

"About Scarlett? What did it say?"

"That she deserved better. What could that mean?"

"It means she deserved better. And she did. Can we talk tomorrow?"

Now, she really was obsessing. "Yeah, sure. I'm sorry. It's nothing, I'm sure. It just, you know, shook me up a little. And I keep thinking about it."

"It's all right. It's been an awful time, God knows. The anniversary is coming up . . . I'll call you tomorrow. 'Night."

"'Night."

Come Monday morning, the message still echoed in Angie's mind, but she convinced herself that pursuing it would be ridiculous. Where would she even start? It was all she could do to remember to take her meds, get to work, stay ahead of the depression, and manage her panic attacks.

She was putting the finishing touches on a pitch memo to Rita when she realized she was ravenous, so she walked the two blocks to her favorite pizzeria to grab her usual slice and then sat on a bench at the playground across the street. It was chilly but the brisk air felt good. Her hunger was a sign that her stress and depression weren't interfering too much with her body's functions. Whenever she began spiraling, the first thing to go was her sleep. The second was her appetite.

"Stop it. I said STOP IT."

Angie recognized the little girl with the pink-and-blue jacket and her nemesis, the same bullying boy from before.

"I'll bet you can't. I'll bet you're scared."

"I am not scared!" the little girl yelled.

There seemed to be some disagreement over her willingness to go down the fireman's pole. Again, the girl's mother came over and tried to mollify her daughter. "Oh, now, sweetie, it's okay. He doesn't mean anything."

Again, the boy's mother apologized to the girl's mother. "I'm sorry this keeps happening," she said. "Billy, we're leaving. Now!"

Of course the girl was upset. An asshole was tormenting her. Why was her mother telling her to not be upset? She should have been telling the asshole kid to knock it off, or the same scene was going to keep playing for the rest of their lives. *What the hell is wrong with people?*

Angie finished her slice and stood to go back to work. But she didn't move. She just stood there. And suddenly, she realized she was angry. Really angry. She reached into her bag and grabbed the envelope she had impulsively shoved in there on her way out the door that morning. It would either lead nowhere or, at the worst, to some pathetic fanboy playing Scarlett's movies on a loop in his parents' basement. But if she didn't check it out, she was never going to have a moment's peace. She pulled out her phone. With Scott by her side, she could walk into a police station and ask about the report.

"Scotty, are you busy?"

"Um, sort of. What's up?"

"Can you meet me right now?"

"I really can't. I've got to prep for a meeting later. Why do you need something right this minute?"

"I just— Forget it. Really." She disconnected, annoyed with herself. *What are you doing? You're a woman in your thirties and you can't go into a police station without your kid brother?*

She steeled herself and left the park, striding down the street toward the building that housed NYPD's 1st Precinct, covering Manhattan's southernmost tip. At the entrance, her resolve flagged and she hesitated, thinking of the cryptic message, "She deserved better." Better than what? Suicide? Everyone deserves better than that.

And Angie deserved answers.

She climbed the steps and went inside to find a bustling station. A beefy cop sat behind a desk that appeared to be an information station. Angie pushed past her anxiety and said as confidently as she could, "Excuse me."

The officer looked relieved to have a reprieve from the sheaves of paper he was thumbing through. "Yes, miss."

"This is the First Precinct?"

"Yes, miss."

"I have a question. About . . ." She didn't really know what she had a question about. She finally pulled the sheet of paper out of her bag and slid it across the desk to him.

The officer checked it out then assessed her more closely. "This is an arrest report number."

"Oh." She forged ahead, needing to know. For Scarlett. They both deserved it. "Can you tell me what it's about?"

"Well, some reports are public, but some aren't. Like if they're part of an investigation. Unless you're an interested party. Are you?"

"Yes," Angie said firmly, quickly pulling out her wallet and showing the cop her driver's license. "It's about my family."

"Okay. Let's see what's up." He typed on his computer keyboard. "Huh. Nothing here. It says, 'No entry available.'"

"Could someone have gotten the number wrong? Or maybe filed the report under another number?"

"Beats me. Sorry, miss, I don't know what to tell you. But if you get another number, come back and I'll see what we can find for you."

"I see. Well, thanks for checking."

Angie was frustrated as she left the building, but her mood had lifted by the time she got back to work. It was some guy's idea of a sick joke. Scarlett probably had lots of fans. But Angie felt proud she'd found the gumption to check, instead of remaining in a state of confusion. She'd walked into that precinct by herself and talked to a cop.

An hour later, Angie was getting absorbed in a new manuscript about an alcoholic priest who uncovers a money-laundering scheme run by his former lover, now the bishop, when her phone rang. She picked up on the second ring tone. "Hello?"

"Hello, is this Angela Norris?"

"Speaking."

"Miss Norris, this is Michael Ridley. I'm calling from LA. I'm an assistant to Daisy Buckman, one of the producers for the Oscars."

Angie froze. A wave of dread swept over her. They wanted to talk about Scarlett but she couldn't. Not after the message with the police number. Going to the police took more out of her than she had realized. "This really isn't a good time," she started.

"Wait, wait, don't hang up. This won't take long."

*Keep breathing, it's just a telephone call, it's not life or death.*

"Miss Norris, we'd love to have you and other members of your family at the Academy Awards this Sunday. Scarlett Norris was such a bright light in our world, you know, and, by the way, let me express my deepest sympathy to you and your family."

"Thank you. So much." Angie had never returned the first phone call she'd gotten weeks ago about the Oscars, and her mother probably hadn't either. No wonder this guy had called.

"Look, Miss Norris, your poor sister took her life. I don't have to tell you how awful that is. I mean, you and your family are living it every day. And the thing is, the last thing anyone wants is for the world to think no one cared enough to show up to honor Scarlett, especially given all the buzz around *Catapult*. You know what I'm saying?"

"Yes," Angie was able to eke out.

"Such a wonderful star, and such a loss for all of us, but of course for your family most of all. Can we count on you to attend? It'll be VIP the whole way. You won't have to worry about anything. We'll handle transportation, wardrobe, hotel, private car from the airport. And, of course, if she wins, well, how special would that be to have her family there to collect this incredible acknowledgment from her peers after—"

"Yeah, okay, I'll come." The words were out before she could stop them.

"What?"

"I said . . . I'll come."

"Well, that's just, uh, great, just great. Just you? Coming?"

"Yes."

"Well, I'm so pleased you will be joining us." Michael Ridley seemed genuinely surprised his pitch had worked. "It will mean so much to the film community. Uh, okay. The awards are March fourth, this Sunday, so you'll be hearing from my assistant with the details—flight, hotel, etcetera. We've got just six days and lots to do, so we'll get things rolling right away. Wonderful chatting with you, Miss Norris. Again, let me express my deepest sympathy to you and your family. We look forward to seeing you out here. Ciao."

He disconnected and Angie stared into space, only jolted back to reality when Rita rapped on her door. "Hey, you got a minute? I don't know what the hell to tell this guy, Jimmy Peterson, about this biowarfare-at-the-Ivy-League-college epic he's got. It's not that it *can't* work, but—"

"Rita, I'm gonna need some time off. Starting tomorrow. I'm going to the Oscars. For Scarlett."

"You're what? The Oscars?" Rita took a moment to process what Angie had said, but then it landed. "Of course! If you gotta go, you go!"

And it suddenly felt real.

That evening at home, as Angie washed her face, the enormity of her decision hit her again. *I agreed to go to the Oscars. What the hell was I thinking?*

She threw on her sweats and wondered if she should call Scott or her mother first. She started pulling potential clothes out of her closet. *What's the temperature in LA in early March? Jesus, do I have any clothes that won't peg me as hopeless?*

She sat on the bed studying her two best dresses. Her face felt sweaty. She had nothing to wear. She didn't know what to wear. She didn't read fashion magazines or watch awards shows. She would humiliate herself on a global scale. *Oh, my God. What have I done?*

She tried to focus on her breathing before a full-blown panic attack took over. *It's fine,* she told herself. *It'll be fine.* Michael Ridley had said they would handle everything. The airport, the hotel, the clothing, what she looked like, what she wore. *It's not a big deal. It's not a big deal.*

But it *was* a big deal. It was a *huge* deal. The Oscars. The most important night of the year for Hollywood, Scarlett had said. The girl who liked nothing more than to watch TV with her cat on a Friday night was going to have to be on the same red carpet as the biggest stars, directors, and producers in Hollywood. *Scar, what have I done?*

She grabbed her phone and called Scott. He hardly got a "Hello" out before she burst in, "Oh, my freakin' God. I told them I'd go."

"You told who—? Wait, what? Where are you going?"

Angie could hear his children in the background. The sounds of normal life. It grounded her. Her breathing evened out a bit. She decided she'd simply go to work the next day and forget all the Hollywood nonsense. And that's what it was. Nonsense. She wasn't a movie star. She wasn't anybody. She'd call that Michael Ridley and leave a polite message informing him she couldn't attend the Oscars after all.

"Angie? Are you there?" Scott sounded distracted. "Where are you going? I just have a minute. I have to put the kids to bed."

"Oh, Scotty, I'm such a . . . oh, God. The Oscars. I told them I'd go."

"What? Oh, my God, Ange, that's . . . Wait . . . That's great! Why aren't you happy?"

"Because I can barely function as it is. I'm supposed to go to the most famous awards show on the planet, surrounded by celebrities who are going to tell me how sorry they are about Scarlett? Everyone will be looking at me. All night long. I can't do that. I'll . . . I'll freeze. I'll fall apart." She gave a small sob.

"Whoa, hang on there, just breathe," Scott instructed soothingly. "Take a few steps back. Why did you agree in the first place?"

It helped to have him ask questions. It gave her something bite-size she could focus on instead of her impending demise. "I don't know. I was at work, and I got a call from this guy, someone's assistant . . . He was going on and on, saying that it seemed wrong that none of Scarlett's family will be there . . . and I think I just . . . wanted him to stop talking?"

There was a beat. Then Scott laughed, Angie felt herself exhale, and she couldn't help but laugh herself.

"Well, I guess you got him to stop talking."

"I did, indeed. But I'm going to back out."

"What? No. It's good you're going to represent the family. I'll help you prepare and, if in a couple of days you still don't feel ready, *then* you can back out."

"I guess."

"No guessing. This will be good for you."

"I guess. I mean, I suppose."

"That's the same thing as guessing!" They both laughed again. "I really gotta go. I'll call you tomorrow. This is so exciting! The kids are going to freak! Once I explain what the Oscars are. Aunt Angie on TV!"

He chuckled and disconnected. Angie put the phone down and looked over to the cat, who was licking her paws. "Brontë, what do we do now?"

She didn't have to wait long for her answer. Her phone buzzed a moment later and her mother's name popped up.

"Honey, we need to go shopping," Ellen said as soon as Angie picked up.

"Why?"

"Why? For you! For the Oscars! I want to help you pick out your dress. Only I can't tell your father."

"Wait, Mom, how do you know—?"

"I just got a voice mail from a reporter at *Newsday* saying she heard you were going to represent our family . . . because Scarlett . . . Well, I haven't called them back, but, honey, when did you decide to go? Look, I can't talk long, your father will be back any minute, but I think it's great. I'm proud of you. And of Scarlett, of course . . ." Her mother paused and cleared her throat. She was obviously trying hard to be cheerful. "Do you have any idea what you want? It's hard to go wrong with Ralph Lauren."

"Mom, can I call you back? I need to figure a few things out first."

Angie hung up and sat for a moment in silence. *Breathe, two, three, four. Out, two, three, four.* She silently repeated the mantra until she had steadied herself. Then she opened her eyes and realized she was almost smiling.

*Hollywood.*

She was going to Hollywood.


The next morning, Angie let herself sleep in a bit and awoke to more phone messages than she usually got in a week:

"Miss Norris, this is Sheree. Mr. Ridley has assigned me to assist you with your preparations for the awards. If you send me your email, I will coordinate your flight on Thursday and arrange transportation to your hotel—the Beverly Wilshire. We use Executive Limousines and they'll be available to you the entire time you're in Los Angeles. What kind of snacks would you like in the car and in your hotel room? Is Perrier okay or do you prefer another brand of water? We can stock liquor, too, if you'd like. Just let me know your preferences . . ."

"Hi, Miss Norris, my name is Jennifer Jensen. I'm a personal stylist. DreamWeaver has hired me to help create your look for the Oscars. Call me back as soon as you can. I want to talk about what kind of dress you're interested in, a classic cut or ball-gown style, or maybe something sleek in a metallic? I can text you some examples. I'm in touch with at least half a dozen designers who want you to wear them. And we'll do jewelry and makeup, too. Also, what's your typical palette? Neutrals, pastels, or primaries?"

"Miss Norris, this is Saffron Markowicz. I run a website and blog about life in LA called *See a Star, Be a Star*. I understand you're Scarlett Norris's sister and you're coming to the Oscars? And you're a literary critic? I'd love to interview you for the site. Please call as soon as you can. Also, could you send us a couple of selfies? One headshot and one full-body?"

"Hi, Miss Norris, I'm Sierra Jiménez. I'll be doing your hair for the Oscars. My email is sierrahairLA at gmail. Can you send me a photo of what your hair looks like right now? Don't worry if it's not perfect. That's what we're here for. Also, are you open to a cut or color or highlights?"

As she sat on her bed gaping at her phone, Angie's stomach clenched. Then she sprang up and ran into the bathroom, flipped up the toilet lid, and heaved up the contents of her stomach. Then she heaved some more, even though there was nothing left to throw up. She pulled the hand towel off its ring and wiped her mouth as she sat there, her skin clammy, her mind reeling.

*What am I doing?*

The trip certainly wouldn't be like her last, two years back, when she'd gone out to visit Scarlett. They'd jogged along the beach in Santa Monica, strolled Rodeo Drive, lounged around the pool at Scarlett's house out in Topanga, and ate so many great meals that Angie lost count. One day, she'd observed a gaggle of teenage girls looking and leaning into one another with urgent whispers a short distance from the Malibu café where she and Scarlett were having coffee.

"Does this happen all the time?" she'd asked.

Scarlett had shrugged. "Sometimes I get bombarded. The series really made a huge difference. A hundred million people watching it. You have no idea. But I've kind of figured out where to go and when, to minimize attention. It's just part of the job. I don't mind as long as people aren't too pushy."

By then, one of the girls had shyly approached. "I'm sorry to bother you, Miss Norris, but do you think I could get a selfie? We all just love you. We've seen *Even Steven* like a million times."

"Of course!" Scarlett had expansively motioned for the rest of the girls to come over and expertly took a couple of shots with the girl's phone, including a silly one where they all made faces.

"That was nice," Angie said when the girls had left.

Scarlett had grinned. "They're kids. Plus, it's good to post a picture now and then with fans. Good for the Insta."

They'd spent a day on the set of Scarlett's latest movie. It was the only day Scarlett was working during Angie's visit and she thought Angie would get a kick out of seeing a real movie shoot.

On the set, Scarlett seemed genuinely well-liked, judging by how everyone from the assistant director to the makeup people to the tech crew greeted her. She hadn't lost her kind, easygoing nature. But Angie was still anxious. *It's okay. It's just the two of us. Follow Scarlett's lead, like in high school.*

Of course, it wasn't high school—they were adults now and this was Hollywood. But Scarlett telling her it was okay was soothing, and Angie had gradually relaxed enough to get absorbed by the process unfolding in front of her. Even during the long stretches between takes, when lights and sound were adjusted, she had enjoyed seeing the myriad people working to bring it all together. Angie had thought that maybe she understood just a little bit of what her sister enjoyed so much about making a movie.

But this time around, she'd be facing Hollywood by herself.

Somehow, she'd gotten herself together and out of New York. Ellen had come over to help her pack, having given up the idea of helping her find a dress, knowing she couldn't compete with the best stylists in LA. Angie's father knew, of course. Gerry may have hated the idea but there was no hiding Angie's decision; stories were appearing on TV, newspapers, and the internet. And obviously, the ceremony would be seen by millions worldwide, which Angie tried not to fixate on.

"You'll be fine," Scott had said, hugging her goodbye before she departed for JFK. "It's just a few days. I know the Oscars are huge, but you'll be great, and remember, you're going for Scar. Call me anytime. We're all rooting for you."

"Dad's not," Angie had replied.

"Dad's Dad. He's not your problem."

*I hope you're right, Scotty.* Her brother's words echoed in her head as she emerged from LAX into the passenger pick-up area that Thursday, pulling her suitcase behind her. *I hope I don't make a fool of myself.*

It didn't take long to spot the man in an immaculate uniform holding a small sign with her name. *Here we go.* She approached him and gave a small smile.

"Miss Norris?"

Angie nodded.

"Right this way, miss."

As she was whisked to her hotel, Angie fretted, unsure what to expect in the run-up to Sunday's ceremony, outside of dress fittings and getting her hair styled. She thought she'd mostly hang out at the hotel, jotting down notes to help her answer questions she anticipated she'd be asked on the red carpet.

The Beverly Wilshire was luxurious and her room wasn't even a room, it was a suite. She had stunning views looking west where she thought she could see the Pacific glittering in the distance. Her bed was a king with sumptuous pillows and sheets. There was a sunken Jacuzzi bathtub in the bathroom. She felt both queenly and out of place.

The next morning, her phone buzzed at 8:00 a.m. She was still on New York time and had been awake for a couple of hours, bone-tired with an aching head. *Maybe I'm dehydrated. Or stressed. Or dehydrated and stressed.*

She reached for the phone. "Hello?" Then came a knock on her door. "Hang on, please, just a moment."

She opened the door a couple of inches, the security bolt still in place. "Room service, Miss Norris. We have breakfast for you. May I wheel the cart in?"

"Um, sure, yes." Angie unbolted and opened the door.

"I'm sorry?" The voice came over the phone.

"Oh, no, I was just talking to . . . Can you just hang on again? For a moment?"

The young catering attendant launched into the menu: "Eggs with crème fraiche and chives, brioche French toast, coffee, fruit." He wheeled the cart in and then turned toward the door.

Wait!" she called. She looked around for her purse. "I just have to find my wallet."

"Oh, no, Miss Norris, that's not necessary. Everything is taken care of. Just ring the desk and we'll be happy to bring up anything you need. Enjoy breakfast."

"Thank you," she blurted as the door shut. The gleaming tray was graced by a small vase holding a bunch of white rose buds.

"Hello? Miss Norris, are you still there?"

*Oh, God, the call.* "Oh, yes, hello, I'm so sorry, room service just came and . . ."

"So, anyway, my name is Candace Blackstone. I'm handling Oscar publicity for DreamWeaver. I'll be meeting with you to prep for the Oscars and then I'll accompany you to the awards."

"Oh."

"Did I wake you? I'm sorry, I was going to call last night, but I wanted to give you a little time to get settled."

"Oh, yes . . . No, I'm fine. I'm just a little, um, well, I guess . . . after the flight and all. What did you say your name was?"

"Candace. Candace Blackstone." The publicist's voice was crisp and assertive. "Travel is exhausting. Luckily, you have a day spa booked for this morning. You can have a hydra facial, body brushing, exfoliation, steam treatment, mani-pedi, waxing, even an eyelash extension. Oh, and a full body massage. It's great for detoxifying the lymphatic system. The limo will come at ten, is that good?"

"Um, sure, yes, I'll be ready." *Detoxifying the lymphatic system?*

By 2:00 p.m., Angie had been thoroughly scoured, steamed, and lacquered and was having lunch with Candace at a trendy restaurant in West Hollywood. The publicist was going through information Angie would need to know for the Oscars. The clean black-and-white lines and open windows gave the place an air of elegance, while her Bibb salad and caviar tart were artfully plated and sleek. Angie didn't feel sleek, elegant, or remotely comfortable.

"We'll do some interviews on the red carpet on our way into the theater and more after the ceremony," Candace instructed. "Every major entertainment news outlet has been given background info on your family and bios on you and Scarlett. Now, here's where we'll be during the event." She slid a Dolby Theatre seating chart across the table. "Because Scarlett is nominated for Best Actress, we'll be sitting with nominees from *Catapult* and other movies, which means a lot of A-listers. You know who's nominated?"

"Um, no, not really . . ." Angie was getting another headache, and the sight of the rich food was suddenly nauseating. She grabbed her ice water and drank.

"Right. David Frobisher Jones, the director of *Catapult*—you know him, of course—and Charles will be with us in the DreamWeaver row but across the aisle. Ferdinand Greco, who's up for Best Director for

*Madrid Song*, the Spanish Civil War epic, his star, Mirabel de Nova, who is up for Best Actress—well, everyone associated with that movie will be two rows directly in front of us." Candace pointed on the chart. "Then, to our right is the cast and crew of *Music Box*. The one about the stalker and the blues singer set in Chicago . . . ?"

Angie shook her head.

"Both leads, Daria Prince and Jeffrey Haddad, as well as the cinematographer and composer are nominated."

Angie nodded but was barely holding on. She was about to ask if they could get the check, but Candace plowed ahead.

"Now, behind us will be the team from *Histronomie*. Tommy Wen Lee directed it and wrote the screenplay . . ."

Angie raised her right hand to her forehead and massaged the ridge over her eyebrows while she breathed deeply. "I'm just here to accept if Scarlett wins. Is all this really necessary?"

Candace stopped talking and folded her hands in front of her. "You know what? I'll just email you the list of all the nominees and where they'll be sitting as it relates to us, okay? Take a look at it, familiarize yourself with it."

Angie nodded.

"The point is that you should expect to see a lot of famous people. Very famous people. Up close. Some may even say hello. You can't just stand there and stammer. You're there for DreamWeaver. They want you to be comfortable, to enjoy the awards, but you need to be on point, and I'm here to help with that."

Candace smiled but the real message being conveyed wasn't so simple or nice. The urge to get back to the hotel and lie down was becoming overwhelming.

"Could we possibly head back?" Angie asked.

Candace motioned to their waiter. "We can go over more of this tomorrow. I'll come to your hotel after your wardrobe fitting with Jennifer." She looked hard at Angie, then softened her voice. "Look, I'm not trying to scare you. I'm just saying, if you're not used to being in a room full of big stars dressed in couture with the press asking you questions, some of them personal, prepare yourself. This is the Oscars."

"Right, of course." *Jesus, get me out here.*

After Candace dropped her at her hotel, Angie was relieved to finally be on her own. She decided to tackle one of the manuscripts she'd brought with her and was quite content to just sit at a table by the pool and read for a couple of hours. She had dinner in her room, and hoped she would fall asleep easily and sleep soundly. A good night's sleep always helped and she was praying the jet-lag didn't mess her up too much.

As she got ready for bed, she set the alarm on her phone. She wanted to get up in time to meditate, hit the gym, and have breakfast—her general stress-relief tactics—so she'd be calm, ready for Jennifer Jensen and her dresses.

Angie woke with a start, her heart pounding, and leapt out of bed so fast she nearly fell. She rushed to the bathroom and splashed cold water on her face. Panting, she looked in the mirror. *I can't do this, Scar, not alone. You've got to help me. You've got to help me get through it.*

Maybe she could channel Scarlett, what she might say or do, to help her focus on the task at hand. Being mindful of what was right in front of her, be it the warmth of the sun, the snug fit of new leather gloves, or the aroma of oregano on a pizza, was a technique she'd learned long ago to stay calm and avert panic. Focusing on the present kept her from panicking about the future.

Later that morning, as she considered a slate-blue taffeta gown, one of the many Jennifer Jensen had rolled into her hotel room, she wondered what Scarlett would think. She'd already tried on a dramatic two-tone purple satin-and-tulle creation. But it was flashy, and Angie couldn't imagine she could pull it off, besides, she worried about the practicality of moving around in the voluminous skirt.

She passed.

The taffeta, by contrast, was cut becomingly close to the body with a diagonally crossed neckline and ruched front.

"I don't know." Jennifer stood back with an expression that reminded Angie of an art critic considering a somewhat disappointing sculpture. "It's a gorgeous color, and you've got a darling figure, but is it really you?"

Angie turned to look at herself from all angles. *Is it me? Well, let's see, I'm a thirty-something depressive who spends her days reading and her nights watching TV with her cat, and who is looking to her dead sister to help her get through the biggest awards ceremony on Earth without collapsing.*

"No, I guess not. My mother mentioned Ralph Lauren," she finally replied as Jennifer unzipped her. "Do you have something like that I could try?"

"Ralph? Sure, but . . . Actually, wait one minute." Jennifer headed to the rack.

Five minutes later, Angie was wearing an ethereal cream-colored chiffon dress that flattered her delicate frame. Its gathered skirt boasted a series of pleats that were interesting but not overdone. It was breathtaking.

"Zac Posen," Jennifer told her. "It's perfect for you. A lot of people wear him at the Oscars. His dresses are beautifully tailored and elegant but easy to wear. I've got the perfect shoes . . . ." She circled Angie. "I'll talk to Sierra about doing old-school Hollywood waves and lighter blond highlights, if you're okay with that?"

Angie nodded.

"Then pale skin, dark mascara, red lips. And jewelry in similar tones, maybe opals. What do you think?"

The Angie in the mirror wore no makeup and her hair was pulled back in a ponytail, but she didn't look ridiculous. She closed her eyes and pictured herself in the gown talking to Mirabel de Nova, the beautiful Spanish actress Candace had mentioned. *I didn't even see her movie, but I guess I could congratulate her on her nomination. What did Candace say? Don't stammer.* When she opened her eyes, Jennifer was smiling with approval.

"It suits you," she said.

Angie realized the dress would be her costume. In it, she would play the role of a woman capable of skillfully navigating a minefield of stress, celebrities, interviews, and photos. And if she wasn't skillful, at least she'd look the part. And maybe avoid total disaster.

"Okay," she said. "I'll wear it."

"Great. Now, it's a little long . . . but I think that will be the only necessary alteration. It fits you perfectly otherwise."

And with that, the seamstress, who had accompanied Jennifer, started pinning the hem with speed and accuracy, raising it up an inch to meet the top of Angie's foot.

As soon as the fitting was done, Candace called from the restaurant downstairs. Angie reluctantly went down for lunch, and they did more prep for the red carpet. Candace threw sample questions at her and when Angie stumbled or just blanked, she attempted to coach her through the answers. She quizzed her on some of the other nominees. She had photos of the *Catapult* cast and others from DreamWeaver Angie would likely meet. The director, David Frobisher Jones, was older than Angie had expected with a full head of salt-and-pepper hair and a round face. The cinematographer, on the other hand, hardly looked to be out of high school. There was a tall, handsome, fashionably-clad man with a trimmed beard, and his straight jet-black hair pulled up in a bun. Candace said he was head of production at the studio.

Then there was Charles Weaver. The man himself. Even Angie recognized him. He was as famous as the successful actors who appeared in his movies. Candace gave her a little background on DreamWeaver. Charles had come from the East Coast and turned his studio, DreamWeaver, into a dream factory. He skillfully navigated the shark-infested waters of Hollywood with aplomb, sniffing out the highest-quality scripts and pairing them with the right director, the perfect actors, composers, editors, producers. He charmed those in and out of the industry when it came to awards season, appearing at screenings and events and parties often with the latest actress on his arm, touting his projects to all who would listen. He had secured countless Oscars, BAFTAs, Spirit Awards, DGA, WGA, and SAG Awards, and big wins at the box office too.

Angie didn't find him handsome by any definition. He was a large man, both in height and girth. His hair was full but unruly and he made no attempts to tame it. His mouth was wide and soft, his nose bulbous, his eyes a little too small for the size of his head. In his late fifties, he appeared a decade older, perhaps due to his paunch.

But Angie looked at the photo of him with gratitude, knowing he was the reason Scarlett had broken through and been on the cusp of real stardom. He had seen something in her, some special spark, so no matter what was going on in her personal life, her professional life had been on fire. And Charles Weaver was the reason.

That night, Angie sat on her bed in the plush terry-cloth robe provided by the hotel. She had ordered a room-service dinner and started a movie but couldn't concentrate. *The Oscars are tomorrow. Scarlett should be here. Not me.*

Her throat tightened. Her grief was a shape-shifter—sometimes a dull ache, other times a stabbing pain that left her breathless and disoriented.

Lying on her side on the bed in the hotel room, Angie considered the quality of the light emanating from the bathroom, how bright it was, how narrow, which parts of the room it illuminated, which stayed dark. She let it draw her in, where she filled the tub, lobbing a fizzy bath bomb into the steaming water. Slowly, as the scent of eucalyptus filled the moist air, she submerged herself completely under the water. When she felt as though her lungs might burst, she came up with a gasp. Then she lay back, resting her head against the porcelain, and closed her eyes. *What if Scarlett wins?*

"All you need to do," Candace had told her that afternoon, "is look good, smile, say thanks, and you'll be off the stage before you even have a chance to get nervous. I'll be right there to meet you backstage for pictures, and then we'll go back to our seats for the rest of the show. Simple and easy."

*None of this sounds simple or easy*, Angie had thought.

When the water turned cold, Angie got out of the tub, wrapped herself in the robe once more, and grabbed her phone.

"What's up, Hollywood? Everything okay?" Scott sounded upbeat even though it was late on the East Coast.

"Can you talk?"

"What's happening?"

"I'm nervous. About tomorrow. The questions I'll be asked. Candace—the publicist—said to say, 'we're still mourning but we're proud of her and that *Catapult* was a,' um, 'a testament to her talent.'"

"That sounds good," Scott said. "Nothing to remember because that's all true. Just remember to tell them Dad does the books for a Mexican drug cartel, and Mom, let's see, she's a set designer for a porn production company, in charge of plumping not only the pillows—"

"Stop! You're useless!" Angie couldn't help but laugh at the idea of their mother in her perfect blouse and pearls as a fluffer of pillows and possibly more for a porn film. Then she grew quiet again. "But really, Scotty, what *should* I say about Scar? That isn't generic?"

"What do you want to say?" Scott got quiet, too. "She was beautiful and bright and easygoing. We all knew she could do whatever she wanted. And she chose acting and Hollywood. For better or worse."

"That's actually perfect. Very genuine. But what about me and my life? What if they ask about me? I don't do anything interesting. I barely do anything at all."

"What do you mean? Look, to you, you read manuscripts in Rita's dusty old office and deal with neurotic writers. But to an outsider, you're an editor for a book agent in New York City who helps put future *New York Times* bestsellers on the market. That's impressive. Say that. Practice saying that."

"Okay. Um, I'm a . . . highly . . . um, influential book editor . . ."

"Jesus, Ange . . ."

Angie took a deep breath and started again, this time loudly and clearly. "I edit manuscripts for a New York literary agency. We have a very talented stable of writers, fiction and nonfiction. And we do everything from editing to pitching to publishers."

"Great! You see, that sounds classy and powerful. Just repeat that a few times so it becomes automatic."

"And Mom and Dad? What about them?"

"Keep it simple. They're watching from our family home on Long Island. They're grateful for the honors bestowed on Scarlett. I mean, what else can you say?"

"Yeah, I guess you're right. Don't make it too complicated. But I'm definitely writing everything down and memorizing it." She paused. "Hey, and what if Scar wins? I'm so worried about going up on that stage. What if I panic?"

"You know what to do. Be mindful. Do the 'focus on what's right in front of you' thing. Stand up. Walk to the stage. Climb the steps. Hear the applause. Take out your notes. Read the words. You have something prepared, right?"

"Yeah . . . I've got it here." She reached for the pad where she had made notes.

"Let's hear it," Scott urged. "The more you say it, the easier it'll be. Muscle memory and all that."

"Candace said to keep it short and sweet." Angie cleared her throat. "'Thank you all so much. I wish Scarlett were here instead of me. But I know she'd be very proud of this honor. We all miss her very much. Thank you again.'"

"That's good. Short and sweet. Everybody knows what happened, so what else is there to say, right?"

"I guess. I figure if I get up there and off as fast as possible, and don't think too much about all the stars watching from the audience, and the millions of people watching at home . . . Oh, God, Scotty, what if . . ."

"Stop right there, do *not* go there, Ange. Breathe, focus on the immediate task, and just get through it."

"Okay," she said, not feeling okay at all. *How am I going to walk up on that stage?* "I should let you go."

"Yeah, I gotta hit the sack. We'll be watching tomorrow. You've got this, Ange."

*I hope so, Scotty.*

Angie slept well that night but woke the next morning engulfed by dread, as if it had seeped into her hotel room overnight, filling every crevice and corner. She called Michael Ridley, whose assistant put the call right through. But when he picked up, she suddenly felt awkward and embarrassed.

"Is anything wrong, Miss Norris?" he asked. "How are your accommodations?"

"Oh, no, everything is wonderful, thank you so much. It's just, I'm wondering if I can really, um, do this. It's a lot, you know, and I don't know what's expected of me—I'm not my sister, after all. I'm not used to being . . . in the spotlight. I don't want to screw up," she admitted.

"Listen, don't worry," he said. "Honestly, people will be gentle with you, given the circumstances. And no one expects you to act like . . . Just be yourself. Have fun."

Angie hung up. As terrified as she was, she was more scared of looking back and hating herself for being a coward. *Either do this or fly home.*

She retrieved a small photo from her suitcase. It had been taken on her trip to LA, and she and Scar were smiling in matching baseball caps. She tucked the photo into the sparkly clutch hanging in the closet with her Zac Posen gown.

*I can't back out, because I'm here for you.*

At 2 p.m., Angie took a last look at herself before heading downstairs, where Candace would be arriving in a limo to take them to the ceremony. She turned to her left, then her right, looking over her shoulder each time to check how the creamy, gossamer dress hung on her frame. It was offset by ruby lipstick, a gold clutch, a pair of matching heels, and a shimmering Art Deco–inspired barrette that was clipped into one side of her satiny, newly lightened waves. Jennifer, the stylist, had secured the loan from Tiffany of a simple but striking opal and diamond pendant with matching earrings. Even with the modern dress, the look was vintage Hollywood and, Angie had to admit, she looked good, better than she thought she would.

She squinted in the bathroom mirror to see if she could blur her image and picture Scarlett instead. They had the same wide-set gray eyes flecked with gold and, if Angie were taller and more athletic with darker hair, then, yes, she would resemble a slighter version of the dazzling Scarlett Norris.

She still felt a little shaky but there was nothing left to do but double-check the clutch, which, along with a lipstick, credit card, and driver's license, held the good luck photo, a vial of lavender essential oil, her phone, and the brief acceptance speech. *That's it, then.* Her phone buzzed with an incoming call.

"Oh, honey, I'm so glad you picked up." Her mother's voice caught her off guard. They'd only had a brief chat since Angie had arrived in LA. Ellen couldn't talk unless she was away from Gerry, who had refused to speak to Angie when he'd heard she was going to the Oscars.

"I'm just heading out, Mom."

"I don't want to hold you up, dear, but do you think you could snap a quick selfie for me? I'd love to see how you look and, well, to be honest, I don't know if I have the strength to watch the ceremony. Plus, your father—"

"It's all right." Angie held her phone up to snap a few different angles that she quickly attached to a message. A few seconds passed, and then she heard a sharp intake of breath.

"Oh, sweetheart," Ellen gasped. "You look absolutely divine. Just beautiful." She seemed overwhelmed by emotion. "I just wanted to wish you luck." She paused. "I'm glad you're there, Angela. And Scarlett is, too. I know it. I see a lot of her in you, you know, the way you look tonight. Just beautiful."

"Thanks, Mom." Angie swallowed hard. *Keep it together. The night hasn't even started yet.*

"You'll call and tell us all about it?"

"I'll call you tomorrow, Mom. I promise."

Her mother's words echoed in her head as she rode the elevator down to the lobby and strode out the hotel entrance, where Candace stood in a shimmery mauve slip dress on the curb near a parked limo.

*I'm Scarlett Norris's sister. I've got this.*

"Well, well, look at you, all old-school glamour," Candace gushed. "It looks great!"

It *looks great, not* you *look great.* But Angie realized the phrasing made sense and was, in fact, oddly comforting. She wasn't herself as much as a beautifully packaged product designed to generate great media coverage. *I'm here to do a job. That's it. Nothing to worry about.*

The limo wound its way to the Dolby Theatre on Hollywood Boulevard, and Candace kept up a lively chatter the entire way, briefing Angie again on what to expect and how to act. Angie listened, but kept her mantras looping in her mind to ground her. She'd never been in a limousine so large or so luxurious. There was practically a chasm between her and Candace. And she hadn't even caught a glimpse of the driver. Colorful, lushly-scented arrangements of lilies and lilacs populated the interior, and in the center sat a bar stocked with liquor so high end Angie hadn't heard of most of the brands. She watched as Candace cracked a bottle of champagne and poured them both flutes.

"I can't drink that right now. I'm too nervous. Do you have any mineral water?" Angie asked.

Candace looked like she was trying hard not to roll her eyes. "Of course. Just remember, the most important thing is to relax and be confident."

Angie nodded.

The traffic through Hollywood was snarled and Angie could see that Hollywood Boulevard was closed off to regular traffic. Once they got close, and the limo driver stopped at various checkpoints to confirm their validity by Academy personnel, Angie's breathing started to become rapid and she became aware of the light perspiration beading on her perfectly made-up forehead. She wished they'd been able to just pull right up to the theater so she could hop out, pop into the Dolby, accept the statue, and fly home. The extended anticipation was torture.

Finally, the driver got in a queue behind other limousines. Angie peered through the tinted windows but could see nothing of note. Somehow that added to her anxiety.

When their car arrived at the front of the line, Candace gestured for Angie to put on a bright smile. It felt silly, but she did it. And then she sat there, frozen. When an attendant opened the door, she could see clusters of celebrities winding their way along the red carpet. Extravagant dresses, stunning jewelry. She even clocked a woman in top hat and tails.

Candace stepped out and gave the attendant their credentials then looked back to Angie. "It's time."

*Right.*

Angie reluctantly took Candace's outstretched hand and climbed out. *Here we go, Scar.*

The attendant closed the door and the limo started back into traffic as another took its place. There were so many people, celebrities, journalists, photographers, even fans on bleachers across the street. The lights were blinding, and warm. Candace took her elbow and led her to the first bank of reporters, who all called her name. They knew who she was. That snapped her out of her stupor. She gave what she hoped was a dazzling smile but feared it actually looked manic.

"Angela, over here!" a photographer shouted.

"Angela, do you think Scarlett will win tonight?"

Angie glanced in the general direction of the question. She had no idea who'd asked it.

"Angela, can you turn a little this way, toward the theater?"

Angie stood and faced the cameras as calmly as possible, answering questions, trying to sound gracious. The reporters seemed genuine and that helped.

Finally, Candace took her by the elbow again, leading her farther down the red carpet. "Now we've got the TV people. They don't need a lot, just a few words talking up Scarlett. You're kinda pretty, so don't hide it. I'm taking you to a stand-up with E! first. Don't forget to smile with your eyes."

*With my . . . ?* "Right." Angie fingered the photo she'd secreted in her clutch.

The pre-show interviews went by in a blur. She was too nervous to focus on any of the famous faces around her. Angie was courteous and tried to smile. With her eyes. It helped that most of the reporters read from the same script: "So sorry about Scarlett. Who are you wearing?"

"Ladies and gentlemen, we are here with Angela Norris, the sister of Scarlett Norris, one of Hollywood's most glamorous stars who tragically took her own life last year," one reporter intoned with too much solemnity. "Miss Norris, why did you feel compelled to come to the awards this year?"

"I'm here to represent my family and Scarlett, who loved acting and making movies," Angie recited gamely.

"You certainly look like a natural here on the red carpet," another said. "Who are you wearing?"

"Zac Posen." She thought about Scott's T.J. Maxx quip and smiled slightly, which helped her relax. "The jewelry is from Tiffany."

"So are we having a good time yet, Angie?" another reporter queried, apparently going off-script.

Angie was proud that she was able to answer off the cuff, despite it being such an obvious question. "I wish Scarlett were here instead. But I'm glad I could be here."

And so it went for what seemed an eternity. She kept hearing the

same questions and repeating the same answers, trying to appear relaxed but interested and also to remember to smile. With her eyes.

When the interviews were done, Candace guided Angie into an
open-air foyer of sorts. Stores on either side flanked a wide staircase
made of gold- and ruby-colored steps, glittering like Dorothy's slippers.
Columns on either side had plaques that bore the title and year of each
Best Picture–winning film.

Angie gasped. It looked positively grand.

"We're in a mall," Candace quipped. "The Oscars are held in a mall."

"But what a mall," Angie breathed.

Ascending the stairs with the rest of the crowd, gowns rustling,
jewelry clinking, perfume trailing . . . Angie couldn't help gawking.
There was the plaque for *Out of Africa*, 1986. *Oliver!*, 1968. *From Here
to Eternity*, 1953. *The Best Years of Our Lives*, 1946. *Gone With the
Wind*, 1939.

Angie wasn't the biggest movie fan, but she knew some of the
classics. Just seeing plaques on the Dolby walls seemed the epitome
of Hollywood glamour to her. And then there were the stars. She
tried not to stare at Tom Hanks, Angelina Jolie, Denzel Washington,
Emma Stone, and others she thought she should know but couldn't
quite place.

And then they got to the top of the stairs where the crowd was
funneled toward a bank of glass doors. Angie felt her breathing become
erratic. So many people. Too close together. And there was last year's
Best Actor winner, chatting jovially with his companion like he was
chatting over a cup of coffee.

Angie had to look away, down, to her hands, anywhere but at
the crowd.

They slowly, slowly, too slowly advanced to the doors, slowed because of the need for tickets, ID, metal detecting. When they finally
got to the attendants, Candace had their tickets in hand, ready to go, a
pro. Angie pulled out her ID and again had to look down at her hands

to calm herself as she walked through the metal detector, literally heaving a sigh of relief she didn't set it off. She looked up to find Steven Spielberg giving her a small smile of understanding. *Whoa.*

Inside the expansive lobby, a sweeping staircase led to a second level, framed images of Oscar moments lining its walls, the entire interior done in tasteful golds, beiges, and whites. Candace led her to the far end where the circular bar was mobbed with attendees all dressed in tuxes and beautiful gowns of all colors. The energy in the air was palpable. It almost matched Angie's anxiety so that she felt a bit of a high, riding its crest without fear for a few moments.

The *Catapult* nominees were seated on the first level, close to the stage, so Candace and Angie made their way toward the entrance back by the bar. When they stepped into the theater, Angie caught her breath. She had never felt like a princess before, but in that moment, she truly felt like Cinderella attending Prince Charming's ball; the dressers and stylists were the singing mice and birds who had transformed her, Candace her Fairy Godmother. She supposed that made the Oscar the glass slipper. And she felt a ripple of apprehension at the idea of whether she'd be taking it home or not.

Several tiered balconies lined both sides of the theater, which had been decorated in gold and purple, that year's theme. An enormous golden arch rose above the curtain with two superhuman-sized Oscars flanking the stage, overseeing the proceedings with silent solemnity. The event had the air of a royal coronation.

And as Candace homed in on their seats, Angie heard an outburst of laughter and turned to see a group coming down the aisle, led by Charles Weaver himself. While he was no Prince Charming, she couldn't help but be starstruck by his presence. He was taller than she had expected, and his bearing, his comportment, made him loom large. People turned and whispered, some pointed, actors and directors and producers alike. Charles was a star among stars. And he knew it.

He and his companions made their way to seats directly in front of Angie. He nodded at Candace as they got situated. Angie finally sat down, and Candace, seated beside her, clutched her arm. "I'll introduce you to Charles and the others after. Right now just focus on enjoying yourself. Breathe, recite mantras, perform Kegels, whatever you need to relax. We've got hours before Best Actress."

Then the lights dimmed, and Angie caught herself clasping and unclasping her hands, unable to avoid her nervous habit in this high-anxiety situation. Attempting to remain in the moment, not in the moments to come, she focused on a woman two rows up and off to the right. She recognized her immediately. Mirabel de Nova, the Spanish actress, and Scarlett's main competition if the pundits were to be believed. She was considered to be one of the most glamorous and beautiful women to ever grace the silver screen. Hard as it was for Angie to believe, she was even more jaw-dropping in real life. She had such lustrous hair, it shone in the overhead lights. When the actress turned to address someone in the row behind her, Angie could see how her black eyes glittered, bright and alive. Her smile was warm and inviting, her pillowy lips painted a dark burgundy that matched her elegant gown.

Angie continued to gaze at the movie star, mesmerized by her presence, and that helped ground her through what felt like an interminable amount of time. She'd have loved to be watching from the comfort of her sofa, Brontë purring on her lap. Finally Candace touched her arm as they went to a commercial break. "You heard that, right? We're just about there."

Angie hadn't. She tore her eyes from the garnet earrings dangling from Mirabel's delicate ears. "What?"

"The In Memoriam segment is on deck. You going to be okay?"

"Yes, I'll be okay. Wait. Do I have to do something?"

"Don't worry. I'll tell you what to do, and when."

That didn't comfort Angie one bit, but she couldn't bring herself to press Candace. Somehow that seemed more daunting than just awaiting the blade of the guillotine she could feel glinting above her. Her heart pounded and even focusing on Mirabel de Nova didn't calm her. *Breathe in, two, three, four. Out, two, three, four.*

The commercial break lasted forever, giving her too much time to create an escape plan in her head. She knew there were seat fillers who took the spots of attendees who stepped out so that it looked like a full crowd no matter what to the viewers at home. Her absence would barely be noted. She could flee. She could excuse-me-pardon-me her way out of the row. She could Uber back to the hotel. Fuck the hotel. She could Uber back to LAX. Fuck, she could Uber all the way back to Queens.

And then a lovely country star took the stage. Angie knew who she was, knew her name, even knew one of her songs, but at that moment she was a blank standing in a spotlight singing a glop of a ballad as a montage recognizing film industry titans who had passed the previous year flashed on screens behind and around.

Scarlett was the last to be projected on the big screen, prompting sustained applause. Angie locked in on her face. *You were so beautiful. Keep breathing.* She was stunned by the reaction. Scarlett had been working in the industry for years but had just broken through in a big way with *Catapult*. She clearly had cultivated good will on her way up the ladder. Angie's terror abated a bit.

Until Candace leaned in and whispered, "Now . . . get up."

"What?" *Oh, my God.* "Why?"

"Stand up and acknowledge everyone. Smile, take it in, be gracious. Do it."

Mortified, a small frozen smile on her lips, Angie rose to her feet and tentatively looked behind her, then to her left, and then her right. The rapturous response from the audience, people she recognized, some she'd seen in movies literally her entire life, gave her an inch of confidence and she stood a bit straighter. "Thank you," she said softly, so softly she could barely hear herself but she imagined everyone read it on her lips, every movie fan around the world sitting in front of millions of TV and computer screens.

And that was when she caught sight of Mirabel de Nova, turned back in her seat, applauding, her eyes glassy with tears. She blew Angie a kiss, a genuine and touching gesture. Angie gave her a nod of acknowledgement.

And then, just like that, the song was over, the segment was over, the moment was over.

Angie took her seat again and was shaken back to reality when the presenter boomed, "And now, our nominees for Best Actress."

"Here we go," Candace whispered.

As last year's Best Actor winner took the stage, Angie pulled the short speech out of her clutch. She felt anxious but not unhappy. It was an odd, unfamiliar feeling but one she was grateful for.

She focused like a laser on the movie star at the microphone, trying to center herself around his voice. His words. A ripple of a thrill coursed through her when Mirabel's name was announced as the second nominee.

And then Scarlett's.

Angie couldn't tell for sure, but she seemed to get the most robust response from the audience.

The actor didn't even hesitate to reveal the winner. He was opening the envelope as he said, "And the Oscar goes to," and then he pulled the card out with a flourish, proclaiming, "Scarlett Norris!"

The crowd roared, rising to its feet as one, applauding and cheering. An enormous picture of Scarlett flashed on the screen behind the stage. Everyone in the row in front of Angie—the *Catapult* cast, nominees, and DreamWeaver execs—all turned to her. And there was Charles Weaver himself, a grin on his face, so wide he was beaming. At her.

She was taken by his gaze, like the sun was shining on her.

And then she remembered. She had to take to the stage.

Amid the applause and cheering, she managed to hand Candace her little gold purse and slip out of her row. She ascended the stairs, and accepted the statuette, but it was a blur. And then, she was standing at the podium. The audience sat down and became quiet. Even though the intense lights were in her eyes, she could feel everyone in the audience regarding her, everything heightened into such sharp precision it almost hurt.

But she knew what she had to do. For Scarlett.

"Thank you, thank you so much, everyone." She glanced down at the paper she was clutching then returned her gaze to the cavernous space and began to recite the words she knew by heart. "I'm Angela Norris, Scarlett's sister, and I'd like to thank everyone on behalf of both her and our family." The words sounded stilted and not at all right.

She took a breath, two, three, four.

*Tell them about Scarlett. Just tell them truth.*

"As you know, Scarlett died last year." Her voice sounded hoarse and unsure. She cleared her throat and continued, clearer and louder. "But she didn't just die. She died by her own hand. And the thing is, none of us realized what kind of pain she was in. She always seemed so strong. She was a wonderful, happy girl growing up. We'd dress up in our mother's old clothes and pretend we were a famous singing duo. We'd pick berries and chase fireflies in summer like every kid on Long Island. Scarlett baked cookies for her friends' birthdays. Once for Halloween, she dyed my hair black because we thought that would make me look scarier in my witch costume, which didn't make our parents very happy."

The crowd laughed lightly.

"What I really want to say is, Scarlett always came through for me. She looked out for me, was my big sister, and I'll always love her." Her voice cracked and so she paused. "But she was hurting. And no one knew. And I know what that is, because I've struggled my entire life. To feel good enough. To find the strength to just get through a day. To wake up and try to feel like life is worth living. But I've made it through so far. One step at a time. So for Scarlett to . . ."

The theater was filled with a silence that boomed back at her.

She took in a deep breath.

"For Scarlett to do what she did . . . Well, it was shocking. I mean, if she can't do it . . . How can I? But in some ways her loss has steeled me. It got me here. Out of my comfort zone. Way out of my comfort zone." Angie gave a little laugh and the audience was right there with her. "I am doing this for my sister. And I want everyone out there who is struggling to know that you're not alone. It's cliché, but it's true. Other people are struggling, too. You just might not know how. So when you're working so hard to just get through the day, I hope you can find some solace in the fact that many of us are doing the same.

"Scarlett would have been so proud of this. Thank you." She lifted the gold statue aloft with both hands.

The theater was dead quiet for a beat. Then came an eruption of applause so strong and sustained it startled her. But she stood firmly on the stage, looking out into the blinding lights, and basked in the adulation because she knew it wasn't for her, it was for Scarlett.

# 4

andace materialized and they were funneled backstage where they were given flutes of champagne. Then they were led out the back of the Dolby to the photo room in the adjoining Loews Hotel, into the presence of what looked, to Angie, like a hundred camera operators and photographers.

Angie turned and quietly asked Candace, "More questions? Aren't we done?" The most stressful part was over, but Angie's anxiety roared at the thought of yet more photos and questions.

"You'll be fine," Candace said into her ear. "You just fucking slayed. This is nothing in comparison! You just wait. Charles is going to be over the moon."

That cut through the anxiety. Was she going to meet Charles Weaver? How could the night get stranger?

When it was Angie's turn, Candace showed her where to stand and how to pose holding the Oscar as hundreds of flashes went off and she tried to keep up with the random prompts the photographers shouted out. Grateful for the adrenaline that was apparently masking every other chemical pounding through her body, she tried to stay in the moment. The lights. Her posture. Holding the shiny statuette. It was heavier than she'd thought it would be.

"Hey, Miss Norris, over here!"

"Can you hold your statue a little higher?"

"Smile over here!"

"Don't block your face! Hold your Oscar to one side, thank you!"

She knew it wasn't her award, but just hearing someone call it her Oscar made her flush. In that moment she felt like a movie star.

"Okay, thanks, everybody!" Candace eventually shouted. To Angie, she murmured, "Now a few press questions," as she pulled Angie to the press room, another required stop for winners before they could head back to the auditorium.

"If we're lucky, we'll make it back to our seats in time to see Best Picture," Candace said, checking her phone. "If not, we hang in the Green Room. Come on."

They entered a room filled with hundreds of journalists. The sheer number of them made Angie's self-consciousness come roaring back.

"Hi, everybody, we only have time for a few questions." Candace checked her phone. She pointed to a dark-haired man in a tux who held up a paddle bearing the number 25. "Yes, twenty-five."

"Miss Norris, you were very brave up there. You opened up. To the whole world." The reporter had a British accent. "How are you feeling now?"

*Oh, wow. Real questions.* And she didn't know the answer. "It's all so overwhelming. I'm not really feeling much of anything at the moment." She was relieved when that elicited chuckles from the assemblage.

Candace pointed to a woman next. "Yes, thirty-seven."

"Miss Norris, do you think your sister may have been helped if she'd heard your speech when she was struggling?"

The question took Angie off guard, and she just stared at the woman for a moment before recovering. "I would like to think so, yes."

Candace checked her phone. "We have to get back to the auditorium. Time for just one more question."

"Angie, is this award the greatest part of Scarlett's legacy?"

"I'd like to think that Scarlett's life and her death will save someone even though we may never know who."

"Okay, gotta get back for Best Picture. I'm sure you understand." Candace clutched her arm and hurried her out of the room, heading back to the Dolby. "Girl, you really can think on your feet."

They sat back down in the theater just as Fernando Greco, the Best Director winner, was wrapping up his speech. When Harrison Ford and Meryl Streep took the stage to announce Best Picture, Angie didn't hear a thing until both actors together called out, ". . . *Catapult!*"

A huge roar went up throughout the auditorium, and the DreamWeaver group in front of Angie and Candace leapt to their feet, exchanging gasps and hugs before filing up to the stage. Some received statuettes and others formed a semi-circle behind them. Charles Weaver emerged from the throng and stood at the microphone. In one hand he held an Oscar. He used the other to gesture to quiet the auditorium. When it did, he placed the statue on the podium and looked out at the crowd. The entire audience was rapt.

"You know, I was thinking today that those of us who've been blessed with success in this industry have tremendous power." Charles's tone was sincere and devoid of bombast. "We create jobs, we make art. We make people a lot of money." Mild laughter rippled through the theater. "Those things are important, of course. But what is our real strength? My friends, we're storytellers. I'm here tonight because people too numerous to mention work tirelessly at DreamWeaver so we can tell stories. From the producers to the set designers to the editors, electricians to craft service. Every single person plays a pivotal part in bringing these stories to life. I owe them a debt I cannot repay. Most of all, I owe one to the late, great Scarlett Norris, whose work in our film speaks for itself and for which you have so rightly honored her.

"Like Scarlett's sister, who spoke so movingly just minutes ago, I wish I had known how much she was suffering," he continued. "Let us all keep working to make movies that reflect people's truths, both the joy and the sadness. We are storytellers. And we have a responsibility to shine a light everywhere, on every aspect of what it means to be human. Thank you all so very much."

The crowd leapt to its feet in wildly enthusiastic applause. Angie's eyes had welled up at the mention of her sister. Charles Weaver was commanding, but he also had that gift seen in great politicians that made you feel as though you were the only one in the room, no matter how many others were listening.

And with that, the ceremony was over. As she and Candace joined the mob heading for the Governors Ball, held in another part of the Dolby, Angie could hear people on all sides of her chattering, the energy level still through the roof. She gripped her statuette tightly, afraid she might lose it in the throng.

Then a flash of burgundy caught her eye. Mirabel de Nova. She was chatting with Fernando Greco, who was gesturing with his Oscar. Suddenly Mirabel glanced over and they connected for a moment. Angie didn't know how to tear her gaze away. Mirabel gave a small smile and a nod.

*She understands. She understands about Scarlett.*

"God, it's always crazy getting to the ball. They need a better system." Candace spoke as much to herself as to Angie as she typed into her phone.

"You gave a helluva speech."

Angie turned to see a tanned man with perfectly combed silver hair on her right.

"I'm Everett. Everett Cox. I was one of the executive producers on *Catapult*. I loved working with your sister. Everyone did."

"Thank you. That means so much."

Candace's back was to her as she talked into her phone. "We're almost there. Where are you? We can come to you."

Everett Cox leaned in a little too close to Angie. "And you look just beautiful, if you don't mind my saying so."

"Oh. Um, thank you," Angie stammered. She glanced to Candace, who was still talking, one hand holding her phone, the other covering her free ear.

"Oh, Christ, Ev," said a tall blonde in a tight, shimmery, cobalt-blue gown. She sidled up to Angie. "Leave the poor girl alone. She hasn't gotten the requisite tutorial yet on industry sleazebags."

Angie turned to her unlikely savior: Patricia Bartlett, a fortyish actress who was considered a "wild child," if the tabloids were to be believed.

"Patricia, how delightful." Everett's voice dripped with sarcasm. "Classy as always. Try to get home before you puke on your shoes, will you?" He shot Angie a look. "Nice to meet you, Miss Norris."

Angie smiled weakly and took in Patricia, who was clearly sizing her up.

"Honey, you are a lamb among the wolves. I'm glad I found you when I did. I'm Patricia. I was friends with your sister, good friends. Nice job with the speech. Jesus, you must have been nervous. I mean, this isn't really your scene, is it?"

Then Candace brusquely broke in. "She's fine. I'm watching out for her."

"You sure didn't save her from Everett."

"Everett's harmless. A pussycat."

"More like a noxious pussy." Patricia clasped Angie's arm. "How about I take over from here? I can show you around the party better than this never-was." She gestured toward Candace.

Angie looked from one to the other. "I . . . don't know. Okay, I guess?"

"Guess? There is no guessing. We're going to the Governors Ball!" Patricia broke into a raucous laugh as she led Angie quickly through the crowd.

"What about Candace?"

"That publicity whore? Fuck her."

Cinderella was fleeing one ball and headed for another, led by a new, very interesting fairy godmother.

Candace had said the Governors Ball was the most glamorous of all the post-Oscars parties, attendees partying and politicking in the most joyous and glittery fashion. And as Angie took in the elegant furnishings and purple and gold—this year's color scheme—that adorned the walls, the tables, the seats, the napkins, the plates, she certainly didn't doubt it.

The room was overflowing with heaping tables of finger food, several full bars, and waitstaff who circulated with trays of bubbly. Angie watched as people broke off into cliques, calling out to friends and acquaintances. It seemed the stress of the ceremony had evaporated and they could all breathe again. Or maybe that was just how she was feeling.

Patricia plucked two flutes of champagne from a tray as a waiter passed by and handed one to Angie. "To Scarlett. And to you." She touched her glass to Angie's with a soft clink. Angie took a sip while Patricia polished her glass off with verve.

Angie was wowed, and still worried she'd lose the Oscar. She held the heavy statuette in one hand, her drink in the other, and her clutch under one arm. Patricia snatched another flute and they made their way through the crowd, Patricia acknowledging people Angie had never seen before and some who were among the most famous faces in the world. She introduced her to some, whispering tidbits and quipping bon mots until Angie felt entirely at ease, unable to keep from laughing at some of the revelations and observations. Many expressed sympathy about Scarlett and commendations for Angie's speech. Hollywood legends seemed genuinely touched by her words.

As Angie took another sip of her champagne, a large, imposing figure approached. He stopped a few feet from them and held out his arms.

"The woman of the hour!" Charles Weaver boomed. "C'mon, bring it in."

Angie couldn't help but be drawn toward his light while at the same time feeling awkward. She hoped it didn't show as he locked her in a tight embrace. Then, over his shoulder, she spotted Mirabel de Nova. Angie's eyes met hers again, but this time Mirabel didn't flash a smile at her. She lowered her eyes and turned away, as if in disappointment.

Angie had no idea how to interpret Mirabel's look before Charles was releasing her from his grip. "My dear, your sister was a wonderful girl, and a terrific actress. We all miss her very much." He took both of Angie's hands in his and focused on her earnestly. "Your speech was so moving and so heartfelt. It was a rousing call to action and I do hope that you have elicited some change. I hope you reached some poor soul who is wrestling with their demons and who will now find the where-withal to take steps forward into the light, the light you have shone on such a delicate and important issue. You did that, Angie. You did that."

He spoke so eloquently, so genuinely, his entire being trained like a spotlight on her, she felt swept up in it, like she was in an energy vortex lifting her off the earth until she was weightless, floating, ready to soar.

"Thank you. So much." Words were inadequate.

For a fleeting moment, her eyes darted to a rugged-looking beefy man in a gray suit who shadowed Charles. He wore mirrored shades that sat above a hard line of a mouth.

Photographers stalked the party and Charles put his heavy arm around Angie's shoulder, subtly turning her toward the clicks, flashes blazing. After a few moments, he thundered, "All right, guys! And gals. That's enough. We need to give Miss Norris some space and some peace."

As if cowed, the photographers retreated back into the crowd and Charles addressed Angie again. "Please, Angela, if I may call you Angela . . ."

"'Angie.' Of course."

"Let me know if you need anything at all." He pulled out a gold business card of thick stock with raised embossing. "Scarlett meant the world to us. And you are her family. So you are our family." He clasped her hands, slipping the card into them. "Hope we see you soon."

He seemed to glide off into the crowd. Angie had never seen such a beautiful, tasteful business card before. The information was simple.

His name and a phone number. Had Charles Weaver just given her his personal phone number? There was no way. It had to be an assistant's. Or the general phone bank at DreamWeaver. She was still thinking about it when she became aware of a man standing nearby as if wanting to approach. Tall and handsome, his dark hair pulled up into a bun, Angie recognized him from the photos Candace had shown her. He'd been sitting with the DreamWeaver nominees during the awards.

She averted her eyes, afraid she was staring, and was suddenly aware of Patricia's absence. When had she drifted off? And where did she go?

"Scarlett was extraordinary."

She jerked in surprise at the voice. It was the bun man, who had been hovering. "Yes," she said, "she was. Did you know her well?"

He gazed at her for a few seconds. He didn't introduce himself. Finally he murmured, "She deserved better." He looked as though he were about to say more but then abruptly turned and walked off.

*She deserved better?* The same phrase that was in the cryptic note she'd gotten in New York. Before she could puzzle it over, Patricia returned with a gaggle of admirers and took Angie by the arm. "The party's moving, and, yes, honey, I'm the party."

"I don't know. I'm pretty exhausted. I think I'll just get a taxi to the hotel."

"Oh, God! First, we don't take taxis in LA. We Uber. And, second, you're not going anywhere but with me." She led Angie toward the exit with her entourage in tow.

"And where would that be?" Angie was getting kind of used to Patricia, bizarre as that would have seemed just hours before.

"You'll see. Where the hell is Tanya? Tanya! C'mon, let's get the hell outta here."

A striking Latina materialized through the crowd wearing a silver lamé gown. Her abundant black hair was pulled back severely. Tanya Castillo. Angie recognized her as one of the *Catapult* group that had been seated in front of her during the show.

"The party's moving, Tanya. Hustle, hustle, hustle!" Patricia called out. Tanya did a silly dance move, eliciting loud laughs from the entourage and then they all headed out the back of the Dolby to a side entrance to the mall.

While they stood waiting for their limo, Patricia introduced the others in fast succession. Angie remembered no one's name, except for Tanya's, though she thought maybe there was a Michael.

When their ride showed up, a Hummer stretch, they all slipped inside, except for Angie. She hesitated, but before she could move, Patricia grabbed Scarlett's Oscar from her hand and shouted, "Get in here, New York!"

Angie slid in next to Patricia, who slammed the door, and the ridiculously long car pulled away from the curb. The inside was cavernous even with nine passengers. The built-in bar was stocked. Neon lights ran around the ceiling and the floor in lines of purple, orange, and green. A circular table in the center offered a surface on which to cut coke, which Maybe Michael set about doing immediately. A petite blonde poured shots and passed them around. Angie accepted a glass, taking a small sip.

"Jesus, Angela, you can do better than that," Patricia chided. "I mean, you're from New York, for chrissake, not East Bumfuck."

"Well, some would consider Long Island East Bumfuck," Angie retorted. Her statement sat there for a second, then the entire group burst into screams of laughter. Angie gave a shy smile. She raised her shot in a cheers and finished it off. But when it came her turn to take part in the coke, she said, "No thanks." She knew where to draw the line.

"Hey, let's get some music going. Jesus, it's a limo not a hearse." Patricia threw back a shot and one of the guys fiddled with the music, dialing it up and flooding the interior with thumping EDM.

Tanya snorted two lines, then tilted her head back, sniffing deeply before turning to Angie. "You gave a great speech tonight, kid. I'm a lawyer at DreamWeaver. I knew your sister, we were friends. You done her proud."

"Thank you. I feel closer to her—"

"Cheers to Scarlett," Tanya interjected. "And to you." She raised a shot glass and downed the contents in one gulp.

"Selfie! Selfie!" Patricia yelled, grabbing Angie and mugging. Then Patricia scooched between Angie and Tanya posing, mugging again, and she snapped another round of crazy photos.

At last, they stopped at a house in the Hollywood Hills. Set off by dramatically lit landscaping, the house was built on multiple levels, and it was vast. Patricia demanded Angie's phone and punched her number into it. "Text me, New York," she commanded ever so seriously, "if you get lost in this house." Then she burst out laughing.

Everyone piled out of the limo, and a man with a clipboard at the front door didn't bat an eye when they breezed in. Clearly, he knew Tanya and Patricia. The party appeared to be an exclusive, lavish after-after affair for the DreamWeaver elite and their friends. The house was furnished simply with chairs and some sofas, and tables that held caviar and blini, elegant canapes, egg rolls, sushi, and cupcakes. Bars had been set up, outside and in, where mixologists mixed elaborate cocktails. Unusual ice sculptures—unicorns, the *David*, what appeared to be Adam and Eve—were set in alcoves under recessed lighting. A DJ in a large dining room spun music, which played softly inside and louder outside, where Angie saw guests gathered around a beautifully tiled pool that glowed aquamarine under the midnight-blue sky.

She was so caught up taking in the atmosphere, she lost Patricia and the group so she wandered the house with a glass of soda water, admiring the dark wood, stone inlays, and metallic touches. Some rooms had strobe lights, some were shadowed, all were occupied by more and more increasingly buzzed partiers. She stepped out onto the main level just as Charles sauntered into the foyer, followed by the muscular man in the gray suit.

A crowd formed as people filed in from rooms that led to the left and the right. A cheer went up followed by resounding applause.

"Hello, friends!" Charles boomed. "What an evening we've had! I

don't want to interrupt the fun, but now that I have everyone's attention . . ." He drew out the sentence so that everyone laughed. Of course
he had everyone's attention, including that of those filing in from the
pool and upstairs. He owned the studio.

"Let's have a moment, shall we? Does everyone have a drink? Good.
Let's raise our glasses to DreamWeaver's incredible success, and to a
helluva year to come."

The crowd cheered and drank.

"And to you, Charles, to you!" Tanya shouted, raising her glass. She
had glassy eyes and her hair was starting to come down from its bun.

The crowd cheered even louder, but Charles held up his hands.
"Thank you so much. Now, I insist, everyone go back to having a good
time. I'll be making the rounds, don't worry."

Charles Weaver was one of those men who naturally commanded
a room. Angie couldn't imagine what it would be like to be that sure of
herself. She was starting to tire of holding the Oscar but didn't want to
put it down for fear of losing it.

As Charles made his way through the crowd, dispensing greetings
and sharing laughs with friends and colleagues, his tough-looking
bodyguard never far behind, Patricia appeared at Angie's side and whispered, "You know Ari was Mossad."

"Ari?"

"The Big Man's *protection*," she giggled.

"Well, in that case, we should definitely abandon our plan to
mug Charles."

"You know, you got a sharp tongue, Angela Norris." Her slurring
was just barely noticeable.

"I have my moments."

That was when her eyes connected with Charles's. He gave a slight
wave, which she returned. She didn't know if she should approach him.
Everyone wanted time with him. Who was she?

"Am I supposed to go up to him?" she asked Patricia, but Patricia had disappeared into the crowd again. And when she turned back, Charles stood before her, with Ari, his silent shadow, just behind.

"I'm glad you came," he said. "Let's sit for a minute."

He led her through a set of double glass doors to the pool, where a cheer went up as soon as he stepped out. Angie had seldom seen someone so at ease with his power and influence. He acknowledged his supporters, his fans, with a nod and directed her to a couple of chairs, and she sat, a bit awkwardly, watching a few partygoers frolic in the pool.

"Listen, how are you doing, really?" Charles placed a gentle hand on her knee as he sat on a chaise longue opposite her, Ari blending into the shadows. "I didn't want to talk in front of too many people, but I want to properly express my sympathy. Losing your sister must have been devastating. And for you to come out here and speak like that, well, it was a real class act."

"Thank you, Mr. Weaver. It all seems surreal now. Even just sitting here with you."

"Charles. Please call me Charles."

"Charles. Thank you." Was she blushing? She didn't know why she felt so giddy in his presence. He was just so famous and successful and kind.

"Look, you were terrific. It's not easy, even for us in the industry, to talk in front of a group, let alone millions of people. I want you to know you can come to me with any problems or questions. Scarlett was special to us. If I can do anything for you and your family, you only need ask."

"Thank you, Charles." Now she really was blushing.

"Don't hesitate to reach out. You have my card. Now, I'd better finish saying my hellos."

He left her with a warm smile and made his way to the other side of the pool where two young women, both willowy and unbelievably tall, were lying side by side on a chaise, their stilettos off and their evening gowns hiked to reveal their legs.

"Well, look at this, double trouble," Charles intoned as he loomed over the duo.

Angie watched the scene unfold, still basking in Charles's light. *God, they can't be more than nineteen.*

Both women stood to greet him. He put an arm around each of them, pulling them close. "I would suggest the three of us get into the hot tub, but I don't want you to go all 'MeToo' on me," he remarked. The girls laughed and one of them quipped, "With both of us, it would be MeThree."

Angie slipped back inside. Her exhaustion was catching up to her, and she had no idea how hard it would be to get back to the hotel. She had the car service but wondered if they'd come out to the Hollywood Hills in the middle of the night. She was pulling her phone out of her clutch to call when she spotted light coming from an open door. Intrigued, she tiptoed up and peeked in. The room, a handsome wood-paneled library, was empty aside from an abundance of book-lined shelves. She immediately felt more at ease. Books were something she understood.

She found some of the usual classics: Proust. Greene. Nabokov. García Márquez. But there was recent literary fiction, too, and she pulled down a volume she'd been meaning to get to. The plot sounded dull, but it had gotten wonderful reviews for style. She scanned the jacket then cracked the book open. She soon forgot about calling the limo service and had no idea how much time had passed when she heard someone clearing their throat. Angie jumped and dropped the book. A beautiful woman stood in front of her, like an apparition. *I must look like a weirdo, holed up with a book at a party.*

But the woman just smiled. "I didn't mean to scare you. Is it good?" She picked up the book and handed it back to Angie. "You seemed pretty engrossed."

"Oh, my God, I . . . I'm sorry, I don't know what compelled me to come in here."

Her visitor looked to be in her late twenties or early thirties. Her skin was a satiny brown and her hair fell in perfect braids around her face. She wore a pale green crepe dress. Angie caught herself staring, embarrassed.

"Don't apologize," the woman said. "With all that's happening out there," she nodded her head toward the door, "you're in here, reading. Interesting." She smiled and extended her hand. "Hi, I'm Nicole Hawkins."

"Angie, Angie Norris." She shook Nicole's hand.

"Nice to meet you, Angie Norris. And you don't have to explain yourself. I know all about the power of a good read. I'm head of development for DreamWeaver. My entire job is to find great books, articles, life rights that the studio can option and develop into films."

"Wow, that sounds like a perfect job. My job is similar, except for the, you know, movie part." *God, I sound like an idiot.* "I work for Rita Ray . . . uh, a book agent, in New York. I read manuscripts and then we take the best ones and pitch them to publishing houses. I spend virtually all my time in the office reading." She gave a small nervous laugh, trying to quell her jitters. "It's just as glamorous as it sounds."

"Oh, I know who you are. I mean, everyone knows at this point."

"Yeah, of course. How silly of me . . ."

"Nah, it's all good. I'm sorry about your sister, by the way."

"Yeah. Yeah, thanks." Angie looked at Nicole shyly.

"So what exactly is this book that had you so engrossed?"

Angie held up the book spine. "It starts off very strong, but . . . I don't need to read it now."

"Feel like raiding the hors d'oeuvre table?"

As they sampled various canapés back in the party, Angie struggled to find something, anything to say. She was always anxious and normally would find a way to absent herself, even if it was awkward. But she didn't want to get away from Nicole. She just wanted to think of something compelling to say.

Before she could dork anything out, Charles wandered by, a different woman at his side, and Nicole called out to him. "Charles, hey! Have you met Scarlett's sister? She works for a New York book agent."

"Angie and I have met and had a lovely chat."

"It's true." Not the most mesmerizing response, but Angie was glad she'd gotten actual words out.

"How great would it be to have someone like her, who's got a bead on hot writers in New York, work for DreamWeaver, huh? We'd get a jump on the best of the best." Nicole was really selling her.

"Well, if she really does have her pulse on the publishing industry, then your job, Nicole, is to steal her away." He raised his glass to toast them. "But watch this one, Angie. She's a vixen."

"Looks like you have a job if you wanna get into the movie industry."

Angie blushed. "He was just being kind. I can't imagine I'd be an asset to you. I know books, and I work with writers, but—"

Nicole clutched Angie's hand and leaned in. "You sound like a perfect fit. And, by the way, just so you know what Charles was talking about, I'm gay, and he never stops warning women about my 'vixenish' ways." She framed "vixenish" in air quotes.

"So, you're not a vixen?" Angie asked with mock seriousness.

Nicole laughed. "Ha! I'm far more comfortable in sweats with a pizza and the remote."

"That sounds better to me, too."

They were both silent for a few moments. Angie wanted to keep talking but suddenly felt nervous again, unable to think of a way to extend the conversation. She needed an escape, just to catch her breath. "Hey, I'll be right back. Need to find a bathroom." She gestured to Scarlett's Oscar resting on a side table. "Would you look after this for a sec?"

Nicole laughed. "Sure."

Wandering down the hall, Angie ran into Patricia. "Well, if it isn't our little literary wonder from New York." Patricia's words were slurred, but she joined Angie in search of a bathroom. "Are we having fun yet?"

"Well, it's certainly been interesting. And, yeah, it has been fun. Thanks for bringing me."

"Oh, Christ, cut it out. This is all such bullshit." Patricia leaned against the wall. Angie hoped she wouldn't pass out. "You seem like a nice girl. Scarlett was nice too. Too nice, you know? She needed to be more of a bitch, like me. Then she wouldn't have gotten *destroyed*."

*Destroyed?*

"Girl, your speech was great. I mean hella good, you know?" Patricia went on. "But, Christ, did you ever talk to Scarlett? Did you know anything about what was going on here?"

They stopped at the door to a bathroom. Before Angie could respond, the door swung open and a drunk woman spilled out, steadying herself before weaving her way back to the party as she smoothed her dress.

"She never told us anything. We were blindsided."

"Scarlett tried to fight. She was a fighter. But you can't fight when you run up against a steamrolling buzzsaw. There's no fighting that." She gave Angie a long look, and then stumbled down the hall.

Angie found herself alone in the bathroom, an ornate space with gold and black trim. She hadn't needed to pee, had only needed a moment, and now that she had it, she was more agitated than before. She braced herself on the sink and surveyed her reflection. She ignored her artfully made-up face, her beautifully styled hair, her exquisite dress and glittering jewelry. Instead, she focused intently on her eyes, looking deep into her irises. What the hell was Patricia talking about? A steamrolling buzzsaw? What had happened to Scarlett? Was it more than depression? Did something happen that exacerbated her despair? Part of her wanted to rush down the hall to confront Patricia, demanding answers, but it wasn't the time. But when would there be a better time? Angie would be leaving LA in a couple days.

She decided she had to act.

Leaving the bathroom, she was surprised to run into Nicole. "Hey."

"Hey." Angie didn't know how long she'd been. "Sorry . . . I ran into someo—"

"No problem." Nicole held up the statuette and handed it back to Angie. "Didn't want you to forget this. Where are you staying? I'm heading out soon if you'd like a lift back?"

Angie felt a wave of relief. There was nothing she wanted more than to get back to the hotel, take off her finery, wash the makeup off her face, and sleep. But what about Patricia? That would have to wait.

"I'd love that," she told Nicole. "I'm staying at the Beverly Wilshire."

"Great."

When they got to the foyer, Angie glimpsed Charles with the tall, attractive man with the close-cropped beard who had approached her at the Governors Ball. She touched Nicole's arm. "Hey. That guy with Charles, who is he?"

"That's Kevin Li. Charles's best friend and president of production at the studio. They go way back from when they were making indies in New York."

"Huh." She didn't want to tell Nicole the cryptic comment he had made. Somehow she felt it was personal.

Nicole put on some jazz . . . as she cruised through the Hollywood Hills. But Angie barely heard the music, or barely felt the wind cutting through the car. She was lost in thought and finally had to ask: "Kevin Li, did he know my sister?"

"A lot of people knew your sister."

"Right."

They drove in silence the rest of the way. Angie couldn't keep her mind off Scarlett and her rarefied life. *Was she ever happy?* She realized how little Scarlett had opened up in recent years. They'd stay up late talking when she'd visited, but thinking back, Scarlett had kept it mostly light. They'd reminisced about growing up, compared LA's merits to New York's, reflected on the glamour of Hollywood. There was one conversation . . .

"It's super sleazy and shallow," Scarlett had said with a laugh.

"Is the casting couch is still a thing?" Angie had wondered how anyone could think they could keep a secret in the age of smartphones, social media, and the twenty-four-seven "news" cycle.

"I'll bet it was easier to hush things up back in the day," she'd said when Scarlett told her about Louis B. Mayer fondling a young Judy Garland, Shirley Temple being sexualized in movies from the age of three and finally getting married at seventeen to evade the advances of many big Hollywood names, and Alfred Hitchcock making life on the set miserable for Tippi Hedren and effectively ruining her career when she rebuffed his sexual advances.

"Men with money and power still think they can get away with anything," she'd snapped, surprising Angie.

*Why had she gotten so angry? Why didn't I ask her more? Like how she really was, and how working in Hollywood really was?*

When Nicole pulled up in front of her hotel, Angie realized she was the first person in LA she'd genuinely enjoyed spending time with. "Thank you so much. I could have Ubered but this was nice."

"I'm in WeHo so just a few minutes away, especially at this time of night."

"WeHo?"

"West Hollywood."

"Ah."

Nicole smiled and extended her phone. "Put your number in here. Maybe we can get together and talk books before you fly out?"

"Oh. That would be nice." Ugh. The second time she'd said "nice" in maybe eight seconds.

They exchanged digits and Angie exited as smoothly as she could. Standing outside the vehicle, she hesitated. "Well, thanks."

"It really was great meeting you," Nicole chirped, casually confident. "You made that party bearable, trust me! I'll text you."

Upstairs in her hotel room, Angie closed the door and leaned against it, heaving a sigh she hadn't known she'd been holding in.

She had done it.

She placed Scarlett's Oscar on the dresser and slipped her shoes off, then hung the Zac Posen gown on its hanger, running a hand down the soft, sleek fabric. She placed the jewelry in their black-velvet boxes, giving the elegant pieces a long look before closing the lids. Who knew when she'd have access to jewelry of that caliber again? Everything went back the next day. Just like a movie, Hollywood was people playing dress-up.

Too exhausted to shower, she washed her face, brushed out her hair, then stretched on the bed. She felt, not just satisfied, but . . . proud of herself.

The evening had been overwhelming and foreign and dazzling, but she had done it. Nicole was fun, so sharp and confident. Charles was so gracious, a real paterfamilias. Patricia and Kevin had known Scarlett and were clearly affected by her death.

That reminded her of the note she'd gotten back in New York.

*Scarlett deserved better.*

Fatigue took over as her mind started pondering just what "better" could mean.

It infected her dreams, and instead of falling into visions of movie stars and gold dust as she slumbered, she was terrorized by a monster that was always just over the horizon.

She couldn't see it.

She couldn't hear it.

But she could sense it.

And she knew it was coming.

# 5

As the car service limo sped along Topanga Canyon Boulevard, Angie watched scrubby grasses and trees pass by her window in a blur. She'd slept late and didn't call for the car until early afternoon but still felt exhausted. She rested her head against the back of the seat and considered closing her eyes for a few minutes. But no, she had to be getting close to Scarlett's house, which was nestled in the Santa Monica Mountains just fifteen or so miles from her hotel. To Angie it felt a world away.

Scott had suggested they sell the house right after Scarlett's death. But Gerry refused to listen to anything that would bring them in contact with LA. Ellen was stuck in the middle trying to keep the peace. And Angie was so paralyzed by grief she was on autopilot, barely functioning, checking off the days as they went by.

So the house had sat empty for the past year but was still being maintained. Scarlett's estate paid the property manager who paid the mortgage, property taxes, utilities, and the upkeep—the cleaner, the gardener, and the pool man. There weren't any practical reasons for Angie to check on the house, but she thought she might stumble across something that would shed light on what had made Scarlett so desperate—or even what was behind the mysterious note she'd gotten in New York.

The driver slowed and turned, and the surroundings started to look familiar. He took another turn at the end of that street, and then another down a craggier road that came to a dead end.

"Here you go," he said when he brought his car to a stop.

Angie recognized the stone address plaque that faced the street. She'd been dreading this moment ever since arriving in LA. "Thanks." She climbed out of the car and watched the limo pull away then turned to face the Craftsman-style bungalow that sat twenty or so yards back. It had been a happy time when she was last there. Scarlett had just bought the place, wanting a retreat, a place to escape into anonymity and silence.

Angie started toward the house, struck by the stillness and the sense of peace. She didn't even know if she was still in LA.

She remembered the landscaping and stone walkway, palm trees offering scant shade. Security cameras surveyed the lawn, both front and back. She approached the door, a bougainvillea-draped pergola looming over it. A tan mat with *BIENVENUE!* in swirly cursive welcomed all comers. Angie still had the key Scarlett had given her the last time she had visited. Letting herself in, she held her breath while it seemed the house exhaled.

The inside was cool, all wood and shadows. Gleaming tile floors added to the crispness in the air. Scarlett's taste in art had a warm quality to it, pieces found on some of her travels adorning shelves and walls. The furniture was comfortable and heavy. Books occupied a shelf in the living room opposite a fireplace. Angie could picture herself curled up with a novel on the overstuffed taupe couch, just across from an abstract painting of flowers that took up most of the wall. Sliding glass doors led to a yard thick with grapefruit and lemon trees, palms towering above the centerpiece—a fifty-foot solar-heated rectangular pool.

Heavy copper pots still hung from a ceiling rack in the brightly mosaiced Spanish-style kitchen. An island that occupied the center of the room. Angie remembered preparing a dinner of squid-ink pasta with those pots and those spices. Scarlett had regaled her with inside stories of co-stars' drunken escapades and on-set temper tantrums. Inset in one wall of the kitchen was a small bank of video cameras highlighting all corners of the grounds so that Scarlett would be aware if there was an intruder. Being so far away from the city, and on her own now in the house with everything so quiet, Angie began to understand.

After a quick look around the ground floor, she climbed the curved staircase that led upstairs. On the right, she peeked into Scarlett's bedroom, with its enormous windows and walls the color of sunflowers. Angie stood at the threshold. She felt tired, and sad. *Are you here, Scar?*

She took a few small steps into the room and stopped, closing her eyes. She took a deep breath, two, three, four, then opened her eyes again and took a few more steps and, little by little, began to look around. Slowly, she moved to the bed and ran her hand along the soft white duvet. She went to the dresser and lifted the lid on a carved wooden box that held Scarlett's jewelry. She didn't have much, especially for an actress who was consistently required to show up on red carpets and talk shows, but what she had was solid and classic. Angie entered the walk-in closet where Scarlett's patterned blouses and silky dresses hung on a long rail, and her jeans and T-shirts were neatly folded and stacked on a shelf. She didn't cry. She told herself she had a mission—to see if anything stood out that could provide a clue to Scarlett's last days. She picked up a pair of her sister's strappy sandals, tried on a straw hat.

*Is there something here, Scar? What am I supposed to see?*

Angie wandered out of the bedroom and across the hall into the room Scarlett had used as a home office and a space for self-tape auditions. She scanned the bookcases holding contemporary fiction, plays, and binders of screenplays. On the wall were photos, including one of Scarlett and Patricia, grinning as they hung off the sides of a golf cart on what looked like a studio lot. The man driving the cart looked vaguely familiar. Angie realized it was Kevin Li, the man Nicole had said was DreamWeaver's production head and Charles Weaver's best friend. His hair was short in the photo, and he wore a polo shirt and glasses, but it was him. *Maybe they were friends. Maybe . . . more?*

She sat at Scarlett's desk. There was an organizer holding pens, pencils, highlighters, Post-it notes, tape, and scissors; a green desk lamp; a box of tissues; and a diffuser with a few bottles of essential oils.

The top drawer was slightly ajar. Angie tried to open it, but it wouldn't budge. She tried to slide her hand in, but the opening was too narrow. She got on her hands and knees to look under the desk. In between the back of the drawer and the wall was the corner of some sort of book. She grabbed it and tried to tug it out, but it was wedged in place. She tugged again, this time pulling on the drawer at the same time, and freed a pink leather-bound book tied with raffia. She untied the cord and opened the slender volume. Scarlett's handwriting—it was her journal. *Is this what I'm looking for, Scar?* Angie's heart was beating fast. She realized she was scared. *I could just put it back in the drawer. It's so personal. I don't have to read it.* But as she ran her fingers along the outlines of the lotus flowers embossed on the cover, she knew that wasn't an option. Not if she really wanted to know more about what happened to her sister.

So she went back to Scarlett's bedroom and sat on the bed, wind rustling in the palms outside, opened the journal, and started reading. Judging from the dated entries, Scarlett had started it a little more than a year before she died.

## 1/14

So great to see Ange. She was here for two weeks. God, I miss her. She's still at Rita's after all these years. But she looked good. She visited the set with me and seemed mesmerized. Glad she came out. I don't see her enough.

1/28

Went out with Patricia last night. Saved her from
the walk of shame. She almost went home with Ben G.
from Tricolor. Yuck. I brought her home with me. She's
still sleeping but later, I'm making paella and Sangria.
Tanya coming by for dinner.

2/2

Groundhog Day but nobody worries about six
more weeks of winter in L.A. LOL. Jeremy wants to
have dinner. I don't know, we tried this once before
and it didn't work but we didn't have much time for
each other either. It seemed easier when I was younger.
There were categories. Family. Friends. Boyfriends. Out
here the lines are blurrier.

3/10

We had dinner & it was great! We both seem
more centered than when we first met. We went up
to Malibu. We were recognized, but he knew a pretty
out-of-the-way place, so it wasn't crazy. They say fame
is fleeting. I wish! I shouldn't say that. I have nothing
to bitch and whine about. But it would be nice for us
to go out sometime and be anonymous.

3/24

Jeremy & I are doing well. He's grown and I don't
feel insecure this time. I'm happy to relax & see where
it goes. He'll be out of town on a shoot for a few weeks,

but I need some time anyway. Feeling a little burned out. The series wraps soon. Sucks that my character won't recur next season but it's been a career-changer. Catapult doesn't start shooting for a while, but I should begin research anyway. Chloe will take all I have and then some.

4/9

Had video conference with Catapult director David Frobisher Jones. I've never met him before, but he came across as true to his reputation of being professional and demanding but fair and not a lunatic. And he's not known as a creep. That's all to the good! I'm REALLY, REALLY stoked. It's the part of a lifetime. A little nervous, too. I hope I can pull off Chloe, not make her a cliche.

5/22

Jer & I were in Mexico & we got into a fight over DreamWeaver. He knows I could never turn down a part like Chloe, but he hates Charles's guts and is worried C. will make my life a living hell on set because he's so volatile and controlling. And he's a womanizer. Trying not to worry. C. won't cross David FJ, not if he wants a good movie, and David will support his cast, I'm sure of it.

6/16

Two auditions this week, and another next week. One is for a TV pilot, one is for an Amazon Prime movie, and one is for a blockbuster superhero gig. Don makes sure I keep getting seen for good projects. An agent who believes in you is so important. My star is rising. For now.

8/25

Just signed another contract for another big role with DreamWeaver! OMG! Supposed to start shooting late next year around when Catapult comes out. Don made sure I was seen for it and was so excited when they wanted me. Gotta get the goods while I can.

11/19

Table read for C., and we all went over David's vision for the story. If I nail Chloe, Don says I can expect to be called in or even offered a lot of great parts in really good projects. But what if I don't nail it? What if I just embarrass myself? Why am I so nervous about this? I have to be careful not to psyche myself out, that will undermine my work.

12/1

Started shooting! C. welcomed all of us but boy, the minute he showed up on set, the entire mood shifted. Everyone stops talking, focuses on their jobs, no joking unless of course he makes a joke, then everybody laughs too loudly. Jeez. Really? Charles made a special point of personally greeting me and telling me how happy he is that I'm starring in the film. He was nice but something about him keeps you on your guard. He's like an unpredictable animal. You don't want to make a false move.

12/10

C. watched the dailies and apparently hated the lighting. And the pacing. We have to redo half a dozen scenes. Then he comes up to me on set. "So, Scarlett, let's pick up the energy today? Even if your character is having a quiet moment, don't lose the intensity. I've talked to David already about the shape the film is taking, so I want to see some more life in this thing. You're great, you know that?" What could I say? I just said, "Sure Charles, whatever you need." David was standing a few feet behind him and looking at me during this entire exchange. He looked pissed. Charles needs to give his directors their freedom, it's ridiculous.

12/14

Had to show my face at a DW party over the weekend but it was suffocating. Everybody pretending to be collegial, supportive. Charles comes over, all warm with that huge hug of his where it's like you can feel every part of him pressed against your body. You have to show your face at these things if you want to get cast. Patricia gets blackballed because everyone thinks she's a bitch and too hard to work with but, as soon as she makes a hit, the offers start pouring in again. Because she makes them money. Being "difficult" in Hollywood means you don't take shit, or you won't sleep with every sleazy producer with an ego the size of the Bowl because they're old, paunchy, bald, and on Viagra. So, I do what I can to not get blacklisted. Don says to show up at the parties – still important.

12/17

Weird night. Wrapped at 6. Went to my trailer to get a few things and change and was about to get a car home when Kristy knocked. Says Charles wants to see me. I ask if it can wait. She looks at me kind of apologetic but I know, of course, it can't wait. It's Charles. I get my stuff so I can leave right after talking to him. He's waiting for me in a makeshift office on the set. Really friendly. "Scarlett," he says, "I wanted to tell you that the dailies are looking really good, you're really bringing your A game, all that energy, I knew it was in there." He offers me a drink. I say I gotta get home. "Sure, you're doing great work, I understand, it's exhausting. Well, I just wanted you to know that I'm happy with how everything's going, Scarlett. And let's have that drink one day. Ok?" So, I leave. And I can't figure out what that's about. Maybe he feels badly for those days he's been such an asshole on set? Jeremy's working in Canada. I'm too tired to call anybody anyway. Came home, had a bite. I'm so tired.

12/23

Nice to be home, see the family this year for Christmas, but so tired. It's hard, always acting like everything is great, everything is fine. I take naps all the time. I tell Mom & Dad I have headaches & am worn out from the shoot. They ask if I'm okay. I don't know. Am I okay? No, not really, I'm not okay but I can push through. I could talk to Ange, but she doesn't need my problems. Depression is hard enough without the rest of your family piling on. Scotty's always busy. I love him but we don't talk about anything real. I wouldn't know what to say anyway. What should I say? Jeremy's worried about me. I told him I can handle everything, the pressure on set.

1/10

Shooting, shooting. Film looks like it will be great. So excited. This could be my best role yet. I didn't know the rest of the cast, some I'd never met, some I knew in passing, but we are really connecting in our scenes. I hope this is as great as I think it is.

2/18

I've made myself very very clear. Why can't I make myself heard? Jesus, does no one listen? Just shut up and take me at my word. Seriously. Back the fuck off.

2/23

Stress, stress, stress. C. had another temper tantrum yesterday. It wasn't only directed at me, mercifully. I hope David doesn't quit. If he does, I'll walk, I swear. He's the only buffer between Charles's bullying & me and the other actors. I don't know how Tanya who works closely with him every day can take it. Of course, Patricia warned me. And how am I gonna make it through the NEXT movie for Charles when I'll be lucky if I survive this one? I have to hang on. On set

I am someone else. On set, there are no worries, I'm tough and positive. I go over the scenes we're shooting the next day, over and over. Then I go over them some more. They are part of me. No, not part of me. They are me. It's in my head, my blood, my skin. My old skin is gone. I'm shedding myself. I'm someone else. That's good.

2/25

Need a break. Need this movie to wrap. Soon. Jeremy came in for the weekend, he's been in New York, but we fought. I was so happy to see him, but he said I looked thin and had dark circles under my eyes. WTF. Yeah, I'm wrapping a major role for a hugely influential studio and the head of it is driving us all insane. Christ, of course I'm stressed, what do you think? Tired of having men dictate how I feel and what I do. Need some space.

2/28

I want to go on summer vacation. There was no school and we just swam and had fun all day. I loved that. You don't get that when you grow up. They take it away. Charles keeps telling me he's talked with David and they agree that I'm not quite doing the role how they want it. I see the ocean from my bedroom window. And the sky. The blue sky. I think about monsters. I never was afraid of fantastical beasts and things like that when I was little. Not like other kids. But now I look up and wonder if monsters fell out of the sky, parachuted into the ocean, and came ashore, would I know? What would they look like? Maybe they look like us. Maybe they wear disguises. Maybe.

3/1

Been throwing up for two days on set but had to keep working. Finally the weekend. Patricia came. She gets it. I can't move. Can't walk. So sick. Want to die. Patricia made her doctor come over. I wasn't up to talking. She did an exam. Gave me pills to help me sleep. Took blood. Patricia's been there, plenty of times, sick, stressed, and still have to get to set. She says everything will be okay. I'll get better, I'll feel better. I'm not sure I believe her. I didn't tell her everything. Called Jeremy. Couldn't stop crying.

3/5

If the world was gonna end, would we get a warning? If I knew I could hide, I could wrap myself up and lay in a ditch. I could dig it in the sand far away enough so I wouldn't be swept out by the tide. Then if a meteor crashed into the Earth, maybe I would survive. There would be a lot to do. You couldn't rest. You'd have to stay busy. To survive.

3/7

You wait in your trailer until it's time for your scene. There are 417 white tiles in my bathroom. There are gray tiles too. 127. I remember Long Island. Mom, Dad, Ange, Scotty, Barry, our beagle. I loved him. High school. We are dumb. No idea how things work. It makes me angry. I can't remember things. Boys I liked. I remember names. But I can't picture them. Their faces are fuzzy. Like someone smudged them in my head with an eraser. 417 white tiles. One night I drank wine and walked outside. Shoot days are long. But it's hard to sleep. If you lie on the ground and look up, you can see a few stars. I count them. Below are ants. Too many of those to count. We can't even feel them. Even though they have these big cities just underneath our feet. I closed my eyes and tried to picture the ground under me softening and me sinking lower and lower and lower, being enveloped by the soft, sweet earth until I arrived in the valley of the ants. I was in their world then. There are 417 white tiles in my bathroom.

3/9

Sometimes you're out of time and place, the place is all wrong, maybe you are from outside? From the clouds? But then you get stuck inside somewhere and it's on fire, you can't breathe, you are a person who can't stay inside. You hold your hands up to your temples, but it doesn't help, it's so hot, it's so hot, why the hell doesn't someone fix it? stop stop stop stop stop stop but it doesn't stop it won't stop it won't stop and it's so hot you have to find the door to outside, but I don't know what the door looks like I don't know

3/19

I have to go. Maybe the ants can all get underneath me and lift me high and carry me away, so I'm gone forever. Or I can float up, up, up, up, and then when I reach the stars, I'll see all the beautiful things below, and I'll see things like they're supposed to be. It's prettier from high up. You don't see ugly things. You don't see cracks and scabs and blood and bad breath and foul ugly ugly smelly gross things. Mean things. Things that hurt. You just see stars and sky and below are lights and then the forever ocean. Soon I could be gone. But in the movies, you can see me. You can always see me. Unless someone takes all the movies I've ever been in and burns them to a crisp you can see me there even when I go. I'll go up up, floating up

Angie sat looking at the final entry. The next day, Scarlett killed herself.

She closed the journal. *Jesus, what the hell was going on?* The last entries didn't even make sense. Scarlett was falling apart, having a nervous breakdown. *Are all movie shoots that hard? It's not possible. No one would survive.*

Angie considered what she'd found out. First off, charming Charles Weaver was a control freak. With a temper. Who pushed people hard. But Scarlett finished the movie. She didn't quit and didn't get fired. *How did you get through it, Scar? Did you just compartmentalize it all?*

Angie flipped back through the entries. Jeremy had to be Jeremy Banker, a handsome model-turned-actor Scarlett had dated some time ago. Angie remembered him but didn't know they'd gotten back together. *She didn't tell me. Did she tell Mom?*

Or maybe she never talked about it because she had more on her mind than her latest boyfriend. *And when were you ever insecure? About anything? You always seemed so nonchalant and self-assured. And Jeremy Banker hated Charles Weaver. Sounds like he had good reason. Why were you sick, Scar? Stress? Flu? And who wouldn't back off?*

The last entries were the saddest, and tears slowly rolled down

Angie's face as she re-read them. Rambling, incoherent, not the musings of a lucid mind. But they also made a sort of tragic sense because Angie had never been able to reconcile the sister she knew with the one who took her life. Now she understood that Scarlett wasn't Scarlett at the end.

She stood, wiped her eyes, and grabbed her phone. She dialed Patricia's number.

When Angie arrived at the restaurant on Melrose Avenue that afternoon, Patricia Bartlett was already buzzed, an all-but-empty bottle of pinot noir on her table. She was graciously signing autographs and posing for selfies with fans. Angie held back, studied her. Patricia was a real beauty, but she could see a bit of the scrappy farmgirl she'd read about in some magazine or newspaper feature. And as lively and lovely as she was, there was something dark in her eyes. She looked worn out, like she was slogging through her life, glamorous though it was.

When the sycophants scattered, Angie slid into the seat across from her. "Hey, thanks for meeting me."

"Well, here's our little New York literary light. Glad you found the place." Patricia flagged down a waiter. "Bring us some calamari and get my girlfriend here a nice chardonnay."

"Just iced tea," Angie told the waiter.

"Iced tea *and* chardonnay," Patricia insisted.

The waiter looked at Angie, who gave a nod.

"So big bad LA hasn't scared you off yet?" Patricia asked. "I suppose that's a good sign. Or a bad one." She took a slug of wine. "Seriously, this was Scarlett's world, a piece of it, anyway. What's your impression?"

Patricia was testing her, and Angie was weighing how much to say. "Everything is beautiful, and everybody has money and nice houses and gorgeous clothes, and the movie business seems terribly exciting, but . . ."

"But it seems fake? And fucked up? Right on all counts!" Patricia raised her wineglass.

Patricia was certainly successful, but it was apparent to Angie how bitter she was underneath the party persona.

"Did you talk to my sister before she . . . before her death?" Angie asked. "I mean, like in the days before, or that week?"

"I talked to Scarlett a lot right up until the end." Patricia turned serious. "Look, it's clear you don't know much of what she was going through. Before she died, Scarlett was a mess. I mean, the girl wasn't herself. She was either not sleeping at all, or sleeping all the time, and she'd call me and go on about things that had happened, obsessing. She couldn't let go of anything and it made her crazy."

"What couldn't she let go of? I found her journal. She seemed incredibly stressed and talked a lot about how hard things were on the *Catapult* set."

"Look, it's a tough, tough industry and you have to learn to roll with things or you will get crushed. Scarlett was getting crushed."

"Did you do anything? I mean to try and reach her or . . . ? I'm sorry, I didn't mean that to sound—"

"Like I didn't intervene and should have? The first time she did a film with DreamWeaver—it was a small role—I warned her about how things work and she just said, 'Not me.' I believed her. I knew better but I still believed her." Patricia eyes became distant before she came back to Angie. "It's nothing I don't ask myself. Scarlett was a good friend. But she couldn't handle it here. Not when it came right down to it, even though she had a great career going."

"How do you mean? I know she was busy and wanted parts she thought were, I don't know, more meaningful or challenging than the typical blockbuster stuff."

"That blockbuster stuff makes a shit ton of money and allows you to do the other stuff, but you're right. She wanted to hold out for roles that would get her noticed. And it cost her."

The waiter brought Angie's wine and tea and a fresh glass of pinot for Patricia. "And bring us two chopped salads with dressing on the side," Patricia said, then eyed Angie. "Okay, New York?"

Angie nodded. "What do you mean, it cost her?" she asked when the waiter had departed. "Cost her what?"

"Cost her everything. I mean, she was making a name for herself as someone to be taken seriously. Scarlett didn't take crap but you can't just tell certain people to fuck off if you want a career in the industry. She doubled down and worked harder when things got tough. And that would wear anyone down."

Angie nodded again, urging her to go on.

"Look, your sister didn't draw a line, she didn't walk away, she just took it all on until . . . until she just couldn't anymore. And, out here, there's a lot riding on these projects. Money, reputations, everyone wants something from you . . ." She took a big sip of her wine as if as punctuation.

Angie wondered if she was talking about Scarlett or herself. When Patricia didn't continue, she considered. *Do I go there? Now?* She lunged ahead before she lost her nerve. "I got a weird delivery before I left New York. A messenger dropped off an envelope in the middle of the night."

"How noir."

"It said something about Scarlett deserving better and had a police report number. I went to the police station, and they didn't have any record with that number. The cop said it didn't exist."

"Of course, it doesn't exist," Patricia said quietly. "Doesn't mean it never existed."

"What do you mean? Like, someone . . . erased it? Why? I mean, it was a suicide, not a murder investigation."

Patricia gave Angie a penetrating gaze. "Yes, it was a suicide. I told you. Scarlett just couldn't handle things anymore. So she took an exit. And you won't be able to handle things either if you keep asking questions."

"What? What can't I handle?" She felt heart start to pound. "I'm not doing anything wrong. I'm not accusing anyone of anything. But I've heard twice now that Scarlett didn't deserve what she got, and I don't know what that means. Were people surprised she was depressed? She wrote a lot about how hard it was working on the movie, and how difficult Charles Weaver was. She said if the director walked, she would, too. It just sounds like the stress of that job really got to her. But why would—"

"Listen to me. I'm only saying this once." Patricia cut her off and leaned in so she and Angie were eye to eye. "Your sister was a sweetheart, and I loved her. I get it. I do. And everyone knows how hard some of these assholes like Charles can be to work for. But that's the deal. You make a movie with a place like DreamWeaver, and you get *everything* that comes with that. Hollywood is full of people with money and power, and they love it. They know how to get people to *do exactly what they want*." The words dripped tartly off her tongue. "And no one in this town has the balls to go after them. If these people can get an NYPD report to vanish, what do you think they would do to you, poking around in the death of your sister? Huh?"

"I don't understand what anyone has to lose by telling me why Scarlett became so horribly depressed," Angie returned. "I'm not here to cast blame. But something weird is going on."

Patricia's expression grew darker. She was obviously losing patience. "Go home, Angie. These people . . . Go back to New York and forget all about this."

Angie started to feel angry. "I can tell you know more than you're saying."

"Go home," Patricia hissed. "Look at yourself. You come out to LA, you get all dressed up and make a big speech about your sister and depression. You think you can take on DreamWeaver? You're nuts. You're worse than nuts. You're pathetic." She stood suddenly, steadied herself, and threw a bunch of cash on the table. "You're nothing. Get out of here. And don't come back."

Angie watched her stumble out of the restaurant, but continued to sit at the table, shocked and hurt. And confused. Patricia's rancor had come out of nowhere, cutting her off at the knees.

Suddenly there was a loud screech followed by a commotion outside. Everyone in the restaurant turned to look. Waiters ran for the entrance and Angie followed, several other patrons on her heels. A small group crowded on the sidewalk and at first Angie couldn't see anything, but there were gasps. Some people in front of her pulled out phones to make calls, others to take video, and finally they moved enough for Angie to make out what was going on.

Patricia lay in the street, her face bloodied and bruised, her left arm was angled unnaturally beneath her back. Oddly she still held the stem of the wineglass she had fled the restaurant with, the remainder of it sparkling in shards in the sun beside her.

Angie heard a click! and turned to find a young man in a white T-shirt and jeans snapping photos. He sheepishly explained, "Tabloids. They pay big money for pics, especially for a huge star like Patricia Bartlett."

Angie was sickened by the depravity. She'd had enough of Los Angeles.

It was time to go home.


As she packed that night, she let the TV drone in the background. "One of Hollywood's biggest names cut down in a hit-and-run," one anchor breathlessly reported in her blue suit and perfectly shiny and cemented blond hair as she fixated on the camera lens. "We'll have exclusive coverage and an update on Patricia Bartlett's condition coming up." The developing story was that Patricia had been drunk and stumbled into traffic. She was expected to pull through, but it was going to be a long road to recovery.

Angie knew there would be no getting near her again. She'd be guarded against any media or other intrusions.

She texted Nicole, thanking her again for her kindness, and made a mental note to keep in touch with her. She had thanked the stylists who had glammed her up, and Candace, who did not respond. Then she carefully packed Scarlett's journal and Oscar and went down to the lobby to await her limo to the airport.

Scott was still in Taipei, so Angie went to see her parents that Saturday on her own. Her father was chilly, as she knew he would be, but her mother gushed over how beautiful Angie had looked and wanted all the details about the Zac Posen dress and the celebrities and all the perks and parties.

"I had more than a few rough moments, but there were nice parts too," Angie told her over bagels in the kitchen. "It's beautiful there, and I was treated to this very luxurious spa, which I'd never be able to afford on my own. The lunches were fancy, and getting my hair and makeup done and wearing that beautiful dress, and the jewelry from Tiffany . . . I mean, it was nice, but it wasn't really me."

Ellen beamed. "You looked wonderful, honey, so lovely. And those things you said about your own depression and about Scarlett and whatever . . . she was fighting . . ." She choked up. "Well, you were just wonderful. I'm so proud of you. Not just for what you said but that you went out and faced all those people on your own. That's really something." She took Angie's hand, tears in her eyes. "You really made Scarlett proud."

Angie let out a breath she hadn't realized she'd been holding. It meant a lot to hear that from her mother. Unable to embrace the moment, she made a joke. "The lights were in my eyes when I got up there—couldn't see a thing. That helped."

They both laughed and Ellen turned to pop a bagel into the toaster.

"The thing is," Angie went on, "it's clear a lot of people loved Scar. They made remarks about her deserving better, and about how hard it is in Hollywood. I think there's more to her story, to what made her . . . do what she did. I just don't know what. Not yet, anyway."

"Your sister was playing in a very powerful league. She was smart and savvy and could handle herself."

Angie gaped at her mother, dumbfounded and suddenly angry. "Obviously, that's not true, Mom. Turns out she couldn't handle it at all."

"Oh, Angie . . ." Her mother was suddenly flustered. "All I meant was—"

"It's toxic, all of those people, all of it." Gerry walked in, having obviously caught part of their conversation. "They're bad news. Scarlett ruined her life. You will, too, if you keep talking to that crowd out there."

Why didn't her parents want to know more? Was it just too painful? "This really isn't about me, Dad," Angie protested. "It's about what happened to Scar. And, honestly, I really can't believe neither of you is the least bit interested."

There was silence.

"We are not having this conversation, Angela." Gerry's voice was practically shaking. He departed without another word.

Angie turned to her mother. *Say something. Anything.* But she knew her mother wouldn't contradict her father. Ellen met Angie's eye for a moment, then the bagel popped up and she turned away.

Monday morning, Angie couldn't help but compare her small, drab-green workspace to LA's sunny vibrance. Rita had given her two new manuscripts and she had started one over the weekend, but she was having trouble focusing. She kept replaying the conversations with her parents and thinking about the weird message with the police report and Patricia and the hit-and-run. The news was reporting Patricia was still in serious but stable condition.

Angie phoned Scott once he was home from his trip and filled him in. He listened thoughtfully as always.

"Look, it had to be really hard for you to be out there. So you heard a few things. You're exhausted. Just let it go. We'll never know why. You have to accept that."

"But Patricia was trying to warn—"

"Patricia Bartlett was drunk, you said so yourself. She likely didn't know what she was talking about. And it's not that extraordinary that someone who's drunk would stumble into traffic."

When he put it that way, it all made sense. *Everything can be explained away.* But it still didn't sit well.

"And look," Scott continued, "even if you were to start investigating, run down every red herring—you'll just drive yourself even crazier."

A heavy pause hung in the air.

"Wait, Ange, that came out wrong. I didn't mean that. I just meant . . ."

"I know what you meant," Angie retorted. "You sound just like everyone else. You think I'm exaggerating and that I can't see clearly what's in front of me because there's something *wrong* with me. You weren't there. I was."

She hung up, angry. *No one trusts my judgment. They dismiss me as a fragile girl who can't distinguish truth from fiction. Impressionable. Naïve. Not able to accept what happened to Scarlett. Unequipped for the world. Unable to face reality.* But she was a grown woman. Not a girl. She coped with depression and anxiety, yes, but that didn't make her impressionable and naïve.

She looked around the office. She had been avoiding life, in a way, safe in her tiny space, where all she had to do, for the most part, was read. Hell, even Scarlett had written in her journal that Angie was "still at Rita's after all these years."

That was Angie's world. But it couldn't be anymore. *I have to stop hiding.* No matter what anyone thought, no matter what they said, no matter how much people doubted her, it was time to be brave. Scarlett had always taken care of her. At home. At school. At summer camp. There was more to her sister's suicide. She knew it. And she owed it to Scarlett to find out.

She quickly picked up the phone, before she had a chance to

chicken out. She was relieved when the call went to voice mail. She left a message. Then she went down the hall and knocked on Rita's door.

"Yeah, what's up?" Rita looked up from the piles of paper stacked on her desk, her glasses propped on her fiery beehive.

"I don't really know how to say this, but there's something I have to do. I'm giving you two weeks' notice, as of today. I'm . . . moving to LA. Maybe I can take an extended leave of absence? I've loved it here but—"

"Honey," Rita cut her off. "I've been waiting years for this." Angie's jaw dropped, but Rita gave her a knowing smile. "It's okay. Just go. Go now. I'll get Joaquin in to help. You know he's always wanted to be you."

Angie couldn't help but laugh.

"And he always needs the money. I'm going to miss you," Rita continued. "No one can really replace you, you know. But, go. You need to spread your wings beyond that shoebox down the hall."

Angie shook her head in amazement. She knew how much Rita relied on her, but she had never known how she saw her.

"But do me a favor. When you go, take a couple manuscripts with you—to read on the plane. When you're done, call me and tell me what you think. Now, get the hell outta here."

# 6

As Angie was going through her things in her apartment that evening, sorting what to take, what to give away, she glanced at her phone and saw she'd missed a call. A return call, from the voice mail she'd left earlier that day. She nervously dialed back.

"Hi, it's Angie Norris. We met at—"

"Hi, Angie!" Nicole Hawkins sounded just as upbeat as Angie remembered.

"I'm sorry we didn't connect before I left LA. I'm back in New York, but I remembered you saying that I'd be good at DreamWeaver. If you, you know, could use someone who can read really fast and connect with writers . . ."

"Are you coming out? Like, permanently?"

"Yes, actually. I'm moving to LA for . . . indefinitely. I'll be needing a job, of course. I mean, everyone needs to work, and I just thought, well, I remembered what you'd said, that I'd be a good fit for that department that looks for books to turn into films."

"You'd be perfect. I'm happy to arrange a meeting with the executive team. The fact you're Scarlett Norris's sister and your Oscar speech—all that will definitely help."

"Oh, wow, that would be great. Thank you so much." Angie felt awkward, unsure how to keep the conversation going.

"Listen, though. You were in town for the biggest night of the year. Everyone was feeling good and being super congratulatory. But that's not how it is here day to day. There's a lot of money on the line, and people have huge egos and a lot at stake, so being nice and not hurting anyone's feelings, all that just doesn't enter into things. It can be tough. You sure you're up for that?"

Angie understood Nicole wanted to prepare her for the reality of the film industry, but she was irritated. Why did everyone assume she was a vulnerable creature incapable of handling any sort of pressure? She had a sharp mind and a good work ethic, but all anyone saw was her reserve and anxiety.

*It's because that's what I project. I have to work on how I come across, always hiding away.* She took one deep breath and steadied herself. *May as well start now.*

"I'm up for it. I read quickly, I know fiction and how to improve a story. I deal with writers, and I know publishing. Plus, I live and work in New York. It's not Hollywood, but it's not exactly the hinterlands." That made Nicole laugh, which gave Angie's confidence a boost. Why not be confident? Everything she'd said was true. She knew good stories. Publishing wasn't the same as movies, but it was all selling stories, one way or another. And selling stories meant selling herself. "I realize Hollywood is a very different animal, but I'll make it work."

"Okay, just wanted to brace you for the everyday realities. Anyway, I'm glad you reached out. Let me make a few calls and set something up, and I'll send you all the details. See you soon."

Angie hung up, pleased she'd connected with Nicole and taken a vital first step. But anxiety was already fomenting deep down. *You've only put out a feeler. Don't panic.*

She lay down on the area rug in her small living room and absentmindedly petted Brontë, who had hopped up on top of her stomach, as she considered her situation.

On one hand, she knew she had the skill to read books and manuscripts quickly and assess what worked and what could be improved. She would be positioned to help writers potentially snag movie options—a huge prize—and steer business to Rita.

On the other hand, was she nuts to think she could work in Hollywood? Securing books for a white-hot studio led by a mercurial control freak? The stakes would be absurdly high even without unraveling the mystery surrounding Scarlett's death.

*Am I crazy to think I can do this?* As intimidating as the move seemed, though, resuming work at Rita's didn't feel right, either. Something had shifted. Maybe forcing herself to go to the Oscars, to see Scarlett's house again, to figure out how to deal with her anxiety moment by moment so she could meet those huge challenges, had taken her to a different place. She was reminded of what Dr. Barker had told her all those years ago in college: Don't be afraid to take a risk. There's no growth without risk.

"I think I'm ready to do this, Brontë. You can stay with Scotty's family, okay?"

The cat blinked and stretched.

Her parents were somewhat less sanguine.

"You're moving to Los Angeles?" her father demanded when she visited them the next day. "Have you lost your mind?"

"Gerry," Ellen attempted to placate, placing a plate of cookies on the kitchen counter. "She has obviously decided it's time for a career change."

Angie looked up from her tea. "I need you both to sit down. Just for a minute."

Ellen sat across from her while Gerry stood, staring at the ground.

Angie felt nervous, as she always did around her father, especially when he was angry. But it was important her parents started to see her as a capable adult. The mantle of the struggling middle child was wearing thin.

"I get that you don't approve of this," she began.

"Honey, it's not—"

"Mom, let me talk." Angie was surprised at the strength in her voice.

"Losing Scar was the worst thing ever, but you guys won't talk about it." She put up her hands to stifle any response. "I need to come to terms with it. And maybe moving to LA will help."

There was a long silence as she looked from her mother to her father and back again. Ellen clasped and unclasped her hands. Gerry glared straight ahead, past his daughter, stone-faced.

"Where will you be working?" her mother finally asked.

"I'm not sure yet, but I have some prospects," Angie said carefully. Her father was reacting so badly to the news of her move that she didn't want to pile on that she was seeking a job at DreamWeaver. "And I thought I would live at Scarlett's. Maybe that sounds morbid, but I stopped by the house when I was out there, so the initial shock of seeing it again is over. And I'll save money that way. Her estate is paying the mortgage—right?—so all I'll have to worry about is food and utilities, maybe a few new clothes."

"What about a car?" her father pointed out. "You can't just hop a subway to Topanga Canyon."

He had a point, but Angie had already thought about that.

"I looked into a car lease. I have some savings . . ." She'd managed to put some money aside, even in New York, because she lived cheaply. She had zero interest in hot restaurants or exclusive clubs where you waited behind velvet ropes to be admitted—the thought of the latter made her shudder.

"We can help you out." Ellen fixed her husband with a stare that dared him to contradict her. "It's the least we can do, isn't it, Gerry?"

But Angie's father wasn't listening. He was looking at Angie with a cold expression. He didn't even seem angry anymore. "You have it all figured out, don't you?" He didn't wait for her to respond before he left the room.


Figured out or not, a week later Angie, a leather backpack slung over her shoulders, was wheeling two huge suitcases behind her through

LAX. She had reserved a rental for a few days until she could get a leased car, and soon was nervously navigating the drive along Pacific Coast Highway to Scarlett's house with the help of the GPS. She kept her lavender oil at the ready, inhaling at regular intervals. When her phone buzzed with a text, she didn't dare take her eyes from the road, calling back via Bluetooth. "Hi, it's Angie. I'm in traffic—"

"Oh, good, you're already in town," Nicole chirped through the ether. Angie's heart was pounding. She had to keep her attention on her driving . . . It was just Nicole. *She's friendly. Breathe. Watch the road. Inhale.*

"Charles and his team want to meet with you this week. I can email you the details." She sounded so self-assured. Angie admired that.

"Sure, sure, that sounds fine. What should I bring? I can draft a list of top-selling books I've worked on and—"

"Yes, that's good, but the most important thing is, be yourself. Remember that Charles likes people who know their mind. Don't be afraid to voice an opinion if they ask you about a film or even a particular actor's performance. You can be diplomatic, but don't be wishy-washy."

*"Turn left ahead."*

"What?"

"Oh, sorry, that's the GPS. I'm—"

"Oh, I should let you go—"

"No, that's fine. I'm on Bluetooth, so it's not a problem. So you were saying don't be wishy-washy?"

"Right. Charles wants to know you're someone who can pick a winner and deal with writers, agents, the whole shebang. I'll email you a list of DreamWeaver's top-grossing films of the past decade too."

"Great."

*"Turn right."*

"Look, I'll let you go, but there's just one more thing." Nicole hesitated. "I know you were just out here, but remember this is LA. We make movies. Image means a lot. If you want this gig, wear something stylish and, you know, a bit sexy. Show some edge. I gotta run. Drive safely, and I'll see you later this week."

Angie hung up. Show edge?

"*Make a U-turn.*"

Angie raided Scarlett's closet and showed up at DreamWeaver three days later in charcoal heels, a tailored gray skirt that hit above the knee, a sky-blue silk shirt, unbuttoned just a bit, and a fitted black jacket. Her hair was clipped back on one side—she tried to style it similar to the way it had been done for the Oscars. Although she was a bit shorter than Scarlett, it all fit well, or well enough. She thought even if she didn't look particularly sexy, at least she looked put together.

The building wasn't a skyscraper like she was used to in Manhattan, but it towered over the neighboring structures along its block of Wilshire Boulevard as it turned from Miracle Mile into Beverly Hills. Gleaming in the California sun, the windows looked like mirrors, reflecting her image back at her as she stood on the sidewalk out front. It gave her the creepy sense of being assessed by unseen eyes, and she felt a wave of anxiety push up from her gut. She tried to brush it aside with a swipe of a hand across her forehead, putting a strand of hair back in place. *Okay, Scar, here we go.*

The corporate offices had multiple levels of security, of course, but she was quickly buzzed into the elevators that led up to the inner sanctum by a friendly security guard who sat in a half-moon alcove just inside the lobby. There was no question they were expecting her.

Nicole had said to ask for her when she arrived, and, as she rode silently in the elevator to the fourteenth floor, Angie hoped a quick check-in would quell her nerves. Each ding as the car passed the ninth, tenth, eleventh gave her pulse a rush.

When it dinged announcing the fourteenth floor, the doors slid open and she was confronted with another person behind another half-moon desk. A tall Asian woman in a fashionable outfit beamed at her. "Welcome to DreamWeaver."

Angie got a guest badge and was told to wait in one of two red leather chairs facing the desk. A large fern sat between them. When Angie took a seat, crossing her legs, she took in the wall of glass behind the receptionist where she could see countless cubicles and beyond them, a wall of windows offering stunning views of the city.

"Hey!"

Angie gave a start and pulled her eyes from the sprawling vista to find Nicole standing before her.

"You look good! Nice to see you." Nicole held out her hand and Angie stood to accept it. "Come on."

She was effervescent and so lovely with her dark ringlets, huge amber eyes, and perfect complexion. But she also had a way of making Angie feel at ease as she led her down a hall lined with movie posters. Maybe it was her open manner and natural self-assuredness. Nicole, Angie considered, knew who she was and was totally comfortable with it.

"Thanks. I wasn't really sure, you know, exactly what to wear." Angie was barely able to get the words out of her mouth.

"Nah, it's great. Now, the job is a CE, a creative executive. I know you're new to the industry so that's actually starting at the bottom in Development and working with a half-dozen other CEs, searching for IP—books, screenplays, articles, new stories. You'd be working under me."

"I brought some printouts with synopses of books I've read and recommended to Rita, my old boss, and that were, you know, published, and they sold pretty well."

"Right. That's fine. Hang on to it as a reference if they ask. What Charles really wants to see is someone who will go to the mat for the studio. That nothing will stop you from closing a deal to get a great book we can turn into a great film. You've already got the eye for books.

Now you need to show them the dealmaker part of it. You know, *Glengarry Glen Ross*, 'Always be closing.' Can you do that?"

Angie swallowed. "Yup, I can do that. I am all about the closing."

Nicole laughed. "Right. Okay, you ready?"

Nicole used a key card to take another elevator to the top floor, where they emerged to face double-glass doors that opened onto a gleaming suite of glass-and-metal tables, blue leather couches, and more gigantic movie posters. Two monster plants flanked floor-to-ceiling windows that afforded even more dizzying views of LA in all its glorious sprawl. They walked through the space and turned down a small hallway that ended at a single wooden door.

Nicole stopped and turned to her. "Okay, here we go. You good?"

Angie nodded, though she wasn't feeling sure at all. Nicole gave a brief knock, and they walked into Charles's office, where he and a handful of DreamWeaver staffers turned to face them.

Angie was half expecting an old-style mahogany room with a humidor and bookcases, but Charles's office was spacious and light with beige walls, carpets in neutral hues, and a huge three-sided desk of blond wood. Off to either side were two strategically-placed minimalist ebony sculptures of the human form, one male and one female. Pops of color came from two paintings that looked like Jackson Pollocks and hung on opposite walls, chaotic explosions of vibrant squiggles and splashes. And in the middle of the room were two large blue leather couches.

Behind the desk, shelves held awards and photos of Charles with politicians, movie stars, and tech titans. One side was devoted entirely to baseball memorabilia: signed baseballs in display holders, photos of iconic images, framed ticket stubs, and a horizontal rack of wooden bats.

"So, you couldn't stay away, huh?" Charles rose from behind his desk and warmly extended a hand. "Nice to see you again, Angie."

She looked at him more carefully than she had at the Oscars and at the party when she was overwhelmed by so many people and the festivities. With his imposing physique, receding hairline, and fleshy face,

Angie decided he made up for his lack of attractiveness with charisma and confidence. He was just as dominating a figure as she remembered.

She tried to meet his confidence with her own, giving him a flash of a smile and firmly shaking his hand. "Thanks so much for meeting with me. I can't imagine what a busy schedule you must have."

Charles put his other hand over hers. "Of course, of course. Look, if we want to make good films—and we do want to make good films"—he glanced around the room to prompt laughter, reminding Angie of old movies where everyone laughed when the king did lest they lose their heads—"then we have to invest in good material. And we need good people to spot that and help us beat others to it." He looked her square in the eye. It was hard to imagine him fearing much of anything. No wonder he was able to build DreamWeaver from nothing.

"This is our executive team." He gestured to the two people who sat facing his desk. "Tanya Castillo, I believe you've met. Tanya is our chief counsel, and this is my right arm, Kevin Li, head of production."

Kevin held Angie's gaze for a few seconds. He still looked every inch the fashionable hipster. His fitted green designer T-shirt was loosely tucked into the front of expensive jeans. He wore dark brown Italian loafers without socks and sported a tan, and, of course, his hair was swept up in a bun. One look at him was like scanning an ad for la dolce vita, LA style.

"Yes, of course," Angie said. "Nice to see everyone again."

"You, too." Tanya gave her an enigmatic smile. Angie wondered if Tanya regretted getting so loose at the after-after party in the hills, or if she even remembered.

"Take a seat, please." Charles phrased it like a suggestion but uttered it like a command. "Nicole, can you join us, or do you have someplace to be?"

Angie thought Nicole faltered for a moment. "I have a meeting with the new Development interns—"

Charles cut her off. "That's great, Nicole. Well, if you have to run, I'll talk to Angie with the team here."

"I'll talk to you again, I hope." Nicole gave Angie an odd expression as she exited, but Angie couldn't read it. One last shot of support?

Charles settled into the leather-bound chair behind his desk—it looked like his throne—and Angie sat on the couch beside Kevin. "Tell us a little about your work in New York. I have your CV here, but tell us more. You worked for a Rita Ray? I feel like I should know that name."

"Rita's a longtime literary agent." Angie felt like she should address everyone but she couldn't take her eyes away from Charles. "She's developed dozens of really fine writers for years and—"

"Right, right." Charles rifled through a script on his desk, his thoughts seemingly elsewhere.

Angie was starting to get a feel for DreamWeaver. In private companies, the leader set the tone, and here, that was Charles. He spoke when he wanted to. He cut you off when he'd heard enough. And the vibe in the room was that no one contradicted him. She could see him pushing people around on the *Catapult* set.

"And you've worked with quite a few good writers, I'm sure. Their books actually sold?"

Angie pulled out her notes. "Yes, I've helped develop a number of writers who've gone on to become pretty big names. I drew up a list here if you'd like to see it. These are some of the biggest names, and books, that Rita's agency handled." She rose and handed him a copy then glanced over at the others, but their eyes were glued to their phones when they weren't keeping an eye on Charles.

"Mm-hmm." Charles perused the paper. "David Tanner . . . I think I read something by him. Not this one, though. It was some thriller. Hellish something. Tanya, do you remember?"

"*Hellish Encounter*. We bought it, but we couldn't get it out of development."

Angie was eager to convince them she could do what they needed. "That book was David's first or second, I think. When I left New York, we were in the process of putting the finishing touches on his latest, which is very captivating, and I think could—"

"Say, Tanya, Kevin, I think you can step out now and I'll have a few words with Angie," Charles announced.

And just like that, the two stood and walked out. It was so sudden, Angie was startled. Tanya had barely had a chance to chime in, and Kevin hadn't said a word.

Alone with Charles, Angie kept her eyes on her list, not sure what would come next. Several moments passed. And then some more. She tried not to fidget. The atmosphere was uncomfortable. *Maybe it's a test? Does he want to see how long I can stand the silence? Should I say something? Is he sizing me up? Maybe he's just distracted?*

"So," he finally said. "You want in, huh?" He stood and maneuvered so that he was behind where she sat, letting his hand graze her shoulder. "Scarlett Norris's kid sister wants into the big, exciting Hollywood scene."

She could almost feel the heat coming off his body. She could hear him breathing. It was weirdly seductive and very unnerving. Maybe that's how things went in Hollywood. Maybe in a place that ran on power, money, beauty, and talent, everyone performed a sort of dance as they weighed who was right for whatever high-stakes project had the potential to make them even more gloriously rich and famous.

"Yes, I want in," she said as clearly and firmly as she could. Charles was still behind her but she kept her focus straight ahead, remembering what Nicole had told her. Don't be wishy-washy. Show some spark. Charles was no doubt testing her to see if she was easily rattled. If she wanted into Scarlett's world, she would have to get past what was comfortable, what she knew.

And so she stood and turned to face Charles. "I know books and writers. I know a good story. I can be an asset to this studio." She could hardly believe that secure and confident voice was hers.

Charles met her gaze for a moment. Then he broke into a grin. "Great. Here, let me show you something."

Angie relaxed. *I was right. It was a test.*

Charles moved behind his desk and pulled down one of the bats from the wall rack. He looked over and saw Angie hadn't budged. "No, come over here, next to me, so you can see what I'm showing you."

*I don't think I have a choice.* Angie joined Charles behind the desk, where he cradled the bat, shifting so he was right next to her.

"You see the writing two-thirds of the way down? Can you read it?"

It was signed and dated, but Angie had no idea who the signature might belong to. She shook her head.

"Rogers Hornsby. The guy hit four-twenty-four. In 1924. Played for the Cardinals. Do you know what four-twenty-four means?"

"Not exactly." Clearly it was something good, but her knowledge of baseball was spotty, at best.

Charles loomed over her and leaned in. "Hitting a fast-moving spinning ball with a piece of wood is one of the hardest things to do in sports. The best hitters bat three hundred in a season. That means the best hitters in the world only get a hit a third of the time. This guy hit four hundred and twenty-four. Incredible."

Angie nodded.

"Do you know how hard it was to find a baseball bat signed by Rogers Hornsby in 1924?" Charles still leaned over her, his face about six inches from hers. "The year he hit four-twenty-four? He even dated it." He brought the bat up so she could see the writing more clearly. "You know where I found it? Some guy in St. Louis had it in his basement. He'd turned the entire room into a monument to the Cardinals. How did I get this, then?" He waited. Then he inhaled deeply. "Nice perfume."

She didn't know what to say to that, so she said nothing.

He broke away and hung the bat back up. "Funny thing is, Angie, I don't even like baseball. It reminds me too much of my mean, ugly father. He was a lousy drunk. Hit my mother. Hit me and my brother. He was a mean sonofabitch. You know what I do like, though?" He turned back around and faced her. "I like collecting things. I like making deals. I like things that have value. I made that guy in St. Louis an incredible offer, more money than he'd see in ten years at whatever shitty job he had in whatever dying industry he was working in. I like making offers people can't pass up."

He extended his arm, indicating she could take her seat again. "So you would be starting out as a lowly CE. You sure about this?"

"I'm sure," she said, baffled and a little ruffled by his baseball analogy. If that's what it was. What had he been trying to tell her? That he got what he wanted even if he didn't want it? Well, she knew what she wanted and she intended to get it too. "I know I can do it."

Charles smiled, seemingly satisfied. "Good. Well, then, assuming our offer meets your salary requirements, let me be the first to welcome you to DreamWeaver."

Angie gaped at him. "I'm hired? That's it? I have the job?"

"Unless you want me to change my mind. Human Resources will contact you with next steps. Come ready to work."

Back at Scarlett's house, Angie was grateful for the quiet of Topanga in ways she never felt she needed back in Queens. She immediately collapsed on the overstuffed couch. When she had first arrived, she had opened up the windows to air it out, shook out the blankets in the bedroom, washed the linens. It felt clean, if not cleared of Scarlett's ghost. Wind chimes on the back patio leading to the pool clacked and clanged through the screen door. Angie felt okay but also a little shaky. She had gotten the job. But what was next? Landing the job was the easy part. Finding out what happened to Scarlett was the thorny part.

She didn't know how to proceed exactly, but she did know that pushing through her anxiety was going to be a full-time job. Setting up routines would give her rhythms and points to focus on, helping her stay stable and not spiral into panic.

She went into the spare room, Scar's office, and wiped clean a whiteboard Scarlett had put in the room. She created a graph for names, dates, numbers, miscellaneous notes. She didn't have much to fill in at that point, but she started with what she knew about Charles, about Patricia, she even included Nicole. Anyone who might know something. And she titled one column with a large X, indicating the person who sent her the note about the police report. She was determined to fill in that column.

Angie's new office was small but airy, and as different from her space at Rita's as she could imagine. Purple chair. Sleek desktop computer. Lucite desk. White walls. She had spent most of the morning filling out paperwork with HR and watching a series of onboarding videos and was decompressing when Nicole knocked lightly on the open door. "So, how's it going?"

No need to tell her about the low-level butterflies that were keeping up a steady patter in her gut. "So far, fine. I've filled out forms and got my security pass. Oh, and IT gave me my log-ons."

"Well, you have to start somewhere. Here, let me get in there." Nicole moved behind the desk, forcing Angie to roll her chair back. She grabbed the mouse, maneuvered to a different screen within the DreamWeaver site, logged on, and brought up a spreadsheet. "We'll get you authorized so you can access this on your own, but for now I just want you to take a look. This is our most updated list of projects in development. There are authors, dates for various development benchmarks, genres, and a lot of other information. We can't have too many films with similar settings like the Old West or Victorian England or whatever, so the default sort is genre, but you can set the parameters however you want." She clicked around the document, so close Angie could smell her perfume. "Anyway, try to at least look over some of that before today's team meeting. I want to make sure you have a chance to familiarize yourself with what's in the pipeline."

Angie nodded as Nicole moved back to the other side of the desk and continued.

"So my team meets every Monday and Thursday, and I meet with Charles every Tuesday. During the Monday meetings, we review the progress on our top three projects in development, sometimes more. Priorities can shift if something isn't coming together or if Charles wants us to light a fire under something else. When that happens, we change gears and focus on what he wants us to. Make sense? Thursdays are when the CEs pitch their latest finds."

Angie could feel the butterflies multiplying. She'd been warned by everyone, but something about Nicole's brisk manner led her to understand, in a way she couldn't have before starting the job, that she was in a whole new world. DreamWeaver was a dynamic culture where everything moved fast and everyone was poised to switch gears at a moment's notice depending on Charles Weaver's whim. She was used to the publishing world, where books didn't move fast unless they were tied to current events.

*Breathe. Focus on the first step. Breathe.*

"You good?" Nicole had a quizzical expression on her face.

Angie had gotten a little lost in thought. "I'm sorry, yes, of course. I was just thinking that since I'm out in Topanga—I'm living at my sister's—I'll have plenty of time to read or work on things when I'm at home. I don't know many people out here yet. So work will keep me busy."

"I hope this isn't too personal, but some people would find it difficult living in the house of a deceased loved one. You're okay with it?"

"It can be a little strange, but I went to the house when I came out for the Oscars. I visited Scarlett two years ago and stayed there with her . . ." She didn't want to get into how she was sad a lot but that being in Topanga also made her feel closer to Scarlett. That wasn't something to share at work and definitely not with her boss on her first day. She tried to lighten the moment. "I've been raiding Scarlett's closet, so there's that," she offered with a little smile.

"Well, you look great."

That was the second time Nicole had said she looked great. It was a new experience for someone to compliment her appearance. Someone who wasn't her mother. Scarlett's clothes and shoes were having an effect, and Angie wasn't sure how she felt about it. She usually faded, quite contentedly, into the background. But she also knew that wouldn't be possible at DreamWeaver. They didn't hire people to fade into the background.

Nicole hesitated, considering. "You know, if you ever feel down or overwhelmed, I'm happy to talk, or just listen."

Angie had mostly seen Nicole come across as friendly but all business. Her concern seemed sincere without being patronizing. "Thanks." She knew she couldn't be friends with her new supervisor, but she appreciated the sentiment.

"Anyway, I've got to get back, but one more thought. I've got the other CEs combing through every script floating around town, so I need you to look elsewhere. You are going to scour books, short stories, magazines, any type of written work for what we need. And I need you to also reach out to authors and their agents, so don't let your contacts in New York dry up. We don't want others to beat us to options or rights to promising new work."

"I'll touch base with Rita—my old boss—and some other connections right away."

"Good. Buzz me with any questions. And welcome."

Later that afternoon, Angie stepped into the conference room Nicole had directed her to for her first team meeting with the other CEs and found them talking amongst themselves. Nicole wasn't there yet, and none of them looked up at her. Angie didn't say anything, just took a seat at the oval table they sat around. They were going on about their weekends, roommates, the latest films they'd seen or screenings they'd attended, and which happy hours had the best and cheapest appetizers. Angie had nothing to contribute and no one asked who she was.

Nicole rushed in and hurriedly dragged out a whiteboard and an easel that had been stowed in a corner. "Hi, everyone. Sorry I kept you waiting. Where are we at?" She uncapped a dry-erase marker.

Everyone snapped to attention, and for the next hour, they went over what was happening with three projects: a serial killer drama set in the rugged nineteenth-century Pacific Northwest; an adaptation of a memoir about one year in the life of a teen in the Haight-Ashbury district of San Francisco during the Summer of Love; and a sci-fi thriller involving romance between androids and humans. Angie didn't say much. She didn't know what was going on, and luckily she wasn't expected to. While she listened, something occurred to her. She had an office. The others all had cubicles on a different floor. She'd seen them during her onboarding tour of the building. Why did she get an office instead of a cube? Did the other CEs resent her? Is that why nobody had been even remotely welcoming or friendly?

When the meeting adjourned, Nicole asked her to stay behind for a few minutes as the others filed out. "So, what's your impression?"

*I'm exhausted and nervous and clearly a fish out of water.* "Everything's fine. I did look over the spreadsheet, but I was a little . . . lost, to be honest, during the discussions."

"Yeah, I realize you've been thrown into the deep end here." Nicole sat on the table in front of her. "I'll show you the source material and treatments for those projects so you can follow what we're doing, but don't worry too much about that. What I really need is for you to scour the Earth for the next great thing."

"Got it."

"And the group?"

"The group?"

"The other CEs, what did you think?"

"Well, I've only just now met them, but they all speak up and seem . . . energetic." She was probably only six or seven years older than most of them, but she felt much older.

Nicole laughed. "Yes, for sure, energetic and hard-working. They're young, of course, and they come here for a few years and work like crazy and hope to parlay this experience into a higher-paying job at a bigger studio or a talent agency. That's usually how it goes."

Angie nodded. *That's not me.*

"Look, I realize you're coming at this from a different place," Nicole said, as if reading her thoughts.

Angie swallowed. *I need to work on my poker face.*

"You're a little older, you're from New York and know publishing, and that's exactly why we hired you. We need to broaden our reach for source material. These guys are great at mingling and networking and figuring out which scripts are floating around town and what's hot and what's not. But you don't have to worry about that. Just play to your strengths. If you want, why don't you head out a little early today? You've got to be exhausted."

Angie hesitated. "Thanks. I'll get back to my office and play it by ear." *I can't look like I can't cut it* . She stood but didn't head for the door. *I should ask her. Then at least it won't be bugging me.* "Nicole, why did I get an office? The others work closely together, literally, but I'm set apart and I'm just wondering if that's—"

"It was Charles's idea. He said he didn't want you to attract undue attention, anything that would make you feel uncomfortable."

*So he decided to isolate me.* "I see. Well, that was thoughtful."

Back in her office, Angie reached immediately for her phone.

"Hello, Rita Ray's agency, may I help you?" answered a familiar voice.

"Joaquin?" She hadn't talked to the thirty-something fledgling fashion designer in a few weeks, even though he was a longtime freelancer at the agency.

"Hello, baby!"

"Oh, my God, Joaquin, how are you? Why are you in the office so late? It's six-thirty there. I was expecting to get Rita."

"Oh, honey, it is crazy busy here. I'm still filling in until she finds someone for your position. And, thank God because I can so use the money right now. She's over at Persea Books. But tell me, how are you? How's LA? Girl, I can't believe you went and moved across the country."

Angie felt a pang of homesickness. For Rita, New York, her favorite pizzeria, her family, Brontë, crazy and fun Joaquin. And she missed the security of her dingy little office, even though deep down she knew she'd left at the right time. "Yeah, I can hardly believe it myself," she finally said. "Listen, Joaquin, I need to pick Rita's brain about what you guys have in the pipeline. I'm responsible for getting rights to new books."

"Hmmm . . . You know, you really have to talk to Rita about this, but do you remember Mackenzie Martin?"

"We sold her manuscript—a memoir—right? Is it coming out soon?"

"It sure is and, honey, it's all about how she lost her mother young and had to go live with her uptight Christian aunt and uncle, and then she falls in love with her first cousin . . . Anyway, it's really good and everyone loves stories about crazy family shit, right?"

"I can't argue with that. Mackenzie Martin, huh? I like it." She made a note to pursue the project. "Can you tell Rita to call me when she's back in the office?"

"Absolutely. We miss you, you know, but I'm proud of you, girl. You're taking a chance. And don't work too hard. Find yourself a cute-ass rich man while you're out there. And one for me, while you're at it. I'll have Rita call you soon. Bye, love."

"Bye." Angie laughed even though the conversation underscored how alone she was in LA.

It didn't matter. She had to give it a chance. She'd been at work exactly one day.

Topanga was just too far away, Angie concluded, as she inched her way back to Scarlett's in her leased car later that afternoon. The bumper-to-bumper traffic that people always joked about seemed to be as real as the shimmering Pacific she saw out the window.

The day had taken its toll. When she arrived home, she kicked off her heels and lay down on the sofa and fell fast asleep. When she woke, it was dark. Groggy, she sat up and reached for her phone. 8:00 p.m. She'd been asleep for over two hours. She went into the bathroom to splash water on her face, then wandered outside to the large illuminated pool. She breathed in the lush scent of evening primrose. It was quiet, but the air felt charged. There were a few stars, and the moon was bright enough to make out a glimmering strip of the Pacific in the distance.

*I'm here, Scar. I did it. Now what do I do?*

# 7

"Mackenzie, listen, I know you're nervous about this," Angie said over the phone, "but DreamWeaver turns out incredible movies, you know that. And you know me."

It was her third week on the job, and she was working hard to convince Mackenzie Martin to sell DreamWeaver the rights to *Peregrine*, which was climbing the bestseller list. Joaquin was right—everyone did love stories about crazy family shit, especially true stories about crazy family shit, so much so that the book had spurred a bidding war. Mackenzie was intent on making sure that when she sold the rights or got an option, she was still protecting the integrity of her project. It was her life, after all.

That was why she hadn't yet accepted Angie's offer. Or anyone else's. She had explained that she'd written *Peregrine* as a form of therapy, to make peace with her traumatic and peripatetic past, and as an offering to a new generation of scared kids. She wanted them to know that they, too, could survive a difficult and tumultuous upbringing.

"Getting published was a dream come true," she told Angie. "And if it's a movie, it can reach so many more people, but God knows how it would turn out. I mean, dramatic license and all that. This is my life."

"Of course your story is important to you," Angie conceded. "But think of it this way: How much control will you have if you sign the rights away to a studio where you know no one? Here, you have me. I worked for Rita. I know what books mean to writers. And your story is what DreamWeaver does best, movies that highlight the intensity and beauty and poignancy of the human experience." She surprised herself—it was a good argument.

"I get it, and DreamWeaver is looking really good. But I don't want to agree to something and then regret it. Can I think just a little more?"

"I understand, it's a big decision. And if it were up to me, you could have as much time as you want. But the studio needs an answer. I can give you a few more days, but then I have to move on. So let me know by the end of the week. And if you have questions in the meantime, just shoot me an email or call."

She hung up after a quick goodbye. She thought she was getting good at her job, the negotiating part. Much to her surprise, negotiating on behalf of DreamWeaver came naturally because she believed in the studio's capability to make an honest, compelling film out of a personal work like *Peregrine*.

There was a light knock on the door, which Angie usually left ajar, and she looked up to see Nicole. "How's Mackenzie? Getting close?"

"Still undecided. I told her I need to know this week. I've stressed that her kind of dramatic personal story is what this studio does well, so if she wants an opportunity to have an artistically great film come out of her book, she needs to sign with us. Or we can option it if that's all she's willing to do. But she's getting a lot of interest, and she's nervous about committing."

"Does it sound like it's a 'no' and she's just toying with us to see if she can get more money from somebody else?" Nicole leaned against the doorframe.

"It's definitely not a 'no.'"

"Hey, there, sorry to interrupt." A petite Asian woman in black stilettos and a becoming fitted pink dress appeared behind Nicole. "Charles wants to see you before his six o'clock."

"Thanks, Kristy," Nicole said as the messenger slipped away as quickly and quietly as she'd arrived.

Nicole addressed Angie again. "I gotta go, but I'm glad you put some pressure on Mackenzie. I don't want to read in *Variety* that someone else optioned it and then have to face Charles. Let's hope she comes around."

"Let's hope." But Angie was barely listening, her heart pounding in her throat. As soon as Nicole was gone, she sprang down the hall, scanning glass-walled meeting rooms that were mostly empty. It was late, and many people were gone for the day.

She took the elevator down a floor to where some assistants sat at desks laid out in quad formations as part of an open plan. A few gathered around a desk, deep in animated conversation, and a woman and a man were typing with headphones on. But there was no one she recognized. *Where did you go?*

She didn't know what she'd say when she finally tracked down Kristy, but she had to find her. Angie had read in numerous news articles that a studio assistant named Kristy Wong had found Scarlett's body. It had to be the same person who'd just talked to Nicole. She'd been hoping to meet her ever since arriving at DreamWeaver, but their paths hadn't crossed and she'd been too damn busy during the days and too exhausted in the evenings and on weekends to go digging.

Angie was in by nine and usually worked past seven. There were meetings with the development team, reports to write, articles and books to scour, writers and agents to contact, and the studio's own records of options and productions—a thicket of paper and electronic files—to wade through. She also had to keep abreast of what other studios and streaming services were producing.

Nicole was always knocking on her door, asking about this prospect or that, and priorities shifted all the time, depending on Charles's mood. One time she stood over Angie's desk dictating one of his whims. "He wants something set in the post-war period, like the 1950s but not the sock hop 1950s, more like . . ." She had looked down at her spiral notebook and read, "'Levittown and the GI Bill and the nascent rise of the middle class.' He's called me four times in three days talking about it. Do we have anything on that?"

"I haven't seen anything," Angie had admitted. "But I'll go through what's upcoming at the big publishing houses—"

"Do more than go through it," Nicole had snapped. "Find something!"

Angie had worked late for days to produce coverage reports on a book, a short story, and an autobiographical magazine article that tapped into Charles's request. Nicole had been pleased, but when she showed Charles, he'd thought the stories were too bland. They were put on a back burner, and he moved on to another idea.

"So, how goes it?" Scott asked one night just as Angie was getting back to the house, her phone propped between shoulder and ear, attempting to fish her keys out of her purse on the front step.

"Um, I don't even really know," she confessed. "I'm keeping up, but it's all I do. I sleep on weekends and try to recharge so I don't totally crash and burn. I'm still dealing with books and writing so I'm not completely out of my depth, but there's a lot more pressure and the pace is fast. I'm not sure how long I can keep it up. And I keep wondering if I'm going to have a panic attack at just the wrong time."

"You can always come back—"

"Scotty, I'm actually surprised at myself. I mean, I think I'm actually doing okay, just really tired."

"We miss you, you know, and, if I haven't said this before, I think this move was good. I mean, I know you have to manage the depression and anxiety, but I'd be sad if you spent your entire life at Rita's. You have a lot to offer, Ange. You know that, right?"

"Thanks, Scotty, that means a lot. I just hope I can last out here, at least until . . ."

"Until what?"

Angie caught herself. She hadn't confided in her brother that she went to LA to pursue her questions about Scarlett's death. She didn't have the energy to try and convince him. "Oh, you know, just until I get the hang of it," she finally supplied, and then changed the subject. "How's Brontë? Adjusting?"

"She's settled right in. The kids love her."

Angie was glad for that, and for Scott's support, but three weeks in she was starting to wonder if she'd ever find Kristy Wong.

As Angie stalked the floor of cubicles, she didn't spot her among the other assistants, and people were starting to notice her lurking. She couldn't risk drawing attention to herself, so she strode away from the assistants' pen with purpose until she turned a corner and nearly slammed into a group of people waiting for the elevators.

"Well, hello. Nice to see you." Tanya Castillo, wearing an elegant beige suit and a bemused smile, stood with two young men who were probably lawyers but could have been bodyguards. There were guys like that all over the offices. They trailed the top executives everywhere and were never introduced. Angie felt like everyone knew what they did except her.

"Hello, Tanya," Angie said, trying to think of something, anything to say. "Nice to see you again. And to be working with you . . . here."

The elevator dinged, and as Tanya's group moved toward the opening doors, Angie, on impulse, joined them. She had no idea where they were headed, but she had to take every single opportunity that presented itself if she was going to learn anything about the studio, meaning Scarlett.

They rode up in an awkward silence until Tanya finally turned her way. "How are you settling in?"

"Fine, thank you." More silence. She wondered if they would win a prize for most stilted elevator conversation ever. "I'm working for Nicole in Development, and I'm using my connections in publishing, so it's working out well."

"Right. I know."

God, of course Tanya knew. She was there when Angie interviewed. Until Charles kicked her and Kevin out of his office.

The elevator doors opened, and Tanya strode out, trailed by her entourage.

It was the top floor. C-suite.

Angie followed. She couldn't have gotten up there without an elevator key, so she was technically somewhere she wasn't supposed to be on her own. *But maybe Tanya doesn't care. She thinks I'm meek, harmless. Good.*

Tanya stopped then. "Angie."

Angie stopped too. Shit.

"Maybe we should make some time to catch up. My assistant will call to set something up." Then she continued down the hall, her goons, or junior lawyers, in tow.

Why would the head of legal want to catch up with a lowly CE? Tanya had known Scarlett. And socialized with her. So perhaps that put Angie in a different league. Or maybe she was keeping tabs on her.

It was impossible to discern Tanya's motive. But Angie could worry about that later. Right then, she was facing the same glass doors she and Nicole had walked through on their way to her job interview. She tentatively held out her arm and gently pushed one door. Unlocked. She looked around. No one in sight. Before she had time to think, she darted through and came to the wide-open reception area that led to Charles's private office. The blue leather couches, the glass-and-metal tables, the enormous movie posters, the staggering views of the city.

*What if someone asks what I'm doing here? Looking for . . . Nicole?*

"I don't give a flying fuck what that asshole says!"

Angie jumped. Charles's booming voice from down the hall to his inner chamber was unmistakable, but it was impossible to tell whom he was yelling at.

"I can buy and sell that sonofabitch ten times over, you know that? FUCK HIM. He thinks he can tell Vivian Reno not to work with me?

Because I'm not *nice*? Jesus fucking Christ. In a few years she'll be lucky to get cast on some shit network sitcom. I want her for this. I know she's right for it. She'll get an Oscar. We just took home a boatload of fuckin' Oscars and she will, too, if she does this. Do we have Gary locked in?"

Angie looked around. Still no one. She moved down the hall toward the wood door that led to Charles's office, her heart pounding in her ears. She thought she could feel her blood pumping through her veins.

She didn't hear anyone else's voice. Charles's got quieter. Was he on the phone? Or were his underlings too cowed to respond? "You call back her fucking agent and you get her to meet with me." A murmur of a response. Then Charles speaking heartily: "We'll have lunch. A nice lunch. Very easygoing. She'll see that I can be very easy to work with. Congenial. I'm a congenial guy. And she will understand that there is no part better than the one I'm dangling in front of her that will ever give her the kind of clout or exposure she's fucking lucky to get at her age."

"Angie, do you need something?"

Angie jumped again. No more than four feet away stood Charles's right-hand man himself—the tanned and funkily tailored-to-perfection Kevin Li.

"Hey, I'm sorry, I didn't mean to startle you," he said. "But I don't usually see you up here."

"Yes." Angie couldn't figure out what to say next. She instinctively backed away from the door to Charles's office. Had it been obvious she'd been eavesdropping? "I was, um, trying to catch Nicole before her meeting with Charles. We just had a meeting, but it can wait. It sounds like he's got people in there."

Kevin held her gaze. "Oh, I see. Well, yes. Nicole's in that meeting, but better to wait unless it's an emergency. Charles doesn't like to be interrupted."

"Of course. No, not an emergency. I can tell her later. Thanks, Kevin. Nice to see you again."

She made her way toward the suite door.

"Angie?"

She froze for a moment then turned back to him. She couldn't get a read on the guy.

"How's everything going for you out here?"

"You mean here at work? It's good. Everything's good, though, you know, a bit difficult at times as I get my sea legs. Lot to learn."

"Yeah, I can imagine." There was a bit of an awkward pause. "Well, I'll tell Nicole you wanted her when she comes out."

"Thanks, that's . . . thanks." Angie moved briskly to the elevator, rode back down to her floor, and walked down the hall and into her office, where she shut the door and leaned against it, finally letting out her breath.

Well, she'd heard Charles Weaver's temper firsthand.

Her phone beeped.

Up for Happy Hour?

Nicole. Apparently the meeting ended moments after Angie fled.

Sure, sounds good.

Angie had been slowly getting to know Nicole better since she'd started. Nicole had started taking Angie to lunches with producers, managers, and writers, ostensibly to expose her to the larger movie eco-system, but Angie thought it was actually to leverage her post-Oscars profile for the studio's benefit.

"This is Angela Norris," she'd say by way of introduction at one of their various meetings around town. "She's just joined our development staff at DreamWeaver. You probably heard her speak at the Oscars this year?"

But Angie didn't care if she was being used. The reality was that she had the right skills for her job and was getting better at it all the time. If she was hired as much for Scarlett's name as her abilities and contacts, so what? It got her where she needed to be. It's not like she didn't have her own ulterior motives.

Though finding answers about Scarlett was even harder than she'd thought it would be. DreamWeaver was a tightly controlled environment. When she'd first arrived, she'd assumed she'd hear some talk about what went on behind closed doors. But no one openly gossiped. Angie only ever heard chatter about the business at hand or innocuous mentions of what was happening at other studios or who had spotted which actors or directors at which restaurant or film premier or screening. And people got suspicious if you poked around too much.

She cautiously broached the topic one morning with Sandra, another CE, as they chatted at the studio's espresso station. "It seems pretty buttoned-up around here." It was an awkward opener and Angie knew it the second it was out of her mouth.

"What do you mean?" Sandra was a bit reserved and smart, a Midwesterner by birth, and Angie and she had become friendly, if not exactly friends.

"I think I was expecting more of an open culture." Angie chose her words with care. "There are so many creative people around, but I never hear any discussions, people giving their opinions about this actor or that project. But maybe it's happening and I'm just not part of it."

Sandra gave a short, tense laugh. "No, you're not missing out, it's just not a place where people talk freely outside their own responsibilities. Charles doesn't go in for a lot of freethinking. He prefers to set the agenda."

*I'll bet.*

"Plus, well, we had something happen once," Sandra said as they sat at a small table with their coffees.

"Something?"

Sandra hesitated, then started typing into her phone. "Someone talked to a journalist who was doing a behind-the-scenes look at how stories make it to the big screen. They were quoted, anonymously, saying that some studios try to lock in A-list actors for future projects that aren't even far along in development yet, just to keep them away from rivals. Anyway, once the story came out, Charles went crazy." She looked around before lowering her voice. "We had all these new people show up around the studio, and everybody thought they were private investigators who were trying to find the leak. Two days later, we got this."

She slid her phone over to Angie. It was open to an email attachment, which read:

To the DreamWeaver staff:

By now we've all seen the *Hollywood Highways* story. I was deeply disappointed to see that one of our own spoke to the press under the cloak of anonymity.

Perhaps I have not been sufficiently clear. For those of you toiling under the assumption that you are free to speak to reporters, allow me to clarify: You are not.

We have a media relations department staffed by professionals who are paid to handle such inquiries. If there is something particular someone outside that department should speak to, the department will authorize an interview, with my express permission and questions approved beforehand.

We work in a highly competitive industry. We guard our trade secrets. They help us succeed and make the kinds of films we can all be proud of.

I'm personally hurt that one of us would breach the trust of the DreamWeaver family. My door is always open if any of you have concerns or questions. In the meantime, I trust I shall never again open a newspaper to find an unvetted, anonymous quote from someone in my employ.

~C.

"Did they ever find who gave the interview?" Angie asked when she was finished reading.

Sandra shook her head. "But, like, half a dozen people were fired. That was the rumor anyway. I think they signed NDAs, so no one talked about it officially, like in the entertainment press. But everyone knew what happened. And after that, no more anonymous comments showed up in the news."

"You're good at this," Nicole said that evening at a trendy bar on Wilshire, all wood and exposed brick with some neon to give it a kick. The crowd was a nice mix of business professionals, hipsters, and, it appeared, screenwriters who sat with their laptops, drinking cocktails, thinking pensively, and then furiously typing when inspiration struck. "You rip through reading and write good coverage reports, but you also handle yourself pretty well with people when we're talking business. You're sure you're an introvert?" She grinned then took a long sip of a blood-orange margarita.

"I'm not great at socializing but talking about books and stories, it's what I know, and how stories might work as films just seems to come naturally."

Angie felt comfortable with Nicole. But she also had to remind herself not to relax too much. She was there for a reason and if she got found out before she could uncover what had driven Scarlett to suicide, everything she had done so far would have been for nothing.

"So, what was it like being an agent? Or an agent's assistant? No offense, but no one likes dealing with agents. Maybe New York book agents are better than the assholes out here?"

"Rita's pretty old school." Angie ran a finger along the rim of her white wine spritzer. "New York is just very different. There's a lot of money, but people don't show off in the same way. New Yorkers are very direct. It's all mean-what-you-say, say-what-you-mean, at least in my experience. They can be real hotheads, too, but you know where you stand. I can't read people out here."

"There's not much to read. In fact, we don't read, per se. We watch. We watch movies, we watch people, we watch famous actors, and then we watch the sun set over the Pacific."

Angie laughed mostly as a cover so she could study Nicole. Her boss's hair was pulled into a high bun with ringlets toppling out. She wore a sleeveless red silk blouse and black skirt, gold jewelry, and dressy open-toed platforms. She always looked great but never tried too hard—that was for the insecure, and Nicole came across to Angie as very secure.

Watching her, Angie wanted to know more about her, like where she'd grown up and gone to school, what kind of books she liked. She wanted to know who she was, not just who she presented to the world. But that would take time, have to happen organically, and she had something far more pressing to tackle.

"I ended up near Charles's office late today," she offered, eager to get out in front of any information Kevin may have relayed. "I overheard part of a conversation. Didn't mean to, but Charles sounded pretty worked up."

Nicole assessed her carefully. "I was actually in that meeting. And, yes, he was worked up. Charles wants what he wants, and he was getting very impatient that this actress . . . Anyway, that doesn't matter. Why were you up there? Were you looking for me?"

"Yeah. Kevin was supposed to let you know. I was going to, uh, call Mackenzie back and I wanted to run something by you before I suggested it to her . . ." Angie felt bad about lying, but she had to gauge Nicole's reaction. She had no idea how close Nicole and Charles were. Did he ever confide in her?

"Hmmm," Nicole said without supplying anything meaningful. "If I can give you a bit of advice: Don't look like you're hanging around. If Charles starts seeing you milling about, he's going to wonder why you don't have better things to do. He's suspicious of people who aren't doing what he thinks they should be doing."

"Do you like working for him?"

Nicole looked at Angie. "It's business. DreamWeaver is one of the best places to be right now, so I make it work."

Angie felt she needed to steer the conversation elsewhere. "Did you always know you wanted to work in movies?"

"Always. My sisters and I would watch movies with my mom and dad on weekends. My folks always had so much to do, so many concerns about jobs and parenting and, you know, all the usual. But then we'd sit down and watch great old movies with Harrison Ford, Will Smith, Michelle Pfeiffer, Angela Bassett, and, of course, Denzel, who is essentially God at our house. I just thought, gosh, if you could make movies, these magical spaces where people could be lovers or killers, from any time or place, doing things they'd never do in real life, why would you do anything else? Everything else seemed hopelessly dull in comparison."

Angie smiled. "Did your sisters feel the same way?" She felt a pang at that word—"sisters."

"Hell, no. They loved watching the movies but mostly because it was fun and we were all together. Jenna, who's older than me, is an accountant. Deidre, the baby, is a physical therapist."

"Did you study film?"

"I actually went to school for nursing." Nicole played with her napkin, ripping small tears in its border. "Fulfilling a dream of my mother's, who's an RN. But I didn't have the focus for science. I switched sophomore year to creative writing and media studies. And after college, I worked in casting for a few years and then talked my way into a production internship at Paramount. When that ended, I was hired full-time and worked my way into development. Then I got hired at DreamWeaver. So that's my bio in under a minute."

"You've done well," Angie said, wondering, *Do I go there?* She decided there was no time like the present. "Did you ever meet my sister?"

"A couple of times, at screenings, that kind of thing. Everyone was excited about *Catapult*. Your sister made a huge leap with that movie. And she was well-liked. I never heard that she treated people on set badly or anything like that. And that stuff gets around. It's really a very small town. You know who's a pain in the ass to work with and who isn't. Patricia Bartlett, for instance, can be a total ass, to be polite about it."

Angie nodded. "I don't know Patricia well, but I know she was tight with Scarlett. And you're right—about Scarlett, I mean. She was the nicest, well, really the best person I knew. She looked out for me my whole life." Her voice faltered.

Nicole put out her hand and covered one of Angie's. "I really am so sorry. I can't imagine."

"Thanks." Angie suddenly felt a wave of fatigue and wanted to get home. But she wasn't done. She took a sip of her spritzer for courage. "I read a journal Scarlett kept," she ventured. "She sounded as though she was losing it in her last days. Said she didn't like the studio but liked being on set. Rambling on and on about all sorts of things, Charles . . ."

"Sorry—" Nicole drained her drink. "I wouldn't know about any of that." She gave Angie a little look of sympathy. "Shall we head out?"

Angie decided not to press further. Prying more information out of Nicole would have to wait.

The next day was the weekly pitch session, and the CEs gathered as usual in Nicole's office, brainstorming ideas and where to find scripts or books to match them. Mackenzie still hadn't called, which made Angie nervous, but she was up to speed with her work so she at least felt confident about that.

"What about an adventure set in the Calico silver mines?" Mark, one of the CEs asked. He was a native Angeleno and knew a lot about Southern California history and heritage. "We could go scout it out, it's just over in San Bernardino. I grew up near there and was always fascinated by the old mine towns."

"I saw at least two westerns in the pipeline already, one of which is moving into pre-production." Angie moved her laptop so he could see the spreadsheet Nicole had shown her on her first day. "*Cabin Fever* and *Whiskey Barrel.*"

"I like the sound of Calico," Nicole said. "We've never done anything local, it would be easy to get press, and the setting sounds novel. But I don't know if we'd want a historic setting. How about a contemporary adventure?"

"I thought we didn't want too many similar concepts at once," Angie countered.

"Sure, but we have to be prepared if those projects fail."

Angie didn't know what to say to that.

"Financing may not come through or something else may unravel to kill a project," Nicole explained.

"But if something is already in pre-production . . ." Angie faltered.

"We need to have the rights to as many interesting prospects as possible so we can move on if something fizzles," Nicole said flatly. "If there's a bunch of sci-fi or westerns or rom-coms somewhere in the pipeline, it's not a problem." She looked at everyone, slowly, her eyes resting on each of them in turn as she spoke. "Possibilities. Charles wants to see lots of great possibilities."

Angie's phone beeped. Email.

Dear Angie,

I've thought a lot about what you said. And I'm going
with DreamWeaver. If I sell my rights to the highest
bidder, I could end up with something I barely recognize as my own work. DreamWeaver didn't offer me
the most money, to be honest, but I believe it will do
the best job with my story. Let me know what the next
step is. Excited for this! Thanks!

~ Mackenzie Martin

She gasped, covering her mouth with one hand. When she looked
up, she realized she had the room's attention. "Well?" Nicole prodded.
"Good news? Bad news?"

"Great news. For us. That was Mackenzie Martin. She's going with
us for *Peregrine*."

Nicole surveyed the group. "That is what I'm talking about.
Possibilities. This is one of the hottest book titles about to drop and
now we have our fingers in the pot."

Angie was a little stunned. Somehow, the victory seemed almost
anticlimactic. *Did I oversell to Mackenzie? Nicole makes everything sound
much more tentative than I thought.*

"This will get made, right?" she asked. Everyone grew quiet.

"What do you mean?" Nicole gave her a quizzical look.

"You just said how so many things can go wrong. I just hope, I
mean, this story means so much to Mackenzie and Rita, and I hope a
really great film does come out of it, that the financing comes through,
and, well, whatever else it actually takes to get it made . . ." Angie
looked at Nicole and her colleagues.

"Oh, my God, Angie, this isn't group therapy," Sandra tossed out
without looking up from her phone. "We can't worry about every

writer. If Charles wants to make a film out of it, he'll make a film. That's not our job. Our job is to lock in the rights."

"Right," Nicole concluded. "Angie, the takeaway here is that you did a great job. You got the rights. The rest is out of your hands. You didn't promise a film."

"I just . . ."

"Your job is to find intellectual property. That's it. But if you have concerns, come to me privately."

"Sure. Sorry." Angie kept a low profile for the rest of the meeting, trying to look engaged. When it finally, mercifully ended, she slunk back to her office, where she sat in silence for a few minutes. The day was drawing to a close, and nothing was keeping her there. But something nagged at her.

She opened her computer and looked at the spreadsheet again. There were more than 150 titles listed. Two were categorized under "Casting." Two were categorized as "Shooting." The others were listed as "Pending." She hadn't studied the categories before as her focus had been on familiarizing herself with the kinds of stories and settings the studio had already gone after versus where they were in the pipeline.

She minimized the spreadsheet and started clicking around the company's internal website, finally choosing one of the titles listed on the spreadsheet—*Alabaster Cove*. She got a one-line result: "The title cannot be found."

She tried a few more titles.

*Atlantic Memories*

*Criminal Error*

*Night Lights and Day Dreams*

Nothing. She clicked around the website some more. There was a huge section about Charles, pages in black and white about DreamWeaver's early days in Jersey City and New York, tabs for each film DreamWeaver had produced going back twenty years to when it had first opened shop in LA.

But who was Charles really? At work, he was so different from the man she'd met at the Oscars. His temper. That bizarre baseball bat story. The way he'd kept Scarlett off-balance on the *Catapult* set by pressuring her one day and fawning over her the next. The intent to cajole that actress, Vivian Reno, to sign after a "congenial" schmoozy lunch. What if something had happened to make him angry with Scarlett, like he'd gotten angry with Vivian Reno? He had sounded enraged. He intended to destroy her if she didn't sign with DreamWeaver. He was used to getting what he wanted, no matter how big or small, no matter the damage. Was Scarlett just collateral damage?

Her breathing grew shallow. Sweat broke out on her forehead, under her arms.

*Oh, God, oh, no, oh, God, not here, not at work, not here, please, no.*

She stood and gripped the edge of her desk before shakily crossing the room, shutting her office door, locking it. She turned off the light, closed the blinds, and sank to the floor. Pulling her knees into her chest, she wrapped her arms around them and lowered her head, focusing on her breathing. *In, two, three, four. Out, two, three, four.*

Breathing wasn't enough. She crawled across the floor to her desk and pulled down her handbag, spilling the contents. She grappled for the vial of lavender essential oil and rubbed it on her temples and her wrists, inhaling deeply. Then she lay down on her side, curled up in the fetal position, breathing rhythmically, four times in, four times out, four times in. She clutched the lavender and brought it to her nose.

*Oh, God, oh, God, oh, God. What made me think I could do this? Oh, God, make it stop. Please, please, please. Not here, not here . . .* She made little rocking movements curled up on the floor.

It took time, but eventually her breath grew more regular. She sat up, drew her knees to her chest again, and gently rested her head on them. The attack was powerful but she realized somehow she was more so.

When it finally ebbed, Angie gathered the contents of her bag and put it all back in. Feeling ragged, she stood, smoothed her clothing, collected her things, and left her office. She just had to get home. She just had to get home.

The offices were dark and hushed. The lights were on in the halls as usual, but most of the employees had vacated.

And it gave her an idea.

Nicole hadn't reacted at all when Angie mentioned Scarlett at happy hour. She wondered what Nicole knew, if anything. If something had happened at the studio, or in the corporate offices, there would be some kind of evidence of it. Right?

She went to the bank of elevators and hit the Up button. A vacuum ran somewhere down the hall and as it got louder, she stifled flickers of panic. She could just as easily be heading down to the parking garage. "Oops, I hit Up by accident. I was looking at my phone," she could say should a cleaning person come by and ask her where she was going. A wave of relief flooded through her when the bell dinged and an empty car presented itself. She slipped inside, and then she realized she needed the goddamn key card to get up to C-suite.

The doors were sliding shut when a wooden pole was suddenly lodged between them, causing them to separate again. A cleaning woman with unruly red hair and sparkling blue eyes stood there holding the handle of a mop, her cart loaded with supplies behind her.

"Going up?" she chimed.

"Um. Yes. Of course. I mean . . ." Angie gestured to the control panel. "My boss needs to . . . needs me to get something from her office. She had to . . . go to a premiere. And she . . . forgot her shoes."

"So you need a scan?"

"A scan?"

The custodian stepped into the car and held up a key card. "A scan." She scanned the card and the doors closed.

Angie hit the button for C-suite. "Thank you so much."

"Of course."

They stood in silence, the custodian keeping her eyes straight ahead.

Angie was terrified she'd ask questions, her name, her clearance on other floors. But she said nothing. Angie held her breath and prayed when she arrived no straggler would be standing there waiting to go home. God forbid if it was Charles himself.

She swallowed down another rush of anxiety as she watched the floors slowly tick upward.

When the doors finally slid open, she inhaled deeply before stepping out into the hall. She looked in both directions and exhaled. Nothing but shadows. The custodian, thankfully, toddled off in the opposite direction to Nicole's office, which was at the end of the hall. Angie could only hope that it was unlocked, but she was afraid she was running out of good fortune.

When she got there, the office was dark and the door was open.

*Do you always leave your office unlocked?*

But it couldn't be a trap. Angie herself hadn't known she'd be sneaking around until just minutes earlier. Still, she felt like she was being watched.

Despite the darkness of the room, she knocked and called out, "Hey, Nicole?" and waited a moment before poking her head inside. Dim lights from neighboring buildings glowed softly through the windows, but otherwise the space was still. She darted into the room, closed the door behind her, and made her way to the desk, where she turned on a small lamp.

But she didn't have time to relax. Who knew why the door had been open? Who knew when a cleaning person could come by? Or a workaholic coworker.

Nicole's desk was tidy, as usual. The clear glass top was barely smudged, a folder and her laptop taking up the only real estate. Two charcoal-gray drawers were on one side. She opened the top one to reveal the usual office paraphernalia: stapler, Post-its, pens, Sharpies, plus one plain key ring with a small brass key.

She closed the drawer and went to open the one beneath it. Locked.

"Shit." She wished she hadn't spoken aloud the second it was out.

Then she had a thought. She opened the top drawer again, withdrew the key, and inserted it into the lock on the bottom drawer. It turned, it clicked, the drawer slid open. At least thirty hanging folders waved back and forth. There were no tabs on top designating the contents, so she flipped through them until she came to one that was thicker than the rest. She selected it, set it on the top of the desk, and opened it. On top of a sheaf of papers was a spreadsheet similar to the one she'd been accessing, but it looked like it contained many more titles and pages. She thumbed through pages and pages of titles she'd never heard of. Options from years earlier?

Despite it not seeming to be anything to do with Scarlett, she sensed she needed to investigate more deeply, so she pulled out her phone to snap images. But what if the flash attracted attention? She really had to get out.

She closed the folder and was slipping it back into its place when something clattered to the floor. She gasped and froze. Nothing more came.

"Fuck."

She got on her hands and knees, shining her phone's light under the desk, across the floor, and there, under one of the chairs for guests, was a small metallic object. She crawled over and grabbed it: a flash drive. Had it fallen from the folder? Was it buried under the documents? Did Nicole even use it?

A muffled voice drifted in from the hall and Angie stood so abruptly she almost knocked the chair over. The custodian. Singing to herself.

In a panic, Angie slipped the flash drive into her pocket and closed the drawer as gently as possible. Opening the door, she startled the cleaning lady who removed her ear buds, putting a hand to her heart.

"Sorry to give you a fright," Angie said brightly. "Just finishing up."

She didn't give the woman a chance to rejoin. She closed the door and strode toward the bank of elevators.

At home, she inserted the flash drive into Scarlett's laptop only to find that it was password-protected. Damn! She couldn't catch a break.

# 8

Jango Davies was sitting in Armina Capetti's plush, overdecorated living room in Alta Loma, taking an earful from his new client. He genuinely enjoyed his P.I. work, the unearthing of information, helping people figure out their messy lives. Before starting his own business, he'd put in twenty-five years with LAPD, the majority as a detective, but lately he felt tired. Maybe a short escape down to Baja with Nola would help. He wasn't sure how much more he had in him. After their son got out of college, he could segue into a less-demanding job, but that was a couple of years off. Until then, he had the corpulent and cross Mrs. Capetti to contend with in her ghastly floral muumuu. And she wasn't making it easy, so he rephrased his question.

"Uh, ma'am, so you don't know what he was wearing. Are there any articles of clothing missing from his wardrobe? Anything distinctive that would help us identify him? The more we have to go on, the better."

"All I know is the sonofabitch took our car and ten grand and left town with that bimbo he was screwing. They're probably halfway to Kentucky by now."

"Kentucky. Good . . ." He wrote down the information. "Why would they go to Kentucky?"

"How the fuck should I know?" she yelled. Then her voice dropped to a seething whisper. "Not literally. They're not literally headed to Kentucky, or maybe they are, I don't know—that's why I hired you."

"So you don't know what he was wearing, but you think he left two days ago in a black BMW with a red-haired woman named Janna O'Hara, about thirty-five years old. Any idea where they would go?"

"He's got a brother in San Francisco and the rest of his family's back in Chicago. Which is where they can bury him after I get through." She spat the words out, then lit a cigarette.

"Okay, Mrs. Capetti, I've got photos, license plate, descriptions, and a few locations to track. Let me do some preliminary checking and I'll get back to you."

She accompanied him to the door, trailing cigarette smoke, her rhinestone-laden flip-flops clacking on the tile of the foyer. He turned back to her before stepping out into the sunshine. "This isn't like the movies, Mrs. Capetti. I may be able to find your husband, but sometimes people don't want to be found. I'm just letting you know. It may cost you a lot of time and money, and you have to be prepared that we may not come up with anything, or we may find something you don't want to hear. But I'll check out a few things and call you."

"Trust me, I'll want to hear. I don't care if I ever see the bastard again. I just want him to know I'm not stupid. Then I'll take him for everything he's worth and destroy him. Simple."

"I'll be in touch."

Jango sat for a bit in his car outside the house. As cases went, this one was about average: missing spouse, missing money from a joint account, could be cheating, could be dead, could be on a business trip. He didn't care as long as he got paid, and it was a nice change from working surveillance for lawyers. That shit made money, but sometimes he needed to break up the monotony of spending his nights drinking coffee and listening to podcasts as he watched people come, go, and take out the trash.

He checked his phone. There was a voice mail from Nola, asking if he'd called the pest control guys yet because she'd found more mice droppings behind the toaster, and another message left by a woman he didn't know.

> "Hi, Mr. Davies. My name is Angela Norris, and my sister was the actress Scarlett Norris. Well, you probably know that she died last year. And, well, I'm trying to figure out what happened to her. It's a long story, but I think I could use some help. I found your name online. Can you give me a call back? Thanks."

Scarlett Norris. Jango remembered hearing about her. A suicide, died on a movie set. Couldn't remember much more, and he doubted he'd seen any of her movies. He was no film buff unless it was classic noir, or Morgan Freeman films. He was told consistently that he resembled the Oscar winner except for his green eyes.

That said, he was happy to take the Morgan Freeman compliment whenever it was bestowed. He knew it was vanity, but, living in LA, everyone got affected.

A quick Google search brought up pictures and stories about how Scarlett Norris's death had been ruled a suicide and she'd won a posthumous Oscar. There were also pictures of another Norris, Angela, with the Oscar statuette she'd accepted on behalf of her late sister and with Charles Weaver, the movie mogul.

*Jesus, all these people with their money.* He knew how miserable many of them really were from working cases over the years. Emotionally unstable. Insecure. Alcoholics. Eating disorders. Overdoses. Affairs that ended one marriage after another. All kinds of kids born to multiple parents and partners. Who could keep track of it all? He didn't judge. But he also didn't get how you could be that rich *and* that miserable. Once you didn't have to worry about paying your bills and you could do as you pleased, what was the problem?

He studied Angela Norris's face. Pretty. Didn't seem the

Hollywood type. He dialed back. "Miss Norris, this is Jango Davies, returning your call."

"Oh, hi. Thanks so much for calling me back."

She sounded breathy and Jango didn't know if it was relief or nervousness. "What can I do for you, Miss Norris?"

"I don't want to say too much over the phone. I know that probably sounds dramatic, but I think there's more to my sister's death than we—my family and I—know. Could we meet? I can tell you more then."

"I looked up your sister, Miss Norris. My condolences. She was a beautiful girl. But it says it was ruled a suicide?"

"Yes, that's right. She was very depressed toward the end. She didn't sound connected to reality anymore, and if she killed herself in that state of mind, well, I want to know how she got there, if something happened to her."

"Hmmmm." She sounded sincere and was no doubt heartbroken. But digging into a suicide on a movie set with a well-known actress? He'd worked in that world before, and a lot of people were reluctant to talk. They were too frightened of bigshot studio owners, producers, directors, agents. "I'm not sure I can help you, Miss Norris. Hollywood is a very tough nut to crack."

"Please. If we could just meet?"

*This is going to lead nowhere,* Jango thought. But something in her voice tipped the balance in her favor. "All right. But I have to tell you, Miss Norris, my time is pretty crunched. I'm working another case so I won't be able to meet you until Tuesday. Does that work?"

"Yes. Thank you. Tuesday is fine."

"Great. There's an Indian grocery with a small restaurant in Glendale. We won't attract any attention there. I can meet you Tuesday evening at seven. I'll text you the address."

"I'll be there. Thanks, Mr. Davies. I really appreciate it."

She disconnected and Jango was left thinking how Hollywood made him want to move to Baja and be done with it.

*\*\**

Angie was heading to a meeting Monday when she glimpsed Kristy Wong heading in the opposite direction. Assessing how tardy she could be, she made the decision to turn and follow.

At the end of the hall, Kristy pushed open a door leading to a stairwell. Angie caught the door before it clicked shut and stealthily followed her up two floors, staying one flight behind. When Kristy stepped onto the sixth floor, Angie allowed the door to close, giving herself a moment to catch her breath, calm herself, and gather her nerve, then pushed it open, intending to move at a quicker pace before she lost her. She nearly slammed directly into her target, who had been waiting on the other side.

"You're following me," Kristy accused and strode rapidly away.

So much for being Nancy Drew.

Angie pursued her. What else could she do at that point? "Please, wait. Please. I don't want to make trouble for you. Truly, I don't. But I want to ask about my sister."

The words came out loudly, too loudly.

"Shhhhh." Kristy turned back and grabbed her arm, leading her into an empty corner office.

The door shut and they stood silently. Angie was nervous, but Kristy seemed nervous, too, that much she could tell. Her arms were crossed, and she shifted her weight from one leg to the other. Then she finally met Angie's gaze.

"Finding . . . your sister . . . was one of the worst days of my life. I mean, I was the one who found her body . . ." She gave an impotent gesture with one hand. "Scarlett, she was one of the nicest actors I ever worked with. Very kind to everyone. She wasn't conceited, she didn't yell at you just because you were a lowly assistant, like a lot of them do. And what happened to her . . ."

"What *did* happen to her, Kristy? Scarlett wasn't herself at the end. What happened?"

"I don't really know. I just know . . . there can be a lot of pressure and . . . it can get to people."

"I read some of Scarlett's journal. She talked about how Charles was micromanaging the shoot, undermining the director, commenting on Scarlett's work, pressuring her to go out for drinks. Did you see anything?"

"Look, this is Charles Weaver's studio, and, well, he wants things done a certain way, but I work for him, for DreamWeaver. I don't have anything to tell you." And with that, Kristy Wong brushed past Angie and out the door.

Angie decided not to follow. If anything, she needed to give her time, some space. She slipped in to her meeting late, giving her colleagues an apologetic look. Going after Kristy had been worth it.

Back in her office, she looked at two reports on books she needed to deliver to Nicole but couldn't stop thinking about the encounter with Kristy. She had seemed uncomfortable, almost afraid.

The knock on the door startled her. She opened it to find Nicole on the other side wearing a slightly bewildered look. "I wanted to focus, so I shut the door." Angie feared she both looked and sounded guilty. Of what, she didn't know.

"Oh. Cool. I was just wondering if you wanted to grab a bite tonight. I've been poring over files to get a handle on how many options we have that are still active. Tracking it all down and getting it organized in one place is proving to be a huge pain in the ass. And I need to blow off some steam."

This was the third invitation from Nicole in two weeks. *Is all this collegial? Or is she suspicious? Or is someone else suspicious and put her on my trail?* Angie wasn't sure if she was being paranoid, but she figured paranoia could only work in her favor. Still, if Nicole was trying to get to her, or get something from her, Angie would have a stronger position on her home turf.

"If you don't mind driving out to Topanga, I could throw a light meal together," she offered, trying to keep her tone casual. "And I'm sure I've got some wine."

"Really? Honestly, I've been dying to see your sister's . . . your place. The traffic will be terrible, but I'm willing to give it a go."

"I'll text you my address!"

After Nicole was gone, Angie realized she was excited to have her over. Not only would she have the home team advantage but she wanted to tap into her knowledge about the studio's inner workings. If Nicole was on the level, maybe they could be friends.

Angie shut her laptop, closed up her office, and headed to the elevators. It was late in the day, and she wanted a few minutes at the house before Nicole arrived to make sure nothing incriminating in her makeshift office was out.

Waiting impatiently for the elevator, she was buried in her phone, checking the commute time on Waze along her regular route, when a familiar voice interrupted her.

"I take it you're fitting in well?"

Angie jumped and jerked her head up to see Charles beside her, smiling beatifically, with the hulking Ari two feet behind.

"Oh, my. I'm so sorry. I didn't mean to startle you," Charles said.

"Just checking the drive home." She held up her phone and spoke as brightly as she could. She didn't trust Charles and was starting to wonder if there was anyone at DreamWeaver she could trust.

"You look lovely today."

"Oh. Thank you."

"How are things? Everyone treating you well?"

"Yes, it's been quite a time getting up to speed, but I'm really enjoying my job, thanks." She was about to splutter something more but the elevator arrived.

Charles held the door for her. "After you."

"Thank you." She stepped in and when he followed, his presence filled the space, making her feel uncomfortable and awkward. Then, of course, there was also the bulk of Ari, who stood in a back corner, silent as ever, reflecting back her discomfort in his shades.

"Which floor?" Charles asked.

"G-3, please."

"Of course." He pressed the corresponding button. "I'm glad you're enjoying the work here. Nicole says you're doing really well, which is terrific."

"Thanks. She's a good supervisor. She helped ease me in."

"You're coping okay? Being here where Scarlett once worked?" He put a hand to his chest. "I apologize if that's intrusive."

"There are hard moments, but I'm getting by."

"You know, I had a close friend growing up, a neighbor kid, Jimmy. And he had an older brother, Jason, who died in a car crash over the holidays one year. And it just devastated his family and the entire community." He was looking at her but it was clear he was a million miles away. "You couldn't get into the funeral home, it was so packed. The line went down the street. I remember waiting with my mother. Jimmy was a great kid, and he idolized his brother. I can still picture Jason. Funny, isn't it?"

Angie gave a small nod but was uncomfortable with this openness. How was she to respond? What was expected? Why was he telling her that?

"I mean, it's decades ago, but that entire week of mourning and services, it was one of the worst things I ever experienced . . ."

The elevator doors opened on the VIP level and he and Ari stepped out. Charles held the door open and continued. "That's why it's important to make the most of every day, Angie. It can all vanish in an instant." He nodded, as if confirming something he'd always known was true. "Well, you have a nice evening."

"Thanks. You, too." *Wow, where did all that come from?*

Just as the elevator doors began to close, Charles put his hand out again to stop them. "Listen, it's crazy running a studio, being so busy.

I'm not always as available to people as I should be. I'd love to treat you to lunch one day soon so we can talk more about how you like living in LA and working with us. My personal assistant will call to arrange it."

"That's really very nice of you, thanks. Thank you."

"Not at all. We'll talk soon." And he stepped back and the doors slid shut.

Angie was grateful to be away from him. She didn't know if he was simply taking an interest in her or if he wanted to keep tabs on her. Wouldn't he direct someone else, a lackey, to track her? Would he really do it himself? Maybe he really was interested in helping guide her career. If so, she could try to leverage that into learning more about what happened to Scarlett.


"He asked you to lunch?" Nicole said with surprise that night, an edge in her voice. They stood in Angie's kitchen with glasses of merlot. A spread of food—Greek salad, chicken skewers, and hummus, the best Angie could throw together last minute—sat on the island, but Nicole hadn't touched it. Charles's invitation seemed to be of more interest.

"I think he's just making sure I'm okay at the studio after what happened with Scarlett," Angie explained, not sure if she believed herself. "He sounded almost paternal."

Nicole gave her a dubious expression. "Charles is not paternal," she said archly, sipping her wine. "There is nothing paternal about Charles Weaver."

"Okay, but what am I going to say? 'Gee, thanks, Charles, but you're not my type'?"

"The problem is not whether he's your type, it's whether you're his, if you get my meaning."

"Oh, come on. It's just lunch."

"Honey, Charles is an operator of the first order. With Charles it's never just lunch or just anything."

"Does he have a wife? A girlfriend?" Not that it mattered. She wouldn't consider getting involved with him regardless. He was the boss, and despite his charisma, Angie didn't find him attractive at all.

"Not that I know of. He usually takes another exec, like Tanya, or an actress starring in one of his movies to events. It seems like it's just business."

"And there you have it. It's just business." Nicole was making her anxious. "I think he asked my sister out once. Casually, anyway."

"I'm not surprised."

"Because she was beautiful?"

"Not just that. Beautiful women aren't hard to come by out here. But your sister didn't seem like the usual paint-by-numbers actress. You know—a big flirt, to put it politely, or a partier. I got the feeling she was someone who wouldn't just crawl into bed for the next gig."

"And Charles . . . would have liked that?"

"Well, it's a challenge, isn't it, to date someone who isn't easy to charm versus a hundred other women who are throwing themselves at you in the hopes of being cast?"

"You always want what you can't have?"

"That's it. Men like Charles like challenges. They want what they can't have because they have so much."

Angie remembered what Charles had said about Rogers Hornsby's bat. How hard it was to get. How much he offered the guy in St. Louis. How gratifying that was. *It's not about baseball at all. It's about winning. Especially when the prize is all but out of reach.*

"Does that sound okay?"

Angie snapped out of her thoughts. "What? Sorry, I was . . ."

"Lost in thought?" Nicole supplied. "I asked if we could have dinner by the pool. It looks so beautiful out there."

They wandered outside with plates and glasses and settled into chaise longues. "It's incredible." Nicole gestured to the artfully lit, landscaped garden. The fruit trees, lemon and grapefruit, were dormant, though they provided shade over the rectangular pool. "Are you getting used to being here? I can imagine it must be hard sometimes."

"I actually find it comforting. It makes me feel closer to Scarlett. I hope that doesn't sound weird."

"Not at all." Nicole looked out at the pool. "It looks so inviting."

"The pool was freezing, but I had the heating turned on and it's finally ready for a party."

"A party, eh?"

Angie didn't know why that made her feel shy. Was she blushing?

They sat quietly, looking out at the darkening twilight, making small talk as they ate. Angie hoped the deepening shadows would hide any awkwardness she felt being alone with Nicole. She didn't know where her self-consciousness had suddenly come from.

Finally, Nicole broke the silence. "Why don't we have that party now?"

"Party?" Angie couldn't even remember what she'd last said.

"You know, a pool party."

"Oh, right!" Did she want to strip down to her skivvies in front of a coworker? Not just a coworker, but her boss? But through the shadows, she could see Nicole grinning mischievously and it empowered her. "You know? Absolutely. Let's break this baby in."

Fifteen minutes later, having raided Scarlett's closet, they were both in bathing suits, Angie's a white one-piece, Nicole's a deep green bikini. Nicole headed to the diving board, while Angie flipped a switch near the house, lighting up the pool from within, rotating colors of blue, yellow, green, orange, red, purple.

"It's the Pride pool!" Nicole quipped, climbing to the diving board, while Angie sat at the side, dangling her feet in the water.

"You're not coming in?" Nicole asked, shivering. "It's warmer in than out!"

"I'm new from New York. May in LA is warm to me."

"Well, it's chilly to the rest of us. So see you when I come back up!" She plugged her nose and jumped into the water, creating a colossal splash. Angie couldn't help but laugh. Nicole had a lust for life that she wished she had herself.

"This is fantastic!" Nicole gasped when she came up for air. She took a few strokes toward Angie. "You really should join me."

This wasn't what Angie had imagined when she'd asked Nicole over. She had hoped to learn something, about Charles, about DreamWeaver, about Scarlett. But she needed a friend. She needed down time. She needed to fucking relax. So she gave a sly grin and slid off the edge into the water.

"You call that an entrance?"

"Maybe it wasn't exactly Oscar-worthy . . ."

"I see LA's already got its claws into you." Nicole swam to the edge of the pool by the diving board, where she hung off the wall with one arm.

Angie swam over and floated alongside her. There was a rush of wind in the palms and then nothing. She let her legs rise in front of her, bracing herself against the edge. She felt light. Like she would get what she'd come for. Like things were right. Well, as right as they could be, considering Scarlett.

"I'm glad you invited me over tonight. It's been a tonic." Nicole raised her left hand up to the side of Angie's face.

Angie froze. Her heart was beating so fast she was certain it would set the water rippling. Was Nicole coming on to her? Did she want her to be? What was happening?

Then Nicole pulled back and swam to the other end of the pool, leaving Angie feeling the place on her cheek where she had been touched. Nicole climbed out of the pool and walked back to the diving board again, and Angie realized it had simply been a tender moment. No more. No less.

As Angie locked up, she closed the sliding glass doors and gazed out over the dark pool, no more rainbow lights setting a mood. The moon cast stark and angular shadows over the yard, and her memory. *Did we really swim?* It seemed unreal. As did Nicole's touch.

Angie realized she hadn't felt so free in so long she couldn't even remember. Was it Nicole? The pool? LA? She felt limitless. Present. Clearheaded. Maybe because she had a purpose that went beyond herself.

"Do you know I'm here, Scar?" she whispered in the quiet. *I need to know what happened to you. That's the only reason I'm here.*


As soon as Angie arrived at the office the next morning, Charles's assistant called. Charles had an unexpected opening in his schedule, and could she have lunch with him that day? She was taken aback by the speed of the invitation but felt she had to accept, though she kept in mind Nicole's comment about him being an "operator of the first order."

At 11:30 a.m., she got word that Charles's driver would pick her up at noon outside the building's main entrance and they would meet at the restaurant. She was downstairs at 11:58 and exactly two minutes later, a sleek, black car pulled up curbside and whisked her away to what looked like a French chalet, with a pitched roof and wooden beams and lots of windows. There was hardly room for twenty guests, making it quite intimate. She spotted Charles at a corner table. She was nervous, her peace of the night before having evaporated with the call from his assistant.

He stood when she approached, something she didn't expect. "Angie, you look terrific." He clutched both her hands in his, totaling enveloping them. The host pulled out her chair and, as they sat, Charles delivered a glance commanding him to pour her a glass of chilled white wine.

"Thank you," she said. "I usually don't drink during a workday . . ."

"When the boss drinks, you drink." Charles gave a throaty laugh and lifted his glass. "Here's to new beginnings." He clinked with Angie and they each took a sip. Then Charles turned his attention to an obliging waiter, who had replaced the host. "Marco, I'd love it if the chef could whip us up some of that fabulous white sea bass, like I had last week? It came with a marvelous salsa. I hope you like fish." He pivoted to Angie.

She nodded slightly.

"Yes, of course, Mr. Weaver." The waiter was obsequious. "It was a citrus salsa, I believe. We can get that for you. May I recommend the chilled shrimp with fennel to start, sir?"

"Yes, yes, I think so. That sounds very nice, thank you."

"Of course, sir." Marco topped off their wine, even though Angie had taken only a sip, then slipped away.

"So, tell me, what's happening for you right now in Development?" Charles focused on her with a direct intensity.

Her nervousness spiked. This was what she had wanted, why she was in LA, and yet she found herself unprepared, emotionally, psychologically. *Careful what you wish for?* Regardless, she had to play the part she'd cast herself in. She had to channel Scarlett's confidence. "We've been talking about so many great possibilities. A drama set in the Calico mines. Another is a period thriller with a female lead, and there's one really hot book we're getting the rights to, a bestseller that's a super-exciting coming-of-age story with a lot of twists and turns." She sounded silly, like a teenager.

"Well, that's terrific."

*Is he surprised? Maybe I don't sound like a frivolous fourteen-year-old. Or maybe he had doubts I could pull my weight.*

"The writer, Mackenzie Martin, is represented by my old boss, Rita Ray, in New York, so I handled that deal." She didn't want to brag, but it was important Charles knew she was succeeding at her job.

"What's the book called again?" His phone dinged and he glanced at it.

"*Peregrine.* It's on the *New York Times* bestseller list and I think it'll make a gripping film—"

"Well, of course. We buy a lot of intellectual property rights and options, but whether any given project makes it to production depends on many factors. The most important thing here is that you maintain close ties with the New York publishers and are in touch with writers. That's what we need, to get the first crack at what's new and hot." He paused to take a large swallow of wine. "Does your writer friend—what was her name again?"

"Mackenzie Martin."

"Well, I'm sure the book is wonderful. You've read it, haven't you? I'm sure you have. I hired you because you have great taste in writing."

"I've read it, twice, actually—"

"Excellent." Charles picked up his phone and began typing.

Was the conversation over? She waited patiently. And then he set his phone aside and looked back at her. "So, this Mackenzie Martin, she wrote, what did you say it was? A coming-of-age story?"

Angie nodded.

Charles drained his wineglass and poured himself another. "You know, my problem with coming-of-age stories is they're all essentially the same. You're young, you get traumatized, you break free, a good thing happens, you move on. The end."

Angie drank from her wine just to have something to do. Getting Charles to green-light anything was obviously difficult, even where a bestseller was concerned. But his track record showed he had good instincts for which stories would make original, compelling movies. So she had to trust he would see the value in *Peregrine*.

"The question is, what makes your coming-of-age story any different?" he asked.

"Well, the crux of it is that this young woman is trying to overcome all these obstacles that never should have been in her path in the first place because she doesn't know the truth about her family background, so she's stuck on this remote ranch—" She was grateful he cut her off because she was babbling.

"Don't worry about explaining the story." Charles finished his wine and wiped his mouth with a napkin. "I mean, we would hire a screenwriter and an entire creative team, plus our attorneys would have to vet anything that implicated real people, all that legal business. But does she get assaulted? Attacked? Does someone die or get beaten? What are the flashpoints?"

Angie felt like she'd been slapped on the nose. She hadn't prepared a bulleted list. "Well, she's emotionally abused, more than anything, but her aunt and uncle also hit the kids as a means of discipline."

"Okay . . ."

"Um . . . there's a sexual relationship between teenagers as they grow up in this harsh environment, there's an escape through the night, a bus ride, mistaken identity. It's got a lot. Plus, they're on this ranch, so there's storms and working the land and cattle and sheep—"

Charles burst out laughing. "Well, say no more if it's got cattle!" His laughter faded and he lowered his voice. "You are really something, Angie. I like your confidence. Honestly, I can't think of anyone else who would have had the guts to pitch me a movie by saying it's got cattle and sheep."

Angie swallowed hard, focusing on her wineglass. *Remember what Nicole said early on: He likes people who speak their mind. You didn't do anything wrong. Breathe. Breathe.* When she looked up, she realized Charles was still amused.

"Yeah, well, we wouldn't have to focus on, you know, the livestock." She attempted to join the joke. "But it's a very American sort of story."

"Hmmm. Well, that is something to consider. I'll have to light a fire under Nicole. I'm having her overhaul a database of IP so everything is in one place and I can see what we have and where we should focus our efforts next."

That was the monumental job Nicole had said she was working on. Marco appeared and refilled their wine. Angie had only drunk a few sips of her glass, but he topped her off again and brought them fresh glasses of water with lemon slices.

"Tell me, how are your parents faring these days?" Charles asked. "I can't fathom such a loss. If I recall, your father is a professor, yes? Has he resumed teaching?"

*He knows my father's job?* "Did you meet my parents? I mean, when they came out here? After Scarlett's death?"

"Very briefly. I wanted, of course, to express my condolences. But I do remember talking to Scarlett, and it was clear how close your family was. She spoke of you with great fondness." He smiled like a kindly uncle, lines crinkling his eyes.

"Yes, we were very close." Angie felt a little shaken.

"So, to answer your question, yes, I only met your parents briefly, but what Scarlett said stuck with me. I knew she grew up on Long Island, had a couple of professional parents, was your typical popular girl."

"She wasn't typical," Angie blurted.

Charles assessed her for several seconds. "I'm sorry, I just meant . . ."

Angie's throat constricted. She tried to swallow.

Then Charles reached across the table, taking one of her hands in his. "I should have chosen my words more carefully. What I meant was that Scarlett was a class act from a good background. No crazy skeletons in the closet, no emotional problems or drug addiction or anything that can create problems in the work environment. I didn't mean to sound insensitive." He gave her hand a squeeze before releasing it. "Everyone has their challenges, myself included. But when someone brings their problems to work every day, it can be a real nightmare. You were palling around with Patricia Bartlett at the Oscars. Helluva girl and actor, but between you and me, she has gotten just impossible to work with. If she doesn't start to behave, she can kiss her career goodbye. No one will touch her. It's not worth the trouble."

Angie had no idea what to say, but she wanted to keep the conversation flowing. "Yes, I know Patricia was friends with Scarlett."

"That was true. But Scarlett knew a great many people. And was well-liked."

"Do you know how Patricia is doing?"

"She's a survivor. I'm sure she'll do just fine."

He drained his wineglass as Marco arrived with a platter of shrimp adorned with fennel shavings. "Shall I serve, sir?"

"Yes, thank you." Charles sat back and gazed at Angie, smiling slightly as the waiter filled her small appetizer plate, added a drizzle of herb-infused olive oil, did likewise for Charles, then disappeared.

"It's a mortal sin to leave good wine, n'est-ce pas?" Charles poured her more, then emptied the bottle into his glass. Angie hoped it wouldn't dull her senses too much. She had work to do that afternoon.

"I have to confess," Charles said, "I find you a charming and intelligent woman. I wanted us to get a chance to get to know one another. I would really love to get together outside of work, perhaps for a late dinner some night, or a screening? I have a screening room in my home. It comes in handy in our business, naturally."

Angie felt her body stiffen and she drew herself up, sitting straighter. "I'm flattered, truly." She was suddenly grateful she'd had a little wine. It made her braver. "But I feel as though my plate is pretty full just now, being out here with a new job and living at my sister's, and I just need, you know, some more time to get settled and all that. I love working at DreamWeaver but it is keeping me busy . . ." She regarded Charles's eyes. There was something unreadable in them. But his voice belied no anger or frustration.

"Of course, that's completely understandable. Take all the time you need. No need to rush."

Angie knew that no matter how much time she took, her answer would never be any different. But she couldn't say that. So she tried to be friendly—all the better to give the impression that it wasn't him, and to keep the lines of communication open. She couldn't alienate him or make him suspicious. "Thank you. It's been a real process to heal."

Charles was quiet for a few moments, taking her in, then suddenly looked around. "Marco?"

The server materialized immediately, as though he had been lying in wait. "Yes, sir, what can I get you?"

"I need to get out of here quickly. Please, get Miss Norris whatever she would like. I hope that's all right, Angie, I need to be getting back."

"Oh. But you haven't eaten yet." She wasn't worried about lunch, she just didn't understand what was going on. What had she done wrong?

"That's all right. I'll catch something at the office. But you stay as long as you like."

"Oh. No. I have so much work to do. I should head back, too."

"Whatever you want." He was already standing.

Marco politely placed the bill on the table. Charles signed the check and handed him folded bills. "Thank you, Marco. Your service was sterling, as always."

Marco almost curtsied as he said, "Thank you very much, Mr. Weaver. I look forward to seeing you again, sir."

Tips like that probably bought Charles a lot of deference. "I'll just pop into the ladies' and meet you at the entrance, if that's okay?"

"Sure. We can head out together." Charles's mind seemed elsewhere already.

She went off to find the bathroom, which had a sign reading FEMMES on it. Just as she pushed the door open, a slender, attractive woman rushed up, followed her into the single-stall room, and closed it behind them, locking it with a click. She turned and nervously faced Angie, oddly out of breath. "You're Scarlett Norris's sister."

"Yes. I'm sorry, do I know you?" Angie found the woman's full dark hair and perfectly contoured face striking. Her vibrant turquoise eyes flashed with an intense urgency.

"I watched your speech. At the Oscars. It was beautiful, very moving."

"Thanks."

"I saw you having lunch with Charles Weaver."

"Yes. I work at DreamWeaver now. Did you know Scarlett?"

"No, I've just come out here from New York. But I want to warn you about Charles."

Holy shit. "Warn me? What do you mean?"

"Listen, I shouldn't say anything, but you need to be careful. Charles is a dangerous guy. Last year in New York, he came to the play I was doing and said he wanted to cast me in a feature he was producing. I knew what he demanded from actresses in order to get cast and I wasn't going to bang some ugly, fat guy every time I wanted a part, so I told him to go screw himself."

"Wait, he wanted you to—"

"I lost my agent a day later. No one would touch me. So I went to Europe and did a couple small films. I'm lucky that I have any career left at all. With Charles, if you don't 'play nice,' play things his way, he lashes out. Get out of there the minute you sense things are going south. Men like Charles have a lot of power. A lot. You have no idea."

"Who are you? I came here to find out what happened to Scarlett. Maybe we could meet sometime."

The woman shook her head. "No. He can't know I talked to you. Just be careful."

She reached behind her and opened the door, looked around, and left, leaving Angie with a zillion thoughts racing through her head. She took a towel, wet it with cold water, and dabbed her face. Charles was waiting. She'd have to sort things out later. But that actress had just given her more information in a ladies' room than she'd gotten in weeks of sleuthing.

She used a towel to blot the moisture from her face, then hurried to the front of the restaurant, but when she got there, she found that Charles had gone. The maître d' approached and told her Mr. Weaver had sent another car for her, arriving momentarily.

Angie waited in the bright Los Angeles sunshine, reeling.

Angie arrived to meet Jango Davies at the small Indian grocery in Glendale promptly at 7:00 p.m. The store was narrow and stacked with items both familiar and unfamiliar, and in the back was a tiny restaurant, just two tables each with two chairs. The dining area was empty aside from a solitary Black man biting into a samosa. He wore a weather-beaten leather jacket and slouchy jeans. On the table before him was an open paperback. He looked relaxed, but when she approached, he looked up and she perceived a wariness in his green eyes. His hair was receding, and his face had wrinkles, but those eyes were intense and bright.

"Miss Norris?" he queried, half standing and motioning to the other chair at the table. "Please have a seat."

She had hardly sunk into it before an Indian woman was there with a notepad. Angie ordered a veggie burger and a large chai, and then introduced herself to the investigator. He was taller and maybe a little older than she had expected, but he appeared astute. That was the only thing that mattered.

Slowly, over the next half hour, she told him about Scarlett and the mysterious message she'd received in New York, the journal, the woman she'd met in the restaurant after her bizarre lunch with Charles, how she knew something was amiss and she needed to find out what. She pulled the note with the police information out of her purse and set it on the table. "The cops said there was no report matching that number when I went to the precinct. But there must be something to it. Wouldn't a crazed fan just, I don't know, post tributes to Scarlett on Reddit? Or conspiracy theories about her death?"

Jango looked over the paper with its scant details. "I think your instincts are good, Miss Norris. Clearly this means something. The question is why wouldn't they just come out and say it? Why hide behind anonymity? Why speak in code? What do they have to lose by coming clean?"

Angie exhaled with relief. He believed her. She hadn't realized she wasn't expecting that until that moment. "Those are really good questions. I hadn't thought about what they might have to lose."

"Even the person on the lowest rung on the totem pole has something to fear from the person on the second-lowest rung."

"So it might not even be some power player, you're saying."

"If someone was involved in your sister's death, this could have come from literally anyone."

What Jango was saying blew open the doors on all of Hollywood.

How would she even move forward? She knew how. By engaging his services.

"I'd really like your insight, help on this," she told him.

"I'm not sure what I can do for you, but I'm willing to make some initial inquiries, Miss Norris. I charge ninety an hour, plus expenses. You all right with that?"

Angie nodded. She would call her mother the next day and tell her she wanted to take her up on the money she'd offered when Angie first told her parents she was moving to LA. She didn't want to be beholden to them, but there was really no choice. Even though she was living rent free, her salary was just enough to keep her in groceries, pay for the basics, and keep the car rolling. She was glad she didn't have to worry about her wardrobe for the time being, thanks to Scarlett's closet.

"Whatever it takes, Mr. Davies. I know something pushed Scarlett over the edge."

"Okay, Miss Norris. I'll be in touch."

# 9

A week and a half later, Angie and Nicole were camped out in Angie's living room, Nicole stretched on the plush carpet, her laptop screen glowing on the nearby coffee table. Angie had mentioned helping out on the IP database project the same day Charles had suggested it during their lunch, and Nicole had quickly brought her on. After work they had set up at Scarlett's. Angie liked being home. And she liked having Nicole there.

The job was as big as both Nicole and Charles had implied. They needed to update the studio's old, incomplete database going back over twenty years by adding missing information, such as dates for options and writers' and their representatives' contact information (why such critical information had been overlooked, Angie couldn't understand), and listing newer IP. Some information was available at DreamWeaver in other forms, such as paper copies, but much of the data they needed had to be obtained or cross-checked by contacting agents, publishers, or copyright lawyers. Charles was putting pressure on Nicole to wrap up the project as soon as possible, thus the need to put in after-work and weekend hours.

"Here's what I still don't get." Angie sat back on the couch, her laptop perched on her legs. "Why were all these options renewed, years back, when none of the stories ever went into development? Almost all the books I've checked had eighteen-month options that were renewed. But virtually none of those titles were produced. We must have wanted to make movies out of them at some point. I mean, why spend money on something you have no interest in?"

"Because it's cheap."

"Cheap?"

Nicole sat up. "Look, a book can be optioned for a year, a year and a half, and then renewed for another year or eighteen months, so you get two or three years to figure out if you want to buy the rights. You're buying time to figure out if it's worth pursuing."

"And if you decide you don't want to make it, you just let the option expire?"

"Or you buy the rights before it expires, or you renew again if you need more time to decide. The key is moving within the time frame to lock in the rights in perpetuity and negotiating a price to do that."

"In perpetuity? Why would you do that if you have no intention of making a movie? Why wouldn't you just let the option run out?"

"Well, we're still deciding if we want to make the movie, aren't we? And sometimes shit just gets lost in the process. And sometimes . . . sometimes we want it to."

"Want it to what?"

"Can I get some water?"

Was she being evasive?

"Sure. There's also a pitcher of iced tea in the fridge." She didn't know how far to push, though it seemed she should know everything so she could do her job. But if Nicole was being dodgy, would she draw attention to herself if she asked more pointed questions?

She grabbed a pile of manila folders that contained recent contracts. Thumbing through an unsigned contract that spelled out the terms for an eighteen-month option with a chance to renew, she realized it was for another writer Rita represented. Alexandra Gold was a native New Yorker who had written a searing account of how domestic violence destroyed three generations of women in her family. The contract specified that a flat rate of one hundred thousand dollars would be paid for exclusive rights to the book during the option period.

"I have no idea if this is a pending deal or was just floated as a proposal," Angie said when Nicole came back and sat beside her. "It's new, too, so there won't be any material in the database."

"Just make an entry and we'll run down the rest of the information."

Angie opened the database document on her laptop and added an entry for Alexandra's book. "You know, there are a lot of titles in here with absolutely no other details. Some of the older ones, I thought maybe they'd been produced years back, possibly with different movie titles, because I didn't recognize the names, but there's not a trace of them in the studio's production archives. It's like they're phantoms."

"That's exactly why we're updating the database. Too much information is missing or scattered, and Charles wants one up-to-date, consolidated place where we can all quickly look and search, by title or author or time period, to see what IP the studio owns. Right now, it's a hot mess."

Angie shut her laptop. Nicole made sense, but she still had a nagging feeling she was being intentionally evasive. She'd have to do some more digging. At the moment, her neck was stiff from hours on the computer, and she started doing half-circle neck rolls.

"Here, let me help with that." Nicole indicated for Angie to pivot on the couch so she was facing away from her and she could put her hands on her shoulders. "I had a roommate once who was a massage therapist, and I learned a few things."

Angie would have usually sworn off an offer of help, especially one as intimate as a massage, but she allowed Nicole to work her fingers into her tightly knotted shoulders. Despite not knowing her real intentions, Angie found herself liking Nicole. Perhaps more than she should.

"Yikes, talk about muscle tension. Girl, you are wound like a spool of thread." Nicole worked methodically from the base of Angie's neck to the outside of her shoulders and back again, then ran her knuckles up and down either side of her backbone.

"Wow, you are good at this," Angie said as she felt herself relax.

"You ain't seen nothing." Nicole laughed and patted her shoulders. "Lie down for a couple of minutes so I can get at this back."

"You don't have to do that." Angie rolled her shoulders back and forth. "It already feels better."

"Nah, let me have more of a go. You'll sleep better, I promise." Nicole stood. "Lie on the carpet, on your stomach."

"Um . . . okay." Angie wasn't comfortable but arguing made her even less comfortable so she stretched out on the floor and Nicole climbed onto her backside, straddling her body so she had more leverage to knead her back.

*This is awkward*, Angie thought, but she didn't interrupt the process. She'd always had a hard time relaxing. At the moment, however, she was growing calmer as Nicole worked the knots out of her back.

Angie considered how spare her life had been in terms of human connection. She had developed few emotional ties to anyone outside her family and a few colleagues. She told herself it was a product of her need to keep her life closely regulated.

*But I have Scotty. And Rita. And crazy Joaquin. I'm not alone in this world.* She breathed deeply. *I can do this. For Scar.* Her mind went back to work.

"What will happen to Alexandra Gold's contract?" She turned her face to the side so Nicole could hear her.

"Who?"

"An author. She's one of those floaters in the database. If we buy the rights, how good are the chances she'll get a film out of it?"

"Hard to say." Nicole put pressure on the hollows under Angie's shoulder blades with her thumbs.

"And if a movie doesn't happen?" She remembered how hard it had seemed to please Charles when they'd discussed book plots over lunch.

"Well, sometimes writers can get their rights back if the contract allows for that and they compensate the studio for any money that went into development. That might be worth it if they had a commitment from another studio. Anyway, these are questions for the lawyers. We find the IP and convince the writers to sign with us. The lawyers handle the details." She hopped off Angie's back and sat on the floor, leaning against the sofa. "How are you now, better?"

"Better, much better. I could probably go to sleep right here." They laughed, but Angie was wondering if Nicole was equivocating, avoiding direct answers to her questions. What was DreamWeaver doing with all these contracts? If they were being consciously buried, why would Nicole be tasked with organizing them?

Angie was groggily making coffee Saturday morning when her phone buzzed. She was exhausted from working in the office during the day and then laboring late into the evenings on the database project but snapped awake when she saw the text.

> Ms. Norris this is PI Davies.
> I'd like to see you as soon as
> possible. Can we arrange
> something for today? Same place?

> > Yes, of course.

> 3 p.m.?

> > I'll be there.

Angie felt a surge of anticipation. She was adding almond creamer to her mug, lost in thought, when the doorbell rang, causing her to jump and nearly drop the container.

What now? Amazon? A neighbor? But when she opened the front door, she faced a delivery man holding an orchid with creamy blossoms and shiny dark leaves.

"Angela Norris?" he asked. She nodded. "Can you sign?"

"Are you sure it's for me? I can't imagine who would send—"

"There's a card. Sign here, please."

Angie did as she was instructed, then took the orchid inside where she placed it on the coffee table and plucked out the card.

Dear Angie,

I've learned that white orchids can mean several things. Humility. Purity. Elegance. Beauty. I can think of no better tribute to such a lovely woman. Enjoy. Until next time.

-C.

*C? Dear God, it has to be. Who else?* Charles would make sure there was a next time, even though she'd been clear she didn't want to see him outside work. The more she looked at the orchid, the more her breathing became erratic.

She got up and paced. *Stay calm, stay calm.* She repeated the mantra, trying to keep the stress and anxiety at bay. *Stay calm. Don't panic. Think. Think it through. There is no real threat.*

*Is there?*

There were two ways to handle it. If she told him to back off, she figured she'd get fired and not learn any more about Scarlett. Or she could thank him but stick to her guns about not dating—maybe a fiancé in New York—buy herself some time. He was a powerful man but he was just testing her to see how far he could get.

Charles could escalate the pressure with calls, invitations, or, God forbid, surprise visits to her home. The last possibility sent a shudder through her. She couldn't help but look at the orchid accusingly. Then she turned her back to it and went outside the sliding doors to the pool, where she called Scott. She needed to hear a familiar voice.

"Hey, kiddo," he answered. "I was just saying to Sarah that I hadn't talked to you in a while. How are you? How's the big bad movie scene?"

"Oh, you know. It's good. I'm kind of confused about some stuff, though, and feel a little lost, I guess."

"That sounds pretty normal for a new job, especially considering you just uprooted your whole life."

"Yeah. I guess."

She heard him say off to the side, "Hang on, I'll be there in a minute, I'm talking to Aunt Angie."

She hesitated to bring up Scarlett. Or Charles. But they were all she could think about. She didn't want to unload on him so much as just have his presence.

"Can you ask your mother?" His voice got louder. "Sarah, can you help Michelle? I'm on the phone with Angie."

"Look, it sounds busy there. I'm going to let you go. I'm doing fine." Something occurred to her. Although Scarlett's clothes and books and other property remained in LA, a lot of her personal papers, including bank statements and calendars and the like, had all been sent to New York after her death so the family's attorneys could sort out her estate and personal affairs. The only reason Angie had found the lotus-embossed journal was because it had been stuck behind that desk drawer. "Scotty, listen, before you go, I need you to do something for me."

"Shoot."

"I want you to go to Mom and Dad's and look through Scarlett's things in the basement—the boxes that were sent back last year. I'm looking for journals, calendars, anything she might have written in."

"Ange, what are you doing? I hope you're not going down some rabbit hole looking for answers. We've been through this. We'll never know why Scarlett did what she did. It's not knowable. You need to take care of yourself."

"I'm fine, I'm doing well, actually, but this is important to me. Please, Scotty?"

He exhaled, loudly. She knew he was considering. "Okay, fine. I'll go over tomorrow. I'll ask Mom when Dad's going to be out of the house. I gotta go."

"Thanks, Scotty. Love you. Miss you too."

"I'm coming!" he shouted impatiently and then back into the phone said, "Yeah, kiddo, miss you too. Talk soon."

Angie hung up and gazed at the pool, the crystalline blue water shimmering from the light wind. The day was quiet, the ocean far enough away she could only imagine its purr. She closed her eyes, willing herself to think of anything but the orchid. The next thing she knew, she heard knocking from the front of the house. What now?

She opened the door to Nicole's smiling face. "I brought avocado toast!" Her smile faded a bit. "Did you forget I was coming to work today?"

"Oh, my God, no," Angie lied. "I just totally lost track of time. I called my brother, and we were talking, catching up. Is it already eleven?"

"Yes, ma'am. Past. Eleven-fourteen to be exact."

*Fuck. I have to push Jango back.*

Once they were inside, she plucked the card off the orchid before Nicole could see it. She didn't want to get into a discussion about Charles. "I'll be right with you, okay?" She ducked into a downstairs bathroom and texted Jango.

> Forgot boss was coming
> over to work.

> Can you meet later?

Twenty minutes later, as Angie and Nicole sat at opposite ends of the kitchen table with their laptops, Angie's phone buzzed.

> How late?

> Five?

Okay, see you then.

"Everything okay?" Nicole had a quizzical expression on her face.

"Yes, I just have to meet someone. Later, though."

"A date?" She seemed amused, but Angie couldn't read her expression.

"No, just . . . some personal business. Anyway, I wanted to ask you about this batch of old contracts I'm trying to input."

They worked through midafternoon, stopping for a quick lunch break, until Nicole had had enough. "Do you think we could have a quick swim?" she asked.

A few minutes later, they were in bathing suits out by the pool. Nicole was poised on the diving board, extending her arms and then circling them up to meet overhead, a motion she repeated a few times.

"What are you doing?" Angie knew a swim would invigorate her but couldn't muster the energy to get into the water so she reclined on a chaise.

"Swan dive!" Nicole shouted. "Muscle memory. Trying to get the arm motion fluid." She raised her index finger as if to say "Wait a minute," moved to the edge of the board, took a few breaths, then leapt forward, her arms thrust out and her back arched. She brought her arms together over her head just as she entered the water with a small splash.

"Not bad, but not perfect either!" she yelled as she surfaced and swam to the side of the pool where Angie sat.

"It looked good to me."

"I feel like I'm eight again, swimming with my sisters. We'd have races and diving contests and inevitably one of my uncles would jump in and make such a huge splash that everyone practically got soaked." She smiled at the memory.

"You had a pool?"

"One of our aunts did. We had these epic summer days over there. All the cousins running around, huge aluminum foil pans of chicken, sweet corn, salad, mac and cheese. The adults would drink beer. It was just great. Innocent and wild and not a care in the world, you know?"

"I don't, actually," Angie admitted. "I mean, I never really felt care-free growing up. Scarlett did, though. And she would try to get me to do things, go along with her and her friends and try to pull me out of my shell."

"Did it work?"

"Did I come out of my shell? No." The confession made her a bit sad. "But Scarlett was great. It made us close. And I think it made me stronger inside to know there was someone who cared so much about me, someone I could lean on." She got lost in her head for a moment before remembering she had a guest. "Anyway . . ."

"I should probably get going," Nicole said. "Just need to change. Is it cool if I take a quick shower? I'd like to get the chlorine off of me."

"Sure. I'll show you where everything is. Follow me."

Angie led Nicole into the guest bathroom, pointing out the linen shelf with freshly laundered towels. "Here's the shower and there's soap and shampoo here too."

"I've seen a shower before." Nicole teased.

Angie suddenly embarrassed, didn't know what to say.

"Unless you were planning to join me?"

Angie stood there for a breathless beat. "Oh. Um. I don't . . . I don't think that would be . . ."

Nicole laughed. "I was totally kidding. It seemed like you were going to jump in there with me."

"Oh, God, no, of course, I'm just . . . I'll get out of your way."

"Try to relax a little. Everything isn't that complicated, trust me." Nicole bopped Angie on the head with the folded towel and waited for her to leave and close the door.


Angie arrived in Glendale and dashed into the Indian restaurant just after five o'clock. Jango was already there, drinking tea. The place was deserted except for another man scrolling through his phone.

"Sorry I had to postpone," she said by way of greeting. "My boss. She . . . um, threw me off."

"Absolutely not a problem. Tea?" Jango offered to pour from a pot on the table as a waiter came over with a plate of naan and a container of green chutney. Angie nodded as she slid into the seat across from him. "Help yourself." Jango indicated the food as he tilted the liquid into a glass.

"Thank you. So did you find something out? About Scarlett?"

"Well, I think I told you, people in Hollywood talk a lot on one hand, gossip and the like, but when it comes to really powerful players, it can be hard to get real information. I'm retired LAPD. I've had many years of dealing with people in the industry."

"So you *didn't* find out anything?" Why was she there then?

"On the contrary, I found a great deal." He lowered his voice. "The person you asked about, the one who may have intimidated your sister, has quite a record. Not a criminal record. But he's a charmer who uses his power and his charisma to get a lot of women to sleep with him. Now that's not a crime. We all use what we have to attract who we want, am I right?"

Angie felt slightly embarrassed. "I suppose so."

"In the case of the person in question, it's not just about getting people in bed. It's about getting them in bed as a prerequisite for work. And threatening to destroy them if they don't comply. A few big names have done quite a few things to stay in this person's good graces, and it's paid off for them professionally."

Jango picked up his phone, tapped the screen a few times, then held it up so Angie could see it: a promo poster for *Wildflower Honey*. The blurb told of a farm girl who's abused by the local sheriff, leaves town, and returns to get even.

"It came out about twenty years ago. Recognize her?"

The farm girl was a young, fresh-faced Patricia Bartlett.

"Yes. She knew Scarlett. She's in the hospital."

"Not anymore," Jango reported. "She's out. And she talked to me. As did a handful of other actresses."

"People talked? Patricia talked? About *him*?" Angie felt breathless.

"It's not unusual for people to want to get things off their chest sometimes when they've been wronged or harmed. Some people, of course, never want to talk. Or they're afraid to. I had a few women hang up on me. One slammed the door in my face. Those who did talk made me promise I wouldn't reveal their identities. But I heard enough to draw clear conclusions. This sleazebag demands all sorts of sexual favors from these women, sometimes before, sometimes after he casts them. If they turn him down, he has them blacklisted so they can't get cast anywhere but middling projects or just crap no one gives a damn about. He's a class-A, number one abusive creep."

Angie both had to know and felt afraid to find out the truth. "And my sister?"

"I'm still working on that part of it," Jango said. "But if your sister had a major role in a film at DreamWeaver, she wouldn't have been able to get there, in all likelihood, without playing the same game."

"She wouldn't have. I know she wouldn't. It just wasn't her. But I know he asked her out during her last film. If she rejected him, maybe he got angry and lashed out?" A new, horrible thought came into her mind. "You think he killed her?"

"No, Miss Norris, I'm not saying that. But your sister was becoming a big-name actress. She was in a hit series, did the talk shows. That's high profile. You have to understand that if I keep digging, I may turn up some unsavory details about her that you may not want to accept." He leaned in. "If she gave in to this guy's demands, that doesn't make her culpable, please understand that."

Angie nodded.

"The movie industry is brutal, and actresses who want to get cast often feel they have no choice but to play the game. They're manipulated by the people who wield the power. And those people are, by and large, men—men who are used to getting what they want, at any cost. I've seen it many times, and not just in Hollywood."

Angie knew he was being straight with her. And it frightened her.

"And it will cost you more if I keep working, so that's something else to consider," he concluded. "Do you want me to keep digging?"

"Mr. Davies, you didn't know my sister. Scarlett would never have done anything sleazy or underhanded or unethical to get ahead. Not in Hollywood. Not anywhere. Whatever you find out, I want to know. And I can cover your fees and expenses, at least for now."

"Then I'll keep digging. I have to get home for dinner. I promised my wife." He gave her a rueful smile over his emptied plate. "You should get something to eat, though, the food here is good. And trust me, you're gonna need to keep up your strength if we dive deeper into the Hollywood cesspool."

# 10

In Scarlett's spare room, Angie focused on the graph she'd created on the whiteboard, a dry erase marker in one hand and a bottle of lime seltzer in the other. Since first filling it in, she'd continued adding names, titles, dates, any new information she accrued, including a list of movies the studio had put out over the past twenty years and every actress who had a leading or significant supporting role. She highlighted entries so she could trace the career trajectories of each actress to see if she could spot any patterns. The burning question—aside from what had happened to Scarlett—was whether the actresses ever worked again at the studio, and if not, was it because they had not given in to Charles's sexual demands?

She had an IMDbPro account at work but she couldn't risk researching contact info at the office, so she'd paid to create her own account at home, paranoia winning out, and was adding that info on a different chart, just to keep some of it separate for clarity's sake. Once she started figuring out some kind of method to the DreamWeaver madness, she hoped to find a through line that would lead her right to Scarlett.

She checked the printout from work and wrote another name on the board.

Naomi England*, lead, *Serious Intentions*, 2014, Oscar nomination, supporting actor

Angie looked her up on IMDbPro. After her one film at DreamWeaver, it seemed she had gone to Israel, where, according to her bio, she held dual citizenship, and ended up starring in a long-running TV series there. She also showed up in films and series in France, Sweden, and elsewhere in Europe.

Angie stepped back to assess her color-coded list. Gray and pink and green and orange and asterisks and arrows and circles. There was so much going on, it read like static. She knew there was something there, but she didn't know yet what it all meant. She hoped Jango would find something that would help frame the jigsaw pieces she'd scraped together.

Hungry, she took the lime seltzer and went to the kitchen to throw leftover mushroom pizza in the microwave. While she waited, she opened Spotify, hit shuffle on a random playlist, and moments later, strains from Judy Garland's iconic performance of "Get Happy" came from every speaker in every room in the house.

When Angie had visited Scarlett two years before, her sister had shared with her some unpleasant Hollywood lore including the grotesque way Garland had been fed uppers and downers as a teenager at MGM, leading to a lifetime of addiction. She continued to have extraordinary success on TV, the big screen, and the concert stage, but those pills ultimately led to her death at just forty-seven.

Shirley Temple married at seventeen to escape the advances of various men at the studios she worked for, and then carved an entirely different path for herself. Natalie Wood said she was brutally raped at sixteen by a major Hollywood star, but her mother told her to keep it quiet so as not to imperil her career. Hitchcock and his obsession with icy blondes led him to proposition Tippi Hedren when they were shooting *Marnie*, a movie where he called for a rape scene to be shot as explicitly as possible.

Angie could still hear Scarlett's voice with that uncharacteristic edge, and thought about all the women making their way in Hollywood since the industry began a hundred years ago. Some naive, some not, but all looking for work and a career in the movies where men headed the studios, directed and produced the movies, and ran the talent agencies. She wandered back to her whiteboard with her rubbery pizza and gazed at the names and DreamWeaver movie titles.

Melanie McClintock, lead, *A Crystal Conspiracy*, 2011
Melanie McClintock, supporting, *The Days and Nights of Fergal O'Grady*, 2012, Oscar nomination, supporting actor

She didn't win and didn't work for the studio again. Angie pulled up her profile on IMDb. Currently she only got the occasional TV gig.

Lisa Ann Jackson, supporting, *The Bird with the Purple Plumage*, 2008
Lisa Ann Jackson, supporting, *Let Them Eat Cake*, 2011

Angie had never heard of her. She did a Google search and found she was living in Santa Fe but had no acting credits after 2011.

Maria Cortez, supporting, *Time Benders*, 2006
Maria Cortez, lead, *A Distant Pier*, 2013
Maria Cortez, supporting, *Back When My Dad Drove a Buick*, 2016

A big name a decade ago, Cortez vanished from the public eye for a time and now only periodically showed up in indie films.

Patricia Bartlett, lead, *The Lie*, 2004
Patricia Bartlett, supporting, *Generation Why*, 2006

Patricia Bartlett, supporting, *Until September*, 2007, Oscar
nomination, supporting actor
Patricia Bartlett, lead, *Statue in the Rain*, 2015, Oscar nomination, best actor

According to what Angie read online, despite still getting cast, her
off-screen antics often got her into trouble and her roles were not as
high profile as they had been. Angie wondered how she was recovering from her accident and made a mental note to reach out. She had
been so kind to her the night of the Oscars, despite her blow up at the
restaurant the day she got hit.

Diane D'Arcy, lead, *Antigone's Sister*, 2012
Diane D'Arcy, lead, *Summerstorm*, 2016

D'Arcy was still working but mostly on Lifetime and *Law & Order*.

Mia Louise Tanner, supporting, *Way Station,* 2017

Smart, quirky, and beautiful with a reputation for going her own
way, Tanner had moved to New York, where she worked in theater and
did voice-over work.

So far, the only former DreamWeaver actor Angie had managed to
talk to was Audra Atkins, who'd moved to Northern California. She
had found Audra's marriage announcement online and tracked down
her husband, a tech entrepreneur in San Jose, via email. Audra had
emailed her back, much to Angie's surprise, and then called.

"My husband never liked me working there," Audra had explained.
"I'm happy to tell you what happened, but I'll only do it over the phone.
I don't trust putting anything in writing."

"I understand. Plausible deniability should the shit hit the fan."

"Oh, it already did that. Basically, Ben, that's my husband, heard things about Charles right after I did *Denim Blues* and didn't want me to work there again. Not that I had the choice."

"What did he hear?" Angie felt a flicker of trepidation.

"What we all heard. That Charles was mercurial and prone to angry outbursts. That his ego was huge, and he demanded complete control over his studio as if he were some sort of feudal lord, handing out roles and jobs in exchange for allegiance and other things. Oh, and then there were the trips. He and a bunch of DreamWeaver bigwigs would book these resort trips to the islands or Aspen, and the starlet du jour would get an invitation. Naturally, it was expected that you'd be Charles's bedmate on the trip. And if you complied, and he wasn't annoyed or bored with you by the end of it, you could expect a plum part in the next best project the studio developed."

Angie remembered the picture she'd seen on Oscar night of Tanya and Charles and a handful of glamorous people at a swanky ski resort. "How did your husband hear about all this?"

"Ben works in tech, and a lot of rich people in tech like to party with Hollywood types, actors and the like. He knows people who've been to parties and on trips and have seen Charles in action."

"I see. If you don't mind my asking, did anything bad happen to you at DreamWeaver? Any bad experiences? I'm trying to figure out why actors who worked there never went back."

"Well, when I first worked at the studio, I had a small part, so Charles didn't really take note of me. Plus, DreamWeaver wasn't as huge a deal as it is now, so he was working himself into the ground and probably couldn't afford as much free time to hang around sets and figure out how to indulge his fantasies. But when I was in *Denim Blues*, in a supporting role, I got a message one day that none other than Charles Weaver himself wanted to see me. Well, I'm not stupid. It was an okay part, but it wasn't Lady Macbeth. I knew he wasn't calling me in to congratulate me on my epic performance.

"Anyway, I get to the little office Charles has on set. We were on location, shooting in the desert for a few days, and it's crazy hot and he's in shorts and sandals, which is fine, and he tells me that he knows I've worked hard, wants to give me a bigger role in his next film.

"So, I'm like, 'Yeah, that would be great,'" Audra recalled. "Then he says he wants me to audition right there and then. And he would set up the scene for me, but I would improvise the lines with him. He says he wants to see how I handle myself, where I can go when I'm not bound by a script—some bullshit like that. And I kid you not, he hands me a robe and says, 'Put this on, and, please, nothing underneath, I need to see some authenticity here.'

"And I'm dumbstruck. Like, how dense do I look? So I say to him, 'Mr. Weaver, if you want me to audition, you'll have to get in touch with my agent and he can set something up.' And I flew out of there and back to my trailer. I call Ben—we were dating at the time. He goes ballistic. Says I'm never to work at DreamWeaver again.

"Well, that wasn't really an issue, because I didn't get called in for anything after that, at DreamWeaver or anywhere else," Audra concluded.

"Wow," Angie breathed.

"Hell, I got lucky. He could have locked the door and attacked me. He's a big guy."

*I don't think Scarlett was so lucky.*

"It hurt to leave LA, but Ben and I got married and moved to Menlo Park for his work. I do theater up here. I'm okay with how everything turned out." But she didn't sound okay with it. "Who knows, maybe someday I'll get back to film work or a series . . . It's a crapshoot—the industry. It can be an *inhospitable* place for women, and some just get a lot of bad breaks." Angie didn't know if Audra was including herself in that. "And, listen, I'm sorry about your sister." Then her voice hardened. "If you find out that sonofabitch had anything to do with her death, you nail him to a cross. And I just might help. Call me back anytime."

Angie was lying on the floor, going over the conversation in her mind as she looked at the whiteboard, but she couldn't keep her eyes open. *I need to get to bed. I can start again tomorrow.* But the next thing she knew, she was jolted awake by her phone.

"Hello," she answered, her voice thick with sleep.

"Did I wake you?"

Angie sat upright as if she'd gotten an electric shock. Charles! Why did she pick up without checking the number?

"Is everything all right?" She scrambled to her feet and ran downstairs to the front door to make sure it was bolted shut.

"Well, let me apologize," he purred into her ear. "I'm not that far from you, and I just wondered if I could talk you into meeting me for a drink. But I don't want to drag you out of bed. No man in his right mind would want to persuade a woman like you out of bed." He laughed lightly.

She ignored the innuendo as she checked the back sliding doors. "No, it's fine. I haven't quite turned in for the night yet."

*Is he here? Would he try to get in?* She broke into a sweat as she snapped off the kitchen light and surveyed the small bank of screens that monitored the property. They showed nothing unusual. Skulking to the foyer, she peeked out at the drive, toward the street. She saw nothing amiss but that didn't quite allay her fears. If he tried to come on the property, he'd trip a motion-sensor light. *I can call security. Or the police.*

"Angie. Are you still there?"

"Yeah. Yes. Of course. I'm just not feeling that great."

"Well, it doesn't sound like a good night for drinks then, but I won't take no for an answer forever." *And I can't put you off forever. Not if I want to catch you.* "Maybe this weekend? I would love to grab a glass of wine."

"That works."

"Glad to hear that, Angie." His tone had grown a bit sharper. "I'll be in touch." He hung up before she had a chance to say goodbye.

She went into the living room and lay down on the couch, pulling one of Scarlett's soft throws over her. It was chilly, and all she wanted to do was sleep and forget the world. Just for a night. The cool night and the warm blanket were cozy and she easily drifted off to sleep.

*She was a kid again, sitting between Scarlett and Scott in the back of their parents' old Land Rover on their way to the beach. Scarlett was to her left, and every time Angie looked over at her, she'd laugh, then turn her head to the window. When she glanced right, at Scott, he'd look at her and smile, then go back to staring straight ahead. The car was flooded with light and music was playing. She couldn't see her parents, but they must have been in front, navigating the family's path. The music got louder. Scarlett started to sing along. Scott chimed in. Angie tried to sing, but she didn't recognize the song. She tried to ask her sister and brother for help, but they couldn't hear her. They sang louder and louder. Soon the music was so loud, it filled the entire car. The Land Rover was going very fast then, hurtling down the road, faster and faster, as the light got brighter and brighter and the music grew louder and louder. Angie couldn't see the road anymore. The car felt like it had lost contact with the roadway. It was flying through the air in a sea of light. She could hear Scarlett, but when she turned to look, she was gone. Same with Scott. Angie started to scream. "Where are we going? Where are we going!"*

She woke suddenly, gasping. A dream about Scarlett, again! She was always there and then suddenly vanishing from reach. Angie tried to ward off her growing panic by rocking gently. *Breathe in, two, three, four. Out, two, three, four.* What was that music that was playing in the Land Rover? She couldn't quite dredge up the tune. But then she abruptly stopped swaying. She was really hearing music. Now

She sat up. It was unmistakable. Classical music, some sort of symphony. Outside. *Charles? He's here?* She wrapped the throw tightly around her and got up to peep through the spyglass in the front door. A white convertible was just pulling away, and in the dark of the night, she couldn't see the driver's face.

The light over the porch was on, meaning someone had walked

up to the front door, triggering the sensor. The vehicle was gone, but she didn't know how safe it was to open the door. Or if there was even reason to.

She turned the lock and slowly creaked the door open.

And there, on the *Bienvenue!* welcome mat, was a single red rose.

# 11

"Who do you think it was?" Nicole had come out to Angie's the next afternoon to wrap up their part of the database project so it could go to IT Monday for the final review and implementation. Angie had shown her the red rose, which lay wilting on the kitchen island. "You have a mystery admirer?"

Angie hadn't told her about the late-night call from Charles or let on that she was worried the rose was from him. She still wasn't sure how connected she was to the studio's leadership so she didn't know how freely she could speak.

"First an orchid, now a rose," Nicole pondered. "What's next?"

"The orchid was from my parents, remember?" Her phone vibrated. Rita. So she let it go to voice mail. She didn't know what was going on with Mackenzie and didn't want Nicole overhearing the conversation until she did know.

"Sure." Nicole gave a knowing smile.

"What does that mean?"

"You've clearly caught Charles's eye. It was obvious at the Oscars party. And then he took you out to lunch. Granted, dropping a rose on someone's doorstep isn't exactly his style, but still, I wouldn't be surprised if he wanted to get to know you *better*, so to speak."

Shit. Did Nicole know something or was she really just sussing it out? To get herself out of the situation, Angie excused herself to check her voice mail, and went out the sliding glass doors.

"Hey, Ange, honey, it's Rita. Call me, will ya? Mackenzie is driving me crazy. She's nervous, she hasn't heard anything since she signed the contract. Now, I know movies take time, but I want to tell her *something*. Hope you're doing well in La La Land. Call me. Bye."

Angie disconnected and walked back into the kitchen. "Let's get started, shall we?"

They set up in the living room, where Angie opened her laptop and called up the latest version of the Development spreadsheet. But she couldn't focus.

"Bad news?" Nicole sat cross-legged on the floor, spreading folders on the coffee table. "The call? You look . . ."

Angie ran her eyes down the column of titles in front of her, *Peregrine* the most recent. The contract for Mackenzie's book had been finalized May 4, exactly a month ago. Not long at all in the world of film development. So she decided to come clean to Nicole. She needed insight. "It was Rita. She says Mackenzie Martin is getting edgy because she hasn't heard anything since the IP contracts were signed."

"So?"

"So she's worried. I think she wants reassurance. She was so concerned about making the right decision on selling the rights."

"Well, her lawyer and agent should give her that," Nicole said a little dismissively.

"Rita does want to give her that, that's why she called me." Angie was already sorry she'd opened up. Looking at the rest of the titles on her list, she said, "You know, I've never heard of one project coming from any of these books. What percentage of the IP we buy is even seriously considered for development? Five percent? Ten?"

"Can we just get the rest of the missing info locked and loaded already? Why are you so concerned about it? Honestly, I don't care what happened to the stuff. You can't worry over the fate of every project."

"I'm not talking about the fate of every project. I'm looking at the big picture of a studio gobbling up rights like Pac-Man and having nothing come of it. And now I'm worried about Mackenzie. Because maybe I deceived her into thinking we were her best shot at getting a good film made when no film will come of it at all." She pointed at the folders on the table. "There are hundreds and hundreds of titles. There seems to be an awful lot of IP that never goes anywhere. I thought DreamWeaver acted in good faith."

"And why doesn't it? Because not everything turns into a movie? Please. You really need to chill out about this."

"Don't tell me to chill out," Angie said, her voice low and serious. "I have real concerns here, and I don't want people who trusted me to get screwed over. What don't you get about that?"

Realizing she was getting angry, she went into the kitchen and inhaled slowly. She couldn't lose her shit like that in front of her boss. Especially about work. She needed Nicole on her side.

She continued to breathe rhythmically, in and out, then closed her eyes and placed a hand on the opposite side of her head, letting the weight of the arm draw her ear down to her shoulder, then repeated it on the other side. The stretching helped alleviate tightness in her neck and shoulders and gave her something to focus on.

"Hey, you okay?"

Angie didn't turn. She had just found a taste of equilibrium and she needed to maintain it. But a moment later, Nicole's arms slipped around her waist and she was being held from behind. It shocked her— she wanted to recoil. She hadn't been touched intimately by anyone since . . . What was his name? Her mother's friend's son. And now Nicole was breaching a space she hadn't been invited into. She was her boss. Her fucking boss.

Angie surprised herself and didn't pull away. She still felt awkward, but there was something nice about it too. It was a gentle intimacy that she hadn't experienced before. Or hadn't allowed herself to experience before.

She breathed into it and gave herself permission to relax. She was very still and closed her eyes. Then she placed her hands over Nicole's, making out the narrowness of her wrists, the knuckles of her fingers. She grasped them and held them to her torso, then released them so she could turn to face her.

Nicole's lips were just inches away. Before Angie could think what to do next, Nicole was kissing her gently on the mouth. Angie couldn't help but kiss back. Nicole's lips were soft, sweet. A strange mix of comfort and passion tore through Angie's core. She realized she'd wanted this since they'd first met, she just hadn't understood her feelings. But she did now, and she wondered if Nicole had been wanting her this whole time or had only just realized it herself. It didn't matter.

When the kiss broke organically, Angie leaned her forehead against Nicole's, grateful neither spoke for a moment. Was this what she truly wanted? Could it endanger her quest to find out what happened to Scarlett? Nicole had as much to lose as she did, maybe more. Yet she seemed to want it just as much.

Angie took her by the hands and led her up the curving staircase and crossed the threshold into the bedroom. She pulled Nicole onto the bed and locked her arms around Nicole's waist as Nicole ran her fingers through Angie's hair. Her touch was gentle, sensual. Angie kissed her again, letting her lips part this time, inviting Nicole in. She let instinct take over, followed the sensations of fingers trailing over her skin like feathers, Nicole's lips exploring her warm, shadowy places. Drops of sweat inched down her neck, her back, her legs. Angie couldn't think straight, and wasn't sure she ever wanted to again.

Afterward, as they lay there, Angie reveled that this kind of passion was within her. It made her feel powerful. And free. And strong. And it had been there the whole time.

"I've never been with a woman," she said, eyes on the ceiling.

"Do you regret it?"

Angie gave a soft, throaty laugh. "No. I do not regret it."

"Well, that's a good start." Nicole laughed too. "But, listen, we have to keep this absolutely quiet. It's okay for you, but for me? If HR were to find out I was in a relationship with a subordinate, I could get charged with sexual harassment and fired. I know it was consensual, but that doesn't make any difference."

"I get it. But . . . relationship?"

Nicole laughed again. "Don't worry. I'm not packing up the U-Haul."

Angie's phone buzzed so she reached down to the floor to wrestle it out of her jeans. There were two texts from Jango.

I have information.

Can you meet?

Yes, when?

Tomorrow morning?
I can come to you.

Okay.

Will send time/place.

Angie got up quietly the next morning, trying not to rouse Nicole, who was still asleep curled up on her side. Downstairs, she poured herself a travel mug of cold brew and almond milk and scribbled a note: Back soon with breakfast. -A

She arrived at the overlook just off Mulholland five minutes early and found Jango already there, waiting in a beat-up brown Volkswagen Beetle. He glanced at her in his rearview mirror, pulled out, and headed down the road. Angie sat there, wondering how long she should wait to follow. Obviously, he wanted to be certain they were alone. A moment later, her phone buzzed.

Don't follow yet.

Go up to Bonilla in five minutes
and take a left.

She did as she was told and found him parked at the end of a quiet residential street. She knew there were houses, nestled at the end of long driveways or hidden behind tall fences or dense thickets of foliage, that couldn't be seen from the road.

"Sorry about all that," Jango said when she opened a creaky passenger door and took a seat. "But I had to make sure we weren't being followed. I have no idea if Weaver's thugs are watching you. Or me."

"He could be watching us?"

Jango gave her an arch expression. "Miss Norris, a man of Charles Weaver's status keeps track of everything that goes on in his world. He has to if he's going to stay on top of the world he's cultivated. Don't you think he wonders why you're out here? You think he thinks you came out to the place where your sister died just for a job, a change of scenery? C'mon, he knew you had more in mind from the start. And now we're both asking questions. It's only a matter of time before he figures out what we're digging up."

Angie gaped through the windshield, surprised she was surprised. It made her feel jittery. "Okay, then we should cut to the chase. What have you found out?"

"You remember we talked about actresses having to give in to Charles's sexual demands?"

"Of course. I heard the same from a woman I spoke with, Audra Atkins."

"Right. Well, it's not just that. It turns out Charles doesn't just want the women who give in to his demands. He wants the ones who won't."

Angie remembered what Nicole had said about powerful men like Charles wanting what they can't have, and the phone conversation with Audra.

Jango shifted in his seat and continued. "No matter how long I do this job, people's ugly behavior still gets me angry. This guy uses his power to abuse, manipulate. It gives him particular satisfaction when they resist. I've heard from at least two people, the more a woman resists, the more determined he becomes to have her, to the point of forcing himself on her."

Angie sat, her gaze fixed straight ahead. A wave of nausea turned her stomach and a trickle of sweat tickled her forehead. "Do you have a Kleenex somewhere?" she asked, dabbing her brow with the back of her hand.

"Uh, hang on." Jango turned around to rifle through papers, files, cookie wrappers, old fast-food bags, and empty coffee cups on his back seat. A McDonald's bag held a prize stack of clean paper napkins. "These work?"

Angie nodded. She took a napkin and placed it across her forehead, gently blotting, before closing her eyes.

"Maybe we should get you some water," Jango said.

"I'll be okay. I just need a minute." Her breathing was rapid and shallow, but she opened her eyes and tried to find a place to focus her gaze so she could steady herself. She settled on the trunk of a slender palm tree and pondered the new information. Scarlett would have never had sex with someone for a part. Certainly not Charles Weaver. He may have been charming and rich, but he was also paunchy, unattractive, and manipulative. She took a deep breath and mustered enough courage to ask the obvious question: "He's a rapist. Is that what you're saying?"

"Yeah. Exactly." She could feel his eyes on her. "You sure you're okay, Miss Norris?"

"Yes, I'm fine. Please call me Angie."

Jango leaned back. "Did you ever hear of a woman named Sari Sunderland? She was a big name about ten years ago. I found her. She had a nice part in a DreamWeaver picture and then went on to have a couple more around town. She was having some success, and Weaver decided he wanted her back at DreamWeaver. She was the catch of the day, if you will. So he promises her a big part, a high school teacher who tries to save a kid from abusive parents and drug addiction. It's a great part, guaranteed to make a splash, get her noticed.

"So Weaver invites this young woman to lunch in a private dining room at a fancy restaurant. And toward the end of the meal, he starts talking about how much he'd like to work with her, and how she has this natural charisma and sex appeal, he knows she'll just light up the screen—all that kind of thing. He stands up and goes behind her chair and puts his hands on her shoulders. She shrugs him off and tries to get up, but he pushes her back down, grabs her hand and pulls it up against his crotch. He tries to kiss her, but she protests, loudly, so he puts his hand over her mouth."

Angie thought of her own lunch with Charles, and her stomach reeled again.

"Well, lucky for her, they get interrupted. Her cell phone goes off—she'd told a friend to check in on her. So it startles Charles, and while he's distracted, she elbows him, grabs her purse, and runs out of the restaurant like it's on fire. I found a woman who worked there as a waitress at the time. She witnessed Sari running out of the private room. She didn't see this incident, but did witness Charles clearly sexually assaulting a different woman another time. The restaurant swept it under the carpet. She didn't dare breathe a word to anyone. So she basically corroborated the story, as did a female friend Sari told at the time. Ms. Sunderland is credible."

"What happened to her?"

"Well, she never got that role, of course. Weaver put out the word around town she wasn't to be cast. The asshole no doubt told people they could kiss any future DreamWeaver collaborations goodbye if they hired her." He shook his head in apparent disgust.

"Is she still an actress?"

"She dropped out after a few years, when work got too hard to come by."

Angie let out a deep sigh and leaned her head back against the seat.

"This guy is sick, twisted, and fucked up, Miss Norris. I mean, Angie. And you work there. You need to be very careful here. He will do anything to protect what's his. And he likes women who resist him."

"He called me late Friday night. Said he was in the area and asked if I could meet him for a drink. And he's been sending me flowers." Angie paused. "He took me to lunch last week."

"He's moving in harder than I realized. He's trying to intimidate you. For the sexual thrill of it, for sure, but also because I can almost guarantee he's worried you want to know more about Scarlett. I don't know yet what happened to your sister, but I will find out. And it's probably not going to be pretty. You know that, right?"

Angie nodded. "I have to get to the truth."

"Okay, then. Don't use the studio phones for anything. Or any kind of work laptop or tablet. Only use your cell and personal devices that DreamWeaver can't access. Change all your passwords. Don't store anything in the cloud. Meet people in public places. And make certain you're not followed. If you are followed, try to lose them, and then get somewhere big and public like a supermarket or pull into a police station."

Holy shit. This was more real than she'd ever imagined.

"You got it? I'll call you in a couple of days."

"Thank you." She climbed out of the car then stood there for a beat before stooping so she could see through the passenger window. "My sister . . . she always looked out for me. And me being me, that was a lot. She always tried to help me, so I can't, you know, just walk away."

Jango nodded. Angie straightened and took a step back, watching as he drove off.

*God almighty, what a nightmare,* she thought as she walked back to her car. Sweet, smart Scarlett, who was as genuine as anyone Angie had ever known, had gotten caught in it like so many others. She blinked back tears as she put on her sunglasses and searched her phone's GPS for a café where she could pick up breakfast to take back to Nicole, who, with any luck, would still be asleep.

Twenty minutes later, she was exiting a popular spot on PCH with muffins and matcha lattes when she heard her name and nearly dropped everything. "Hey, Angie, what's up?"

She turned to face Kevin Li, who was sporting black jeans, a yellow jersey, and expensive sunglasses.

"Hey, sorry, didn't mean to startle you, especially not holding your breakfast." He was eyeing her to-go tray for two.

"Kevin. Hey. Wow, sorry, I was lost in thought." *Is he following me?* The look on his face was friendly, and she didn't get any malevolent vibe off him. But he was Charles's friend. "You live in this area?"

"Nah, I got a buddy out here. We go riding on the trails. It's nice getting away from it all, you know?" He gestured toward a shiny green motorbike parked in front of the café.

"Yeah, for sure." Angie looked at him, not knowing what to say. "Well, I'm meeting a friend. Don't want the matcha to cool down. See you Monday. Have fun."

"See you."

Angie scurried to her car where she pretended to check her phone in case Kevin was watching.

She didn't feel threatened. But what if her instincts were wrong?

"Hey, I brought muffins!" Angie called out a little too brightly when she breezed into the kitchen.

"Where did you go for them, Vegas?" Nicole was dressed in a pink tank top and shorts and was grinding beans. "I borrowed some clothes. Hope that's okay?"

"Of course." Angie handed her a latte. "I brought you matcha with soy milk and sweetener. But please make that pot. It's going to be a caffeine-heavy morning, I can tell."

Nicole opened the bag Angie set on the counter and pulled out the treats. "Well, you've redeemed yourself with breakfast at least." She wrapped her arms around Angie's waist affectionately. "I was a little disappointed, I have to say, when I woke up and you were gone." She kissed her neck then reached down, broke off a piece of a muffin, and popped it into Angie's mouth. "So, why did you cut out of here?" The question seemed an obvious one. Nicole turned back to grinding coffee beans. "I wondered if you woke up and felt weirded out by me being here. Or last night."

"No. I liked having you there when I woke up." Angie spoke shyly, but she was being truthful. She hadn't had much time to process what had happened between them, considering she had to sneak out as soon as she woke up, but she did know she had been happy to see Nicole sleeping next to her. She'd always assumed she was straight, though her depression and anxiety took up so much mental energy, she'd never embraced any strong sense of sexual identity at all. She'd dated men and, when none had proved particularly interesting, she figured she just hadn't met the right person. And that's what finally happened. Only the right person turned out to be a woman.

"I just woke up restless," she added, silently chastising herself for being so vague. "I bumped into Kevin." She hoped she sounded as nonchalant as she intended.

"Kevin Li?"

"He said he and his buddy go dirt biking out in the canyons." Angie broke off a piece of a muffin, just for something to do, not meeting Nicole's eyes. She felt like she was lying when that part of her story was actually truthful.

"The canyons, huh? Maybe we should do the same. I mean, we don't have dirt bikes, but what about a bit of a hike? Get some air? Might help you decompress from work and Charles and everything else you've got going on in there." She tapped the side of Angie's temple with a finger.

Angie needed time to contemplate her next move. She had to coordinate calls to more former DreamWeaver actresses and absorb Jango's information. But she didn't want Nicole to get suspicious, and getting some fresh air out in nature did sound good. Yesterday they'd mostly been cooped up, hunched over computers and stacks of paper.

"Sure," she finally allowed. "I probably need to clean up around here later, but let's get out for the early part of the day at least."

"Don't worry, I won't monopolize all of your time, I promise," Nicole teased her. "But right now, I'm gonna need to borrow some sturdy shoes. I hope we're the same size. And a water bottle."

An hour later, Angie was panting a few feet behind Nicole as they made their way up the four-mile trail known as Skull Rock Loop in Topanga State Park. She felt like she was burning up; she wasn't used to the strong Southern California sun. As they ascended, they passed other hikers, enormous rock formations, and thickets of dense overgrowth, stopping periodically to take in panoramic coastal and mountain views that blew Angie's mind. She didn't see anything like this in Queens.

When they climbed an outcropping near the top of the trail, they stopped to take a break. Nicole uncapped her water bottle and took a long draw. "Can I ask you something?" she asked when she'd swallowed. "Why did you come out here, really? Was it just for the job?"

"Isn't that enough?" Angie was suddenly on edge. She leaned against the rock formation she was perched on and kept her gaze on the vista.

"I guess. I mean, a lot of people would kill to have your job, work in the industry, work at DreamWeaver. Don't get me wrong, you've settled in really well. But I have to say I was surprised when you said you were actually moving to LA. I'm happy you're here, like, very happy." She rested a hand on Angie's leg. "But I can't help thinking, now that I'm hanging at Scarlett's more, just how hard the move must have been. Living here, where it all went down . . . I don't know what I would have done if it were one of my sisters."

Angie focused on the pale dirt path, the scrubby desert brush, the expansive blue sky. "I feel guilty. For being alive. For being here to enjoy Scarlett's house and for stepping into her world while she's not here to enjoy it with me." She thought a simpler truth, or part of the truth, would do for the time being. "And like I've said before, I feel closer to Scarlett out here. Plus, it was time for a change."

"So do you know what happened to Scarlett? Why she . . . ended her life?"

Angie drank from her water bottle and then shrugged.

"I'm sorry. I shouldn't pry. You probably don't want to talk about this."

"It's fine," Angie said and thought she meant it. "I don't know, really. Scarlett wasn't someone who fell apart. And yet, she did. She wasn't insecure or desperate. Yet she felt so trapped she took her life. Her suicide doesn't make sense. But I suppose all survivors think that."

She extended a hand to Nicole, who squeezed in next to her, and Angie raised her phone so she could take a selfie. Then she saw a text that had come in minutes ago from a number she didn't recognize.

> I want to talk about
> Scarlett. 8 p.m. Thursday.
> Geoffrey's Restaurant in Malibu.
> I'll find you.

They continued along the trail, chatting about the weather and work and colleagues. But Angie only half listened. She couldn't stop thinking about the text.

"I still don't understand what she hopes you'll find in there," Ellen complained to Scott as he dragged a box out of the basement closet. "She should focus on her new job and life in LA. Honestly, she's chasing ghosts."

As much as he himself had warned Angie not to obsess over Scarlett's suicide, Scott felt an urge to defend her. His mother's obstinance was getting annoying. He expected that from his father, but not Ellen. And so what if he wanted to go through some of Scarlett's belongings?

"Mom, the reason Angie is in LA in the first place is Scarlett." He knew she didn't need reminders, but hiding from reality, refusing to even try and understand what Angie was trying to do, wasn't doing anybody any good. "She's working at the last place Scar worked before . . ." He cleared his throat and his mother looked away. "She's living at her house. Obviously, it's going to bring up a lot of things. You know how sensitive she is. And how much she idolized Scar. So let me just do this for her."

"But what does she hope to find?" Ellen pressed on.

"She doesn't hope to find anything in particular, Mom, I think she just wants to know what's here. Don't *you?*"

The front door opened, and a voice rang out above them. "Ellen, where are you? I got a loaf of that olive bread and a bottle of that red you love. We can crack it before dinner. Ell, are you here?"

"I'll be right up!" Ellen called. She turned to her son, who had started to open the box, and dropped her voice to a whisper. "I've got to go. If he finds out you're going through Scarlett's things, oh, God, I can't even—"

"I know, Mom," Scott whispered back. "I parked a few blocks away on a side street. He'll never know I was here."

Ellen hurriedly left the room, calling to her husband as she went upstairs. Scott could hear them from the basement.

"Hey, there, so where's that bread?"

"I'm slicing you some right now," Gerry said. "Where were you, anyway? What were you doing?"

*Jesus, has Dad always been so controlling?* Scott wondered. What did it matter what his mother was doing in their own house? Did she have to answer to him for her time? How had he not noticed that before?

"Oh, just sorting through some old sweaters and jackets I need to get rid of," Ellen replied. "Why don't we put on a movie?"

Their voices faded as Scott distracted himself with the contents of the box. There were mostly file folders with bank statements and other business documents, but underneath the paperwork he found a cell phone and two photo albums, one of Scarlett's college years and a second from when they were kids. He started to leaf through that one, finding images of their birthday parties with Ellen's homemade cakes. Angie had always wanted strawberry with white icing, Scarlett had loved devil's food with fudge frosting, and Scott's favorite had been carrot. There were the three of them in swimsuits, running through spray from the hose in the front of the house, like brightly colored summer fairies sprung from the lawn. The Christmas pictures were the same each year—Ellen always picked out coordinating sweaters, pants, and skirts, and they would pose dutifully in front of the tree—except they got taller over time. There was a shot of Barry, Scott's beagle, who'd followed him to elementary school every day and then walked back home on his own. Barry had lived to be fourteen. Scott could feel his throat tightening at the memories, but he pushed the emotion down. They'd been a happy family, but it had been derailed, first by Angie's depression, then by Scarlett's suicide.

He remembered a bad dream phase he'd had as a kid, maybe six or seven. He'd call out in his sleep and his mom or dad would usually hear him and come. But one night, Scarlett opened his bedroom door. "Hey, Scotty, it's okay," she reassured him, slipping into his room. "What happened?" He told her he was being chased by an old man who was kidnapping little boys. "But I don't want to go! I want to stay here with you and Angie and Mommy and Daddy!" he'd sobbed.

"Oh, Scotty, it was just a bad dream." Scarlett sat next to him on his bed and embraced him. "That mean old man isn't real. And even if he was, I would never, ever let him take you. Not ever. You and me and Angie and Mommy and Daddy stick together, and that's always the way it's gonna be."

He remembered how she'd wiped the tears off his cheeks and told him to close his eyes and had stroked his hair until he fell asleep. He remembered feeling safe, because Scarlett would never let anyone take him or hurt him, not ever.

Another time, when he'd just turned eleven, a few older boys began taunting him on his walk home from school. They'd wait for him at a corner a few blocks from his house and close in, pushing and jostling him, throwing his books around, knocking him down. Scarlett, then a senior in high school, got wind of it and one day she followed him. When the bullies appeared, she stalked up and glared down at them, now being a head taller than the twelve-year-olds. "You guys got a problem?" She went to the biggest one, shoved him, and, with a menacing tone, told him, "If you ever bother my brother again, I will beat the living shit out of you so bad your mother won't recognize you. Then I'll drag your ass home and tell your parents that you attacked me first. And if you don't believe it, just try me, you little shit!"

The boys never bothered Scott again.

He could still see Scarlett so clearly. The way her full dark brows curved over her wide-set gray eyes. The chain with the "S" dangling around her neck. Her long skinny legs. The way she could eat a cupcake in two bites and would gulp iced tea out of the glass pitcher in the fridge, much to Ellen's consternation. He could hear her loud laugh and remembered, at Christmas, she'd gleefully sing carols so loudly in church that everyone, including the rest of the family, cast wary glances at her. But Scarlett had never cared. She was always herself, everyone else be damned.

He shut the album and put it back in the box, then slid the box into the closet, exchanging it for another, equally as full. Then another. And another. More memories he didn't allow himself to get lost in, but no insight into Scarlett's state of mind.

When he had gone through them all, he felt numb, kind of hazy at the nostalgia. He quietly made his way up the stairs and escaped through the front door, turning down the street. Half a block down, he started to run, first one block, then two. Then he kept going, block after block, until he could no longer breathe. He stopped, hot tears running down his face. He tried to curb them, but he couldn't. He cried and cried as his body shook, gripping a stop sign for support. It was a quiet Sunday afternoon, and he was grateful there were no passing cars. His sobs slowed, and he stood there, catching his breath, and letting himself feel everything he'd been avoiding since the initial shock of Scarlett's suicide. He understood why Angie wanted to figure out what had happened, and he felt ashamed. It was true, he didn't want Angie to upset herself. But more than that, *he* didn't want to upset *himself*. Maybe there were no answers, but at least Angie was trying to be brave. He felt around in his jacket pocket for his phone and texted her.

> Didn't find anything. Love you.
> I am so fucking proud of you.

Then he slowly made his way to his car and drove home.

# 12

"Look, honey, I trust you," Rita told Angie over the phone. "But something's fishy out there, and it ain't the sardines, all respect to Steinbeck. Of course, that was Monterey, but anyway, Mackenzie's worried and, frankly, I don't know why her lawyer or I can't get through to anyone at that place."

Angie felt a growing sense of dread and her head was starting to ache. Two days after getting Rita's message, Angie was still trying to figure out what to say. Nicole would know if something got fast-tracked, but she hadn't heard anything, and Angie had the distinct feeling that people were getting tired of her questions about IP. The decision on developing the book at all would come from the very top. *And I can't very well ask Charles.*

"I'm sorry," she finally went with, weak as it was. "Let me ask around and see if anyone knows anything. It could take a while, but I'll dig a little bit." She hesitated. "Rita, by the way, did another one of our—sorry, your—writers, Alexandra Gold, sell DreamWeaver her rights or maybe get an option? I saw a draft of a contract, but I haven't been able to find out anything else."

"We haven't cut a deal on that yet. I don't know why they'd draft anything. Maybe so they'll be ready in case we move forward. But we're also talking to two doc and one indie producer."

"Listen. Hang tight with Alexandra. Don't sign anything yet. I'll talk to you soon."

"Okay, kid. Jesus, now I know why I stayed in New York. At least here if someone is yanking your chain, they tell you."

"I'm sorry. I may have . . . overpromised. Let me see what I can find out."

She hung up. Who besides Charles or Nicole might know something?

She opened her email and scanned her inbox. One message caught her eye; it had come from legal about reorganizations in that department. As unusual as it would typically be for a low-level creative exec to reach out to a top attorney at a studio, not every lowly CE was the sister of a well-known actress who'd killed herself while in the studio's employ and had shared a cocaine-fueled limo ride with said attorney after the Academy Awards.

She opened a new email and started to type.

> Dear Tanya,
>
> I hope this finds you well. I wondered if you were still interested in getting together some time. I'd love to pick your brain about a few things now that I've had a chance to settle in. I also wondered how Patricia is doing.
>
> Best,
> Angie Norris

*Now we wait.* She tried to get back into the groove of work, but it was hard to focus. She was behind in her reading because the database project had soaked up so much of her schedule, and while she wanted to spend as much time as she could with Nicole, she also had to devote hours to finding projects for the studio. And she had to locate and contact women who might shed more light on Charles and

DreamWeaver's tactics. She was in regular touch with Jango, who was worried about keeping Charles off her trail, and she needed to return a message from Scott.

She covered her eyes with the heels of her hands. *No wonder my head's killing me.*

When she got home that night, she went into the guest bedroom to assess her whiteboard. In addition to Audra, she had tried to call several women who had only done one or two movies at DreamWeaver, but so far they weren't returning her calls.

She was looking at contact information for an actress on IMDbPro when her phone buzzed with an incoming text from Jango.

> Can I stop by?
> Will be out your way
> for another case.
> Found something interesting.

> Sure. I'm here.

She was in the kitchen when she heard a car pull up outside. She rushed to the door and opened it before the bell could ring, only to find Nicole on her front step. Nicole had said she might come over if she didn't have to work too late, but since she usually didn't come over during the week—it took too long to get to Topanga Canyon in traffic—the tentative plan had entirely slipped Angie's mind.

"You look surprised." Nicole beamed at her and held up two big paper bags, her rose gold hoop earrings glinting against the caramel skin of her slender neck.

Angie *was* surprised, but mostly she was stunned at how sexy Nicole looked in her satiny sleeveless blouse.

"Expecting your other girlfriend?" Nicole joked. "Anyway, I brought Middle Eastern. Hummus, pita, tabouli, the full mezze experience. Any wine left?"

"Absolutely." Angie kissed her as she stepped into the foyer. "And you're in luck because my other girlfriend just left." She grinned in jest.

The shot of happiness she felt whenever she saw Nicole always took her by surprise. It was so new, that sense of excitement. On the surface, it seemed ordinary enough: People dated all the time, moved in together, got married. Yet to her, it was special, unreal, the first time in the history of the world anyone had ever felt such a thing.

At that moment, however, she couldn't revel in their specialness. How was she going to keep Nicole and Jango from meeting?

She got plates that they filled with dips, olives, dolmas, and salads before she casually tried to introduce the subject of Jango. "Hey. I've got someone coming by." She busied herself pouring a glass of wine so she could focus anywhere but on Nicole's face.

"Aha! So your other girlfriend is coming back!" Nicole grinned, then added, "You know, the other woman, as it were?" She dipped a piece of pita into the baba ghanoush before the plates could even be set on the dining room table.

"Ah. No, she's been and gone," Angie teased. "It's the person who's been helping me out with some family business. He's in the area tonight, so he's coming by to update me. It shouldn't take long."

"I see." Nicole sat at the dining table, fiddling with the stem of her wineglass. "You know, you can tell me things. Confide in me."

"What do you mean?" Angie hoped she sounded more natural than she felt. She carried in the plates and took her own seat at the table. "I mean, it's nothing like that. It's just something my family needs to . . . sort out. About Scarlett's estate."

Nicole reached over to rest a hand on Angie's arm. "I really care for you, Ange. I haven't felt this way in so long. And I want us to be able to talk."

Angie looked into her golden-brown eyes and sun-kissed face. But she wasn't ready to let her guard down. Her phone buzzed, and she quickly checked the text. Then replied:

Outside. Come around side.

I'll unlock the gate.

"Okay, that's him." She stood, ready to break away. "I'll be back in a sec."

She slid open the door at the back of the house and slipped out to find Jango at the side gate. "Sorry to barge in on you like this," he said.

"No, it's no problem. I want to know about anything you find." They heard faint music from the kitchen and looked over. Nicole was standing by the doors holding her glass of wine. She waved through the sliding glass door at Jango, who gave a sort of half-wave back.

"I'm interrupting," he said. "I'll make it quick."

"It's just my boss."

Jango looked at her with raised eyebrows and a skeptical smile.

"Let's go over here." Angie led him to two patio chairs and a table beside the pool. Wind rushed quietly in the palms.

"Someone close to Charles wants to help. He gave me a lot of information about actresses and other leads including the name of a producer in town, Christo Holland, who hates Charles Weaver's guts." Jango pulled back a chair, the wrought iron screeching against the flagstone tile that surrounded the pool, and sat. "Seems Holland goes way back with Weaver. A few years back, this guy was in serious talks with the writer of this killer sci-fi mystery novel, but somebody at DreamWeaver got to the writer first, who was so enticed by the idea of getting a DreamWeaver movie made from it that he sold the rights outright. The writer was on cloud nine by the sound of it. But the book never saw the light of day. No movie, no nothing. And the writer couldn't get the rights back, not even with an IP lawyer, and this producer said the writer hired the best, spent a whole lot of money. So the producer got locked out and the writer is totally screwed, too. The thing got taken off the market—buried—like for good."

Angie gazed out at the night sky. Another deal that locked a writer out from getting his book turned into a film. Anywhere. Ever.

"You following me?" Jango asked.

"What? Yes, sorry. It's just . . . This is the same thing I've noticed. We—DreamWeaver—buys options and rights and none of it ever goes anywhere. I don't know why."

"What do you mean?"

"I mean we're in the business of making movies. So why do no movies get made out of a large majority of the books and IP we own?"

Jango looked at her hard. "Angie, you're smart, but you still don't get it. It's not just about making good movies. Your stuff not only needs to be good, it's gotta be better than what your competitors are churning out. It's got to be the best movies in town. That's how you get box office, audience, awards. You getting me?"

*How could I be so dense?* "He's locking them down so no one else can buy them. Because he doesn't want the—"

"Competition," Jango said, finishing her sentence. "Exactly. This producer says Weaver does it all the time. Buys up the rights to books, articles, you name it, just to bury them, so no one else can have a crack at them either. It's a classic catch-and-kill situation."

"Catch and kill? I thought that was a tabloid thing, what a celebrity's lawyer does to kill an embarrassing sex scandal."

"It can be. But it isn't always about burying damaging information, scandalous behavior. This is about burying books to deprive your competitors of content. Now, there's lots of content around town, original screenplays, all sorts of things being written all the time. But this is one area, published books and stories, that the sonofabitch you work for is trying to control. And this guy, Charles Weaver, he likes to have control."

Angie heard the sliding doors open. Why was Nicole coming outside?

"Didn't mean to startle you. Just wanted to see if I could get you anything." Nicole joined them, extending her hand to Jango. "Hi, I'm Nicole Hawkins."

"Nice to meet you, Miss Hawkins." Jango shook her hand but didn't introduce himself in return. "I'm fine, thanks. In fact, I need to get going." He turned to Angie. "Enjoy your evening. I can see myself out."

"Thanks. Let's talk soon."

Jango held up one arm in a goodbye as he walked away, disappearing through the gate.

"Should we get back to dinner?" Nicole suggested. "Wait until I tell you Charles's reaction when he toured the database. It's still being tested, of course, but I think he's really pleased."

"Why did you come out here?" Angie demanded.

"What?"

"Why did you come out?"

"I just thought I'd see if your guest wanted a drink or something. I didn't mean to do anything wrong. I mean . . . I guess shouldn't have intruded."

Angie softened a little. Was she being paranoid? "It's fine. I'm just feeling a little tired. Let's eat."


When Angie got to work the next morning, staggering her entrance with Nicole's so they wouldn't draw attention, her mind was still reeling. She hadn't been able to sleep and found herself sitting up at three in the morning gazing at Nicole sleeping peacefully in the moonlight streaming through the window. She wondered what was going on behind those eyes fluttering through a dream. Was she sent to investigate Angie? Was their relationship solely a ruse? *If so, what will I do?*

When she plopped into her desk chair, exhausted, and brought her computer awake, Angie found an email waiting from Tanya. She'd entirely forgotten that she'd reached out. It made her anxiety spike even higher. She clicked it open, unable to bear the suspense.

> Nice to hear from you, Angie. I meant to follow up
> after we met that day in the elevator. A little free time
> opened up later today. What about a coffee around four?

She fired off a reply.

Sounds fine. Let me know where you want to meet.

Angie showed up at an airy café near the studio at four o'clock on the dot. Tanya, impeccably chic in a slim gray pantsuit, was already waiting and waved her over. "Have a seat." She motioned for a server who breezed by to take Angie's order.

"Well, I'm glad we've finally had the chance to do this," Tanya said smoothly. "Word is you've settled in nicely."

"I think I've gotten my sea legs." Angie played nervously with a packet of Equal. She'd truly thought she had settled in when she wrote to Tanya, and she hadn't expected that bombshell from Jango. Overnight she'd realized she didn't have her sea legs at all.

"That's great, though I wouldn't have necessarily expected that after meeting you the first time." Tanya gave her usual unreadable smile. "No offense, but you seemed rather shell-shocked that night. Not that anyone could blame you. You were thrown into the deep end without so much as a pair of water wings."

*Be direct. Be confident.* "Yes, well, I suppose I was. It seems so long ago now." She wasn't going to make mention of the party limo again unless Tanya did.

Both of them paused as the server swooped in with Angie's coffee.

"But here you are!" Tanya raised her cappuccino in a little salute.

"Yes, indeed." Angie saluted back with her own steaming cup.

Tanya checked her phone. "So what was it you wanted to pick my brain about? By the way, all I know about Patricia is that she's home and getting physical therapy."

"That's good to hear." She knew she needed to cut to the chase before she lost Tanya's attention, or her courage. "I'm trying to get a better handle on how all the departments at the studio work together. I thought you might be able to shed some light on how fast properties can move into development once the IP contracts are signed. I recently closed a big deal with a writer back in New York who has a bestseller."

"Congratulations. But I'm afraid I can't really help you. I don't have anything to do with it once our attorneys wrap up their part of the work. What's this bestseller?"

"It's called *Peregrine*. It's a memoir." Angie wondered if Tanya had even heard of it. "I just thought that being one of the top people at the studio, you would have a sense of which projects Charles wants to fast-track."

"I have a slew of attorneys reporting to me who draft contracts and handle a zillion other legal tasks. The studio owns a lot of IP. I can't remember what happens to every book."

"Of course not. I just thought this one might ring a bell because it's a recent acquisition. And Charles knows about it. I told him personally."

"What are you getting at, Angie?" Tanya looked at her watch.

Shit. She was losing her. "Just that I recently helped wrap up the huge IP database project—"

"Angie, let me give you a little advice. To be honest, normally I wouldn't even bother having this conversation with an employee working at your level. But you're Scarlett's sister. I liked Scarlett, I did. We were friends. Something you no doubt know and are using—"

Angie started to speak, but Tanya held up her hand.

"Not to worry, I admire you being assertive, trying to get some inside knowledge that may help you succeed in this industry. But all you need to know is that DreamWeaver runs based on what one man wants." She leaned in. "One. It's not a public company. We are not beholden to shareholders. We do what Charles asks of us. It's that simple. So if I were you, I wouldn't try to figure out too much beyond your job. If something moves into development, you'll hear about it." She looked at her phone again. "I really must get back." She stood. "Nice catching up with you, Angie."

*** 

That night, Angie headed directly upstairs to the guest bedroom with her whiteboard where she dropped her jacket, bag, and keys on the floor. She needed to prioritize her search. She'd been so busy with work, the database update, and her deepening relationship with Nicole, that tracking down and cross-referencing actresses to contact had slowed practically to a crawl.

She turned the light on and headed to the whiteboard, leaning against the desk, a Sharpie in her hand. She had been there for twenty minutes and was filling in contact information for an actress who hadn't been active for eight years when something caught her eye.

On the floor was a glinting object. A delicate rose gold hoop earring.

Nicole. Had she been snooping? If she'd seen the whiteboard and not said anything, the jig was up. Angie sank to the floor, pulling her knees close, her breath thin and gasping. Had Nicole already reported to Charles? Were they going to arrest her? Had she done anything illegal? Should she leave town? Just get on a plane to New York?

*Breath in, two, three, four. Out, two, three four . . .*

Her blood coursed hot and fast, rushing in a burst of static into her brain. She was fucked. And she'd gotten fucked over in the most stupid, stereotypical way—by a pretty girl. Had Nicole always known? Had Charles? *How could I have been so stupid? I'm such a patsy.* All over again, Angie felt like the weak, shy middle child who had never achieved anything and never would.

Tears burst past her lids and she wept, for herself, for her ignorance, her stupid innocence . . . for Scarlett.

Her phone buzzed and she pulled it out to silence it but there was Scott's beaming face. *Scotty, thank God.* He was the only one she could fall apart in front of.

She didn't even recognize her own voice when she answered. She eked out his name but the tears wouldn't stop.

"Ange!" His voice came through the speaker. "What's wrong? What happened?"

Angie couldn't tell him the truth. She couldn't tell him about Nicole. Or her true intentions in working at DreamWeaver. Or her fears for Scarlett.

"Angie? Remember to breathe."

*In, two, three four. Out, two, three four . . .*

"I don't know what's happening out there, but I know you're doing something you're not telling me about. And that's okay. I'm proud of you, Ange."

Angie's breaths slowed as she focused on his words.

"Just know that I am behind you a hundred percent. Scarlett would be, too. She always believed in you. And you going out there, trying to figure your shit out, figure out Scarlett, you are so much braver than I am. All I wanted to do was hide from it all. You are rushing headlong toward it. So no matter how scary or fucked up things are, you are the bravest person I've ever known. You have balls of cast iron."

Angie couldn't help but laugh. "Balls of cast iron, eh?"

"Absafuckin'lutely!"

She laughed harder, and Scott laughed, too.

"So what's going on? Why are you freaking out?"

"Oh, GOD. There's just. So. Much. Charles Weaver is . . ."

"Yeah?"

"He's just a lot."

"Okay. You're used to dealing with egos, though, right? All the authors you've worked with?"

"Yeah."

"He's just another ego."

*You can say that again. Times ten.* "Right."

"And who's got the balls of cast iron?"

She chuckled to herself. "I do."

"That's right. It's not Charles Weaver, no matter what kind of blow-hard he is, how much he squawks."

"Thanks, Scotty. I feel better now."

"Good. You let me know if you need me to come out there and kick some Hollywood ass, okay?"

"Oh, I will. Absafuckin'lutely."

Both of them were laughing when they hung up and Angie realized she really did feel better. More solid. Scott heartened her, steeled her. She wasn't searching for the truth about Scarlett, about Charles just for herself. Scott and their parents deserved to know too. She was doing it for them. And for all the actresses Charles had threatened, assaulted, buried through the years. It was bigger than she was.

It seemed Scotty was seeing her through new eyes . . . perhaps it was time she did too. She wasn't just trying to emulate Scarlett any-more. She was finding her own strength. And that was what she needed to draw from so she could stand up, dust herself off, and try again, even though part of her wanted to pack up and run. Run from the rhine-stone world of Hollywood, from powerful, controlling Charles, from Nicole and her lies. But it had been a full day since Nicole had been at the house. That gave Angie pause.

Nothing had happened. She hadn't been aware of a change in Nicole's demeanor. She hadn't been arrested. She hadn't been fired.

It didn't take the sting out of the betrayal. Obviously, she would have to keep an eye on her while she pretended nothing had changed, but clearly Nicole was biding her time too. Two could play that game.

But she needed help.

So she dried her eyes, steadied her breath, and reached out to the one person she thought she could trust in Los Angeles.

> Hey, Patricia.
> I hope you're healing.
> I'd like to stop by.

> You were right.
> I'm out of my depth.

Angie kept herself busy at work for the next two days, her guard up around not just Nicole, but everyone. She distrusted every person she worked with. If Nicole was a plant, anyone could be. The hardest part was keeping Nicole at bay without raising any suspicions. Wednesday night she begged off, saying she had an upset stomach. Thursday, she claimed "family business," though she was aware that hadn't stopped Nicole from barging in on her and Jango, which now made sense.

Her "family business" was actually the meeting in Malibu with the person who'd texted her during her Sunday hike with Nicole. Someone needed to know where she was should something go down, so she had confided in Jango, who had not been pleased.

"You're going out to Malibu at night to meet someone who sent you a text, but you have no idea who they are?" he'd said over the phone earlier that day. "Your sister, we think, was driven to suicide working for a guy who is controlling and dangerous and for whom you now work. It's a high-stakes industry full of sex, power, and money, and you're trying to bring the dark underbelly to light. And you think that this meeting is safe?"

"It's safe," she assured him, and herself. "I don't know why, but my instinct tells me it will be fine. And if someone out there really knows something about Scarlett, I can't afford to pass up a chance to find out. Plus, if someone wanted to kill me, there are less risky ways than throwing me off a cliff in Malibu in the middle of dinner."

"Whatever you say," Jango said. "Just be careful."

Driving out that night, she was so preoccupied she almost missed the turnoff to the restaurant. After she'd given the valet her keys, she fingered a small bottle of pepper spray in her purse. Earlier, she had programmed her GPS with a few public places she could go on her way home if she thought she was being followed.

*It's okay. It'll be okay.*

Despite some nervousness, she felt strong. And brave. She reminded herself why she was doing this, and that Scott had said he was proud of her. Plus she had balls of cast iron, which forced a smile and calmed her butterflies—a tad, at least.

"Hi, I'm Angela Norris," she told the host. "I'm meeting someone. I'm not sure if they've arrived yet."

"No one has mentioned you, Miss Norris. But I will happily seat you and bring the rest of your party over when they arrive."

He was so solicitous it struck Angie he might recognize her from the Oscars speech. Or maybe he just thought she was meeting someone from a dating app.

She sat and looked around. Two young women, very thin and very blond, were at one table, talking excitedly. At another table, a man in sunglasses sipped a cocktail as he checked his phone. Two middle-aged couples were dining at a third. No one looked familiar or paid her any attention.

She decided to walk to the restroom so people could see her and she could survey the restaurant. As she headed back, she caught sight of someone she recognized being ushered to a table. Her breath caught in her throat. Could that be who she was supposed to meet? She didn't see how it could make sense.

"Hi, Tanya," she said, approaching the table her coworker had been seated at.

Tanya looked up, her brow knit in surprise. *Obviously not expecting me. Coincidence.*

"Angie, hello. How . . . interesting to run into you out here."

Angie nodded and started to say something but a younger woman was suddenly brought to the table.

"Ah," Tanya said. "Angie, do you know Dominique Spencer? Dominique, this is Angela Norris. You may have heard her marvelous speech at the Oscars this year."

Angie recognized the beautiful dark-haired woman—the same one who'd approached her in the restroom when she'd lunched with Charles.

Dominique looked at Angie and chimed in quickly. "No, I don't think we've met. How do you do."

Picking up the cue, Angie extended her hand. "So nice to meet you."

Dominique sat down and Angie stood silently for a moment before Tanya said, "I'd ask you to join us, but we have some business to go over."

"I've got to get going anyway. I'm meeting a friend." Angie gave a gracious smile. "Nice to meet you, Dominique."

Angie could swear her heart was pounding loud enough for Tanya to hear as she walked back to her table. She was tired and jumpy. The mysterious stranger was either delayed, had changed their mind, or never intended to show. Maybe it was just a deranged fan of Scarlett's toying with her.

She was walking out of the restaurant when her phone buzzed, startling her. It was her mother. She hit the Accept button as the host opened the door for her and she moved outside.

"Angela!" Ellen's voice was chipper, too chipper for Angie's mood.

"Hey, Mom." She was already regretting picking up.

"We're coming to visit!"

*What?* She didn't even have a chance to process the announcement before her mother charged on.

"But don't you worry. We won't cramp your style. We're renting an Airbnb in Santa Monica. Your father agreed to come only if we didn't stay in Los Angeles proper. We know you're busy with work. We don't want to get in the way, so we'll entertain ourselves. It is the entertainment capital of the world after all!"

It was then that Angie detected the strained note in her mother's voice. They weren't coming for a vacation, not with the way her father felt about LA, especially after what happened to Scarlett. They were coming to check up on her. They didn't believe she could take care of herself.

"You have *some* time for us, right, dear? We arrive a week from Friday and want you to come see our place that Saturday."

"That's . . . great! I'll clear my social calendar," she joked but then realized she actually did have a social life. Sort of. With Nicole. Shit. One more thing to pile on the stress percolating through her veins.

"Perhaps you can introduce us to a movie star."

"Mom. That's not what LA is like. You don't just see movie stars standing on street corners. But we can go to the tourist spots. I haven't even been to them yet, so it will be fun for me too."

She said goodbye to her mother and then looked out over the Pacific. As she waited for the valet, the clouds streaked across the horizon, outlined in gold as the sun lit them from behind. She was thinking it was easy to see how people would never want to leave the Southern California coast when she heard footsteps crunching up behind her on the gravel parking lot.

She turned quickly to face a very handsome man in his late thirties. Sporting a full beard and mop of wavy dark hair that reached the bottom of his ears, he had brown eyes and a chiseled physique. And he looked vaguely familiar.

"Angie?"

She started to bring out the pepper spray hidden in her purse. "Yes."

"Sorry I'm late. Traffic."

"And you are . . . ?"

"Jeremy. Jeremy Banker. I was Scarlett's boyfriend."

# 13

Jeremy popped the top off a beer bottle and downed half its contents. Angie had followed him a mile or so down the coast to the small one-bedroom guesthouse he was renting in Malibu. She could hear the waves rolling in, crashing on the beach below. She perched on the sofa, looking out the big picture window. Just blackness.

"How are you? I watched the Oscars, of course. You were great." He sat in an easy chair across from the sofa.

She couldn't help but smile at him. He seemed like a decent guy. "Thanks. I wasn't sure I would pull it off. But I had to—no one else in my family could go. Or wanted to."

She tried to picture him without his beard and shaggy hair. With those changes, she would probably have recognized him as the man Scarlett had pointed out in magazines and movies, back when they'd dated the first time around.

"How did you get my number?" she asked.

"When Scar was having such a hard time, I borrowed her phone one day, told her mine was dead, and rifled through her contacts. I forwarded your number to my phone. She asked me not to call, that her parents wouldn't understand, that her brother had his own life, wife and family, and that you . . . well . . . you had had a difficult time and whatnot . . . I wanted to call but . . ."

Angie tensed, suddenly angry. "I keep beating myself up over the fact that Scarlett didn't think I was strong enough to help her. It's true I've had issues my entire life, but I've learned to cope. And I'm living out here now and working at DreamWeaver, as you obviously know."

"Yeah, it was in *Variety*. You were *the* story at the Oscars, you know. You and Scarlett. Anyway, I knew you were out here, and I'm sorry it's taken me this long to contact you. To be honest, I think I was afraid to talk to you. I was afraid you'd think I should've done more for Scarlett, to help her." Angie was touched to see his eyes glistening, and not surprised when he suddenly got up and walked to the kitchen, presumably so she wouldn't see him wipe his eyes. "I've been shooting a series in Vancouver. That's why I've got all this." As he pulled a beer from the fridge, he looked back at Angie and gestured to his unruly appearance. "Working on the series, being that busy . . . Well, it's very convenient if you want to avoid . . ."

Angie waited for him to complete the thought, but when he came back and sat down in the chair opposite her, she realized he wasn't going to.

"Why reach out now?"

"I'm not sure. Maybe I just wanted to talk about Scarlett. I did wonder why you came out here. You don't seem like someone who'd move to LA after her sister died and start working at the same studio just because you wanted a change of pace."

"True enough," Angie conceded. "But I do like being here. It makes me feel connected, still, to Scar. If that doesn't sound weird."

"Nah, I think the same things. I rewatch movies we watched together, order drinks she liked, get her favorite sandwich when I go to this one café, anything that reminds me of her." He mindlessly picked at the label on his beer bottle. "I took some things of hers from the set, you know, after she died."

"Really?"

"Yeah, I raced down here when I heard. On my series, they gave me a couple of days off. We were almost done shooting the season but they let me take a few days. Anyway, I get to Scar's trailer and these guys are carrying out boxes. I mean, I get it, they've got to empty it, but all her things were being lined up outside her trailer like someone was waiting for a freakin' pickup from Goodwill. I kind of went nuts. And some stupid young assistant comes up to me and she's all, 'We're so sorry for your loss, but I'm going to have to ask you to leave, this is DreamWeaver property.' I wanted to wring that girl's neck, but I just stared at her, and then all my rage just disappeared, you know? And I remember getting really quiet and just looking at her and saying, 'Sure, I'll go. But have a little fucking respect. It's not a goddamn yard sale.' And I stormed off and went to a bar, drank two shots of whiskey and two beers, and had a buddy pick me up. I must have scared the hell outta that girl. Serves her right. Who do these fucking people think they are?" he asked, more to himself than Angie. Then he looked over at her. "Hey, sorry, I didn't mean you. But you don't seem like the type to work in the industry, for Weaver, no less."

"Yeah, I surprised even myself."

"So why did you come out here?"

"There are things about Scarlett that don't add up."

"I agree."

"You knew what Scar was like. She was strong, confident. I can't imagine her being driven to suicide."

"It all started with *Catapult*. She became really moody, but she wouldn't talk to me about it. And then she cut me out entirely. I got angry, defensive, like an idiot. I didn't know if she needed space or if she was ghosting me or what. But I know it was about that fucking movie. Making movies, shooting TV, is work, hard, tedious work. And sometimes it can be exhausting and a fucking nightmare. But *Catapult* . . . She just fell apart. There was something else going on."

"Do you know him? Personally?"

"Charles? Everybody knows him. Or of him. A great part in one of Charles's movies will get you noticed. Not just for your work but because he campaigns the hell out of things. That helps with the awards. Hell, that *wins* awards. But I wouldn't work there, and even if I wanted to, I couldn't get hired at DreamWeaver. I'm persona non grata and that's fine with me."

"Why?"

"Because I publicly humiliated the bastard—my finest hour." He wryly lifted his beer in a toast.

"What happened?"

"After Scarlett died, about two weeks or so later, I was on hiatus from the series. I had nothing to take my mind off of her. I was barely functioning. So, Dan, my agent, wants to meet for lunch. And we're sitting at this restaurant, so I can 'be seen,' and in walks Charles Weaver. And Dan keeps talking, but I'm not hearing him anymore—it's just noise, because Weaver comes in with this young chick who's falling all over him. And it makes me sick. And just like that, I get up and go over. He looks up. And he recognizes me, I know he does, but he plays dumb. And I say, 'Hi, Charles, we've met before. I'm Jeremy Banker, Scarlett Norris's boyfriend.' And he gives me this patronizing smile that just infuriates me. So, I grabbed him by the jacket and lift him up. He's a big guy, but he's a fat fuck, not strong. And he was afraid. Truly afraid for his life. And everybody just gasps, and Charles yells, 'Get him off me,' and his bodyguard is on me in a second. Then Dan grabs my arm and I yell at Charles, 'You killed her, you sonofabitch! I know you did!' And then Dan dragged me out of there."

They were both quiet a moment.

"Jeremy, did you send me a note in New York?"

"No, I never had your address. Just your phone number."

"So it wasn't you."

"What wasn't me?"

"I got a weird note late one night, when I was still in New York, right before the Oscars. A courier dropped it off. It had the number of a police report with a note that said Scarlett deserved better. But I couldn't track the report down. I went to a precinct in lower Manhattan, and they had no record of it, couldn't find the number."

Jeremy shook his head in bafflement. "Wish I knew."

"I read some of Scarlett's journals," Angie admitted. "She wrote about a lot of things, about her work, about you and her."

A flash of concern crossed Jeremy's face.

"It was good stuff, don't worry. Mostly good anyway."

Jeremy gave a small laugh.

"But it was clear Charles's micromanagement on the set and the way he treated the director were stressing her out. And then she started rambling toward the end. I have no idea what happened, but she wasn't in her right mind. And I've heard that Charles is a real predator when it comes to women, and that he doesn't back off. I started wondering— about Scarlett. Do you think that's possible?"

"Anything's possible with that fucker, and somehow, some way I know he's responsible. If you find out that he touched her . . . Jesus." He took a long slug from his beer.

Angie gave him a moment to process before venturing gently, "Her journal said you fought the last time you saw one another."

He sighed and lowered his gaze, shook his head. "Yeah. I wish it wasn't true, but we did. We were having these great weekends, and I realized I didn't want to be apart from her. So we had been talking about moving in together. But then she started to change. And the last time I saw her, she was so brittle and she snapped at me for everything. She said she was confused and didn't know what she wanted, meaning me, I thought, which left *me* confused. And I responded in kind. Which was oil on a fire, of course. So I went back to Canada and we talked and texted on and off after that, but she would give terse replies or not reply for days, and I wasn't sure what was going on. I should have asked more questions or just flown back down. It's Hollywood, after all. I should have known how bad things were."

*God, Scar, why did you have to be so strong?* "You couldn't have known if she didn't tell you." Angie realized she was assuring herself as much as she was Jeremy. "None of us could. All we can do now is move forward and, if anything horrible did happen to Scarlett, make sure some sort of justice is done on her behalf."

Jeremy nodded softly, clearly lost in thought, and a silence settled over the room. He broke it a few moments later. "I think part of the reason I finally texted you is I wanted to make sure you were okay. I didn't do enough for Scar, and then when I read you were working at DreamWeaver, I thought I should . . . I don't know, check in? Does that sound ridiculous?" Jeremy focused on his beer bottle, the label almost entirely shredded. "I mean, you're a grown woman, and now I can see you have your shit together."

"What?" Angie laughed out loud. "Oh, my God, my shit's never together, but thank you." Jeremy laughed, too. "Since coming out here, I've been doing a little research. I can't get into it all right now, but I know there are actresses who wouldn't go along with Charles's advances, and they got blacklisted."

"Christ. I'm not surprised."

Angie was beginning to feel tired and decided it was time to go.

"Thanks, Jeremy. I appreciate you contacting me." Angie stood to leave before remembering one more thing. "Hey, have you been out to the house at all? Scarlett's. I mean, have you driven by or anything?"

Jeremy shook his head as they moved toward the foyer. "Why?"

Angie took a beat. "Nothing, it's . . . nothing."

Angie hugged him goodbye and drove home.


Angie woke up feeling restless. The meeting with Jeremy had comforted her, but it had also shined light on Scarlett's state of mind and exacerbated the state of her own. She had so much to do, but first she had to get through the workday hoping Nicole or Charles or Tanya wouldn't lower the boom. Thank God it was Friday. And somehow, she had no meetings scheduled. Which meant she finally had a moment to track down Kristy Wong.

She pulled up the company directory and skimmed the listings to find that Kristy Wong was in cubicle number 1408—on the same floor as both Nicole and Charles.

She snatched a folder to look official and headed to the elevators, where two employees she'd never seen before stood waiting. She counted that as good luck. If she didn't know them, they likely wouldn't know her. Or at least not enough about her to think it suspicious she was on her way to an upper-level floor.

They hardly glanced at her when the door dinged and they entered the car, gossiping about someone. The taller of the two swiped a key card and hit the button for the thirteenth floor. Shit. It wasn't the one Angie needed. But the other employee casually swiped his card for the fourteenth floor. Bingo. The car started ascending, and their conversation hushed for a moment, but then they quickly returned to dishing the dirt. The door opened on thirteen and the first guy got out, giving a quick wave to his companion. The short ride to C-suite was silent, and the second guy didn't seem to give her a moment's thought.

When the bell dinged on the top level, she took a deep breath and stepped out with what she hoped was a confident air. The same double-glass doors let on to the suite of glass-and-metal tables with the blue couches and film posters. No one was there.

She counted that as more good luck. And hoped she wasn't using it all up.

She turned left and headed down the hall to a pen of cubicles. To her surprise, the first space she came to was number 1400, followed by 1401. She was going in the right direction. But when she got to 1408, the cube was empty. Now what? She couldn't very well stand there and wait. What if Nicole saw her?

She was suppressing her rising panic and was about to head back to the elevators when movement down the hall caught her eye and she observed Kristy coming out of what appeared to be a kitchen area. In a mauve skirt and white blouse, she was carrying a cup of coffee, her heels clicking softly on the tile floor. She was alone and focusing on her phone. She was still several cubicles away when she looked up. A flash of recognition—followed by, what, fear, annoyance?—crossed her face and she immediately deviated her course, slipping into a door on her right. The women's restroom.

Angie followed her inside to find a clean white room with four stalls and two sinks. Only one stall had its door shut. Angie leaned against the counter, the folder held tight against her chest. She spoke quietly.

"Kristy. I know you're in there and I know you saw me." When there was no response, Angie added, "I know it must have been hard for you to find my sister." She waited.

The bathroom was so quiet she could hear the air conditioning thrum through the building. Finally, there was a scuffling of shoes and the stall opened. Kristy's face was blotchy, her eyes wet.

"I liked Scarlett," she said, her voice a whisper. "But I can't lose my job."

"I don't want to endanger your position here. But I need to know what happened that day. You can understand that, can't you?"

"Of course. I told the police everything."

"But something happened to push Scarlett over the edge. Do you know *anything*?"

"I know she was stressed. There were a couple days when she really wasn't feeling well, but she kept working. She seemed kind of distract-ed. I had the feeling she wasn't eating or sleeping enough, so one night I went to her trailer with some tea, thinking it would relax her. But when I got there, I heard voices inside. I didn't mean to eavesdrop but you know how sometimes you can't help it? You just hear something?"

"Sure, of course."

"Right. And Scarlett sounded upset and scared, but she was stand-ing up to whoever was in there. She was saying something like, 'You need to get out. This can't happen again. I won't let it.' And then I hear a man's voice, very clearly. He says—I still remember the words—'It isn't up to you. You should know that by now. I always get what I want.' And it's Charles. He sounds . . . menacing. And I panic. I try to think what to do. I'm not really supposed to be there and not supposed to hear their conversation. Right then my phone goes off. Very loudly. And I'm literally standing on the steps to the trailer. So, I freeze. And then I hear the doorknob turning. And then Charles is standing there, looking angry, and he says, 'Kristy, can I help you?' And I say something I'm like, 'Scarlett wanted some tea.' And I can see her right behind him, over his shoulder. And she smiles at me. And then she says, 'Thanks, I'll text you if I need anything else' and comes forward, takes the tea, and then Charles closes the door."

"What did you do?"

"I left. But then I got a text from Scarlett asking if I would call her in thirty minutes. So I did, but it went straight to voice mail. Then the next day on set, she was even more distracted, short with people. She snapped at her assistant. That wasn't like her. I mean, she was always a pro, she hit her marks, knew her lines, could modulate her performance for different takes, but once the director said 'Cut' she started wandering off to her trailer. Normally, she was easy-going, she liked to hang with the crew or rehearse or just watch the process. But after the thing in her trailer, she was, like, gone. Just vacant."

Kristy's eyes met Angie's and then she started to cry. Her next words came out haltingly. "I shouldn't have left her there with him. I should have gone back or called the police or . . ."

"The police? Why?"

"Because . . . that was just the first time he was in her trailer with her."

Angie knew her next question would cut, but she had to ask. "Do you think he raped her?"

Kristy turned away, tears glistening on her face. "Oh, God. I'm so sorry. I didn't know what to do."

*Sweet Jesus.* Angie tried to contain her own tears. "You couldn't have done much. What would you have told the police, you overheard parts of conversations? Scarlett herself said she was okay. We both know who the responsible party is, and it's not you."

"You can't tell anyone. Please. My parents . . ."

The door opened and Tanya strode in wearing a red power suit, her expression one of surprise when she saw them.

"Just washing my hands," Kristy murmured, turning on the tap at the nearest sink. She ran her hands under the water for a moment, dried them on a paper towel, and slunk out, leaving her coffee on the counter.

Angie picked it up and went to follow, but Tanya held up a hand. "Leave her be." It wasn't a suggestion, it was a command. Angie set the cup back down and, still clutching her prop folder, pushed the door open, but Tanya spoke again, arresting her with just her voice. "Angie, don't let me catch you up here in C-suite unless you're with someone who belongs here. This isn't your place."

Angie released a shaky breath. She was caught. But what did Tanya suspect? "Right. Sorry. Never again."

And she stole out into the hall, letting the door close with a soft rush.

Angie stared numbly at her computer, unable to focus on the screen in front of her. She was seething and unsure what to do. She started scanning her inbox. Screenplay pitches. Queries from writers. Agents seeking meetings. An automated message reminding her of an upcoming performance review. And a message from Charles, checking in to see how she was doing, and could she meet for a drink?

She decided it was time to set a trap now that she knew what kind of animal she was trying to catch. She had to get him talking about Scarlett. She hit reply.

Hi, Charles,

I'd love to get that drink. How's tonight?

The response came almost instantaneously: Come up to my office at 7:00.

Angie's mouth was dry and her heart hammering when she slipped into the ladies' at 6:48. Peering at herself in the mirror only confirmed how wan she looked. She applied a little lipstick and blush and mascara, then used drops to get rid of her bloodshot eyes. By 6:54, she was shaking. She gripped the marble countertop to steady herself and met her gaze in the mirror. She had been told a number of times how much she reminded others of Scarlett. She was finally accepting that there were similarities in how they looked, and, more importantly, she felt she was developing some of Scarlett's strength, too, if only a little.

At seven o'clock, she approached Charles's door. Apparently, his assistant was gone for the day and his bodyguards elsewhere. She knocked. "Come on in!" His voice was gravelly yet mellifluous. It only made her more anxious.

She swung the door open and stepped inside. She didn't know what she had been expecting, but it wasn't what she found. Charles sat almost primly at his desk, his hands folded in front of him, the light of the sun in the west flooding him through the tinted windows that looked over the city to the ocean. His baseball memorabilia, balls and bats, gleamed behind him, polished to a shine. When she entered, he hopped up and went to the wall, which he slid open, surprising her with a hidden bar: vodka, tequila, wine, red and white, whiskey, gin, even Kahlua. "Have a seat," he said. "Let's take in that sunset."

Oh. That was when she caught sight of the settee that was facing the window. It was upholstered in a pale green and before it was a small coffee table.

"What's your poison?"

"Vodka, straight." Had she just said that? She didn't really drink.

Charles chuckled.

She stood in front of the window, the setting sun warming her face. She hadn't planned anything beyond getting closer to Charles, to gain his trust so that he'd leave himself vulnerable. Vulnerable for what, exactly, she wasn't sure. But that meant she had to be relaxed, gracious, maybe playful. "I find a good, stiff drink at the end of the day really relaxes me." And where did that come from?

She heard liquid being poured and a moment later, he was offering her a glass with two fingers of vodka. He raised his glass in a toast.

"I can think of another stiff thing that might relax you even more."

She tensed, shocked by his disgusting remark, but raised her glass and they both drank. The alcohol scorched her throat, but she worked to keep her expression neutral. She wasn't mousy, ineffective, frightened Angie. She was assured, determined Angela.

"Why don't we have a seat." Charles indicated the settee and they sat. He left only an inch of space between them, placing his free hand on her knee. "So. We finally get some time alone. I'm glad you came around."

"I've been looking forward to getting to know the boss."

"That's what I like to hear." His hand moved up to her thigh.

She could smell onions on his breath. Her stomach roiled, already sour from the vodka. "Now, Charles. We're just having a drink," she said coquettishly with a little smile.

"That's right. We're just having a drink. At the moment." He sat back and took in the floor-to-ceiling view. "This always makes me hard. You know? Being king of the world, the city spread out in front of me for the taking." He angled his eyes back to Angie. "Just like you."

Oh, fuck. She was in over her head. She was certain there were still people in C-suite, but would they hear her if she screamed?

She stood, approached the window. The sun was starting its slow descent toward the horizon. Soon, the twilight and then the darkness would engulf them.

Charles approached, standing behind her. "You know, Angie." She didn't turn back at his voice. "I'm having a fantastic year. I feel like Rogers Hornsby. Maybe I'll hit four-twenty-four this year."

Then she felt his erection pressing against her ass. He nudged it in a circular motion.

Shit. "Charles. I think this is inappropriate."

"Honey, this is what you came for." When she hesitated, he added, "Don't you want to be like your sister?"

She froze. *That* was why she was there. Her sister. She couldn't acquiesce, but she couldn't scare him off either. She sipped more of her vodka and finally turned to him. "How well *did* you know Scarlett?"

"Oh, very well. She and I were very close."

"She never mentioned you. Aside from getting the part. You know, in *Catapult*."

"Maybe she's not the type to kiss and tell."

She was outraged at how glibly he was talking about a woman he had driven to suicide, how he was implying she had been into it, that it had been an affair, not rape. She slipped out from her place between Charles and the window and made like she was heading to the bar, but before she got more than a few steps, he gripped one of her wrists, pulling her back toward him.

"Oh, no. Don't think you're getting out of here that easily. We still have some business to attend to." His gaze skimmed down her body and back up. "I mean, you're not Scarlett, but you'll do. In a pinch."

She wrested her wrist from his grasp. "Charles. You're right. I'm not Scarlett. I do things differently."

He stared into her eyes for a prolonged moment. "You look a lot like her, you know." Then he headed to the bar himself. "Actually, you're more like her than you think."

"What does that mean?"

He spoke over his shoulder while he refilled his glass. "She took some convincing, too, you know, to play *nice*."

Angie's heart pounded in her wrists, her feet, her throat. "What kind of convincing?" Her voice sounded like that of a frightened child's, weak, vulnerable, breakable.

"Ah, you know. Sometimes you gotta show 'em what they like before they realize they like it."

He suddenly stopped. Angie followed his gaze to find Tanya standing in the doorway, a folder in her hand.

"Charles." Tanya's enigmatic smile was gone. "Hello, Angie. I see you're making the rounds today."

Oh, fuck. "Charles wanted to meet . . ."

"What do you want, Tanya?" Charles was clearly not pleased.

"Oh, I don't want to interrupt your . . . *meeting*, though I may have some information you might like."

*Shit fuck piss. She's referring to Kristy. She must be.* A scalding rush of panic shot through her temples, and she staggered toward the door, hoping she didn't look crazed. As she slipped past, Tanya gave her a withering look. "Have a good night."

Angie didn't wait for the elevator and instead rushed to the stairwell, her feet making too much noise on the concrete steps as she raced away. Once she got to her floor, she practically ran to her office, and that was when she realized she was still holding the tumbler of vodka.


When she got home, Angie took a blisteringly hot shower, wishing it would wash her skin off. She felt like she'd never be clean again, like she was destined to taste the shitty flavor of vodka and Charles's sexual aggression for the rest of her life. She had been with men who overstepped, who were entitled, who were flat-out repellent, but they had been nothing compared to Charles Weaver. She scrubbed her face, her body, her hair and came out feeling only somewhat less dirty.

She then scoured her teeth, hoping it would wash away the residual revulsion.

It didn't.

Finally, she was ready for a Xanax and a night of dreamless sleep.

Then: Nicole.

She showed up unannounced, fueling Angie's suspicions. Had Charles instructed her to go keep an eye on her? Specifically, that night? What might he have told her? And had Tanya told Charles about her conversation with Kristy?

God, she really wanted that Xanax.

But despite needing to be alone maybe more than she ever had in her life, she let Nicole in. She wanted to keep an eye on her as much as she suspected Nicole was there to keep an eye on her. Thankfully, Nicole didn't press her to chat or for sex. She seemed content to just be there. Which confused Angie even more. Did she really just want to spend time together? Or was she there just to report back to Charles? Or maybe she truly did want to be there, *and* she was also doing her job, which meant simply being in Angie's presence, nothing more required.

They curled up in bed and Nicole drifted off quickly, but Angie tossed and turned despite the Xanax. She so desperately needed sleep, she needed to rest, to refuel. She didn't know how she'd have the strength to get through the following day without it.

Finally, sinking into a shallow, restless slumber, she dreamed.

*She found herself in the middle of a forest. The trees were so tall, she couldn't see where their tops vanished into the sky. Hearing shouts and the thunderous hoofbeats of horses, she ran to hide behind a particularly large trunk, flattening herself against it to stay out of view.*

*The sounds grew louder and then abruptly stopped. When she peered around the tree, she saw riders on horseback in a circle formation. A heavy-set man with his face obscured rode in and took his position in the center. He was followed by two lines of women. The man lifted his face and Angie gasped. It was Charles. A bow and arrow materialized in one woman's hands. She drew back and fired, hitting Charles, who vaporized, his smoke curling toward the sky. Angie started rising, too, until she was floating above the clearing. Suddenly Charles was floating across from her. "Have you seen enough yet?" he asked, breaking into laughter.*

*Angie looked down and started plummeting back to Earth.*

She shot up in bed. Nicole turned over but didn't wake up. Angie quietly crept out of the room and tiptoed downstairs to the kitchen, poured a glass of cold water, and peered through the sliding doors into the night.

Angie realized she needed her sister's strength more than ever. *Please look out for me, Scar.* Hot tears trickled down her face, but she didn't wipe them away. She wanted to feel them. This was her life now. Not a break from her real life. This was it. She was a woman in LA in a relationship with another woman who had been commissioned to spy on her and enmeshed in a high-stakes game of chicken with one of the most powerful men in the film industry.

*Inhale, two, three, four . . .*

"What are you doing?"

Angie jumped. She turned to see Nicole, clad in an oversized football jersey, padding down the stairs, and she squinted when Nicole flipped on a floor lamp.

"You look like you're in a trance."

She spun away, the glare of the lamp and the sight of Nicole too much to take. Angie didn't feel sad anymore. She felt rage. Rage that she had been deprived of her sister. That Scarlett had been deprived of her life. Because of a monster.

"Scarlett left me here alone. There's no one now to count on. And I just don't know how this could have happened. It wasn't supposed to turn out like this. I'm the one who should be dead. Me. Not her." She addressed Nicole's reflection on the sliding door. "I was the one who was sad. I was depressed. I didn't have the promise of a brilliant future. But I'm still here, more alone than I've ever been."

"You're not alone." Nicole approached and turned Angie gently so they were face to face. "I'm here. I love you. And I'm not going anywhere. I know I'm not Scarlett, but I'm here. Only you have to let me in."

Angie strode to the kitchen and pulled Nicole's rose gold hoop earring out of a drawer. She held it up as she returned to the living room. "Oh, I think you already let yourself in."

Nicole gaped at the earring for a few seconds. "It's been missing for days. Where did you find it?"

Angie couldn't tell if she was honestly surprised or just concentrating on what she should say next. "In the spare room. Got any questions about my whiteboard?"

Nicole gave her an odd look. "Really. I was looking for toilet paper and I popped my head into that room. And, yeah, the board got my attention. Who are all those people?"

"Actresses. Actresses who were manipulated and assaulted and then blacklisted."

Nicole looked confused. "Assaulted? Blacklisted? What are you talking about?"

Angie wanted to believe that Nicole's reaction was sincere. That she really didn't know. But if she had been sent to track her, of course she'd be pulling lies out of thin air once confronted. Maybe if Angie threw it all out there, full force, Nicole might be overwhelmed enough to tell the truth.

"Hey." Nicole took one of her hands. "You do know I'm not the enemy, right? You've been really distant the past few days and now you're being really sketch."

"*I'm* being sketch? You're the one who was caught snooping in my office. And it's awfully convenient how you befriended and then seduced me."

Nicole dropped her hand and stepped back. "Whoa, whoa, whoa. I thought this was mutual. You didn't think you had to do this for your job, did you? Did I ever put any conditions on our relationship?"

Angie didn't know what to say.

"I am real. This"—Nicole gestured in the space between them—"is real. I could lose my job if this went sideways. Do you really think I would risk that?"

Angie let her shoulders sag. Nicole sounded genuine. And it was true she had never expected anything from Angie. And she was risking far more in the relationship than Angie was.

"I don't even care what the whiteboard is about," Nicole continued. "We need to fix us. Or break this off now."

Shit. Angie didn't want to lose her. Not until—unless—she found out for sure that Nicole was just using her.

"So, what do we do? Right now?" Nicole gave her a soft, imploring look.

"You're really on my side?"

"Who else's side would I be on?"

"I don't know." Angie sat on the sofa. Nicole joined her but kept some distance between them, holding a throw pillow in her lap. Angie wanted to believe her. But she needed leverage. "All right. I'll tell you. But just remember what you said. You have more to lose than I do."

"God. Okay. My lips are sealed."

Angie took a breath and dove in. "I'm out here because I think something or someone pushed Scarlett so far that she killed herself. And I think that someone is Charles. The whiteboard is a chart of actresses who refused Charles, refused to sleep with him, to be overpowered by him, so he made sure they didn't work anymore. Not for DreamWeaver or, essentially, for anyone."

Nicole had a look of shock on her face. "Wow. Okay."

"It's a lot, I know."

"I mean, Charles can be a tyrant. I've seen him lose his shit on sets, in the office, even at parties. But I have never heard of him outright assaulting anyone."

"There's a pattern. And I have someone, a private eye, doing some investigating. He's made some connections himself."

Nicole scoffed as if in disbelief. "You have a private eye investigating Charles?!"

"Welcome to my mind."

"Jesus Christ, Angie. Do you know what he would do if he found out!"

"That is why he can't find out."

"Fuck."

"Scarlett never told us anything about her difficulties out here or her depression. She hid everything. You had to know her. For her to commit suicide is just unfathomable. So, yes, I came out to see if I could figure it out."

"I don't think most people ever know why someone commits suicide."

"Well, I also got a weird message in New York, an anonymous note that said Scar *deserved better* and pointed me toward a police report that I wasn't able to track down. It was enough to convince me something had gone on that we knew nothing about. So I had to find out what I could. And here I am!"

"I don't know what to think." Nicole pulled at the fringe on the pillow in her lap. "I mean, like I said, Charles is temperamental and demanding and can micromanage things on set, and everywhere else, but that's how a lot of powerful men are. And he's a creative genius. But actual assault?"

"I'm reaching out to those actresses, trying to build a case. Because it seems, yes, there have been actual assaults."

"Fuck." Nicole shook her head and then looked deep into Angie's eyes. "You have to be very careful. This isn't just fire you're playing with. This is a runaway firestorm."

# 14

"I can't believe this." Mackenzie had called right as Angie entered her office Monday morning, and Angie had no choice but to fill her in on the status—or lack thereof—of *Peregrine*.

Angie paced listlessly, wondering what she could say to make things better. "I thought DreamWeaver acted in good faith. I was certain that if they bought the rights, it was because they wanted to make a movie, and they still might. It hasn't been that long, not really."

"But why won't anyone talk with me or Rita? Why doesn't anyone just say, 'Hey, we're backed up for another year, but we've assigned a screenwriter and we'll keep you posted.' This radio silence makes me nervous. It's like they forgot about it once they got the rights. So be honest with me. What do you think the chances are this will actually get made?"

"I hate to say this, but I don't know what the chances are. When we spoke in April, and you agreed to sell us the *Peregrine* rights, I didn't realize the sheer amount of IP the studio owns that doesn't go anywhere. Obviously, everyone knows not everything gets made, but I really thought *Peregrine* was a shoo-in because it was so hot. Turns out, that's no guarantee."

"I had better, bigger offers, you know that."

"I'm so sorry. I wish I had more to tell you. We'll just have to wait and see if Charles Weaver lights a fire under it. There's still a chance. It's just a lot more uncertain than I thought at first. I'm really sorry."

"I'm going to try to get the rights back." Mackenzie's tone was hot, angry. "I don't trust these fuckers. I'll give the money back. I'd rather make less and see a good film come outta this than see the damn thing languish altogether." Then her voice softened. "I had all these visions of a great film."

Man, this sucked. It wasn't what Angie had wanted for Mackenzie at all. "I did too. Even if I seem the bad guy right now, I really believe in your story."

"I hope so. Because you talked me into this."

"I know, I know. Look, just keep the pressure on. Call your attorney now. Have Rita keep me posted. I'll let you know anything I hear on this end."


That night, Angie carried her dinner salad, grabbed her laptop and the flash drive she had found in Nicole's office, and went to the spare room to plug the drive into her computer's USB port.

The blinking password prompt taunted her. She typed "IP". Nothing. She typed "Development". Nope. She knew trying endless combinations of letters, numbers, and characters was a waste of time, and too many failed attempts would lock her out. She didn't have the computer firepower or know-how to run millions of combinations until the password was cracked, like in the movies.

She stared at the screen, thinking of her conversation with Charles, and typed in "nice" for the hell of it. She didn't get an automatic rejection. Then an arrow started swirling and, to her amazement, a document appeared on the screen. It was a blank page but she clicked it and a second page opened behind it. It was a spreadsheet with dates, titles, and initials. Some of the dates went back a decade or more. Was it an old IP list? What were the initials? Authors? Agents who handled the sale? Did any of this get developed? Did DreamWeaver buy it?

She picked a set of initials arbitrarily. SB. It was next to a project called *Neon Rose*. She double clicked on the title, but it wouldn't open. She Googled it along with the term "movie" and more than eighty thousand results popped up, but nothing seemed to be what she was seeking. She scrolled down to another title, *Maggie's Dilemma*. Significantly fewer results, a couple of books, a short film, but not what she was looking for. She did the same with both titles with the term "book," and while there were results, none of them were the bull's-eye she needed.

Then she started to think: maybe they were working titles for movies that never got made or were developed into shorts rather than feature films. DreamWeaver would have started out small, and that could explain why the titles were difficult to track down. Angie checked a few websites geared toward film buffs but, again, nothing turned up.

She opened a new browser tab and went to Patricia's IMDb page, where she scanned her credits. Patricia had starred early in her career in a DreamWeaver movie called *Wildflower Honey*. Angie opened another tab and pulled up her Wikipedia page. Born Susan Patricia Babbington, she had changed her surname to something more marketable and used her middle name as a stage name.

*Wait, Susan Babbington. SB. The initials. They're not writers or agents or titles. They're actors' initials.*

Angie went back to the spreadsheet and clicked on the letters. An envelope icon appeared. She clicked on the envelope and a document opened.

She scanned it, her skin prickling.

NDA 9-1-2008 Susan P. Babbington DBA Patricia
Bartlett #65988

NDA. Non-disclosure agreement. *Oh, my God, that's it. Hush money.* That was why the women wouldn't talk, or couldn't talk. Charles paid them off.

Unfortunately, there were no other links. No actual NDAs. Just a reference file. Of course, Charles wouldn't be stupid enough to store them electronically. Too much risk they'd wind up on the internet or emailed to some tabloid journalist. But the paper files had to be somewhere. They were contracts. Tanya would know about them. Charles too. Where would they be?

Angie sat back in her chair, her salad forgotten. She was avoiding thinking too hard about one obvious fact—that she'd found the drive in Nicole's desk drawer. It had nothing to do with development. So why was it there?

Jango pulled up in front of a row of dingy storefronts. When Nola was away, he allowed himself a splurge. And right then, hitting up a terrific falafel place was just what he needed before heading to his meeting with a new client.

His hunger was battling for attention with flashes of Charles Weaver's atrocities as he pulled into the small strip mall with a smaller parking lot.

He parked and hopped out of his car, debating the merits of lamb over chicken when he woke up in darkness. The back of his head pulsed with the rhythm of his heartbeat. He didn't have to touch it to know he would find blood. Not that he could have seen it anyway.

He could hear a smooth motor from inside the car's trunk, its vibration all around him. He fumbled for his phone, realizing as he patted an empty pocket that of course that was the first thing they did. Well, second, after they had knocked him unconscious.

He felt real fear for maybe the first time in his life, and he thought of Nola and how her heart would break if they never got that holiday in Baja.

***

The first thing Angie did when she got to work the next morning was plow through her inbox. She was hoping to find something regarding Mackenzie's project, but there was nothing. Someone rapped sharply on her open office door and she jumped. She looked up and blanched.

Charles loomed in the doorway with Ari in tow. But this time, Ari was accompanied by a lookalike: another beefy bald bodyguard in a gray suit with mirrored shades. What was going on?

Charles strode in, but Ari and Ari 2 stayed just outside. She was trapped.

"Oh, Charles, hello." She tried to sound casual, but she knew he had seen her jump when he knocked. To cover, she blurted, "Are you pleased with how the database turned out?"

"Oh, yes. Nicole did a terrific job of heading that up." He didn't break eye contact but hesitated a beat. "Turns out there was a terrible murder in the city last night."

Angie exhaled. A murder? What did that have to do with anything? There were countless murders in every city around the world every day, especially Los Angeles. "Oh?"

"Yes, some private eye was found shot to death in an abandoned lot. But he had some contacts, as it turns out, in the movie industry. It's all very murky."

Oh no. Jango. The room started to spin, and Angie broke into a cold sweat. She could practically feel the blood draining from her face, and she was probably growing paler by the second. *Charles knows.*

"Are you all right, Angie? I didn't mean to shock you."

"I'm—I'm fine," she sputtered, a little too loudly. "I just, I haven't had any breakfast, so I'm a bit light-headed."

"Please don't worry. About that murder, I mean." He took a step toward her and leaned in. "I've got everything under control here."

He abruptly departed, followed by Ari and Ari 2.

As soon as they were gone, she Googled "Los Angeles" and "murder" and "June 26." *Please, no, please, no . . .* She didn't have to look any further than the top entry:

Private Investigator Found Shot to Death on Skid Row

*Oh, no, oh, no. Oh, please, God, no. Oh, my God, oh, my God . . .*

But she knew what she'd find even before she clicked the embedded video about how former LAPD detective and private investigator Jango Davies was found dead the night before in an abandoned lot with a bullet through his head.

Angie's heart raced. She leaned back in her chair and closed her eyes. *Breathe in, two, three, four. Out, two, three, four. In, two, three, four . . . I have to get out of here, I have to get out of here, but I need to be calm first, I need to breathe, be calm, be calm so I can move.*

She opened her eyes, a surge of nausea threatening to erupt. She darted out of her office and down the hall to the women's bathroom, flung open the door, ran into a stall, and immediately threw up. When she was sure there was nothing more, she flushed the toilet, wiped her mouth with tissue, and leaned against the stall door.

*Oh, my God, they know. They know. They killed Jango and they're going to kill me.*

She wiped away tears with a shaky hand, thoughts ricocheting from Scarlett to Patricia to Jango to the women he'd interviewed. Jango was always so careful. They'd met at that small, out-of-the-way Indian grocery and café. He'd made certain no one followed them that morning in Topanga. But someone knew.

Was it Kevin? He'd been on his motorbike at that café after she'd met Jango. Was he following her? Or was it Tanya? Maybe Kristy ratted her out. But she wouldn't have known about Jango. Maybe it didn't matter. Charles knew. His little visit to her office was a warning. He was telling her to back off. Did he know she was the one who had hired Jango?

She stood, smoothed her skirt, and went out to wash her face and rinse out her mouth in the sink. As she was spitting out a second mouthful of tepid water, a woman pushed open the door and glanced her way. She grimaced at Angie through the mirror, and Angie looked up at her own reflection. Yikes. Messy hair. Runny eyes. Flushed face. She looked as terrified and fucked up as she felt.

"Are you all right?" the woman asked.

Angie dabbed at her cheeks with a damp paper towel. "Oh, yes, fine. I just . . . I think I'm getting a migraine."

"Oh, God, those are awful. My mom gets them. They make her sick to her stomach." The woman tutted sympathetically and went into a stall.

Angie exited the bathroom, focusing on taking one step after another. She could leave. Pack her bags. Fly home. Charles wouldn't follow her. She could cut off contact with the studio. She'd be all right. Jango was gone. With her back in New York, there would be no one else to dig up Charles's dirt. He would win.

Back at her desk, she found she'd missed three texts from Nicole.

Where are you?

Your phone is on your desk.

Everything OK?

Just a little nausea.

Stepped away.

Angie opened Kayak in a browser tab and checked flights for New York, but her thoughts stayed with Jango. He shouldn't have died like that. He deserved better. Just like Scar. She hadn't been friends with Jango. It was a professional relationship, but they had grown to like one another. And more, she trusted him. He was the only person in LA she had felt she could trust completely. She felt utterly wrecked when she thought of his stoic demeanor, his innate sense of decency. Some people never have to ask what's right or wrong, they just know. Jango and Scar. Where would this end?

Her throat tightened and she closed the Kayak tab. She, too, knew the difference between right and wrong. And Charles was wrong. He was a monster. She wasn't going to let him win this time. She was going to stay. And make him pay.

That night in bed, Nicole turned to her. "Are you going to tell me what's going on?"

Angie didn't answer right away. Finally, she said, "I heard a man was murdered last night." *The same man you met out here by the pool.* But Jango had never introduced himself to Nicole so she wouldn't be able to put the name and the face in the news together. She'd be none the wiser.

Nicole frowned. "And . . . ? Did you know him?"

"No. Just . . ."

"Just what? Jesus, it's a shitty world. People are murdered every day."

"I guess."

They were silent for a bit, lying on their backs. Angie's eyes focused on the ceiling as she pondered her bedmate. *What do you know, really, about Charles's catch and kill operation? About any of it?* Finally, she said, "Do you remember a producer by the name of Christo Holland?"

"Doesn't ring a bell, but I deal with a lot of people. Why?"

"We bought the rights to a sci-fi book he was keen to option. He was in talks with the writer, but he lost out on a chance to buy the book because the writer was apparently bedazzled by the DreamWeaver name. DreamWeaver bought it and buried it and now both the producer and writer are out of luck. No one will respond to his calls or emails."

"Okay. And?"

"Nothing." Angie was disappointed yet unsurprised by the lack of interest or concern. She rolled to her side, facing away from Nicole. "Good night."

The rest of the week felt like a slow blur and when Friday arrived so did Angie's performance review.

As she waited in a chair outside Nicole's office, a statuesque blonde strode down the hall in an aquamarine power outfit. Angie thought she was going to pass right by but then she stopped, towering over her. "Mr. Weaver is ready for you now."

Surprised and alarmed, Angie stood. "But— What?"

"Miss Hawkins will not be assessing your review. Mr. Weaver will be. Come with me."

She stalked away so Angie had no choice but to follow. Nicole hadn't said anything about this. Had she known? The elevator ride was weirdly silent, the blonde focused straight ahead. Then something occurred to Angie and her heart plummeted. "Um. Where is Kristy? Charles's exec assistant."

"Kristy's no longer here." She gave an insouciant shrug. "More than that, I don't know."

Fuck. Fuck fuck fuck. Kristy had been fired, maybe paid off, maybe forced to sign an NDA. And it was Angie's fault for pursuing her into that bathroom. Tanya. She had told Charles. But what else had she told him?

When they got up to the executive floor, the woman led her into Charles's outer office. "He'll be with you in a sec." She departed, leaving Angie to take a seat beside the closed inner office door.

She pulled out her phone and scrolled through industry news from *The Hollywood Reporter* to look busy and that was when she became aware of muffled voices coming through the door. Charles and another man were speaking heatedly. She cocked an ear in that direction as subtly as she could, afraid to get caught eavesdropping, by Charles or anyone else who happened by.

"Someone in this company talked to that private eye!" Charles suddenly boomed. "And I'm going to find out who. Until then, these files are safer at my place than here. So fucking get them and don't offer your 'insight' again. I don't pay you to think."

The other man rejoined but Angie couldn't make it out. She strained her ears but heard nothing more. Angie fought to keep her fear at bay, but she could feel her heart palpitating, sweat on her brow. She wanted to flee but she was trapped. And desperate to know what was in those files. What did they have to do with Jango?

When the door opened, she jumped. Ari and Ari 2 strode out so quickly and with such purpose she didn't even know if they had seen her. She stood and poked her head inside. Charles sat behind his massive desk like a king on his throne.

"Sit." He was being purposely gruff. Was he pissed she hadn't disappeared after his implied threat the day before?

She sat.

"So. Nicole has told me about your work performance."

He let it sit there. She didn't rush in to fill the void mostly because she had no idea what to say. Was that another threat? He continued to eye her, unblinking. He clearly was not going to take up the thread again. She had to do *something*.

"I hope I've been satisfactory."

He leaned back in his chair, steepling fingers beneath his chin, and assessed her. "Well, that depends on your learning curve. How well you read a room. How well you adapt."

She wasn't quite sure how to take his remark. "I think I'm pretty flexible."

She hadn't intended the double entendre but Charles grinned with the veneer of the Wolf about to feast on Little Red. He stood and approached her, nudging his erection into her shoulder. "You know, I'm sorry Tanya interrupted us the other day."

"I am too." Her mouth dry as sand, she swallowed a shudder. "Why don't we start again tonight?"

Charles looked at her sharply. Was that too much? Had she over-played her hand? Then he said, playfully, "Yeah?"

"It is Friday. How about a drink after work?"

"That works. I'll bring the car around front. Six-thirty?"

A wave of relief washed over her, followed by one of anxiety. "I look forward to it."

At 6:29, Angie slipped into the back of Charles's sedan and Ari whisked them away toward Westwood. Apparently he was chauffeur as well as bodyguard. Ari 2 sat in the passenger seat. Not much was said on the ride. She glanced at Charles's briefcase. If he was taking those files home, they had to be in that briefcase.

Charles placed a proprietary hand on her thigh, and she gave him a small smile she hoped read as coy rather than terse.

They pulled into a parking lot under a tall building on Wilshire and Ari parked in a reserved spot right next to a bank of elevators. Ari opened her door and she was led to an express elevator to the pent-house that opened onto a vestibule with one door, soft light emanating from above. Charles used a key card and buzzed them in, the door opening to an expansive, open-plan apartment with windows looking out on the city from every direction. Evening light from the sinking sun made the living room feel like a wonderland. The furniture was all white leather, a sofa, a loveseat, two chairs, and a fully stocked bar stood against one wall. A fireplace was in the center of the room and Charles flicked it on with a remote, dropping his key card on the man-tle. "Ari." It was all he said, but both Aris turned and left, closing the door behind them.

"No need for protection tonight."

Angie wondered if there was a double meaning in his use of the word "protection." She set her bag by the couch where she slipped out of her jacket, then moved toward the bar, taking the lead. "Why don't you get comfortable. I'll make drinks. Vodka straight good for you again?"

"Lady's choice." Charles moved into what Angie assumed was the bedroom with his briefcase.

She dropped ice into two tumblers, reached for a bottle of Tito's, and poured four fingers' worth. She could hear Charles in the other room as she popped two Xanax out of her pocket and dropped them into one of the glasses, swirling the contents with a forefinger. She moved her finger faster. The pills weren't dissolving as quickly as she hoped. She cast a look toward the room Charles had entered. She heard a drawer close from within. She stirred faster. The pills were halfway disintegrated, then two-thirds. Then he was back, his rank breath on her back. She popped her other forefinger into the other glass—hers—and stirred that as well.

"Just adding a little flavor," she said, hoping she sounded quippy just as the pills dissolved completely. She turned and offered him the tumbler, surprised he was in nothing but boxers and a silk robe that was open. And socks. He was, inexplicably, wearing black socks.

"Bottoms up." He downed the entire thing in a gulp, much to her relief. If anything tasted off, it was too late. She took a dainty sip of her own, aware she didn't know how much time it would take for the drug to take effect. He was a large man. Maybe she should have given him three?

Luckily, instead of dropping his shorts or grabbing her, he poured himself two more fingers of Tito's, downed that, and poured two more. "Hell, why not? It's the weekend." He finally grasped the bottle and went to sit on the sofa, leaving his glass on the bar.

Angie joined him, sitting at the opposite end. He wasn't as aggressive as she'd expected. Likely because he thought they had all night. But she knew she didn't. She kept wondering about the Aris. Were they just outside the door? Had they taken the elevator? Were they headed somewhere to get drinks and try to pick up UCLA students? Were they watching her on video screens in some hidden room?

She shook her paranoia off and sipped at her vodka. She had to keep Charles talking until the Xanax took effect.

"So you and Scarlett, eh?"

The topic was so distasteful, but she had a feeling he'd like the chance to gloat about it again and she was hopeful she could glean some information.

"Oh, yeah. She liked it rough. I always wonder what a girl's childhood was like when she likes it that rough. When she's that dirty." He filled his glass again from the bottle and offered it to her.

The revulsion passed through Angie like in a tidal wave but she kept her face neutral. She wanted to murder him. She wanted to gut him, for him to feel pain before he died. She was grateful she didn't have a knife. There were things she needed to do first.

"We had a pretty good upbringing. Long Island." She didn't know how much to say, how personal to get. She didn't want to sully her memories by talking to Charles about them but she had to give him something. "A nice house, good neighborhood, good schools." She started to think about how she had had all that. Yet she still hadn't been okay. She'd still flailed.

"Yeah, that tracks, knowing your parents."

"What do you mean?"

"Oh." He sat up straight and took another generous swallow of the liquor. "Just that I met them once. When they came out to see Scarlett."

When had they come out to visit?

Before she could press the matter, Charles pushed on.

"But we're not here to talk about all that, are we? Why don't you come a little closer, help me relax?" He cocked his head at her and put a hand on her thigh. "I'm sure we can figure out a few ways to make that happen. And I can make you relax too, Angie. You'd like that, wouldn't you?"

Angie cringed inwardly, but she played along. "I guess we can all use some relaxation."

He moved his hand farther up her thigh until his fingers were smack in her groin. "Scarlett always had a hard time relaxing. But I think it could be different with you. Couldn't it, Angie?"

"It could, but first I need to freshen up. Maybe slip out of these restrictive clothes." She stood before he could restrict her himself.

He sat up, clearly a little drunk, and slurred, "Don't freshen up too much. I like my girls musky."

She forced a chuckle, then found the bathroom on her fourth try. It was a spacious room with an enormous window letting onto the city. She figured there was no concern about anyone peeping in so high up. There was a shower in the center of the room. Beyond it was a bathtub and Jacuzzi positioned right in front of the window. A walk-in closet branched off in one direction and a counter lined an entire wall with two sinks and various lotions, creams, and colognes. She approached the closet and peered in. It appeared to lead to his bedroom. She crept closer, past suit jackets and slacks and button-downs and shiny shoes, and craned her head through the doorway. His room was large, a circular bed at the center of it, black wood and black bedding. Windows looked out over the city, toward the ocean. A dresser and a desk, both in black, took up opposing walls. His clothes had been dropped in a heap at the base of the bed. He'd clearly been in a rush to get back to her.

And there, right there, leaning against the foot of the bed was the briefcase. It practically gleamed in the light as if winking at her.

The butterflies in her gut took flight. She had to check it out once he passed out. If he passed out.

She went back into the bathroom and turned the faucet on in one of the sinks to create a wall of sound. She didn't know what else to do to kill time. Catching sight of herself in the mirror, she realized she looked as frightened as she felt. Her eyes were bloodshot, her face splotchy, her lips dry. She automatically applied lip balm before realizing she didn't want to be appealing to him. Though, clearly, he didn't care.

Ugh.

She hardly recognized herself anymore. Who had she become? What was she doing there? If it hadn't been for Scarlett, she never would have found the mettle to do any of what she'd done in the past weeks. She felt good about how she'd shifted her foundation, though she didn't know if it was worth it yet. She hadn't prevailed. She hadn't brought Charles to justice.

But she was there. Doing something. Not just existing like before, running down the clock with only Brontë for companionship, turning to Scott when she was overwhelmed. She didn't recognize herself because she wasn't the same person.

And she was liking who she had become. And who she was still becoming.

It dawned on her, she didn't know how long she had been gone. So she ran her fingers under the faucet for a moment and patted them dry on a plush towel, before cracking the door, as quietly as possible, and slipping back to the living room.

She found Charles unconscious, the bottle dangling precariously from one hand.

She stopped abruptly, stunned that he was out. She took a couple of steps forward and leaned in, still four feet away. He was snoring so loudly, she was surprised she hadn't heard him from the bathroom. She moved closer yet and peered at him to confirm he was indeed passed out rather than just dozing.

Finally convinced, Angie moved fast. She hustled into the bedroom and moved with laser focus toward the briefcase. She placed it on the bed and tried to snap it open, but it was secured with a small padlock. A small rush of relief briefly overwrote her fear.

She just needed the small key.

And then she remembered his clothes at the foot of the bed. Could the key be in his jacket?

She scooted over to the pile of fabric and rooted around in his coat, both inside pockets and out: nothing.

Then she spied his trousers.

She grabbed them, hearing the clinking of keys as soon as she did. He had a handful of keys on a ring in one pocket. She pulled them out and one, small and gold, glinted in the dim light.

She turned back to the briefcase, casting a glance over her shoulder at the door to the living room. It had been left ajar. She could make out the soft purr of his snores.

The key fit the lock perfectly and turned almost without effort. The case opened with a click. Inside were about thirty files sitting there like treasure. She opened the top one to find a nondisclosure agreement. It was lengthy.

Shit. What was she going to do with them?

Her phone. It was in her purse. In the living room.

She slipped to the door and peeked out. Charles was still unconscious on the sofa. She moved as quietly as she could to her tote, which sat at the opposite end of the sofa. It took her a moment to find her phone at the bottom and she checked the volume. It was on silent, like usual. Good.

She set the bag back on the floor and was just passing Charles when he let out a rough snore. His eyes fluttered and he reached for her hand, grasping her fingers firmly. She froze, fearing her heart would explode out of her chest. Then he gently let go as he drifted back into blackness.

She stifled a sigh of relief that he hadn't grabbed the hand that held her phone.

Back in the bedroom, she snapped a photo of the first page of the first NDA. She flipped to the second page and was about to take another shot when she heard Charles make a grotesque sound through his nose. She almost screamed but managed to maintain her composure and went to the door to check on him. He had rolled over and was about to fall right off the sofa.

Shit, shit, shit.

If he fell, he'd probably wake up.

She made a snap decision. She scooped up all the folders and secured them under one arm, closed the briefcase lid with a quiet click, set it back at the base of the bed, and slipped out into the living room.

And then she had a thought that sent panic through her like she'd been struck by lightning. What if there were cameras?

She froze, as if that would somehow save her. Straight ahead, she could see the dining area, but no lens, no tell-tale red light. She looked to the left, the foyer, and nothing. To her right was the wall of windows. She decided it didn't matter. If she was being taped, it was too late.

She strode purposefully to her tote bag, stuffed all the folders inside, grabbed her jacket, then headed for the front door. She had one hand on the doorknob when she paused.

Would the Aris be on the other side? She put her ear to the door and heard nothing, which didn't surprise her. They were almost always silent even when actively on the job. They wouldn't be having a party in the hall.

She turned the doorknob, silently opened the door just a crack, and peered out with one eye. She could see only the elevator directly across.

If the Aris were there, just out of sight, she could always tell them Charles had had too much to drink and passed out. Which was half true. Or she could imply that their rendezvous was complete. Would they buy that? How long did Charles usually take? Did the women leave like Angie was, or were they in tears, clothes torn, bruised, anguished?

She had to take her chances.

She swung open the door and stepped confidently toward the elevator, not intending to look back unless she was accosted. She didn't even know if she needed a key card to get into the elevator and her heart plummeted as she hit the button, hearing the apartment door close behind her. The key card was still inside. She turned back in horror, terrified she might be stuck in the hall only to be caught red-handed. At least she was able to confirm the Aris were not there. She was alone.

And then she heard a musical *ding!*

She exhaled and faced the elevator doors just as they slid open. Still, as she rode down, she knew she wasn't out of the woods yet. The Aris could have been watching on cameras she hadn't detected and be waiting in the lobby. Security could be waiting for her in the lobby. Charles could have roused and sounded the alarms.

When she got to the ground floor, the doors dinged open and she hesitated. No one greeted her. She heard no commotion. The lobby—what she could see of it—was hushed.

She finally stepped out and turned a corner into the full foyer. One security guard, in his fifties in a blue uniform, sat behind a desk, a bank of computers behind him. He looked up from his iPad and nodded at her as she passed, easy breezy, through a revolving door into the heavy evening air.

She turned to the right, no clue where she was headed except for away, as quickly as possible, and didn't stop until she'd gone four blocks. Then she took another right, down a quiet, shadowy tree-lined residential street. No one had followed her, either on foot or on wheels. She was pretty sure of it, but she continued another two blocks before stopping and calling an Uber, just to be extra cautious. It took more than ten minutes for it to arrive and she felt every second like a life sentence.

When she was finally ensconced in the car, being whisked back to DreamWeaver, she realized Charles or the Aris could be waiting for her in the parking structure, possibly with the police. But she found it quiet and got into her car and drove away, one eye in the rearview for any suspicious activity, but nothing unusual happened.

She made it home, exhausted but still wired from the adrenaline of her escape. She felt dirty.

Again.

She set the security alarm, checked the lock on every door and window, dropped all the blinds, and looked in every room, closet, and under the beds. She turned on every light in the house before taking a shower so hot she hoped her skin would peel off in strips. Jango was dead, and it was her fault. She had just drugged one of the most powerful men in the city. She had stolen from him. And her parents had just arrived in town. How was she going to fold them into her ongoing crazy juggling act?

Once she was as clean, or as cleansed, as she was going to get, her body screamed for rest. But she sat at her kitchen table, pulled the bounty out of her tote, and opened the top folder. It was an NDA with a payment of two hundred thousand dollars issued seven years ago to a woman. Angie didn't recognize the name but assumed it was an actress. She put it aside and opened the next one, which detailed a three-hun-dred-and-fifty-thousand-dollar agreement with another woman.

She flipped through folder after folder until her tired eyes could barely focus. But when she opened one that was labeled "De Nova, Mirabel," a jolt of electricity shot through her. And then she read the name on the next file: "Norris, Scarlett."

It made no sense.

> I, Scarlett Norris, the party of the first part, agree to keep strictly confidential as per the requirements and conditions outlined in this agreement any infor-mation regarding the personal, social, and business activities of Charles Weaver, Founder and CEO of DreamWeaver LLC . . .

Angie couldn't believe what she was reading.

> . . . the party of the first part furthermore hereby acknowledges and states without reservation that all sexual activity, including any and all sexual acts, were consensual. . . .
>
> . . . In exchange for the agreement . . . the party of the first part will receive a sum of one million dollars . . .
>
> This contract is binding and irrevocable.

Angie read the agreement over and over until the words became a blur. A knot of rage at the very bottom of her stomach traveled up through her body until her heart pounded so hard she feared a panic attack or maybe even a heart attack coming on.

She went to the sliding doors, needing air, and stood looking out at but not seeing the pool and the night sky. *Consensual?* It was inconceivable. *You were raped. That bastard raped you. And then he paid you to shut up.*

She had looked through at least two dozen NDAs. *There's enough here to destroy him. And I'll get more proof. He's not getting away with it.*

But something didn't make sense. It was entirely out of character for Scarlett to have been bought off. If she hadn't signed, she would have been blacklisted, true. Charles would have spread rumors, created false stories about her in an attempt to destroy her career. A clear-thinking Scarlett would have seen she had other options: indie films, TV, stage work. But Scarlett wasn't thinking clearly at the end. Those journal entries were not from a lucid mind. She was broken.

Wind rustled in the palms. Angie had had her moments of sorrow, anger, and terror, but now she was calm. And resolute. *I won't let him get away with it, Scar. But why did you take that check?*

# 15

"I'm sorry, what?" Angie had missed her mom's question, too distracted about the NDAs and when Charles would figure out she'd taken them to focus on Ellen's chatter. She'd come over to their Santa Monica Airbnb around eleven. Surely he was up by now. What was he plotting?

"We want to drive up to Malibu," Ellen repeated as she sliced avocados for a salad lunch.

The Airbnb suited her mother perfectly, Angie thought, an airy bungalow with an open floor plan, prints of beach watercolors, comfortably padded furniture, a fireplace for cool evenings, and a bright kitchen that afforded a sliver of a view of the Pacific. Her dad sat in the adjoining living room reading a newspaper.

"And we definitely want to eat at Chateau Marmont," her mother continued. "The history behind that place is unreal. And we're going to go down to Laguna Beach. Maybe you could join us for that." She looked up from the cutting board. "We can go next weekend. You said you hadn't done any of the tourist sights, but have you explored at all?"

Angie took a sip of her green tea. "Yeah, I've been a few places, but I just work a lot."

"You can't work all the time. And your father has been navigating the rental car like a pro, haven't you, Ger?"

"What's that?" Gerry lowered his paper. "The traffic out here. Jesus, I thought I'd lose my mind. It's like a goddamn war zone every time you get in the car."

"It hasn't been that bad. C'mon. You drive in New York." Ellen went back to slicing, her tone directed at Angie. "Everything all right, dear? You're awfully quiet."

"Of course everything's not all right." Gerry stood, dropping the paper on the seat of his armchair, and joined them. "She's out here trying to make a living in this ugly, ugly industry that killed her sister. How the hell could anything be all right?"

"It's not that, Dad," Angie said sharply. "My job is fine. I'm actually very good at it, if you must know. I wouldn't have thought it, but I have real skill working for a movie studio."

It was clear from the surprise on their faces that they hadn't expected their shy daughter who could barely make it out to Long Island on a Saturday to skillfully navigate the shoals of Hollywood.

"Well, that's great, dear." Ellen was tentative. "We're happy you've made a positive change in your life."

Angie looked carefully at her parents. They seemed older and frailer than she remembered. Maybe it was because she hadn't seen them in months. Or maybe Scarlett's death had aged them in ways she hadn't noticed before.

She needed to redirect the conversation. To show she was accomplishing something. So she approached the subject they had danced around for more than a year. "I learned something out here, about Scarlett, about what led her down the road to . . . to take her life—"

"I told you, we won't talk about this," Gerry interjected.

"You need to hear this, Dad." Angie's voice rose. "I'm not a child you can just shut up and send off to her room. This is important."

"Gerry, let's just hear what she has to say." Ellen patted him on the arm.

He backed down, leveling his gaze on his daughter. "Fine. What is this spectacular news about your sister?"

"Well, you were right, Dad, in a sense. This place did kill Scar, but not how you think. It wasn't the movie industry as a whole. Scar had her head on straight. She had her moments of insecurity, but overall, she was doing all right. Until *Catapult*. Until Charles Weaver, the head of DreamWeaver assaulted her. Attacked her."

"And you know this how?" Gerry demanded.

"I found Scarlett's journal."

"You wha—?" he started.

But Angie cut him off. "Scar wouldn't play the casting couch game, and Charles . . . sexually assaulted her." Her voice wavered. It was wrenching telling her parents what that monster had done, but they had to know. "Scar signed a confidentiality agreement, that anything between them, any sex or anything, would be kept quiet. He paid her off." She waited for a response but when none was forthcoming, she aired her own feelings of perplexity. "I can't understand that. It's not like her. But I read the NDA. I think it must have driven her over the edge."

Ellen's eyes teared up and she fidgeted with her hands, clasping and unclasping them. But Gerry's glare was icy and unbending. "Is that it?" he spat. "That's your news, that your sister was assaulted and took some hush money?"

Angie gaped at him, confused, then turned to her mother, who refused to meet her gaze, then back to her father. "What do you mean, is that it? Yes, that's it. Isn't that enough? Charles Weaver raped Scar, then called it 'consensual sex' and made it so she could never speak about it. She couldn't go to the police, she couldn't sue. She couldn't go to the press. She couldn't tell anyone. It's horrendous. Not to mention this is a crime we're talking about. A felony!"

Her father pursed his lips as if trying to swallow something bitter, then stomped over to a back window and stared outside.

Ellen followed him with her eyes then turned back to Angie with a brittle smile. "Well, I'm sure that was very upsetting to hear, but, you know, Scarlett knew this industry very well, and she must have thought that signing that paper was the right thing to do. I mean, if she hadn't, the publicity could have killed her career."

Angie gaped again in disbelief. "Killed her career? What about killing *her*? The silence killed her, Mom. What is wrong with you guys?"

"Angie, that's enough!" Gerry wheeled around. "We do not need to relive this nightmare. Now, you wanted to come out here to work and do whatever the hell else in this cesspool without regard to how that would affect anyone else. It was total self-absorption on your—"

"Excuse me?"

"You heard me, self-absorption. Selfish behavior. You come out here, you trace Scarlett's final days, dredging up all sorts of sordid details, and I won't have it. Whatever you know, you keep it to yourself, you understand? We don't want to hear any more about any of this."

Angie's stunned silence fell over them like a blanket smothering all that was left unsaid. Her father had always been intractable and difficult, especially when it came to Scarlett's death, blocking every overture to talk about it as a family, to share their grief to help them endure it. But this was too much.

As Angie struggled to come up with what to say next, the silence was shattered by the violent clinking of crashing glass. Angie jumped from her stool as her parents instinctively hit the floor. "What the hell was that?" she cried.

She glanced up to see the living room window smashed, a brick lying on the rug in a pile of glittering shards. She inched over, carefully avoiding the biggest fragments, and craned her neck to see outside.

"Be careful, they may still be out there." Gerry rushed over and pushed her out of view. "Don't stand in front of the window, for Chrissake."

"Who may be out there? What is going on?" Angie demanded.

Gerry bent down to Ellen, putting an arm around her to help her stand. She patted his hand and spoke softly. "I'm fine, Gerry, honestly. It was just a terrible fright, is all."

"Angie, get your mother a glass of water." His voice was low and tense.

Angie ignored him. "Are you going to tell me what's happening? We need to call the police!"

Her father sighed. "We don't know, exactly, but there's been a dark SUV circling the house since we arrived."

"What? An SUV has been circling the house since yesterday?"

"At first, we thought it was a neighbor or maybe security for a celebrity, but something didn't feel right." Gerry glared at Angie, his anger palpable. "We think we're being watched, and it's your fault."

"My fault? What did I do?" Angie yelled.

"You've stirred up a hornet's nest," Gerry hissed. "We told you to leave it alone. I know Scott told you we would never know what drove Scarlett to kill herself. But did you listen? No, you had to come out here and get involved with the same people she did."

"I'm trying to figure out what went wrong! Why does it seem like I'm the only one who cares?"

Ellen gasped. "How can you say that? How can you say we don't care?"

"I'm not saying you don't care that it happened. I'm saying you don't care about the reasons why."

"So what *are* you saying?" Gerry demanded "You're poking into other people's business, trying to find out more about Scarlett? Is that why you're here?"

"Yes! I'm trying to do something!"

"You're just going to piss off the very people who hurt your sister," he retorted. "How can you be so naïve? You don't think they can hurt us too?"

"So you're admitting something happened?"

"I'm saying, paying a million dollars doesn't mean it's necessarily over."

Angie narrowed her eyes at him. "What did you say?"

Ellen looked at her husband, her expression frantic, then at Angie.

"You said 'paying a million dollars,'" Angie clarified. "But I never told you that. I just told you her silence was bought."

"Well, you must have. I don't know how I heard it, but the point is—"

"Oh, my God, you knew?" Angie gasped. "You knew! Stupid me, here I was worried about upsetting you, and you knew all along. And you did nothing to help her."

"It's not like that." Ellen was desperate to placate. "We didn't know what had happened. Not specifics. When the studio approached us, we were just told that Scarlett was having some issues on the set. We thought we were doing the right thing. We only had her best interests at heart." Her voice choked as she brought her hand up to her mouth.

"DreamWeaver approached you!? What other secrets have you been keeping?"

"Well . . ." Ellen wrung her hands.

"Ellen, don't."

She gave Gerry an imploring look. "Ger. We have to." She turned to Angie and gestured to the sofa. Angie followed and sank down into the middle cushion next to her mom. "They offered us some money. To help convince Scarlett to sign the NDA."

Angie was dumbfounded. "What! Who the hell are you?"

Gerry took a seat opposite her. "We didn't want money. We were worried about Scarlett. You can't understand what it is to see one of your children suffering."

"You don't know how many nights we've spent worrying about *you*." Ellen patted her hands.

"Don't you dare put this on me."

Ellen pulled her hands from Angie's. "We didn't keep the money, you know. We gave it to Scarlett."

"So she could add it to the million dollars? You think that makes it BETTER?" She rose in a hurry, grabbed her bag, and headed for the door.

"Angie, please, wait," Ellen pleaded.

Angie turned to face her mother, the mother she'd tried so hard to protect. "Does Scotty know?"

Ellen shook her head.

Angie pivoted to leave, unsure if she could believe anything either of them said.

"Just listen, just for a minute." Ellen's words tripped over one another as they tumbled out. "We didn't think going to the police was a good idea. Signing the contract seemed like the best choice. For Scarlett's well-being. We told her to stay quiet, we told her it was for the best, that she could come back home after the movie and take some time, but she was so angry. Then she said we abandoned her." Ellen's voice sounded small and distant. "But we didn't mean to. We had no idea . . . the impact."

Angie looked across the room at her father, who had also risen and was standing at a distance, his eyes fixed on her. "Do you have any idea what you've done?" she said.

With that, she fled the house, the sun burning through the ocean fog.

Angie pounded on the door of Nicole's West Hollywood apartment, tears burning her cheeks. Once they'd started falling, they hadn't stopped. The door opened, and Angie collapsed into Nicole's arms.

"What's the matter? What's wrong?" Angie let Nicole loop her arm around her waist and lead her to a couch, where Angie crumpled into a sobbing mess. Nicole's palm made smooth, soothing circles on her back, and Angie started to catch her breath. "Here, I'll be right back," Nicole said, and a moment later she returned and said, "Close your eyes." A cool, wet cloth moistened Angie's face as Nicole gently blotted her eyes and forehead. "Better?"

Angie nodded, the tears having evaporated as if Nicole's tenderness had wiped clean her emotions. Angie gave her a half-hearted smile and watched Nicole walk to the kitchen, where she put on the electric kettle. When she returned, she sat down beside Angie, taking Angie's hands in hers. "Now tell me. What happened?"

Angie let it all spill out: her night with Charles, Scarlett's NDA, her parents' betrayal. "What could they have said to get to my parents? Jesus, I would hope that, if Charles's lawyers had come to me, I would have spat in their faces and taken Scarlett to the police. But I have no idea what they told my parents, or maybe they were threatened?"

She rose from the sofa, stalking around the room, thinking aloud. "This needs to be exposed," she said, her voice stronger. "All of it. I'm not waiting anymore. I'm calling the *LA Times* with this entire story. I'm sending them copies of all the paperwork, the NDAs, everything. No more sweeping Charles Weaver's crimes under the rug."

The kettle whistled and Nicole got up, speaking from the kitchen. "You have to slow down and think. You're really emotional right now, and I don't mean that's a bad thing, but you have to think about this rationally. What you've discovered is horrible. I'd be angry too. Very angry. But blowing this open in the press won't bring Scarlett back. And you could get hurt, like really hurt." She rejoined Angie, placing a tray with a teapot and mugs on the glass coffee table. "You don't know how far these people will go to protect what they've built. You need to think very hard about what you do next."

Angie picked up her mug, gazing into the pale, hot tea that warmed her hands she hadn't even realized were so cold. What had Patricia said? That she was crazy to think she could take on DreamWeaver? Was she crazy?

"Listen," Nicole continued. "You want to take down one of the most powerful men in Hollywood. You won't win. Think about the jeopardy you'd be putting your parents in. And for what? To get even with Charles? You can't get even with Charles. He will always be one up on you. Always."

Nicole might be right, but Angie had to live with herself, with her choices. Scarlett had been silenced. Angie wouldn't be. "Are you worried about your job?"

"I'm worried about *you*," Nicole stressed. "But, yeah, I don't want to be destroyed as part of some crusade, obviously."

"Nicole. My sister is dead."

"I know. But we have to live in this world. And Charles is a big part of it."

Was Nicole serious? "I can't believe what I'm hearing! He attacked women. And then he bought their silence. He's gotten away with sexual harassment, assault, rape. He's destroyed careers. He's destroyed lives. And he's probably still doing it!"

"Where is your evidence?" Nicole queried.

"I told you. I've seen the paperwork. The NDAs. And you saw the board in my house yourself. You saw the names. I've talked with some of those women."

"I've never seen a scrap of proof. I don't know what that board is, not really. A bunch of names? That isn't proof. That's a list. What I do know is that Charles makes great movies. He signs my checks. He hangs out with beautiful women like every other rich or powerful man in town. And you don't cross him. That's what I know."

Angie was certain Nicole was being evasive. And even though she had virtually no inhibitions left after what she'd heard that day, it was still difficult to say what she did next. "I found a flash drive. In your office. I couldn't get in at first. And when I did, it just looked like a random collection of project names. But then I realized, there were initials of actresses who had signed NDAs."

"What do you mean you *found* a flash drive in my office?" Nicole faced her, eyes blazing.

"Actually, yes," Angie confessed. "I'm embarrassed to admit it, but it's true. This drive fell out of a folder. And I took it." She opened her purse and placed the drive on the coffee table. Nicole took it in in silence. "I guess you didn't miss it, huh?"

"I don't even know what that is. I'm only involved with contracts for options and rights. You know that."

"Well, those projects, the ones on the flash, are books that are never going to see the light of day. And there were contracts for women, to bury their stories of assault. I shouldn't have snooped, you're right. But somehow that doesn't seem as bad as being a consensual part of a culture of harassment and rape, does it?"

"I don't know what the hell you think you found, but I don't know anything about buying off anyone!" Nicole was suddenly angry, up in Angie's face. "My files contain contracts for IP rights. Copyright agreements. Options. That's it. That's the job. Whatever else you 'found'"— she made air quotes with her fingers—"has nothing to do with me. I don't know how it got there. You got that?"

"Oh, I got it. Loud and clear." Angie snagged her bag and walked out, letting the door slam behind her. She was in tears again before she even got to the elevator.

Angie had never felt more alone. Jango was dead. She didn't want to talk to Nicole, or her parents. She called Scott, but it went to voice mail. As a last resort she tried her sister-in-law, who answered.

"He's in Amsterdam," Sarah said. "He had to meet with some engineers about a joint research project. Wait, Brendan, don't jump off that! We're at the park. Hey, I gotta run before Brendan fractures something. I'll tell Scott to call you if you don't talk to him first. Bye."

So much for connecting with family. Angie wandered into the spare room to look at the stack of NDAs piled near her whiteboard. She flipped through them absent-mindedly. Charles still hadn't been in touch about the missing files, and that made her nervous. But she needed to act. She just didn't know what to do. Call a lawyer? Get the files copied? To who, a journalist? The police?

Tanya probably knew about the stolen NDAs. God knew who else did. Angie thought of the two Aris and shuddered. And she had no idea what to do about Nicole.

She decided to go for a run to clear her head. The hills offered a perfect variation of incline and decline to work her heart and burn off nervous energy. As she turned into the pathway back up to Scarlett's house, she picked up the Sunday paper, which had been dropped on the sidewalk.

Inside, she got a bottle of water from the fridge and took a long draw as she unfolded the *Times*, and gagged. On the front page of the entertainment section was the picture of Tanya, Patricia, and her in the Oscars night limo under the headline: From NY to LA: The Downfall of Scarlett Norris's Sister. The story detailed how Angela Norris, a reserved but powerful literary agent from New York, had headed to Hollywood on behalf of her dearly departed sister but got caught up in the crazy Tinseltown lifestyle and went on a cocaine-fueled binge on Oscars night.

Angie bolted to her laptop and tried to sign in to her DreamWeaver account, but her password no longer worked. *Of course. They've already fired me.*

She checked her personal email on her phone and found a message from HR sent earlier that day, apparently to coincide with the story's publication.

Dear Miss Norris,

We're sorry to inform you that your Creative Executive position is being eliminated. The studio is reorganizing as it adopts a more integrated approach to the pursuit of content.

Thank you for your contributions to DreamWeaver. Your final paycheck and two weeks' severance will be mailed to the address we have on file.

Sincerely,
Doreen Lopez
Human Relations Director

She texted Tanya, whose number was in her contacts and who was in the best position, next to Charles himself, to have engineered her demise.

What the hell is going on?

You're an attorney.

That story is libelous.

Then she went outside and sat on the front steps. She watched hummingbirds flit back and forth around the magenta bougainvillea. Had all of her efforts led to this absurdity?

Her phone buzzed. Tanya.

Don't blame me.

You knew where my loyalties lay.

But I wasn't the one who knew you were going public.

Angie gave a start. Tanya was right. She would have had no way of knowing Angie had threatened to go to the *Times*. There was only one person who knew that.

Angie stabbed the buzzer furiously, but Nicole's door stayed firmly closed. "Nicole, open up! I've been fired! I need to talk!" As she paced the hallway in front of the door, debating what to do if Nicole didn't answer, her phone buzzed with a text.

I thought we were done.
You walked out.

Do you know
what happened?

Tanya told me you were fired.
I'm sorry it turned out that way.

                                    What do you mean?

                                    Did you tell her
                                    what I was doing?

I told you I wouldn't be
part of your crusade.

                              At least have the guts
                                    to face me.

                              Did you tell Tanya I was
                              going to expose Charles?

Charles figured out you &
I were together.

I had no choice.

                                          What?

                              What do you mean you
                                    had no choice?

                              There's always a choice.

It's not that simple.

They would have destroyed me.

Have you been spying on
me the whole time?

Feeding information to Charles?

I have to go.

I'm sorry.

Angie slumped in the driver's seat of her car for what felt like hours. She was too depleted to be angry. She just felt empty. She thought about who she could call, besides Scotty again, and dialed Jeremy, wondering if he would have any ideas about what to do or if he would at least let her stay at his place in Malibu for a few days—as long as she had the NDAs, she wasn't safe on her own. And now that Charles published that story and she had been fired, who knew what else he might do. But Jeremy's voice mail message said he was on a remote shoot and would be hard to reach for the next few weeks. *Is there anybody left in LA I can trust?*

She was considering her next move when she observed two women walking down the street toward her car. It was Nicole and another woman engaged in what looked like a lively conversation. Angie slunk down with her back to the door, hoping Nicole wouldn't spot her car. But when she lifted her head to peek out, Nicole was typing into her phone. Then the other woman checked her phone. *They're exchanging contact information.* Angie's throat tightened. *Replaced already. Did you ever give a damn, or did you become my girlfriend so you could keep tabs on me for Charles?*

Nicole gave the woman a quick hug and headed back toward her apartment while the other woman took off in the opposite direction. Holy shit—Angie recognized her. She waited until Nicole was out of sight, and then pulled out, following until the other woman stopped at a bright blue Porsche and pulled out the car fob. Angie double parked, turned on her flashers, and hopped out.

"Dominique? Do you remember me?" The car. It was too expensive for the average young actress.

Dominique started, dropping her fob in the gutter. "Oh, my God, you scared me." She crouched to rescue her keyring. "You're . . . Angie? Yes, I remember. What are you doing here?"

"Listen, Dominique, I need people, women, to talk about what Charles did to them. I want to go to the police and the newspapers and expose him, and you were the first person to warn me. Do you remember that day when you saw me having lunch with him?"

"Look, Charles and I . . . When I was in New York . . . I didn't mean anything I said to you, and if you tell anyone, I'll say you're lying, that you made up the whole conversation, and considering today's *Times* . . ."

"Tanya made you sign an NDA, didn't she? And they paid you." Angie gestured to the Porsche.

"I need to go."

"Are you working for them? Is that why you were with Nicole?"

"Don't follow me." Dominique unlocked the door, slipped behind the wheel, and slammed the car door shut. After she pulled out of the spot, Angie stood and watched the sports car roll down the street and then recede from view.


Back home, Angie's paranoia and self-doubt skyrocketed as she paced across the living room. Had Scotty been right? Was going to LA a waste of time? Knowing what she had discovered made her feel worse than the black hole she'd been left with when she had no answers at all. She was jumping at every turn, afraid of every swaying tree branch, every stray cat, every tick of the clock. She didn't know when Charles would pull the trigger. And why hadn't he already?

She needed some grounding, so she pulled her brother up on her

Favorites and lay on the couch. He didn't pick up, so she left a voice mail, hoping to sound, if not upbeat, fairly stable. "Hey, Scotty, it's me. I talked to Sarah. I know you're away, but can you call me when you get a chance, even for a few minutes? Things out here have gotten . . . complicated. Bye."

She closed her eyes, clutching her phone to her chest. She missed Brontë. And she needed to get back to those files, her whiteboard, her search. But she was exhausted from the sheer panic of waiting for the other shoe to drop. When would it drop?

The vibrations of her phone woke her up. "Scotty?" Her voice was thick from the nap.

"Not Scotty, I'm afraid."

Angie bolted upright at the sound of Charles's voice.

"You have something of mine."

The shoe had dropped.

"I'm right outside. Why don't you just open the door, and we can talk."

Angie sprang up to check the locks on all the ground-floor doors then hurried into the kitchen to check the bank of video screens. They were all off. She surveyed the control panel. The lights were all green, meaning the system was working. Why couldn't she see anything on the screens?

She dashed to the backyard and peered out. She didn't see anyone, so she went back to the front hall and stood still, listening. Silence except for the sound of her breathing. She gingerly peeked out the peephole. Charles was right there, standing on her front steps in a baseball cap, white polo shirt, and track pants, the two Aris flanking him.

*He's trying to scare you. Just breathe. He wouldn't commit murder here in broad daylight. He has too much to lose. You can call the police.*

"Trick or treat," she heard Charles sing-song. "If you give me a treat, you won't have anything to worry about. Maybe we can even get you your job back."

She punched 911 into her phone but didn't hit Connect. Instead, she responded. "You're going to rehire me after engineering that bull-shit news story? What would be the point?"

"Oh, Angie. News stories come and go. We could easily suggest a follow-up about your 'come to Jesus' moment, how you were a wreck, pushed over the edge by your sister's death, hobbled by grief, but are now back on track and a success in your own right out here. It's the same old story. Please open the door. I don't like talking this way."

Angie confirmed the door was double-locked then pressed her ear against it. Her heart pounded, but she didn't say a word.

"Never mind then. We'll just have to talk like this," Charles said. "I want my files. I'll even move toward the street if you feel more comfort-able that way. You can keep an eye on me as you drop them outside the door. Then let's see if we can't come to some sort of agreement, hmmm? I'd love to give you your job back, and with a tidy bonus, but first we have to iron out all these misunderstandings. I hate to be misunder-stood. You can appreciate that, can't you?"

"I know what you did to Scarlett. And I know you manipulated my parents to get them to talk Scarlett into taking your fucking money! If you think I'm going to sell out my sister after she's dead, you don't know me."

"This can be easy, or it can be hard." Charles's voice took on an edge. "Very hard. I'll sue you. I'll plant more stories. I can ruin you in ways your piddling little mind can't even fathom." Then silence.

Angie waited a few seconds then looked again through the peep-hole. Charles and the Aris reached the end of her front walkway, got in the car, and disappeared.

She heaved a sigh of relief and hurried to the spare room to get the files. She would copy everything and send it to the *Times*, just as she'd planned.

Her phone buzzed again. It was her father. "Angie, come quick. It's your mom. She's in the hospital. She collapsed and isn't doing well." Gerry's voice was husky. "I'm so sorry. Please come now. We're at Cedars-Sinai."

Angie hurriedly gathered her tote bag, snatched her charger, and rushed out. As she turned to lock the door, she looked up at the security camera. She gasped when she saw the lens had been painted black. That must be why the image inside was dark even though the green light was on. All the cameras must have been tampered with. *That son of a . . .* But she didn't have time to check the others or do anything about it.

By the time she got to the hospital, her mother had been taken to intensive care. She found her father standing in the waiting room, his countenance grim, a pallor cast over him like a shroud. The room was gray with fluorescent lighting, black plastic tables, and orange plastic chairs. A vending machine offering coffee and tea was against one wall.

"It was a heart attack," Gerry explained as soon as Angie came into the room. "She just slumped over at the dinner table."

She took his hand and guided him into a chair.

"I don't know what I'll do if I lose her." He buried his head in his hands.

Angie sank into a seat beside him. She had no idea what to say beyond empty platitudes. So she said nothing.

"I've ruined all our lives," he whispered. "I never meant for any of this to happen. We didn't care about the money. It was just all so terrible, I wanted it to go away. We thought it would be easier that way, but Scarlett, she was so upset when we told her. I didn't see that, to her, it looked like we were just two more people betraying her. I never should have dealt with that man."

"I know, Dad. I know." It wasn't his fault. She knew her parents had just wanted to help. So many people had been complicit in Scarlett's death, consciously and not. Even she had not been there for her sister.


Ellen's doctors emerged three hours later to say she was stable. Angie drove her father to his Airbnb and slept on the couch. The next morning, Monday, she headed back to Topanga with a promise from Gerry that he would call with updates.

She was dragging on the drive back home, but even with her dulled senses, as soon as she approached the house, she knew something was off. The doormat was askew but there were no packages outside to explain it.

She tried the doorknob. Locked. She let herself in slowly. "Hello?"

She went straight to the spare room. The entire space had been ransacked. Shelves emptied of books, papers strewn over the floor, chairs on their sides, closets raided. And the files containing the NDAs and her laptop were gone. On the whiteboard, someone had erased the actors' names and replaced them with a huge red "X".

Angie sank to the floor in the middle of the mess. *Gone. All gone.* Now there was no hard proof against Charles. Only those he'd assaulted could attest to it, and they had obviously been pressured to shut up.

Charles had put himself beyond her reach.

# 16

Angie was too afraid to stay home but had nowhere to go so she drove aimlessly around LA. She sat in traffic, numbly staring at the cars in front of her, not caring if she ever moved. She killed an hour watching the Ferris wheel on the Santa Monica Pier, envying the tourists, the kids, the lovers their freedom. She knew they didn't have perfect lives, but from where she was standing, she also couldn't see a single blemish.

Her father called and said her mother's condition hadn't changed, and as angry as she was at them, the thought of losing her mother overrode her resentment. She burst into tears at a red light in West Hollywood, the pressure of it all exploding.

Eventually, the day having long ago bled into night, she found herself in an unfamiliar neighborhood where she spotted *Catapult* on the marquee at a repertory cinema. Her heart lurched, as did her foot on the gas pedal, and she was thankful she didn't crash the car. Seeing an empty parking spot on a side street, she made a sharp turn and slipped into it.

She'd never seen her sister's last movie, *Catapult*. It had been released after Scarlett's death and Angie hadn't been able to bring herself to watch it. But she didn't feel safe going home after the burglary and things were so fucked, she needed a distraction. While the film might not provide that, it might provide some clarity, and it was time she could spend again with Scarlett.

So, after reading the labyrinthine parking rules, she got out of her car and popped into the convenience store on the corner. She bought herself a candy bar and, fuck it, a pint of Jack Daniels, and went to the movies.

She found a seat just as the trailers were ending and unscrewed the cap on the whiskey. The audience was sparse, which felt safer than a crowded theater, but she flinched when the DreamWeaver logo appeared. Once the opening scene flashed on the screen in a blur—a soft, multicolored haze that slowly came into relief as headlights reflected off wet pavement—she allowed herself to let go. Of her fear, of her anger, of her frustration.

Inching into focus, the camera moved in on Chloe, Scarlett's streetwalker character, and her smeared eye makeup and purple lips. Neon signs for pawn shops and Chinese takeout glowed in the night, and the fluorescent glare of cheap liquor stores was tastelessly brash. Chloe shivered and tried to keep her pink fuzzy jacket closed over her micro-mini silver skirt and slinky tank top with one hand while she smoked with the other. She finally tossed the cigarette butt onto the sidewalk and stomped on it with her cheap, platform heel as a black luxury sedan slowed and neared the curb. As she approached the expensive car, a dark window came down and she leaned in to talk to the driver. "Seventy-five for an hour."

He shook his head. "Not me." He motioned to the back seat.

Chloe stepped toward the rear window, muttering to herself. "Shit, he's got a driver. I should have asked for more."

But when the rear window came down, Chloe found herself looking at a fifty-something woman with a smooth gray bob, double strand of pearls, and tasteful suit that matched her hair. The woman smiled. "I've been looking all over LA for you. Get in."

"Representative Santoro?"

The reaction on Chloe's face was so genuine it moved Angie to tears.

She could see hope and grit and despair and suspicion all at once. She didn't know how Scarlett had been able to create a moment so complex and so authentic. How could she have done this while dealing with the monstrous behavior of Charles behind the scenes. He flashed in her mind's eye while Scarlett loomed over her, thirty feet tall. She wished Scarlett had been that big in reality. She would have squashed him, the disgusting insect that he was.

She took a slug of whiskey, suddenly aware the pint was almost empty. She hadn't even opened the Kit Kat yet. Her eyelids felt unnaturally heavy. She pulled her jacket around her in the dark space. It was warm and the cushy seat invited her to curl up. Chloe's face grew distant, and it wasn't long before Angie drifted off to another warm place.

*It was a bright day, and she and Scarlett were running into a lake, laughing and splashing with a bunch of other kids. The sun was blinding, glinting and glittering off the water. Then Angie looked around to find the kids fading one by one until she was standing alone. "Scarlett? Scarlett, where are you?" she called as she spun around in the water, frantic. Then she heard a man's voice call out. "Angie? Angie, is that you? Can you help me?" He sounded gentle, but Angie felt dread. Where was Scarlett?*

Angie jolted awake. The credits were rolling. She didn't know how long she'd been passed out. She grabbed her bag, stumbled out of her row, and made her way through the lobby. It was nearing midnight, and she was drunk. There was no way she could drive. So she crawled into the back, took off her shoes, and curled up on the seat, hoping she wouldn't throw up. She would only sleep for a bit, just enough so she could safely make the drive back to Topanga.

A trickle of sweat dripped down Angie's neck, waking her up. Her mouth was dry and tasted awful. Her head throbbed. She blinked into the hot morning sun, amazed she'd slept all night in the backseat. She crawled into the front and caught sight of a parking ticket tucked under the wiper. Figured. She retrieved it and got back behind the wheel. As she put the key in the ignition, she glanced into the rearview and was appalled by her reflection—dull skin, cracked lips, unkempt hair. But the worst thing was her dead eyes. She looked as hopeless as she felt.

Her phone was almost dead, so she rooted around in her purse for a charger, thinking about what to do next. She couldn't go to the hospital, looking how she did. Jeremy was out of town. Jango was dead. Charles had the files. Nicole was complicit. Tanya wanted nothing to do with her. There was nowhere to go and no one she could turn to.

Charles had won.

When she finally got back to the Topanga house, she let out an audible sigh of relief. The place looked as she'd left it, but she did a search anyway of every room, every closet, even—ludicrously, she knew—the linen closets. No boogeymen. No goons out to get her on Charles's behalf.

She took a couple of ibuprofens, drank two glasses of water, checked the locks twice, and then went upstairs to start packing. It dawned on her she should call her father. Pulling her phone out of her purse, she saw a missed-call notification and a voice mail. Mackenzie Martin. She spoke briefly to Gerry, who reported no change in Ellen, both a blessing and a curse, and then she listened to Mackenzie's message.

"Jesus, Angie. I still haven't heard anything from those fuckers at DreamWeaver, and when I tried your work line just now, it went to somebody who told me you don't even work there anymore? What the hell? You sold me out. What the fuck am I supposed to do? I swear to God if that DreamWeaver lawyer bitch doesn't tell me or Rita in twenty-four hours what is going on with my book, I will hire the best lawyer I can find. And your name will be in the lawsuit."

Angie didn't even care about the threat of being sued. Mackenzie had every right to be furious. Angie didn't have the wherewithal to call her or Rita back.

Instead, she went to the bathroom, where she splashed water on her face. She hadn't showered since the morning before and, worse, she hadn't brushed her teeth. She reached for her toothbrush in its cup by the sink, but accidentally knocked both to the floor.

"Jesus Christ." She squatted, reaching into the gap between the sink cabinet and the wall, and touched soft fabric. She pulled out a white one-piece swimsuit. She hadn't seen it since the first night she and Nicole had gone swimming. She sank onto the floor, her back against the wall, as a childhood memory flooded in.

Angie was out on the lake in a rowboat at the summer camp Scarlett had finally convinced her to go to. The other campers in her eleven- and twelve-year-old group were in the water, on the shore, playing on the grounds. Clouds suddenly gathered dark and thick, and the counselors blew their whistles to signal that everyone should get to their cabins on the double.

Angie used the oars to navigate back to the dock, and by the time she'd safely secured the boat to the dock, she was the only one still out there.

She had started up the dirt path toward the cabins when a man's voice stopped her. "Angie, can you help me for a second?"

She turned to find Mr. Stratton, one of the camp counselors, working to secure a few other boats. He smiled at her. He smiled at her a lot. It made her self-conscious. "Um. I, um . . . I think I should, I should go back up now," she stammered.

"This will only take a minute." Mr. Stratton continued smiling.

She gave an awkward smile back. And, too timid to refuse again, she approached his boat.

"Great," Mr. Stratton enthused. "Now if you lean over here and grab the bow and just hold it steady near the dock while I tie it, that will be a big help."

"Okay, I guess. I'm not sure I can hold it in place that well . . ."

"Oh, sure you can," Mr. Stratton assured her. "Get right in here."

So Angie slid in front of the counselor to hold the cold metal bow of the boat flush with the dock while he tied it, looming over her shoulder.

"Can I let go now?" she asked once the boat was secure.

"Yup, that's fine."

But Mr. Stratton didn't budge. He stood so close to her back that she could hear his rapid breathing and feel the warmth coming off his body. Then he placed a hand on each of Angie's shoulders. "Thanks, Angie. You were a big help, you know that."

"I better go now." She tried to slide away, but Mr. Stratton slid both thumbs under the straps of her one-piece swimsuit. He was standing flush against her, and panic rose within her.

"There's no real rush," he purred, and started guiding her toward a thick patch of trees.

"It'll be dinnertime soon," Angie protested weakly. She glanced around, but there was no one in sight.

"Oh, we'll be back in no time," he assured her. "So what do you like to do, Angie? Tell me a little about yourself."

Just as she and Mr. Stratton entered the woods, she heard her name.

"Angie? Angie, where are you?"

Angie turned under his grip. Scarlett had run down to the dock and was searching for her.

"Don't worry about your sister," Mr. Stratton urged in a soothing voice. "We'll be back soon."

Angie's heart seemed to thump louder than the thunder that rumbled overhead. She couldn't talk. One of Mr. Stratton's hands had drifted down to her stomach and he was pulling her close to him. She started to cry. "Let me go. Let me go."

"In a minute, Angie, in a minute." He continued trying to guide her into the cover of the trees.

When she saw Scarlett start to return up the dirt path toward the cabins, she was overcome with terror. *No, Scar, don't go, please, don't go, please, don't go.* But she couldn't make a sound. Her frantic words were only in her mind.

As her sister's lanky frame retreated out of sight, overwhelming desperation rose in Angie. She took a deep breath, mustered all the energy she had, and screamed so loud that it startled both her and Mr. Stratton, who released his grip. Angie tore out of the cover of trees and raced toward her sister. "Scarlett, Scarlett!" she sobbed, slamming into her arms.

"Oh, my God! What happened?" She stroked Angie's hair tenderly, reassuringly. "Oh, no, it's okay, you're okay."

"Scarlett, hello." Mr. Stratton strolled toward them as if nothing out of the ordinary had happened. "Angie just helped me tie up a few boats since we had to come in so fast from the storm. She was a big help. Isn't that right, Angie?"

Angie, standing so close to Scarlett she was practically standing on her feet, nodded.

Scarlett scrutinized the counselor with hard eyes. "You should get adults to help you, Mr. Stratton. Not eleven-year-old girls." Then she turned to her little sister. "C'mon. We'll be late for dinner." They started toward the cabins but Angie was trembling so hard she stumbled and nearly fell. "Are you okay?" Scarlett asked.

Angie nodded furiously and whispered. "I just tied up a boat."

"Why were you over near the trees?"

Angie didn't know why. She couldn't say.

Scarlett didn't stop until they were outside the cabins, where she crouched so she was at Angie's height. "Did he ask you to walk into the woods with him?"

Angie looked at her with scared eyes.

"Did he touch you?"

Angie shook her head.

"But he asked you to go into the woods?" Scarlett pressed.

She nodded slightly. "I'm sorry, I didn't want to, but he . . . he . . ."

"Listen to me," Scarlett said. "This is not your fault. You did nothing wrong. I don't know what he wanted to do, but it can't be good. He's a creep. And there are a few girls who have mentioned feeling weird around him. Now, I'm going to wait for you to change, and we're going to go to dinner. And this is going to be the last time that pervert bothers you or anybody."

The next day, Mr. Stratton was gone, due to a family emergency, the campers were told. Angie didn't find out until they got home that Scarlett had confided in two junior counselors she'd gotten friendly with and who, themselves uneasy around Mr. Stratton, immediately told the camp's director. Scarlett had not only saved her sister but countless other kids.

She'd sworn Scarlett to secrecy and blamed herself. If she hadn't been so timid, so lacking in confidence, a predator like that wouldn't have targeted her. He could see she wouldn't fight back. She wouldn't tell. And he was right. Not even their parents found out. They never knew why Angie refused to ever go back to summer camp. Over the years, whenever the ugly memory of Mr. Stratton floated to the surface, she'd pushed it aside. Eventually, she'd buried it so deep it was forgotten. Until now.

Angie got up off the floor and assessed herself in the mirror. She had wallowed in despair, terrified by Charles, upset by the false news story, angered by her firing, betrayed by Nicole, and shocked at her parents' complicity in Scarlett's unraveling.

But what of it? What did that mean for her? Was she going to unravel too? She hadn't been able to save Scarlett, but she could avenge her.

She opened the tap and filled the sink with cold water then plunged her face into the iciness, holding her breath for as long as she could. Then she did it again. A third time. When she brought her head up next, the woman who regarded her, water running down her face, had life in her eyes.

In the shower she washed her hair and scrubbed her skin, enjoying the pounding spray on her body. After drying off with a fresh towel, she slathered lavender lotion on her arms and legs and put on clean clothes, feeling like she had shed a skin. Then she scrolled through her contacts and sent a text.

I haven't wanted to bother you
but leaving town soon.
Need to talk once more. Please.

She was surprised at the calm she felt crawling into bed that night. She had a newfound faith in herself. She wasn't worried about Charles or his goons or the press. She was going to prevail. She was going to take down Goliath with her slingshot.

The next thing she knew, she was sitting up in bed. 2:00 a.m. A dream. A beautiful, glittering dream with music, a mirrored ballroom.

Then she heard a noise from outside. That must be what had woken her. She tiptoed downstairs in the dark. Was Charles and his goons back? She grabbed a chef's knife from the block next to the stove and dropped to her knees, crawling toward the sliding glass doors overlooking the backyard. Clutching the blade in one hand and her phone in the other, she was poised to call 911 as soon as she saw anything or anyone. But all was quiet.

She got up and peeked out the front window. The white convertible was there again, and a figure in a brown leather jacket was walking back toward the street. Adrenaline pumping, she bolted out the door. "What do you think you're doing?"

The man reeled around in surprise. It was Kevin Li. "Jesus, Angie. Hang on." He put one hand out as if to stop her approach. "What are you doing here?"

"What am I . . . ? You're creeping around Scarlett's house and you're asking me what I'm doing? I'm living here." She gripped the knife in front of her, now just a foot from his faded Nine Inch Nails T-shirt. "Did Charles send you here?"

"What? No! No, no, no, it's not like that, I swear. I just . . ."

"You just what?" Angie erupted into a shout. "I'm calling the police."

"I loved her."

"What?"

"Scarlett. I loved her. And I wanted to tell you—I did—but I just couldn't. I didn't know if you even wanted to know, and then I wanted to warn you when you started working at DreamWeaver, about Charles, but I . . ." The words tumbled out until Kevin finally took a breath. "I didn't know you were living here, in Scarlett's house. I come here sometimes, leave a rose, the smallest gesture, but I didn't know—"

"What? You leave flowers?"

"Roses." He motioned to the house. She turned back and spotted a red rose resting on the porch just outside the door. She'd rushed out so fast, she hadn't even seen it.

"It's YOU? You're the one who's been leaving roses?"

"Please put the knife down. Please." He gently placed a hand on top of hers and lowered the blade. "I'm sorry I scared you. Okay?"

Kevin Li, the handsome guy with the snazzy wardrobe and cool hair, who headed DreamWeaver's production unit, had been mourning Scarlett all this time. Leaving roses. And working with Charles.

"What the hell, Kevin!"

"I'll tell you everything. But can we go inside? I would never hurt you. I swear. I'm not him."

Angie finally took him in, noting his disheveled appearance, tired eyes, and serious expression. She let out a breath, and turned and headed back toward the house. Kevin followed.

# 17

Angie turned on the kitchen lights and Kevin took a seat at the island. "Wait here." She rooted around in Scarlett's liquor cabinet, pulled out a bottle of bourbon, and placed it and two glasses in front of him. She poured each of them a couple of fingers and sat on a stool next to him. Kevin raised his glass and knocked it back. "Thanks."

"What are you doing here?"

He combed his fingers through his hair. "I couldn't sleep tonight. I got in the car and started driving. Ended up here."

Angie took another sip of bourbon then looked hard at him. "So, start."

He indicated his empty glass. She capitulated, giving him a generous pour, which he downed again. "There are things about Charles I should have faced years ago," he began. "But we were doing so well, making money, making great films, lots of awards. It was all so good, being on top of the world. And he wasn't so bad, not in the early days. And neither was I. But things got worse and worse over time, until I couldn't look away anymore."

"Because of Scarlett?" Angie asked tentatively.

Kevin nodded. "Even before Scarlett. Charles and I met in New York. I was just out of film school and we worked together to get DreamWeaver off the ground. We started to have real success—this was before we moved the company out here. I was the perfect loyal confidant and right-hand man." He sounded rueful. "He was married a long time ago, you know, in New York. She was sharp and funny, a graphic designer turned film promoter. She really helped his movies make a mark, succeed. Looking back, I can't say what she saw in the guy. Anyway, he got successful and then unfaithful. So that was that."

"And in LA?"

"Same thing, but worse and more of it. He became a real player. We'd take trips to St. Moritz, the Caribbean, all sorts of spectacular places, and he'd have to have one or more beautiful actresses join us. Once I asked him about it, whether he thought it was right to dangle all these opportunities in front of young women who knew he had the power to make their careers."

"And what did he say?"

"He said they knew what they were getting into. That if they want-ed to play in this league and work for him, then they had to do what it took. If they didn't, they 'lacked commitment.' I think he almost believed that." Kevin shook his head. "Then I started to hear more things, snippets of phone conversations. He'd demean women. Joke about how some woman really 'wanted it,' even if she said she didn't. I played along," he admitted. "Tanya, too. We knew. I realized one day looking in the mirror, when I was shaving before work, that I couldn't stand the sight of myself anymore."

Angie took another sip of her bourbon. "What happened with Scarlett? Did you really love her?"

Kevin nodded. "Yeah, but I never told her, and I don't know that she ever picked up on it." He turned the glass in circles in his hands. "I could see the toll *Catapult* was taking, and it broke my heart to see her deteriorate like that. She was so beautiful, talented, but her spirit was the thing. She was so independent and turning into a really fine actress. She wasn't forcing it, and she could come across as both strong and vulnerable. It was great seeing her blossom. It's rare, but someone like Scarlett . . . she didn't really need Charles. I mean, yeah, he could have helped make her a huge star, but she was the type who would have carved out her own path and gotten there anyway. And the fact that she wasn't desperate for Charles's help or approval drove him nuts."

Angie couldn't suppress a small smile. "Yeah, that was Scar." Then the journal entries came to mind. "But I think she worried more than she let on about getting good, better parts, really making her mark."

"Obviously, she was a lot more fragile than any of us knew, and this isn't an easy business at the best of times." Kevin shook his head and blew out a sigh. "I told Charles he should back off, that he didn't need to bag every beautiful actress in town, just let Scarlett do her job on the film."

"But he didn't."

"No. He didn't. And he saw right through me, too. We were having lunch one day and talking about *Catapult*—it was the middle of the shoot—and Charles says, all of a sudden, 'You're getting soft, Kev. A zillion gorgeous women in town, and you can't take your eyes off Scarlett Norris?' Then he gets this look on his face. It was weird. I can still picture it. And he says, 'You might want to stay in your lane, pal. Remember that.'" Kevin scoffed again. "Here I am, a good friend, we've worked together for twenty years, I built the studio with him, and he's warning me to keep away from a woman like he owns her."

"So what happened? I talked to Kristy Wong."

Kevin took a moment, looked down at his hands, and sighed. "Kristy and I were both worried. Charles was around Scarlett more and more as the shoot wore on, hovering on set, hanging around her trailer, putting his arm around her as she walked off set. I tried to distract him with calls and business meetings, all these excuses. I could only do so much. But if I had spoken up, she'd still be alive."

Angie looked him directly in the eye. "I found an NDA. He raped her, probably more than once, and then paid her off to keep quiet. She felt abandoned. That's what did her in."

Kevin stared at Angie, his mouth open. "Charles raped her, and then she signed an NDA?"

"Charles got to our parents. They agreed to get Scarlett to sign for a million dollars. They thought they were being helpful. You know—avoid a scandal that would end her career . . ."

"Christ. I knew there were others, but Scarlett?"

"Who else knows about all this?"

"Charles, me."

"Tanya?"

"Tanya, absolutely."

Angie went to the sink to get a glass of water and poured one for Kevin too. "So, did you talk to anyone about your concerns about Charles's behavior?"

"Not exactly, but Charles got wind of that PI you were working with, he told me about him. So, I got in touch and sent him the names of women I'd seen Charles move in on over the years."

"You sent information to Jango?"

"I decided it was time to put a stop to this. I was a coward for a long time—not like you."

Angie remembered Scott's comment about her balls of cast iron and chuckled. "Honestly, I had no idea what I was doing. But one night in New York, I got this mysterious note dropped at my house. It got me wondering about things because it said that Scarlett deser—"

"—deserved better," Kevin finished.

Angie set her glass on the island. "You."

"Yeah. After Scarlett died, I wanted you to know there was more to it. But I never thought you'd move out here, get dragged through the studio machine, possibly risking your life to figure it all out."

"But why me? How did you even know who I was?"

"Scarlett spoke so highly about you. She was so proud of you. She said you carved out a nice career for yourself in one of the hardest cities in the world."

"She was proud of me?" Angie's hand rushed up to her heart.

"Absolutely. She was happy you were making your mark in the world. She said you were shy, so it was harder for you than it was for her. I thought someone should know something about the shit that went down here, but I didn't want to give too much information. I was afraid Charles would find out it was me."

"That police report, it was real?"

"When Charles was in New York last year doing PR for *Catapult*, he started to put the moves on a young woman, a stage actress he'd seen in a play. He told her he wanted to work with her. But she wasn't interested. Smart lady. He shows up at her apartment one night un-invited and he attacks her. But he doesn't realize her boyfriend's there too. So the boyfriend walks out of the bedroom and surprises Charles and coldcocks him. They throw him out into the street. And she filed a police report. She wasn't playing."

"Maybe she'll talk to me. Do you remember her name?"

"Yeah, Dominique Spencer. She's in LA now, I think."

"Shit," Angie breathed. "She tried to warn me—she saw me having lunch with Charles—but then I saw her meeting with Tanya and I just saw her driving a brand new Porsche. I guess he gets to everybody eventually."

She went back to sit on the stool beside him. "You know you have to come forward now, right? We can't help Scarlett anymore, but there are other women . . . I stole a bunch of NDAs from Charles's brief-case. NDAs from actresses, a ton of legal documents. Charles actually showed up here trying to get it all back. Then, the next day when I left the house, his goons broke in and took everything, even my laptop, before I could copy any of it."

"Angie, you are extraordinary, and brave. But after your PI turned up dead, I copied all those documents—it's everything I need. Just sit tight. Or better yet, go back home to New York. Safer there." He yawned. "Sorry, I should go."

"You could just stay."

He shot her a look.

"Not like that," she said, prompting a smile from him. "You can stay in the guest bedroom. Don't drive this late. Especially if you think you might be followed."

"Good point." Kevin's tone became serious again. "Charles is capable of anything. You be careful."

Angie needed to know one more thing. "Kevin, what's with the roses?"

"I love roses. So did Scarlett. I grow them in my yard. They're offerings, I suppose. Sometimes I would come by, bring a rose, and just sit and think. Talk to her, say I'm sorry."

"Yeah." Angie's voice was a small whisper. "Yeah, I get that."

"I really didn't know you were living here. I thought the house was empty. I never saw lights, never saw a car."

"I always park in the garage."

"Makes perfect sense." He gave a little laugh. "Listen, I'm really sorry about earlier. I never meant to scare you." He looked around the house and with a wistful, sad note in his voice said, "You know, this is the first time I've been inside."


Kevin was gone by the time Angie woke up. She found a note: Thank you, Angie. I've got to leave town for a while. Check the news. K.

Angie grabbed her phone, opening her local daily headline email:

> Studio Security Head Held in Murder of LA PI
>
> The head of security for DreamWeaver Studios has been arrested for the murder of private investigator Jango Davies.
>
> Ari Acker was taken into custody early today. Acker served on the studio's private security force for a decade and as a personal bodyguard for studio head Charles Weaver for the past four years.
>
> Police declined to comment on the arrest beyond

confirming that it had taken place. A spokeswoman for DreamWeaver said the studio had no comment.

The story was accompanied by an old picture of the bulky, unsmiling Ari holding the door of a dark sedan for Charles.
Angie fired off a text to Kevin.

Did you go to the police?

Her phone buzzed almost immediately.

Trying to make amends.

Too little too late.
But you were the impetus.

Be careful.

I'm okay. Met with my lawyers.

Be safe.

Will be in touch.

Angie tried to get some breakfast down, scanned various websites for flights to New York, showered, and was starting to slowly get her things together to pack when she decided one last time to try Patricia.

It's Angie. Can I talk to you
for a few minutes?

She was folding a sundress for her suitcase when she heard a chime indicating a response to her text.

Sure, NY
You're welcome to come out
Will send address

Just before four o'clock, Angie pulled up in front of a two-story yellow stucco house that sat behind a tall wrought-iron gate. She got out and pressed the call box button. No answer. She pressed again, worried that she was being toyed with, but then she heard a click and the gate started to swing open. She made her way up a winding path lined with small lanterns. The front gardens were heavy with palms, orange trees, flowering jasmine, and birds of paradise.

As she climbed the front steps, a huge espresso-colored wooden door swung open. Patricia looked younger than she remembered. She wore faded jeans, a white shirt, and was barefoot. Her hair was pulled back in a ponytail, and she wore no makeup.

"You look good," Angie said. "How are you?"

"Well, I'm not dead, obviously. No thanks to that asshole who ran me down." Patricia gave a wry grin. "You don't look so hot, though. You look fuckin' exhausted."

"Yeah, well, things have been . . . not great."

"You don't say."

"It's been a ride."

"I can imagine. Kevin called. We talked for an hour before he fucked off to God knows where. Wouldn't tell me. Better that way, he said."

She gestured for Angie to follow as she entered an airy foyer with cream walls and a tiled floor. A sweeping staircase led to the second floor. To the right was a sitting room, done in browns and greens. A brick fireplace dominated one wall, plush chairs and a settee offering seats that they took. Angie glimpsed through an adjacent dining room a wall of glass that looked out on a swimming pool glittering in the afternoon sun.

Patricia pulled out her phone. "Have you seen the *Reporter*? The story *just* dropped."

Angie leaned closer and they both peered at her screen. Sure enough, the *Reporter* had, twenty minutes earlier, published an item about DreamWeaver's top legal executive, Tanya Castillo, who had been fired for engaging in bad faith business practices.

> Sources also tell the *Reporter* that Castillo ran an un-savory scheme in which actresses were promised plum roles in exchange for sexual favors.
>
> "This sort of behavior will not be tolerated," said studio head Charles Weaver in a statement. "We great-ly value our employees as well as all the creative talent we work with. And the idea that we would hire or fire an actress based on some salacious exchange of sex for work is utterly abhorrent. We will leave no stone un-turned to get to the bottom of these rumors, and we will waste no time in clearing out the perpetrators."

"He threw her under the bus," Patricia said. "If it all comes out now, Charles can say he had nothing to do with any of it, that his name was forged on those NDAs, and he knew nothing about it."

Charles, naturally, would continue to be quoted as being horrified by the disclosures, Angie knew. But the real story of Charles's crimi-nality? Unlikely to ever see the light of day. He made too many people too much money.

"I'm sorry I yelled at you that day at the restaurant." Patricia put her phone away. "And I'm sorry I've blown you off since. I couldn't face it—all the humiliating things that scumbag made me do over the years. Then it happening to Scar. You made it all too real again."

"I get it, I do. You're strong, though. I wish Scarlett had been as strong as you."

"Scarlett was strong, but too good for this place. I don't have that problem." She gave Angie a small smile. "All right, New York, I'm forgetting my manners, you want something to drink? I'd offer you a belt, but I'm off the hard stuff. We could have tea. I got this whole infuser thing. Trying to live clean and all that. It's boring but nice in its own way. But I'm not doing any goddamn yoga."

"Tea is good." Angie followed Patricia through the dining room to a large farm-house style kitchen with a rustic wood table. Despite its grandness, she found the house surprisingly homey.

"I've just signed on to shoot an indie thriller in Finland," Patricia said. "Who knows? Maybe I'll become a big star in Scandinavia and shack up with some studly twenty-something ice sculptor named Sven."

"You know, Patricia, if anyone could pull that off . . ."

They shared a dry chuckle.

Then Angie cut to the chase. "I need your help with something . . ."

Angie had another stop to make. She didn't care about settling a score. She just needed a favor.

When Nicole opened her condo door that evening with a fresh pixie cut, sporting a pale pink T-shirt and black leggings, Angie's heart lurched. She hadn't stopped thinking of her, but seeing her was harder than she'd expected. She took a deep breath. "Can I come in?"

Nicole stepped aside and Angie entered the living room. Nicole closed the door and joined her. "So?"

Angie's stomach clenched. "I have to ask you something, a favor. But I want to know first. Why did you tell him? He looted my house. He took all the documents. He stole my laptop."

Nicole gave it a few seconds before responding. "He knew we were together. And he knew you were on to something. He'd called me into his office a few times. I never told him anything about you looking for answers to Scarlett's suicide, but then . . ."

"What?"

"After you left here, that last time, I didn't know what to do. I wanted to support you, but I was already unnerved, and then he called me. He made threats. How it would be a shame to lose my job. How gay people were absolute equals now, but women could be accused of sexually harassing women just as surely as men could be. And getting involved with a subordinate was, of course, forbidden. And anyway, didn't everyone know what a 'vixen'"—she made air quotes—"I was? He said I'd be accused of harassment, exploiting my position, and trading sexual favors."

"So what happened?"

"I told him to back off." She looked down. "And I lost my temper. I told him he'd better not say anything about you or me, and he sure as hell better not start lying about me, because you had enough information to bury him."

Angie gaped at her in surprise.

"I just blurted it out. I know he's dangerous and I should have just hung up and played it cool, but he had me rattled, and I . . . I lost it and caved."

Charles's reach was never-ending. He'd gotten to her girlfriend. He'd gotten to her parents. He'd gotten to Scarlett. "You shouldn't have told Charles I was going to expose him. That was my battle, not yours. It wasn't right to assume you'd go down fighting with me."

Nicole took both of Angie's hands in hers. "I'd go down fighting with you any day. For the record, I never covered up any crime. I knew Charles could be sleazy. But I also knew there were women who welcomed his attention because they wanted to make it and knew that was a way in. Welcome to Hollywood. And I'm sorry for what happened to Scarlett, truly. As gross as Charles can be, he wouldn't have wanted Scarlett dead."

"I'm not so sure about that. What about the codes to the NDAs?"

"That shit on the flash drive? I didn't even know that was on there."

"Why was it in your office?"

"When I took over IP, all the departments sent their files to me with books, movie titles, writers, agents, all this information that was scattered all over the place. That folder must have gotten mixed in with everything else. I probably thought it was dated, expired material, and stashed it away."

Angie evaluated her. And decided she believed her. She also still loved her, she realized. But her heart was a jumbled mess of longing and disappointment. She wasn't in a place where she could be present or authentic in a relationship. She had to focus on herself before she could focus on anyone else. Except for Scarlett.

"So, that favor?"


Her last stop was the hardest one.

She found her father in the same waiting room at Cedars, the same fluorescent lighting, same black plastic tables, same orange plastic chairs. He looked like he hadn't moved since she'd last seen him. He looked haggard. Old. Lost. For all of his blowhard tendencies, he was nothing without his wife.

He gave a start when she sat in the chair next to him, an empty paper coffee cup gripped in his hand. His face was drawn, gray like the room, his eyes red and bleary.

"Hi, Dad." She took his free hand and held it, something neither of them had ever done before. He squeezed hers in return but didn't speak.

She was about to do something that would change her forever, and she wanted to make things right where she could.

"There's no way I can forget what you and Mom did," she began, "but I know you thought you were doing what was best for Scar, you thought you were helping her. I also know you hold yourself responsible." She made sure to look him in the eye. "And you should."

He gave a slight nod and turned his face away.

She continued, "What you need now is support. Empathy. And I'm going to be the first to extend that."

He looked at her with a vulnerability she'd never seen before, and also like she was an adult, possibly for the first time. "But you have to respond in kind. You've always been distant. A tyrant. To the whole family. And we never understood why. And you're a literature professor, for shit's sake. I got my degree in English and I'm a book editor. Why have we never talked about that?" She stopped and waited.

He removed his hand from hers, wiping it across his face.

"It's not brain surgery, Dad."

He gave her a sharp look, then softened. "I know. That doesn't make it easy."

"Life isn't easy. You don't know that yet? I'm half your age and I know it all too well. Why do you think I've hidden in books since I was a child? Maybe that's something we have in common?"

She took his hand again, and he squeezed hers and said, "I'd like to talk about literature with you."

"We could have always done that."

He nodded again.

She'd said what she needed to, even if it had taken Scarlett's suicide and Ellen's possible death for her to say it and him to hear it. She just hoped what she was about to do wouldn't endanger the tenuous connection they'd finally made.

Back at Scarlett's, she poured herself a glass of sparkling water and went to stand out by the pool. She watched as the sky darkened into shades of crimson. There was no wind. The fronds of the palms were silent and motionless. The pool wasn't illuminated, its depths murky in the twilight.

Angie stood in the shadows, willing herself to summon Scarlett's self-belief, her fortitude, her backbone. *I need you more than ever tonight, Scar.*

She went back inside and changed into jeans and a hoodie she'd brought from New York but hadn't worn since she'd been in LA. She fished a pair of Scarlett's driving gloves out of a drawer. She made sure she had a pair of sunglasses in her purse. She Googled the nearest Home Depot on her phone.

Then she called Charles.

# 18

Charles Weaver pulled into his reserved spot at the DreamWeaver underground parking garage and cut the engine. He didn't see any other cars, but Angie had said she'd meet him there. Finally coming around, the little bitch. Even harder to tame than her sister. But he had broken her. And the wait had, in the end, made the chase more satisfying. He adjusted himself, then hopped out of his car with anticipation, locking it with a chirp.

"Oh, Charles."

Her voice came out of the shadows of the structure. He smiled at the way she said his name. He couldn't see a damn thing, but he liked this game. This was going to be fun.

"Angie?"

A figure materialized, wearing jeans, a hoodie, sunglasses, and black leather gloves. "That's not quite the outfit I had in mind when you said you wanted to meet to 'make up'. I expected much less." He chuckled. "Come here, into the light. I want to see you. You're not the first bitch to come crawling back after I put her in her place."

"What did you call her?"

Charles turned to his right. Another figure was emerging from the shadows, the face obscured by a hoodie. What the hell? "Who is that?"

"Don't you recognize me?"

"Patricia? Angie, did you plan a menage-a-trois? You dirty girl. So, Pattycake, you're back for more. You always were insatiable."

"You and your twisted fantasies."

A third woman? What was going on? Charles peered into the shadows and finally made out a figure in the dim light. "Dominique? What the fuck?"

Patricia started to circle him like a slow-orbiting planet. He swiveled his head to track her, the skin on his arms prickling. He'd been caught off guard, and he didn't like the feeling.

"Pattycake, I'll bet it still hurts where that car ran you down, doesn't it, you fucking lush? Maybe if you weren't day drinking, you would have seen it coming." He laughed and felt a surge of power as it reverberated in the cavernous garage. He felt like he had the advantage again. "Jesus Christ, I can break you in half. All of you. With a flick of a finger. Don't you dare fuck with me."

"No one ever wanted to fuck you."

He spun around. Angie had moved closer. What was she holding behind her back?

"And you're never going to fuck *with* anyone ever again."

"All right, this is bullshit. I'm out of here. And you all are fucking DEAD in this town." He fumbled for his key fob when Patricia materialized on the other side of the car. She raised a baseball bat and brought it down on his windshield before he had time to even process it. "You fucking cunt! Do you know how much this car cost? It's worth more than your fucking LIFE!"

"It's not worth much now, is it?"

Charles whirled around to face Angie. She raised her own bat, gripping it with both hands, letting it hover over her shoulder like a champ. "This may not be a 1924 Rogers Hornsby, but I think it'll do the trick."

He looked to the security cameras for help. Where were the fucking security guards? He didn't know their names to call out but he couldn't bring himself to simply shout "Help!" surrounded by four fucking cunts.

He turned, left, then right, then pivoted to his rear. He was surrounded. Angie, Patricia, Dominique, and . . . where the hell had the fourth one come from?

"Who are *you*?" Charles tried to keep his voice level, in control. But a distinct quaver betrayed him.

"You don't remember me?" She gave a low laugh. "You'll remember me now."

Four baseball bats raised in unison.

That was when he realized in a crush of terror that even if the assault was caught on camera, their faces covered by hoods, and the shadows of the garage would obscure their identities even more.

"Pattycake . . . ?"

"Don't worry, Charles." He could hear the smile in Patricia's voice. "As I recall, you always took care of business, um, quickly. And we will, too."

As Angie lifted her bat high above her head, she whispered, venom dripping for her lips, "This is for Scarlett."

And they descended.

# EPILOGUE

A month later, on a bright, sunny Saturday afternoon, Angie was laughing so hard that she nearly choked on her iced coffee. She walked through SoHo with Joaquin, her arm looped in his as he regaled her with tales from the fashion world.

"Well, girl, I told him, 'Your work is just shameful. Do not ruin this beautiful fabric and my gorgeous creations with stitching you wouldn't use on your mother's kitchen curtains.' Puh-lease."

They continued laughing as they careened down the street toward the park where they were meeting Scott and his kids. "So are you going to get some sort of show next season?" Angie asked.

"Well, it won't be Bryant Park, baby, but I got a few fashion websites interested and two buyers for smaller chains, and I'm working on getting an interview in *Women's Wear*. And Marc Jacobs almost made eye contact with me at this opening last week, so I'm getting there, sweet thing, I'm getting there."

Angie's phone buzzed. "It's Rita," she told Joaquin before answering. "Hey! Joaquin and I are near you at Vesuvio. You wanna meet us for coffee?"

"Oh, I can't, honey, I gotta color my hair. But you kids have fun. I'm thinking of going more burnt sienna than burgundy. You remember that color? Burnt sienna? From the Crayola box?"

"I do. I do remember burnt sienna," Angie said with a smile, looking at Joaquin and pointing to her head.

Joaquin made a face of mock-horror and mouthed *burnt sienna?!*

"Anyway, honey. Can you come by this week? I'm drowning in manuscripts. Which is a good thing. If it doesn't kill me."

"I can help out," Angie told her. "But, Rita, what's up with Mackenzie? I've left messages and sent texts but she's not responding. I feel awful."

"I know, honey. There's a new head of legal at the studio and we're trying to renegotiate and get her rights back so we can shop it elsewhere. But listen, I got this other book, a thriller. I think it'll sell. It's about this young reporter who's bored out of her mind covering local zoning meetings and whatever when she overhears a conversation . . . Well, you know—the usual, but it's very good— good story, *very* good writing."

"Sure, I can come in Monday and pitch in however you need."

"Okay. I gotta go and get this damn hair done. See you Monday."

"See you Monday." Angie disconnected and Joaquin looked up from his phone with a sassy grin.

"I just got a text from that painter! The one I met that time at that party, so I gotta jet. We'll meet up Friday, though, yeah, with Mr. Hottie?"

Angie laughed. Jeremy Banker was in town rehearsing a play off-Broadway, and the three of them were getting together for dinner. Joaquin was almost giddy with excitement.

Joaquin dashed off, and Angie wandered over to the park playground on her own to meet Scott, who had the kids for the afternoon. Angie observed Michelle, who had just turned six, proudly pushing Brendan on the swing set. She pulled Scott into a big hug and then they sat on a bench to watch the kids play.

After a moment, Scott asked, "So, how are things? You're getting by?"

"I'm getting by."

"What about LA? Do you miss it?"

She and Nicole had texted for half an hour the night before. Nicole had suggested coming to New York to visit her next month, and, while Angie was considering it, she was still raw from everything that had happened. Ellen had been released from the hospital and was now back home, but the road was going to be long until she was back to her usual self.

Angie was still trying to accept what she'd learned about her mother and father in LA. She'd lost more than just Scarlett. But they were her parents, and while she could never look at them the same, they had all made efforts to repair their broken bond. Gerry had even suggested Angie come out to the house once a week for a book club, just the two of them. He was so animated when she went, so delighted to talk about books and literature with her, she almost didn't recognize him.

"What happened in LA is part of me," she finally said to Scott. "Just like what happened to Scar will never leave me. Or any of us. But life goes on, doesn't it? And now I'm back here, and I can honestly say I feel good these days. Happy, even."

"Yeah?"

"Yeah. I grew a lot when I was out there. I feel pretty . . . almost . . . okay."

"Okay is good."

They both laughed as Michelle came running up, her little brother in tow. "Daddy, that boy said Brendan had to get off the swings. Then he pushed me!"

Angie realized it was the same bratty boy who'd pushed the little girl in the pink-and-blue parka last winter.

"Oh, honey, he's just crabby," Scott soothed his daughter. "Just ignore him. It'll be okay."

"No. No, it won't be okay." Angie couldn't look away from the scowling boy standing at the swing set.

Michelle looked at her aunt, her mouth open, her mind working. And then, just like that, she walked right up to the bully boy and punched him.

Other books by
EDEN FRANCIS COMPTON

*Emily*
A world-famous playwright becomes obsessed with Emily Dickinson,
believing she has left clues in her writing of her trauma. He is forced
to come to terms with his own difficult past as he begins losing his
grip on reality.

*Death Valley*
In a dark and seedy part of Las Vegas that few know about, two
brothers with a violent past, battle over a woman they love and the
money she wins at a casino.

## Stay up to date:

Follow Eden on Amazon & Goodreads

https://www.amazon.com/author/edenfranciscompton